SPILLED COFFEE

J.B. CHICOINE

Straw
Hill
Publishing
SHP

strawhillpublishing@jbchicoine.com

ISBN-13: 978-0615823775
ISBN-10: 0615823777

Printed in the United States of America

ACKNOWLEDGEMENTS

Many thanks to my writing partner, Robynne Marie Plouff, for her constant support and willingness to read through each draft—and to my writing buddy, Liza Carens Salerno. Thanks also to Dan Zenas at Georgia Prosthetics for his generous technical support, and Gary Johnson for tweaking my aviation skills.
Above all, thank you, Todd, my ever-encouraging, always-willing-to-listen husband. My stories are all for you—without your support, I would never have published them.

For my brother Pete

Spilled Coffee

J.B. Chicoine

Straw
Hill
Publishing

CHAPTER 1

I **TAP** THE CRYSTAL OF MY POCKET WATCH, AS IF jarring its works might synchronize it with the time on my dashboard—10:00 AM. The old analog is eighteen minutes slow. I should have given the watch a fine-tuning when I received it, but the idea of tampering with its works seemed sacrilegious. Besides, what's a mere eighteen minutes?

Climbing from the rental Saab, I fumble with the timepiece like an awkward memory. Sunlight glints off gold as I ease its cover closed and shut the car door. I press the watch to my ear, listening for a heartbeat, and then return it to my vest pocket. I need one of those vintage watch fobs, something proper to go along with this pinstriped vest.

Approaching the entrance to Rockette Diner, I gather my hair behind my ear, trying to compensate for having missed my barber appointment—as if anyone here cares that I look like a throwback to the hippie era. I've just stepped into a pocket of New England where the artsy mingle freely with local farmers, and although these college and prep-school communities foster individualism, I still feel a little off. Maybe it's just the weirdness of being back here—or that my twitch has intensified. I rub my eye and adjust the perch of my shades.

My foot catches the curb. I stumble into an old lady as she steps through the diner door. Reaching out to steady her, I gasp, "I'm so sorry."

She frowns, slapping my hand. "Watch where you're headed, young man! You could hurt someone."

I wag my head. "Sorry."

The door slams on my elbow, disrupting my sunglasses. In a wave of self-consciousness, I scramble to catch them in midair—I meant to take them off anyway—and tuck them between my shirt and vest.

Stepping inside, I squint at the fluorescent light. My eyes flinch. The dense aromas of bacon, maple syrup, strong coffee, and cigarettes hit me first. As my sight catches up with my olfactory senses, the black-checkered floor, red vinyl stools, and chrome-edged counter send me from 1987 back to 1969, back to my fourteenth summer. It's as if the world hasn't changed—as if I were eighteen years early for this appointment.

I scan the counter and tables for Oscar in his soiled work coat. I'm not sure if Oscar is the guy's first name or last. He seemed like a nice enough fellow, even if he did remind me that I'm a "flatlander." I guess that much is true, although I didn't bother to explain that I had just flown in from the Rockies. Here in New Hampshire, the saying goes, "Once a flatlander, always a flatlander." All the more reason why I don't take for granted that Oscar has agreed to show up at the lake with his truck, tomorrow, on Memorial Day weekend—*and* a Sunday, no less.

A few patrons peer over their coffee mugs. Avoiding eye contact, I make my way to an empty stool at the counter. I wipe my sweating palms on my blue jeans, smooth worsted wool over my torso, and then fold each of my crisp, white cuffs. I doubt anyone will recognize me after so much time. I hope no one does. My beard should help, even if it is close-cropped. I twitch. *Oh, cut it out!* I have every right to be here.

I breathe deep and pull out my pocket watch. The hands remain unchanged. Eighteen minutes—eighteen years. Ironic.

To my right, a grisly old man in overalls—smelling of barnyard—sops egg yolk with a crust of toast. As he raises

2

an eyebrow at me, I turn to my left, toward the slender lady wearing a patchwork vest. She's writing something on a pad, as distracted as the old guy. I'm blending. *I'm fine.*

A burly figure wedges himself between the old farmer and me.

"Hey, how ya' doin'? Sorry I'm late," Oscar says. "I got caught up at the town clerk."

I swivel my seat, extending my hand. "Oscar. Thanks again for doing this on such short notice. Any problem with the permit?"

"Nope." His gaze travels from my face to my attire and back—he ought to be more concerned with his own fashion statement. "We're all set for tomorrow, but I'll give you my home number in case you come to your senses."

Come to my senses? I resist the urge to chuckle. At any rate, I won't have a way to contact him once I arrive at the cottage, but I don't want to come off as unappreciative, so I accept his offer. He pulls a business card from his wallet and pats a non-existent pocket on his too-tight polo shirt. "Got a pen? Seem to have misplaced mine."

"No." I glance at the woman beside me, at her pencil. "Excuse me—" I hope the tone of my voice conveys my sincere smile. "Mind if I borrow that for just a second?"

The curvature of short black hair carves into her cheek, obscuring her profile. Her eyes don't meet mine as she passes the pencil and picks up her coffee mug, bringing it to what I imagine are rosebud lips—the one feature I've always been a sucker for.

"Thanks," I say, lingering for a moment, hoping for a better look.

She swivels away and folds her arms, perhaps to give us more room. Or I might have annoyed her. Disappointed that she hasn't allowed me at least to smile at her, I pass the pencil to Oscar. As he scribbles, I glance at her shoulder and left hand clutching her arm. I can't help noticing the lack of rings. With a recent ex-fiancée, I'm not in any condition to pursue a romantic interest. It's simply force of habit. Just the same, she does have pretty hands. Long, slender fingers and nails that aren't all painted and fake looking like my fiancée's—that is, *ex*-fiancée. Just trimmed and natural. Don't they say you can tell a lot about a person by their hands?

She lifts the coffee cup. Too bad she won't allow me a glimpse of her lips. *Oh, honestly!* Why am I even checking her out? I'm no better than a fourteen-year-old.

Oscar passes me the card and pencil. As the pretty-handed woman shifts toward me, I twitch and bump her arm. Coffee sloshes, as if in slow motion, rolling up and over the side of her mug. From the perfect curl of a wave, droplets break away, tumbling past the buffalo china's pink floral pattern, and splashing, no, crashing all over her pad. She gasps, her mug thumping to the counter, wobbling just enough to dump any remaining coffee before it comes to rest. I hold my breath as tightly as the pencil.

"Oh God, I am *so* sorry." Heat rises from my neck to my ears as I yank paper napkins from the dispenser. *I'm such a moron!* Fumbling and blotting coffee from her pad, I sop up enough to reveal a sketch of her mug, and from what I can tell, a pretty good one. I choke, trying to form words, but nothing comes out.

As she lifts the pad, layers of paper curl in front of her. I catch just enough of her cheek to see crimson as she stares straight ahead.

"Sorry," I blurt. "What can I do? How can I fix this?"

"*Fix* this?" she shoots back, still focused on her drawing. "Seriously?"

I have no idea what to say. On a heated impulse, I pull my wallet from my hip pocket and open it wide. "You could buy a new pad—I've got a fifty—here, sixty, sixty-five, six, seven, eight, sixty-nine dollars—"

She plucks the fifty from my hand, slaps the pad on the counter, and scribbles across the bottom.

"There! You just bought yourself a drawing pad," she says, then up and whisks her way toward the door. Without looking back, she pushes through the exit.

In all of twenty seconds, I revert from a thirty-one-year-old man to an awkward kid. I'm sure my eyes have been twitching the whole time. I let out a long, strained breath and shake my head. Serves me right for gawking. Oscar's chuckle tightens to a wheeze as he pats my back.

I glance at the notepad. Across the bottom she's written, *Spilled Coffee*. Well, there's a twist to the old cliché—I guess there is no use crying over it.

Chapter 2

THE STATE ROUTE WINDS UP AND AROUND, under shady trees that give way to a clearing, cutting through cow-dotted pastures. With one hand on the steering wheel, I put on my sunshades—a rip-off on old aviator goggles. My tape player blares "Lifetime Piling Up", one of my favorite Talking Heads tunes.

This rental Saab grips the pavement as though it knows these roads better than I once did. I like the way it handles, although I do miss my old Chevy conversion van with its customized levers and switches. Maybe I'll replace "The Transformer" with one of these foreign jobs.

The farmhouse I'm passing looks familiar, but I'm not sure if it simply typifies so many of the old homesteads on the town outskirts, or if I actually remember it. I slow to the thirty-miles-per-hour speed limit through the center of the old brick and clapboarded village, splitting Elmore Academy's campus. There are only a few students milling around, now that it's the end of May. I brake again as several stragglers step into the crosswalk and shuffle past in army boots and dyed hair. Their Grunge and Goth attire—albeit toned down to acceptable prep school protocol—looks a lot different from the preppy students of eighteen years ago. Kids of every generation revel in their originality. I can't help chuckling at my own pair of Doc Martens that I've been wearing since those kids were toddling around in baby booties. Even so, I am the melting pot of unoriginality.

At the edge of town, I accelerate. Will I recognize where to turn? I could double-check the map, but I'm winging it, hoping to engage my memory—after all, that's what this journey is about.

Sure enough, as I round a bend in the road and continue straight for about a mile, I look for—the name returns to me—Switchback Road. I turn left. I'll soon come across the old country store if it's still there. I'm taking a chance on that, too, since I need to pick up a few groceries, though only enough for one day.

In the distance, I spot the yellow and red Shell sign and the gas price: $0.95. As I approach, I steer past the single pump and into the parking space in front of the weatherworn porch. The Garver's Market sign hanging over the entrance is peeling and faded. Garver's is the first place we always stopped at on our way to Safe Haven. Funny how the names of summer houses and camps sound so much like mental institutions and cemeteries.

I shiver. Now the memories start encroaching, wicking their way in. I don't have to close my eyes to conjure the visual.

MY GAZE DARTED PAST MOM'S BOBBED blond hair and over to Garver's Market. She steered our station wagon to the gas pump and parked, while Dad's Falcon pulled up to the storefront ahead of us. Dad always drove the company car up to camp, leaving Mom the Galaxie so he could return to his job, selling junk to housewives. We kids always rode with Mom, even though the Falcon had plenty of space for a passenger. Dad had said there was only room for one kid, and he didn't want to play favorites. *Yeah, right!*

My big sister, Penny, brushed her hair into a ponytail and then daubed pale lip-gloss over her already glossed lips. She glanced back at me and smiled with a spark in her eye—the assurance that no matter what, we were going to have the best summer ever.

Still behind the wheel, Mom flipped the visor mirror

and applied hot pink lipstick as Dad climbed from his driver's seat and approached her open door. He ran his hand over his buzzed hair that melded into a dark five-o'clock shadow. I shuddered at the thought of "the buzz." This was the first summer Mom let me grow my hair out— "but not past your ears," she had said, "or you'll look like a girl with those pretty dark curls." Penny always wished she had my mop instead of straight, dirty blond hair. At least we both inherited Mom's modest nose and not Dad's beak.

My little brother, Frankie, kicked his door open, wiping his nose on his sleeve as he sprung from the seat. As disgusting as that was, at least he wasn't picking boogers again. The kid was a veritable snot factory. Frankie zoomed past the fuel pump where Dad grabbed the gas nozzle, flexing his grip as if anyone but him were admiring his biceps. He glanced from the pump display and back at his muscles, as Mom wiggled her way out of the car.

"Thirty-three cents! It's highway robbery!" he said loud enough to draw attention. I cringed.

"Oh, Frank, just pump the gas," Mom said as she dug through her purse. She looked like she had been peeled off a page of the Sears catalogue, pressed and color coordinated, from her bright pink headband down to her toenail polish. Her puffed-up hair gave her an inch of height over Dad, not that he was short, but he wasn't tall, either. If I had to define the word average, I could point to Dad.

I should have moved quicker, because as I scooted from the back seat, Dora Garver stepped outside and sat on the front porch rocker. Her gap-toothed smile splayed between pudgy cheeks, sinking her eyes deep into half-moon sockets. She was twenty but seemed half that age.

I followed Penny up the steps. Even though my siblings greeted Dora first, her husky voice singled me out. "Hi, Ben!"

I forced a smile. "Hi, Dora."

"You can call me Isadora."

I sighed, wishing I had never started calling her Isadora in the first place. That was when her crush began—I had been trying to be nice after she butchered her hair, cutting her bangs so short they stuck out like pine needles. This morning, it looked as if she had snuck the scissors again.

She grinned. "I cut my own hair."

"You did a good job," I lied.

Behind me, Mom's heels clunked the wood steps as I passed Dora and pushed through the jingling door. It slammed behind me.

Mom waited until we were inside before pinching my arm. "You be nice to Dora. Just be glad it wasn't one of you kids that was born with Downs." As if I needed reminding.

Mr. Garver glanced over his black-rimmed reading glasses from behind the counter, straightened his back, and offered a half-sad-half-chipper smile. It seemed to me that if Mom were so concerned about the Garvers, she would have been a little more discrete about always bringing up Dora's disability. At least she saved the gossip about how "the Garvers were both close to fifty when they had Dora" for the privacy of our car or at camp, like we needed reminding for the hundredth time.

Mr. Garver smoothed his thinning pompadour and rubbed his dimpled chin.

Mom gave her hair a gentle lift, as if it weren't already Barbie Doll perfect, and waved. "Hello, Mr. Garver."

He nodded, his gaze shifting to the stock room and back to Mom. "Mrs. Hughes—good to see you and your family here for another summer. Just let me know if there's anything I can help you with."

Mom smoothed her blouse and flowery pedal pushers, too tight to have any wrinkles. Why couldn't my mother dress frumpy like all the other moms?

While she tried on a wide-brimmed hat at the apparel

display—Garver's sold a bit of everything, from trinkets to ammo to Spam—I moved to the reading rack, cautiously checking for the latest *MAD* magazine. Did I dare sneak it? Since Mom was distracted, slipping in and out of an assortment of flip-flops, now was my chance. Not that either of my parents cared about my lighter reading any more than they did my H.G. Wells or Jules Verne, but Mom hated *MAD*'s cartoons with "bosoms bursting out of their clothes on every page." No, it was too risky, too early in our vacation to screw things up. It wasn't so much Mom and the mood it might put her in, but she had a way of needling Dad into handling matters.

Instead of grabbing the *MAD* magazine, I picked up *Popular Mechanics* and scanned a few pages. As I put it back, some guy in an Elmore Academy blazer brushed past, shoving me into the display. By the time I turned to scowl at him, he was a blur of forest green, stepping up to the front counter. *Jerk.* Again distracted, I moved on to the snack aisle. Studying the selection and then grabbing a bag of barbecue potato chips, I headed to the counter, now that Elmore's 'elite' had stepped outside and there was no line.

Mr. Garver grinned. "And how are you, Ben?"

"Fine, thanks. How are you?"

"Just dandy." He looked me up and down. "You've put on a little height since last summer—about six inches, wouldn't you say?"

"Just five, actually." At two inches short of six feet—an inch taller than Dad—I felt like a freaking giant.

"I guess you'll be the tall one of the family."

I shrugged. "I guess."

He winked. "Now you'll have to beat off all the older girls."

"Doubt it," I said under my breath. He probably meant Dora.

"Will that be all?"

I eyed the penny candy. "Five Tootsie Rolls and five Mary Janes, please."

"You bet." With a grin, he shoved two huge handfuls of each candy into a small bag as I stared at the white roots of his jet-black hair. He winked again. "With the chips, that'll be twenty cents."

"Gee, thanks Mr. Garver." I acted like it was the first time he had ever given me a whole lot more than ten-cents-worth of candy, but on the rare occasions when he, instead of Mrs. Garver, had waited on me, he always loaded up my bag. I laid down two dimes and made my way toward the exit. Mom and Penny approached the checkout.

Mrs. Garver's lilting call traveled from the stockroom. "Earl! I need you back here."

"Yes, Dearie," he responded with a smile.

In a moment, Mrs. Garver greeted Mom, "I'll ring you up."

I pushed open the front door, sneaking a peek in the bag as I stepped outside and walked smack into the back of a green blazer. The tall blond guy, a little taller than me but outweighing me by half, whirled around.

"What the—!" He scowled. Coffee from his Styrofoam cup spotted the front of his Oxford shirt as he held the dripping cup away from him with one hand, while the other pinched a cigarette butt.

I gasped. "Sorry."

"You freaking retard!"

I winced as he flicked the glowing butt at my face and stormed off the porch, brushing coffee from his sleeve. I glanced at Dad, behind his newspaper shield, as the Elmore creep slunk into his sporty little Mercedes. To my side, Dora whimpered. Big fat tears welled from her eyes and escaped down each cheek, meeting her quivering chin.

The heat I had felt in my own cheeks, a second ago, dissipated. "He meant me, Dora, not *you*."

She wrung the fabric of her skirt, wet with tears.

I shoved my hand into the candy bag and pulled out a fistful. With a gentle nudge, I said, "Here Isadora. Never mind him."

Like squeezing off a hose, the tears quit and her usual smile spread across her face. "I like Mary Janes."

As the Elmore kid peeled away from the storefront, I replaced Dora's Tootsie Rolls with her favorite. "Don't eat them all at once, okay?"

"Okay," she smiled.

Just then, Mom called out, "Ben! Come help your sister carry bags."

I opened the screen door for Penny. She passed me a paper sack full of groceries as Mom stepped through with an armload; a big orange sunhat topped it off. As I headed toward the car, Frankie barreled through the door.

Dad looked up from his newspaper. "What did you do, Beverly, buy out the store? I told you, that paycheck needs to last until July."

"Then I guess *you* can do the shopping next time," she huffed as I put the groceries in the back seat. Dad finally budged after I took my place, sandwiched between Frankie and Mom's new summer outfit—like she had anyplace to wear it.

Frankie squirmed beside me, fiddling with a BB in a five-cent maze. He sang out, "Ben's in love with a retard, Ben's in love with a retard."

From the front seat, Penny reached behind and swatted my brother. "That's not nice, Frankie. How would you like it if I went around calling you a bed wetter?"

"Shut up. I am not."

"Are too," I said under my breath.

"Ben," Mom spoke up. "Don't tease your brother."

I stifled a huff and an eye roll and then glanced down at my white T-shirt, at the singed hole right in the middle of my chest. *Great.*

CHAPTER 3

How LONG HAVE I BEEN SITTING BEHIND THE wheel, staring off into space? I check the Saab's clock. It feels like hours have passed, but it's been just a few minutes. Technically, my journey into the past has only begun, but already my anxiety is mounting. I steady my breathing, unhook the seatbelt and pull myself from the car.

As I make my way to the Garver's Market porch, a small swarm of black flies gathers around my head. The step creaks the way it always did. A poster advertising the August carnival is skewed, taped to the inside of the window beside the screen door. The overhead bell jingles when I step in.

Next to the checkout, they've installed a sub deli. Behind the counter, a familiar gap-toothed smile spreads across an aging face. Straight, salt-and-peppered hair frames her pudgy cheeks. The familiarity of her is at once disconcerting, yet comforting.

My breath falters, catching words in my throat as I say, "Hello, Isadora."

She squints hard until I remove my shades. Now she smiles with recognition, as if seeing past my beard and erasing two decades. "I know you—you're—you're Ben! Ma! It's Ben!"

Mrs. Garver, her hair now feather white and still wearing the same old rhinestone cat's-eye glasses, steps out from the stockroom. A warm smile colors her entire countenance. "Why, Ben Hughes, is that really you?"

I draw in a deep breath—"Yeah"—and let it out slowly—"it's really me."

"How *are* you?"

I twitch and paste on a smile. "Good enough."

"Well, now isn't this a treat?"

Dora, breathing with effort, hasn't quit grinning, but Mrs. Garver's happy smile wanes. "And how is your poor mother?"

Another lungful. Hold. "She passed away last year."

"Oh, I'm so sorry to hear that."

I doubt she'll ask about the rest of my family, but I still hope to divert her attention. "And Mr. Garver?" I remember his dyed hair, like black polish on white orthopedic shoes, but mostly I remember his kindly disposition.

"He passed ten years ago—at seventy-six. Sudden heart attack, don't'cha know. Killed him instantly—no suffering."

"I'm so sorry. That's very sad. How have you and Dora been getting on?"

"Oh, we're just fine. Earl—God rest his soul—made sure that we'd be well cared for."

"He was a good man."

"Yes, a very good man. Now tell me dear, what can I get for you?"

I give the cold cut selection a once-over, wishing for sushi—or at least something semi-organic. *Oh, what the hell!* "Pastrami on rye, a pint of potato salad, please, and a cup of coffee." I think twice about the coffee—I don't need the caffeine, I just feel like something warm. "Make that a decaf."

"You got it."

As Mrs. Garver assembles my sandwich, I stroll up one aisle and down the next on the same old speckled and chipped linoleum. I grab a jug of water from the glass-doored refrigerator and stall at the sight of Marshmallow Fluff and Spaghetti-Os. As reminiscent of childhood as they are, they won't make much of a supper or breakfast, although since I don't know what shape the cooking facilities will be in, I'm better off buying something that doesn't need heating. I pick up a can of Spam and read the label—this stuff is about as far from organic as I've eaten since before we moved to the farm. I deliberate, tossing the can from one hand to the other, weighing my options. Well, for the nostalgia of it, why not? I grab a loaf of Wonder bread while I'm at it. If I'm going to deviate from my health-food diet, I may as well do it up right. When I pass the Marshmallow Fluff on my way back, I grab a jar.

The *MAD* magazine on the rack catches my eye. Alfred E. Neuman hasn't aged one bit. I resist the temptation to buy the latest copy.

"You certainly look dapper in your white shirt and vest," Mrs. Garver calls out.

"Why, thank you."

"Special occasion?"

"No." She doesn't realize that the white shirt and vest with jeans has become my standard attire. Being 'all buttoned up' feels comfortable to me.

"I heard there's a storm rolling in," Mrs. Garver says. "But not till after midnight."

Great. My body temperature rises as I head to the checkout. I wish I had ordered something cold, but Dora is already pouring coffee.

"Would you mind adding a couple extra mustard and mayo packets to my bag, and some utensils?" I say to Dora as I glance behind me to the back corner of the store, to a narrow hallway where the cord of a pay phone catches a glimmer of light. I swallow hard, shifting my tense jaw. There's no point in trying to suppress my tick; my eyes flutter.

"Here you go, Ben." Dora looks at me askance. As she drops condiment packets and plastics into my bag, she bumps the coffee cup. I'm quick enough to salvage it before more than a single drop sloshes. Now *that* was a rescue.

15

She winces. "I'm so clumsy."

"No, you're not." I hold up the cup to show her it's still full. "See? No damage."

"I *am* clumsy."

"Well, you should have seen the mess I made of someone's coffee this morning—spilled it all over some poor lady. Now *that* was a disaster!"

Dora's giggle puts me at ease. Mrs. Garver rings me up between sympathetic glances.

"That'll be eleven, thirteen." She folds over the bag's top.

I fish out a ten and a couple ones. As she makes change, I give Dora a quick wink, pocket the 87¢, and then grab the bag.

Mrs. Garver pats my hand. "Will we be seeing you again, Ben?"

"Probably not. I'm just here overnight."

"Staying locally?"

My heart fibrillates. "At the camp. I just bought it back."

Her brows narrow into one continuous tuft. "Oh … I see…."

I force a smile. "So good to see you again. You too, Isadora." I leave without giving them a chance to ask further questions. When I step back out onto the porch, a breeze cools the sweat running along my sideburns. Black flies gather as I head to the car.

As I sit in the driver's seat with the door still open, hot Styrofoam warms my hand. What was I thinking? Well, I paid for the coffee—I should follow through and drink it. That's my nature; commit and don't let go, even at the defiance of logic. Some call it stubbornness. I've always considered it fortitude.

I could drink the coffee now and burn my lips, or forget about it until it's tepid—or, given the way my morning has been going, I'll spaz and spill it all over myself. With resignation, I flip off the lid and pour the coffee onto the ground. There—that wasn't so hard. Without ceremony or further contemplation, I put the Saab in gear, leaving the spilled coffee behind.

Ten minutes later, I turn onto Rockette Lake Road. Before long, I pass familiar landmarks. The boat landing. The public beach. The overgrown, still creepy-looking picnic area gives me a shudder. The pavement ends where a boulder forks the road. A sign, Swaying Pines—Private Drive, signals my turn. Ahead, on the winding dirt road, an SUV approaches. I pull over as far as possible, struck at the narrowness of the passage compared to what I remember.

I meet up with another car, not unusual for Memorial Day weekend. As I continue driving, swatches of the lake become visible, and sunlit reflections flicker between evergreens. Through my open window, a light breeze carries the crisp scent of water—that trigger is sufficient to send me back.

BAD ENOUGH THAT I HAD TO SIT BESIDE Frankie for the entire three-hour drive from Southeastern Massachusetts, but by the time we left Garver's, he had used up the half-roll of toilet paper Mom had given him for his runny nose. For the hundredth time, I caught him with his finger up his nostril.

"What are you going to do with that?" I asked as he studied what he had dug out.

"Wipe it on the back of the seat with all the others."

"*Mom!*"

She huffed, "Ben, you're going to make me miss my turn."

"But he's—"

"That's enough!"

"*Gross.*" I leaned as far away from him as possible until Mom turned onto Rockette Lake Road. As soon as water came into view, Frankie turned into an overgrown Labrador retriever, prancing around the back seat. He rolled down his window, scuttling to his knees, his sneakers grabbing the hairs on my thighs.

"Get off me!" I shoved his feet away as he stuck his head out the window, eager to lap up rushing air. In many ways, my little brother was like a family pet—he could get away with anything, in spite of his wet nose and bladder problems.

Mom glared via her reflection in the rearview mirror as her hot pink fingernail shook in my direction. "Don't be so intolerant, Ben."

I was more annoyed that Frankie blocked my view than I was at his feet in my lap. We were coming up on Whispering Narrows, 'cottage' of the richest man on the lake, Doc Burns. Our car, leading the Falcon, slowed at the first set of large cement lions perched atop stone pillars that marked a half-circle-driveway entrance. I craned my neck, hoping for a glimpse of curly red hair. For as long as we had been coming to camp, just a peek at Doc Burns' granddaughter made my heart race. Over the past few years, she had traded her pink sundress for hot pants, and then last year, a two-piece bathing suit. I could never hope for a wave, but her mere glance at our station wagon would be the perfect beginning to my summer.

As we approached the second pair of lions, the overhanging porch of Whispering Narrows came into view. Doc's Land Rover was parked in front. Off to its side sat two other cars I had never seen before—a new, black Jaguar Coup and an old, blue Rambler station wagon with a red driver's door and multicolored tailgate.

As soon as I had a clear view of the massive pillars that supported the porch roof, the front door flew open and shut. Amelia skipped down the granite steps, halting when her attention landed on our caravan. Penny leaned across Mom's lap, waving like an imbecile until Amelia waved back. My whole body heated to such an uncomfortable level that if I burst into flames, at least my embarrassment would end, once and for all. Why did big sisters have to be so conspicuous?

As we passed, I couldn't help glancing over my shoulder, catching one last glimpse of Amelia. Penny reached back and gave me a knowing shove. I ignored her, now lost in lust. Amelia Burns. Love of my life. Maybe this summer I would get up the courage to talk to her.

Chapter 4

As I maneuver the Saab past Whispering Narrows, the estate soon disappears beyond a stand of blue spruce, which hides two other camps and separates Safe Haven from Whispering Narrows. Thick greenery buffers a sharp, uphill turn in the road. One sweaty hand grips the steering wheel, while my other fist tightens on the stick, grinding gears as I downshift. It hadn't dawned on me how much shorter the incline would be, let alone how diminished our cottage might seem. In fact, the old place looks so small, hidden in the overgrowth at the top of the hill, that I overshoot the driveway. Shifting into reverse, I watch eighteen years catch up in my rearview mirror.

I pull into the clearing between the cottage and a lean-to that is literally leaning. We used to call this nondescript driveway "the dooryard."

I check the dashboard. 11:00. I wonder what Gretchen, my ex-fiancée, is doing right now, "On Saturday, the Thirtieth of May, Nineteen Hundred and Eighty-Seven, at Eleven in the Morning." Probably her sisters are offering consolation, or more likely, congratulations on having cut me loose. It's ironic, how I have inadvertently traded one life-altering day for another. Granted, it remains to be seen whether the next twenty-four hours ends up altering my life. I didn't plan that bit of melodrama, it's just how the days fell. Either way, it seems auspicious somehow.

Pushing Gretchen out of mind for the time being, I climb from the car. The smell of decaying leaves hangs in the midday air, and pine needles crunch underfoot as I walk the path toward the cottage. Spotty moss covers the roof except in those places where shingles have fallen off. The chipped and peeling layer of asphalt brick siding makes an apt statement about Safe Haven. Even with the crumbling facade and rotting sill, I can't help seeing potential. I shake my head and move forward.

This property has changed hands once since we lost the place. I was told that after the foreclosure it sat for ten years. The young couple who bought it ended up in divorce shortly thereafter. If anyone made improvements to the cottage, I'm sure they've long since slipped into disrepair.

Even though I've braced myself for the impact of so much time away, I didn't anticipate how the years would rush past as if they were Frankie and Penny racing each other to the water. I twitched at the sound of birds swooping down the path, weaving between overgrown limbs. I pick up my pace, careful of the roots at my feet, and hurry down a rickety stretch of moldering stairway to where I played as a boy.

This piece of property sits upon the highest point of the lakefront and slopes down into the deepest curve of a sheltered cove. Whispering Narrows' waterfront eats up half of the cove's north side, then pinches it off before curving back out into the lake, where Doc Burns' floatplane used to moor. The "Narrows" closes up the cove just enough that it muffled the rumble of the Cessna, while allowing passage to the rest of the lake. Unfortunately, the Narrows also enhanced all acoustics within the cove. We used to cringe at Mom's grating censures that returned as an echo: "Bad enough we have to hear that god-awful contraption, but we have to look at it, too!" Yet, I loved having the plane in sight beyond the Narrows, just as much as I relished light-handed piano sonatas that rolled down the Burns' lawn like an early morning mist.

I would have ventured down our dock, but too many planks have disintegrated on the sagging, narrow walk. It looks like a sad old smile with unsightly gaps between teeth. My boots feel heavy now that I'm standing on a small patch of beach, kicking at some loose gravel. I drop to my rear end. With my laces untied, I pry off my boots and then peel off red-and-white-striped socks. I can't help grinning, which is why I wore these socks in the first place. I was told they would help me keep my sense of humor.

I smooth each sock and roll them into tidy balls before sticking one in each boot. Giving my tattered hems a couple folds, I trip toward the water's edge. If I fell face-first into the cove, now *that* would be funny.

I slosh out far enough to wet my ankles and then hop onto a small boulder, which leads to another a little farther from shore, which leads to several more, until I land on the "launch pad" where we would dive into the surrounding black water. As soon as I plant my feet, the sun recedes behind a cloud. The treetops quit rustling. Not even a water bug disrupts the lake's glassy surface, and all the black flies vanish. My own pulse seems to pause. It's as if every creature in the cove holds its breath.

Out on the main lake, a small island reflects on the water. I push back a bittersweet memory. Bit by bit, the sounds of the lake revive. The swelling blat of a bullfrog ripples across the water; as if eighteen years suspends its reverberation, the echo finally rolls back to me. The frog sloshes in the reedy pool, but I could swear it's Frankie. Traveling through time—through eighteen years—I hear Penny's voice.

"**GET** THAT DISGUSTING THING AWAY FROM me!"

"Kiss him," Frankie said, shoving the bulging creature at her face. "Turn him into Percy Wade, your Prince Charming."

She gave his flaxen head a good-natured swat. "You are the most annoying seven-year-old alive."

"Sweet sixteen and never been kissed," he chanted, narrowly missing a not-so-gentle smack as he fled toward the boat shack.

Penny turned her attention to me. "C'mon, Ben, let's help Dad get the float in the water. I want a couple hours of sun before supper."

I check Whispering Narrows, hoping for another glimpse of Amelia. Would she notice that I now towered over every other fourteen-year-old on this planet? I wouldn't have minded the height if I had gained as much girth, but I planned to work out over the summer and hoped for improvement.

Amelia was a no-show, and so I followed Penny over to where Dad surveyed the float. The sheathed platform sat on blocks, right where we had left it last Labor Day weekend. As Dad scratched his head, the rolled-up sleeves of his T-shirt cut into his biceps. That didn't make him look any tougher—just made his shirt look too small.

Frankie tugged the tattered canvas, snuffling boogers.

"No, Sport, like this," Dad said, demonstrating how the corners needed lifting before removing the cover.

Frankie mimicked the maneuver.

"Good job, Sport." He cut a look toward me. "Ben, don't just stand there like a moron, help your little brother."

I knew the drill, so I would have stepped in sooner, but I always hesitated around Dad. One screw-up and he would cuff me upside the head.

With one of us at each side, we waddled the float toward its summer mooring place. Within a half hour, we had it secured a few yards from the end of our dock, which was enough time for swimsuit-clad Amelia to find her way down to her beach. After Dad's dismissal, I swam to the float, while Penny retrieved her sunbathing necessities and soon joined me. Open water frightened Frankie, so he stayed at the shoreline with the frogs.

Hoping to shrink my spindly new height, I sat at the float's edge with my chest and shoulders slumped over my knees, careful not to face Whispering Narrows, as if I wasn't spying on Amelia. Penny lay close by, wearing a modest one-piece bathing suit, the style she had to settle for because Mom didn't want her "attracting boys from a fifty-mile radius," as if Penny filled out her top the way Mom did. The fact was, Penny couldn't help attracting boys, and it wasn't just her figure or face. She was a genuinely nice person, even if she had become a little touchy at times.

The scent of perfume-tinged baby oil wafted from her glistening white body. As if waking from sleep, she sighed. Moving only her lips, she said, a little louder than a whisper, "I hate to burst your bubble, Ben, but Amy is way out of your league."

I cringed at her intrusion upon my daydream but was grateful she had kept her voice down. We both knew how sounds carried across the cove.

"I mean honestly," Penny said. "Money aside, look at her—she's got boobs bigger than mine, and what is she, barely fifteen?"

"You're just jealous 'cause you're flat as a board."

"And you're just jealous because she and I are friends."

"You are not."

"Okay, well, more like acquaintances—but at least I've actually been over there. Besides, I'm not flat as a board, at least not *this* summer." She glanced approvingly at her chest. Rolling to her side, she tossed a glance toward Amelia on her stretch of white sand. "You know, I'm not saying that about Amy to be cruel, Ben—"

"I couldn't care less about her." My voice hit two octaves in a split second. I sprung to my feet and then dove into cool water, cutting through midnight velvet. My eardrums compressed as the lake enveloped my body in murkiness that splintered with light as I rolled and darted

24

back to the surface. With a splash, I emerged halfway into the cove. Sucking in a deep breath, I flung water from my hair and wiped my eyes.

Amelia sat cross-legged on her towel, reading a paperback in her lap. She was now nearer to me than Penny. Her eyes responded to the spattering water and settled on me. Confident of her attention, I did my best front crawl. I hoped she was watching, but I didn't have the courage to check. When I dove in again and came up, she had set the book down. I think our eyes met. Then she stood and I took in a real good look at her. For two seconds, I thought she would wade out to meet me, but instead, she picked up her towel, shook it, then wrapped it around herself and walked up their expansive lawn to the house.

Chapter 5

I'M OVERGROWN, STANDING ON THIS BOULDER that once required effort to climb. I've put on another five inches since I was a spindly kid, which seems to have shrunk the entire cove, but not Whispering Narrows. As a boy, the vastness of it captured my imagination, like volumes of Robert Louis Stevenson and H. G. Wells. Treasures of far away places filled its rooms, and the most beautiful creature in the world walked its halls. I spent many hours wishing I could peer into the second-story windows of the west wing, which faces the cove. The far, eastern-facing wing looks out over the lake and hides most of a four-car garage. Just beyond that, at the water's edge, a short dock once moored the floatplane—the second greatest mystery of the lake.

Back in the day, Doc Burns always had Whispering Narrows opened up before we arrived at Safe Haven on Memorial Day weekend. Dad had three weeks off every summer and spent them with us at camp—the first and third around Memorial Day and then Labor Day, and the second during the middle of July. The rest of the time, it was only Penny, Frankie, Mom, and me—until our last summer; more people came into my life, and left, than during any summer before that.

Now, the quiet over at Whispering Narrows is conspicuous. So is the absence of Doc's floatplane. I assume it never came out of winter storage this year. Or perhaps it went up for sale—if that's the case, I wish I would have known; I might have considered buying it myself. Learning to fly—legally—is still on my To Do list.

As for Whispering Narrows, I hope the place stays in the Burns family. I should have asked about it, but I didn't have the presence of mind. Once I'm done with this place, I'll have to look into that. On second thought, perhaps not. It's too much just knowing Doc is no longer around. Besides, I'm not here to grieve him. That will have to wait.

I swat a black fly and turn my attention toward camp. The eagerness of my drive to Safe Haven has devolved into that too-familiar feeling of measured anticipation, never daring to cross the line into all-out excitement. It's difficult to unlearn disappointment. In this case, I can deal with the physical dilapidation of the cottage; I need only to brace myself for the unrecalled memories awaiting my return.

I slip my feet into my socks and boots, leaving the laces slack. Heading up the path, I dig inside my pocket for the key—the front door key. I do not intend to bat my way through insects and other debris suspended in spiderwebs that ensconce the rear basement entrance. The stairway, slick with lichen, adds to the odor of rotting pine needles, decaying asphalt shingles, and mold. The mixture stirs a memory—a fleeting sense of childhood—of me as a child, the innocent who had not yet gained a broader perspective. That child inserts the key and turns it. The adult, the man who understands that nothing stays the same, pushes the door open.

A thin band of light streaks down the length of particleboard paneling, widening like a path as I step inside. A haze infiltrates the grimy windowpanes above the old chipped sink and sideboard beside the door. I move through the shadows to an overhead light bulb in the center of the room and pull the string. Twice. No such luck.

I push back dingy curtains above the sink, illuminating some of the only remaining pieces of furniture, the same old table and chairs that always sat there. I close my eyes and breathe the musty odor, the scent of summer and hope and fantasy—the scent of not knowing.

I walk the perimeter of the round oak table, a sentinel of the past, dragging my fingertip through a film of dust, right over a burn mark. I had forgotten about that. It was the most recent mar, not there long enough to make a deep impression, but significant enough to spark the mental image of a burning cigarette. *Don't dwell on it.* Moving to the opposite side, running my hand beneath the table's overhanging edge, I feel around for a familiar carving—*BH.*

The defacement of family property. My secret rebellion. It would have earned me a beating, for sure. The tactile memory stirs voices—the familiar din of suppertime. Frankie reaching over my plate for bread, without reprimand.

"ELBOWS OFF THE TABLE, BEN, AND STOP slouching," Mom said as she passed the green beans. "And button up your blouse, Penny."

Penny rolled her eyes. "I'm wearing my halter top under it, Mother."

"I don't care. It looks sloppy and gives the wrong impression."

Yeah right. I stifled a snicker. Mom kept her shirts buttoned up, but men still stared.

"Gives the wrong impression to who?" Penny asked, surveying all present.

"Easy on the attitude, Sweet Pea," Dad said.

Distracted by Mom and Penny going at it as usual, I hadn't moved my elbows fast enough.

"Ben, you heard your mother." Dad swung, grazing the back of my head.

I ducked and slid my elbows to my side. Mom's penciled brow spiked. "What is that on your shirt, Ben?"

I had forgotten about the scorch mark. "I bumped into someone's cigarette at Garver's."

She kept one brow arched while squinting. "You haven't been smoking, have you?"

"No, Mom. I just wasn't looking where I was going." I didn't dare mention that the kid had flung it at me. That would have brought up the whole bullying lecture and how I shouldn't let kids push me around, and that I needed to stand up for myself and give it right back.

Dad jumped in. "Well, I don't appreciate having to buy new clothes because you can't be bothered to watch where you're going."

"Sorry," I said, anticipating another swing. "I'll be more careful."

Penny gave me a nudge. "You could just tie-dye it, and no one would notice a little singe."

I let out a huff. "Not likely." What I really wanted was to change the subject. "Can I ride my bike after supper?" I asked, directing my question to neither parent specifically.

They exchanged a look. Before Mom could object, Dad said, "After you help with dishes."

In hopes of avoiding further stipulations or leaking any eagerness, I nodded without making eye contact.

An hour later, I skidded out of our driveway, calculating the lean of my stingray bike with its brand new banana seat. It was impressive. Back in the development where we lived, it was the bossest bike on the block. Its best feature was caliper brakes. I had installed them myself. Everyone knew me as the go-to bike man. I could take any piece-of-crap bike and give it a complete makeover, paint job included. Since there weren't any hills in our neighborhood, only square grids of pavement, I couldn't wait to give it a spin on the inclines and declines of the dirt roads around the lake.

Taking a left turn onto the road, I pedaled the downward slope. I had grown too big for the bike, which made the whole contraption top-heavy and sent me reeling side to side with each pedal thrust. Before the steep drop-off, I locked up the rear brake, shooting a gravel fishtail behind as I 'J' skidded to a halt. From there, the road gradually ascended until the road peaked in front of our camp. If I gained enough speed, I could catch a little air as

I headed into the hairpin curve beyond our driveway and then zip down toward Whispering Narrows. Sure, it was risky, but for months, I had been imagining my moment of triumph, envisioning myself as Evel Knievel.

I took off, speeding up as I breached the curve and gained some air. With a twist of my handlebars, I righted myself and landed as Doc Burns' vehicle came out of nowhere. I hit both brakes, skidding into his Land Rover's front tire. It was more of a scrape than a collision, but it disabled my chain as I careened off to the side of the road. We both came to a halt.

His head lunged from the window as his voice thundered, "Jeeze, son, you alright?"

I brushed gravel from my leg with one skinned hand, and gripped the handlebar with the other. I panted, "Yeah, I'm fine—no biggy."

"You ought to take it easy on that curve, you know." His bushy white brows furrowed as his fingers raked a shock of silver hair.

Awaiting his rebuke, I quickly replied, "Yes, sir, I'll be more careful. I didn't hurt your car, did I?"

He cocked his head and exhaled a chuckle. "I'd be more concerned with your bike, if I were you."

I nudged the slack chain with my sneaker. "I think that's the worst of it—I can fix it easy."

"You sure?"

I didn't know if I should read his squint as disbelief or approval.

"Oh yeah—" my voice pitched a curve. "I fix all sorts of stuff."

"Is that right?"

"Yeah, bikes and all kinds of other mechanical crap—I mean, *stuff*, sir."

"Mechanical, eh? Like what?"

"Lawn mowers," I said and then thought of something more impressive. "And I fixed a clock that I bought at a junk shop—with gears and everything."

"A clock, did you?"

This time I detected a distinct glint of approval. "Yes, sir."

"You're Ben, the lad from Safe Haven on the crest."

"Yes, Mr. Burns."

"I almost didn't recognize you. You sprouted a few inches this past year."

"Yes, sir." I tried to keep my face from cracking a too-eager smile.

He extended his meaty hand and enveloped mine like a baseball mitt. "Good to see you, son."

I squeezed with all I had, a tiny mouse in a steel trap.

One corner of his mouth curled. "That's quite a grip you've got."

My ears flashed hot and I nodded my modest best.

"How's your family?" he asked.

"Good, sir," I said, suddenly aware of how often I had uttered the word *sir* in the past two minutes.

He winked. "You come on by my house tomorrow morning. I've got an old clock that my brother-in-law gave me, years ago—a relic as far as I'm concerned. But if you can fix it, you can have it."

My jaw dropped. Nothing came out. I needed to reply with something clever—something memorable, something that didn't include the word *sir,* but all I could come up with was, "Gosh, sir, I don't know what to say, sir."

"Don't say a thing. Just come by before noon, 'cause I've got an appointment after that."

My ears flamed hotter. "Yes, sir."

"Will that be okay with your parents?"

"Oh yes, sir," I lied.

"Alright then. You sure you're okay?"

Gravel still clung to my bloody knee. "Yeah—I get these all the time. Thank you, sir."

As he drove away, I reveled in having just received an invitation from the most impressive man alive.

31

Chapter 6

YEARS OF MILDEW CONSTRICT MY AIRWAYS. Exerting some muscle and leverage, I pry open the window sash above the sink. *Gah*! More insect carcasses and spiderwebs. Now that my eyes have adjusted to the dim light, it's easier to make out other features of the dining-kitchen area. Aside from a 'new' avocado-colored refrigerator replacing the old, white Frigidaire, much of the cottage appears the same. Scuffs and gouges mark the 1950s kitchen linoleum, and the tired old floorboards in the dining area don't show a whole lot of extra wear. There doesn't appear to be any structural alteration, which provides an illusion of stability, of unchangeableness, as if everything about that last summer would continue like all the summers before it.

When I jump a little to see if the floor still bounces, the glass in the front door rattles, and the bare bulb sways overhead. A huge water stain sags the sheetrock ceiling above me. I fear it may give way, splitting open and dumping eighteen years of vermin feces and fallout. Metaphor and filth aside, now *that* would be funny. I hop again, just to tempt lingering ghosts. *Nothing?* I guess it's safe to proceed.

Making my way through the kitchen and down the short hall, I pass Penny's closed door—I will visit there, but not now. At the end of the hall is my parents' room. I would rather not go in there. It's not the focal point of why I'm here; just the same, I stare at their door—eyes twitching—wishing for X-ray vision. At least that way I would know if there was any reason worth my venturing in. No hurry. I'll think about that later.

The room I shared with Frankie is nestled between my parents' and Penny's rooms, which always seemed stupid to me. What sane parent puts a pair of rambunctious boys only two sheetrock layers away and the quiet little bookworm out of earshot? Granted, Penny's floor space was four inches less than ours was, and we boys needed every bit of elbowroom available.

I push open my door and step inside. The walls close in around me. The metal-framed bunk bed against the near wall eats up most of the cubicle that now feels no bigger than a closet. Two steps away, a small corner window offsets the bed. The bare mattress of the upper bunk looks like the same one I slept on, back when I didn't care how lumpy the bedding was. I usually dozed off easily at camp, although, now that I think of it, I had a hard time sleeping that first night, and it wasn't because I would be sneaking to Doc's in the morning. The problem was Mom and Dad. Even over Frankie's snoring below me, I detected contention in their hushed voices.

" ... **WELL**, BEN'S AT THAT AGE, YOU KNOW," Mom rebutted.

My ears perked.

Dad's deep sigh penetrated the wall. "And what would you have me do? Search his room?"

My cheeks heated. I would have to find a new hiding place for my *MAD* magazines. Good thing I had already transplanted the bulk of them before we left last summer.

"You need to do something about your son. I don't want him smoking—like father, like son."

"Like father, like son? That's a stretch."

"I know you have a smoke every now and then, Frank."

"The *smoking* isn't what I'm talking about.... "

Through the pause, I envisioned Mom's glare. "We are not having *that* discussion again."

33

Something clunked the floorboards—a shoe, maybe, followed by a second thud. "No, I suppose we don't need to, now that you're up here in the boonies, away from—"

"And what's that supposed to mean?"

"Nothing." I pictured Dad knotting his arms with finality. "Fine. I'll talk to Ben."

If I hadn't heard that phrase, "Fine, I'll talk to Ben," a hundred times before Dad brought up any of Mom's pet topics, chances were, I would never receive the Why-Smoking-Is-Bad lecture. It would be a refreshing change from the Stand-Up-to-Bullies spiel. I would never forget that speech.

Dad had waited until a neighborhood barbeque when my friends and their parents gathered around the picnic table and grill. "Ben just needs to learn how to stand his ground, like his old man," he'd said, smacking his fist to his palm. "He's got to earn respect the old fashioned way."

It wasn't as if Dad were some tough guy who went around getting into brawls. He wasn't violent so much as always on the edge. Although I never knew when he might lash out at me, his full-blown hairy fits usually coincided with one of Mom's moods. And even when he booted my rear end or smacked me upside the head, it wasn't hard enough to really hurt. But he always chose the worst times, like when I was around my buddies. As much as I would have liked a friend at camp, at least there was no audience for Dad's belittling—that was a perk. And so far, Mom was in a relatively good mood. At least she had been until they started bickering tonight. To my relief, their argument didn't last long. Mom ended it with her predictable, "Quiet or you'll wake them …."

As I lay there, hoping that was the last of it, I couldn't help thinking about exactly *which* discussion Mom and Dad were 'not going to have again.' Why were adult arguments always so cryptic? And why did so many of my parents' disputes begin or end with my name? If I hoped for any sleep at all, I needed to quit thinking about stuff that made my heart pound. If I was going to dwell on any of life's big mysteries, I was better off fantasizing about Amelia Burns—the ultimate mystery. My thoughts jumped from her to Doc to Whispering Narrows, and how I might sneak down there undetected. Halfway into formulating a plan, I fell asleep.

The next morning, my plotting picked up where I had left off. My strategy would be to play it cool and draw no undue attention. I never had much to say at the breakfast table, so I didn't appear any different from usual, but I thought for sure someone would notice my excitement. I chewed slowly, made no eye contact, brought my dishes to the sink, and even volunteered to sweep pine needles off the stoop. That might have been a mistake.

Mom grabbed my sleeve. "Are you feeling alright this morning, Ben?"

"Yeah," I said. "I'm just gonna ride my bike—that okay?"

She looked me up and down like a schoolmarm, and I half-expected her to inspect my fingernails for tobacco stains or check my breath.

"Just be careful, stay off the main road, and be back by lunchtime," she said.

It never occurred to me that I should bother to ask if it was okay to go to Doc's place. My mother disliked him, although I didn't recall that she ever came out and said so, but I did have some recollection—more like an out-of-focus snapshot—of some falling-out between them. And, why provide one more opportunity to prove that my parents delighted in disappointing me? Besides, Mom never said I couldn't go to Whispering Narrows. In my book, omission was as good as permission.

In case Mom or Dad might have observed me from the window over the kitchen sink, I headed away from Doc's and then calculated my turnaround. A few minutes later, I zipped back past our dooryard and coasted downhill. For the first time in my life, I ventured between the grotesque lions atop the large stone pillars and onto pea stone gravel. The lions would have been scarier if they didn't have their paws up, like Lassie. Doc's Land Rover was parked in the half-circle drive in front of the grand entryway, between the west wing and the east.

I didn't want to leave my bike lying in the driveway, but my run-in with the Land Rover had snapped off my stingray's kickstand. I dared not lean it against any of the large concrete planters, the sculpted shrubs, or the wrought iron railing that curled up either side of three steps to the front door. I opted for the large oak tree near the road, tucked out of sight from passing vehicles.

I climbed the wide granite steps between two pillars, twice as tall as me. The faint roll of piano scales penetrated the wooden door. Standing under the huge porch, I stared up into the fearsome eyes of a cast-iron lion's head. I hesitated to lift the large ring and looked for a doorbell. Surely, the richest man on the lake had a doorbell, but no, I had no choice but to use the knocker. With two timid raps, the sound of piano notes ceased. As I waited, I imagined Amelia at her piano, wearing a bikini, with her strawberry locks tumbling down her arched back—a side view of course. I continued waiting, hoping that she might be sauntering toward the door at that very moment—that the door would open slowly, that she would blush and take my hand ….

The heavy door flew open, displacing enough atmosphere to cool the sweat collecting at my hairline.

"Ben—Good," Doc bellowed from within, his voice as vigorous as his stature, which loomed like a sequoia. "How's the knee?"

"Good, sir," I said without moving. Before I could add anything, he walked back into the house, leaving the door wide open.

"Don't just stand there," he called. "Do you think I want to air condition the entire lake?" Was that an invitation to step in? He half turned, his voice booming in the large foyer. "Inside, son! And shut the door behind you!"

"Yes, sir," I said as he exited into a doorway that seemed to narrow as it enveloped his girth. I stepped inside, onto slate. Although I stood indoors, everything surrounding me—the wood and iron, the earthy colors, the smell of pine—felt like outdoors. Overhead and in front of a balcony, a massive iron chandelier hung like an eagle descending upon its prey. An oak rail and balusters wound around the upper foyer and joined a staircase that landed to my right. Opposite the main entrance, a set of double doors was cracked ajar. Stained-glass panes shrouded the room's contents but could not obscure an outline of a grand piano.

Music had not picked up again. The figure sitting at the bench shifted. Her back faced me. I thought she might have turned around for a look, and so I moved just out of sight, although I'm not certain why. Perhaps I felt out of place—perhaps standing in the grand foyer brought Penny's words back to me: *She's out of your league, Ben* ....

My throat tightened with an involuntary cough—it ricocheted off a hundred surfaces and came crashing back like thunder. The seconds hung forever. With stealth, I moved just enough to snatch a view between the doors.

She wore a sundress. Tendrils escaped from a ponytail atop her head and swept across her shoulder as her face turned toward me. A piano keystroke cut the silence like shattering glass, and then another stroke, a note lower. As if in time with a metronome, her notes repeated: one-two—one-two. Tick-tock—tick-tock—tick-tock, drawing blood to my face. Our eyes met. I resisted the impulse to look away. To endure her tease without a flinch was the lesser humiliation. She seemed to be smiling. Was it at me, or at my discomfort?

Rescuing me from torment, Doc's voice reached the foyer before he did.

"Found it—seems to be all here," he said as he approached, carrying a box with flaps askew.

I moved from Amelia's sight and met Doc, my heart pounding. He shoved some crumpled old newspaper from the box to my hand. I stretched my neck for a peek at a pointed-top, beehive-shaped clock with a plain, porcelain face and mahogany-looking case. I bet it was old. My confidence bolstered at the sight of the manufacturer's stamp, Seth Thomas—I had heard of that clock maker.

"Well? What do you think? Fixable?"

"Don't know, sir. I'll need a closer look."

He thrust the box at me with a wink. "You got tools?"

"No, sir—I mean, yes, but not at camp."

"Follow me," he rumbled, heading back through the narrow doorway. I obeyed.

From what I could tell, it was a service hall—a long one, unadorned and emptying into a room that dwarfed under his presence. A door to the right remained open, exposing a kitchen. We exited through another door directly ahead, leading to the garage. It looked nothing like any garage I had ever been in, and it didn't smell like gasoline and oily rags, either. I stayed close at his heel, counting off four cars sheathed in canvas—except for the Jag, which sparkled even in the dim light. Side by side, we stood in his workshop, tucked in a corner that was the size of an entire room.

Benches lined the wall, over which a set of windows peered out at the lake, providing a view of not only Amelia's beach, but also Doc's floatplane.

I scarcely noticed when he asked, "Ever been in one of those?"

I shook my head—with my mouth agape.

"Every boy's dream, I suppose."

"What is it? I mean what kind of plane?"

"She's a Cessna 185 with their new 300 horsepower Continental engine," he said as I gawked. *She*. I had never heard anyone refer to a plane as 'she'—a boat, yes, but I hadn't ever thought of a plane the way he apparently did. All at once, his Cessna took on female characteristics— beautiful and curvaceous, while elusive and full of mystery.

He bent to a low drawer, pointing. "In there."

I gave him a curious glance, hesitant to come off as presumptuous.

"Yes, open it! Don't make a tired old man bend."

"Yes, sir," I said and pulled the drawer.

"You see what you need?"

"Yes." A full set of jeweler's screwdrivers and assorted other fine implements sat arranged in a wooden base. I had never seen such sparkling tools outside of a catalog.

"Well then, now you know where they are. Work on the clock for a little while this morning, if you like. When you're done, leave through this door," he said, opening the portal leading to the world outside—to the airplane dock. "Come back tomorrow if you'd like. Use this entrance. The key's under the rock by the door."

"Really?"

His brow crinkled with dismay. "Was I unclear?"

"No, sir," I replied, bracing myself for his rebuke.

"You are trustworthy, aren't you?"

"Yes."

"Then we'll get along fine," he said, jabbing his hand toward me.

Apparently, he liked me. I shoved my hand at his.

"So, you *do* know how to smile, young Benjamin Hughes!"

He winked, exited into the yard, and shut the door behind him. Through the window, I watched him come into sight as he ambled down the dock toward his Cessna and all but disappear behind its fuselage. It barely rocked under his weight as he stepped up onto its torpedo-shaped float, which jostled for a few moments afterward. I imagined him checking all the controls, flipping switches, tapping gauges, and talking to some staticky voice in his headphone as he cleared everything for takeoff. Before long, the engine engaged and it started its forward lunge into the middle of the lake. After skimming the surface, it rose from the water, cleared the trees within inches, and then veered sharply to the southeast, disappearing from my view. He must have been the richest man on the East Coast!

Alone now, awe overtook me. The shop may as well have been a sanctuary for the reverential feelings it evoked. Light streamed in from the double window, as if through cathedral stained glass, and reflected off a set of hand ratchets of ascending sizes, gleaming like pipes of an old church organ. I was surely in heaven.

The clock drew my attention. I set it on the workbench and pulled the small brass knob on its back access door. A pendulum lay in the bottom of the case with a long and bent wire still attached. Its spring had cracked and split off. I had to think on the remedy, but before I tackled that, it needed a good cleaning. Of course, that would require at least several more trips to Doc's shop. I glanced at my watch. Time was running short. I didn't want him to think I had abandoned the project, so I wrote a note, letting him know I needed some mineral spirits, and that I would be back.

I slipped out the door and gazed at the spot where the plane had sat. How would it feel, moving forward over the water, gaining momentum, and lifting skyward? My imaginings soon wandered around the corner of the garage shop, across the back lawn, and down toward Amelia's unoccupied beach. I kept out of sight, hidden from Safe Haven.

Penny sat reading on the float and Frankie played at the water's edge. Mom reposed in her recliner, her head tipped sunward. I assumed that some project over at our shed kept

Dad busy and out of sight. Our camp's appearance from Amelia's perspective excited me, but Frankie's laughter rippling across the water, as if he were only feet away, reminded me of our precarious proximity. How many of our conversations had Amelia overheard? At the thought of it, heat pulsed from my neck up, intensifying as I recalled the look on her face as she played Tick-Tock on her piano.

CHAPTER 7

I T'S STRANGE HOW EVEN AS AN ADULT, THE memory of Amelia turns me into an insecure kid and twists my stomach. I'm not sure if my intensified mood is the result of staring out the window at Amelia's beach, or because I'm standing in my old room, but the atmosphere now feels heavier—gloomier. As I crank the casement window open, a glint of light from the sill catches my eye. An aggie marble. Rubbing off the film of grime, I hold it up, marveling at the simplicity of it. I pop the marble into the air and catch it, grinning at the happy memento, and then stick it in my pocket. A cool breeze follows me out of the room.

Next, I need power and water. Or I could spend the evening in the dark. I walk toward the basement stairway, considering that option, and stall. Rather than succumb to cowardice, I give myself a rehearsed speech: *All you have to do is walk downstairs, go directly to the utility closet, take care of business, and get the hell out!* My eye twitches. Sucking in a long breath, I give my vest a fortifying yank and straighten my spine. *Just do it.*

I step onto the first tread. The second squeaks. From there, my nerves steady, and I continue down the narrow stairway. Humidity and the odor of mildew strengthen as I descend into the dimly lit basement. The exterior door, separating me from the hovering bug graveyard that I bypassed earlier, provides hazy illumination. As soon as I step onto concrete, the temperature drops. Although the fieldstone fireplace in the corner is swept clean, the acridity of ash still lingers in the air. How many rainy days did we warm ourselves in front of that fireplace, playing cards or monopoly? How many times did I stare into flickering embers, wondering how my life would turn out? What career would I have? Whom would I end up marrying?

Gretchen comes back to mind. If all had gone according to plan, I would be wearing a wedding band at this moment, kissing my bride in front of 278 guests. God, I miss her. And yet I'm also relieved—not because she broke the engagement, but because she's no longer dependent upon me. Not that she was a burden—I would have gladly followed through. Bittersweet, how you can build someone up, help her discover her own value, and then realize you've given her wings. The hardest part has been accepting the notion that *I* am no longer enough, that *my* emotional baggage has caught up with *me*. Watching her fly away gave me an odd satisfaction and the deepest pain I've ever known. Okay, that may be a little melodramatic. In reality, the pain of our breakup is farther down the list.

I focus on the utility closet opposite the fireplace. Inside, the water pump and the rusty, paint-peeled water heater look as if they've been here since the sixties. I turn levers, light the pilot, and flip the main breaker, working mechanically, going through the motions like checking off a mental list before takeoff. *Clear.*

I back out of the closet. Beside me, the door to an adjacent room at the rear wall—a flaking particleboard partition—remains shut. We called it the "unfinished room." It housed a washer and two-by-four-constructed shelving with exposed rafters above. As soon as I catch myself lingering, I let go of the breath I've been holding and swallow back a wave of nausea.

I need air—*now*! Turning on heel and trotting upstairs, I trip on the laces I didn't tie. Now *that* would be ironic, if I slipped and broke a leg and couldn't climb back up. I would laugh myself to death, right here on the stairs.

Continuing my sprint, I soon hit the upstairs and rush to the door, out onto the front stoop. Only two deep breaths later, my stomach simmers down, and my pulse slows. I shake off my nerves. *I'm good.* While I'm outside, I may as well gather up my few things from the car.

In two steps, I pause in the dooryard, lulled by the chirps of crickets and peepers. I close my eyes. How could I feel so panicked in one moment, and then two seconds later, breathe so easily, as relaxed as a kid at the outset of summer? I move forward. *Why did I come out here?* That's right—to retrieve my overnight bag.

My stomach growls. Rather than reach for my clothes and overnight luggage, I snatch the lunch bag on the back seat and my Birkenstocks from the floor. Better grab the fold-up lawn chair I bought on my way up from Logan Airport. Distracted by the coffee-spoiled drawing pad on the dashboard, I roll my eyes. I'm not sure if I feel worse about ruining the lady's sketch or insulting her with a fifty. I can't say I would have been any less ticked than she was. *Oh well.* I'm glad she took the fifty. For the money, I should at least thumb through my purchase—maybe later.

Down on the beach, I set aside my lunch, wrestle open the contraption-of-a-chair and sit. With the Birkenstocks at my feet, I leave my 'Dr. Seuss' socks on and slip out of my boots and into the sandals. Wiggling my red and white toes, I reach for Pastrami on rye. Seconds later, I'm squirming as my rear end numbs. Makes me think of our old aluminum chairs and how we sacrificed Adirondack aesthetics for supposed utility and style, and ended up with a nylon-weave pattern engraved in the backs of our bare thighs.

I open the potato salad, finishing it off in a few minutes. Chewing the last of my sandwich, my eyes close. Perhaps I'll doze for a minute; but no—as if the image of Mom's outstretched body on her lounge chair were burned into my retinas, I not only 'see' her, but my heart rate spikes, just like that morning when I returned from looking at Doc's clock. I'm awash with excitement and guilt for having gotten away with something.

I APPROACHED MOM FROM BEHIND HER lounger while keeping an eye out for Dad. Part of me hoped to hang out with him even if it entailed a lecture on smoking. Maybe we would end up fishing or something. Not that we had done much fishing over the years, but it seemed to me that's what fathers and sons were supposed to do at camp.

"Hey, Mom," I said in a low voice, in case she was snoozing. She didn't respond. I cleared my throat. She flinched, sloshing the lemonade in her paper cup.

"How many times do I have to tell you not to sneak up on me like that?"

"Sorry. I was just wondering where Dad is."

She heaved a deep sigh and shut her eyes. "He had to take care of some business for a few hours."

"What? We've only been here a couple days."

Her lips pressed, forming thin, bright pink lines as her jaw tensed, and her eyes again flew open. "Something unexpected came up at work. You know, someone has to pay for our vacations here—we're not like the Burns, who come and go as they please and have everything handed to them on a silver platter."

My focus cut across the cove toward Whispering Narrows. Fortunately, no one had taken up sunbathing on Amelia's beach. Why did Mom's voice have to be so shrill whenever she spoke of the Burns?

Mom's whole body shuddered as she raised the cup to her lips. Her eyes rolled and shut as she sipped and then slid back into her seat as if all tension drained in an exhalation.

As she snoozed, I went for a swim. Penny joined me. We raced, from the float to the mouth of the cove and back again, enough times for me to win just once. She was a great swimmer, way better than I was, but every so often, she would throw me a victory. Out at the mouth of the cove—at the Narrows—we treaded water.

"You wanna try for the island?" I asked.

"Mom would have a fit—besides, it's too far."

"Like, only a quarter mile."

"In your dreams. It's a mile if it's a yard."

"Is not."

"Who'd wanna swim out to that mound of brush and trees, anyway? It's smaller than our float."

"Is *not*! It's at least ten times the size of the float."

"Big whoop! It doesn't even have a beach," she said and splashed water at me, swimming backward toward shore. Again, the race was on, and I beat her by a hand's width. It was a pity win, but I didn't care. I was just glad to have someone to hang out with while I waited for Dad, even if she was my big sister.

Mom slept most of the afternoon, which gave her plenty of energy for slamming pans and cabinet doors around the kitchen at dinnertime. Dad still hadn't returned by the time we sat down to eat. It wasn't until after I went to bed that I heard the Falcon's transmission grind into low gear and the engine quit in the dooryard. I waited for the car door to shut. A few minutes later, careful steps moved toward our room. Our door closed with a quiet click and then came the muffled clunk of my parents' door. Soon their voices began, low and hushed at first. All I could make out were Mom's usual accusations—*Frank, you always ... You never ... You said ... Leaving me alone with the kids*—and Dad's mumbled rebuttal, *Now, Beverly ... Don't be ... I'm not ... You're so ...* before the closet door slammed, sending a tremor through the wall.

Frankie snored loudly on the lower bunk as I climbed out of bed, my *MAD* magazine falling to the floor. I cranked open the window overlooking the cove, letting in a burst of air that shrank my skin, tight over my chattering bones. The breeze had felt too cold earlier, yet now provided relief. Moonlight scattered across the water. I thought about sneaking down to the beach, but with two parents in a foul mood, why risk it?

I glanced at Frankie. Bluish light washed his sweet little face, giving it an eerie and devious tinge. I tugged his blanket from his ankles up over his chest. Crickets and bullfrogs chirped and blatted like a pubescent chorus. They sounded way better than the feebly stifled argument next door. I waited until Mom's voice cut through the muddle, as always.

"Quiet! You'll wake the children."

From then on, it was just the usual scuff against the wall or a muted thud. It would soon quiet down. I scooted between my sheets, letting them settle at my waist. Now all I needed was a fantasy about Amelia, and I would drift off in no time.

We kids were the first ones up the following morning. Frankie grabbed a piece of toast with jam before hurrying down to the water, ever oblivious to anything that had happened in the night. I never knew anyone who slept more soundly.

Penny sat at the table with me, eating a bowl of Rice Krispies. When something inside our parents' room rustled, we both glanced at their door and then at each other.

"Did you hear 'em last night?" I asked.

She rolled her eyes while nodding, her cheeks bulging. A dribble of milk escaped the corner of her mouth, and we both smirked as she tried to catch it, making it worse.

"You are so gross for a girl," I said.

Still chewing, she stuck her finger up her nose, trying to restrain a close-lipped grin. She was the only girl I knew who could do that and still not look completely disgusting. Amelia could, but I was certain she would *never* do a thing like that.

47

Dad stepped into the kitchen, carefully closing their bedroom door behind him. Penny brought her bowl to the sink and sidled past him toward the bathroom. He pulled a folded paper from his breast pocket.

"We're going to the market for some groceries," he said and shoved the list at me. So much for going to Doc's this morning, but going to Garver's wasn't a bad tradeoff.

My gaze shot toward his bedroom but I didn't dare ask.

"Your mom's sleeping in," he said. I waited for him to blame it on me, as if somehow having a middle child the likes of me might frazzle any mother. But he said nothing more except, "Meet me out at the car in five minutes—and make sure you brush that crud off your teeth."

So what! I had forgotten to brush the night before.

I tapped the bathroom door.

"I gotta brush my teeth to go to Garver's," I said in the loudest hushed voice I could without rousing Mom. I tapped again and the door flung open.

"I'm going too." Penny pulled her hair into a ponytail. "Don't let Dad leave without me."

As if he would ever do that to his Sweet Pea.

A minute later, I climbed in the back seat of the station wagon. Dad cocked an inquisitive brow.

"Penny's coming," I informed him.

He nodded but said nothing, as if my words didn't register. We waited a few minutes, and then Penny slid into the front seat. The knot at the nape of her neck meant that she wore her halter-top beneath the buttoned-up, button-down shirt. Of course, Dad didn't notice. He simply stared ahead, twisting the corners of his mouth. As he pulled out of the dooryard, he didn't even react when he nearly clipped the Falcon's bumper.

We drove past Whispering Narrows, where Doc stood in his driveway. He flashed a friendly wave, but Dad seemed not to notice that either. I offered a discrete wave, glad that Doc could see I had plans for the morning, and that's why I wouldn't be showing up to work on the clock, that I wasn't a slacker. Although it embarrassed me that Dad didn't wave back, I was just as glad he had missed my exchange with Doc. Penny, on the other hand, turned her head all the way around, flipping her ponytail and raising one brow. At least I could count on her not saying anything in front of Dad. We had an unspoken pact.

Our car pulled into the parking spot at Garver's Market. Dora sat in front of window advertisements for Yoo-hoo, Coca-Cola and Orange Crush. Dad tucked a newspaper under one arm as he climbed from the car. I followed him up the steps, keeping some distance between Dora and me.

Penny lingered behind. "I'm just gonna sit out here and enjoy the sun."

"Sure thing, Sweet Pea," Dad muttered, still preoccupied as he stepped through the jingling door.

"Hi, Ben," Dora called out.

"Hi, Dora. You didn't eat all those Mary Janes at once, did you?"

"Yes."

I shook my head and smiled.

Mr. Garver grinned through the window as he taped a poster beside the door. Colorful letters and brightly illustrated rides announced the annual carnival, August 22nd through 24th. Every year, carnies assembled the event out in the field behind the store, where it brought business for the Garver's and provided a diversion that broke up the summer monotony of swimming, fishing, and rowing around the lake. It was the highlight of our summers, the one event Mom always agreed she would take us to.

I went inside as Penny sat at the edge of the porch, stretching sun-pink legs as she undid all her buttons and tied the shirttails in a knot at her waist. Through the screen, I glanced at the pickup across the street and the longhaired hippie in bellbottom jeans that climbed out. Percy Wade— the lifeguard at the public beach last summer.

"I've gotta make a phone call, in back," Dad said, grabbing my arm. "You got that list?"

"Yeah, Dad."

"Have Mrs. Garver put it on our tab," he said as he pulled out his wallet. My eyes gaped at the sight of more greenbacks than I had ever seen crammed into any wallet in my life. He pulled out a five.

"Get me a dollar's-worth of dimes," he said with urgency. He studied my face for a moment before saying, "And keep the change—get yourself something."

My jaw dropped.

"Don't just stand there like a moron."

I walked straight to the cash register where Dora had joined her mother. Mrs. Garver made change. I stuck four singles into my pocket and, with a handful of dimes and a shopping basket, I headed toward the back of the store. Dad tucked the phone between his shoulder and chin, scribbling something on his newspaper. He waved me over. Even while I was depositing the coins in his open hand, he turned away, falling into the shadows of the narrow corridor leading to the rest room. That was my chance to grab a copy of *MAD* and move on to the groceries.

With my magazine in the basket, I scanned the list and headed to the third aisle from the storefront. Even from there, Dora's heavy breathing alerted me to the likelihood that she was watching my every move. I glanced across aisles of chest-high shelving, catching her big grin. She let out a throaty sigh. I returned a hesitant smile and got down to the business of shopping. Rice Krispies, margarine, green beans, ginger ale, Spaghetti-Os, hot dogs, *Marshmallow Fluff —What?* Since when had we started buying Marshmallow Fluff? Four dollars in my pocket and now Fluff? I smiled, looking for Penny. Out on the porch, the hippie paused in front of her, stroking his goatee as they talked. I felt Dora's continuing stare.

As I flopped a loaf of Wonder bread into the basket, the front door jingled open. I expected the hippie, but instead, Amelia walked in, all backlit like an angel—until Doc's large figure overshadowed her. She tugged her sleeveless, white blouse and smoothed her plaid pedal pushers. On impulse, I glanced at Dad. He had disappeared into the shadows. I stood motionless and then snatched the first thing in front of me.

"Well, good morning, Ben," came a deep voice that would certainly draw Dad's attention. I didn't dare check.

"Good morning, Mr. Burns," I said as Amelia stepped over to the magazine rack between the register and the door. I stared at the coils of her ponytail as she thumbed through a *Seventeen Magazine*.

"Didn't I tell you to call me Doc?" he said.

"No, sir," I replied as she replaced the magazine and then turned her attention to the paperback rack.

"Well, I'm sure I meant to."

I nodded, mustering the courage to monitor Dad's attentiveness. He remained absorbed in his phone exchange. I relaxed a little.

With each groan of the carousel, Amelia picked one book, perused the back, returned it to its place and picked another. With her final choice, she moved to the outside aisle. Froot Loops, laundry detergent, and cookies separated us. As she picked up a package of Oreos, I tried not to stare. *Act casual!* I kept her in my peripheral vision. She must have been aware of me only three aisles over— after all, her grandfather had just talked to me.

"Ben," came his booming voice again as he held up a pint of mineral spirits. "Will this do?"

I recalled the note I had left in his shop and nodded, now certain that I must have had his granddaughter's attention. I glanced her way. Our eyes met at the very same moment—her gaze far steadier than mine, as if it were nothing to stare at someone she had never uttered one word to, in all the years we had been aware of each other. My resolve weakened as the corners of her mouth rose simultaneously with her single brow. If I had tried to smile, my lips would have trembled and splintered, falling right off my face, and so I only returned her raised brow. She bit her moistened lip.

"Ben," Dora's voice cut in. "Mommy says I'm allowed to swim. Could I come and swim at your beach?"

My gaze darted from Amelia to Dora and back. *Gah! Why does she have to talk to me in front of Amelia?* "Um—" I huffed, rolling my eyes. "I don't think so—" My snotty tone surprised even me.

Before Dora could respond through her tears, Mrs. Garver interrupted, "Dora, it's not polite to invite yourself. Besides, we already talked about this. You'll have to wait to go swimming with Lenny and the group, remember?"

With a big sniff, Dora's chin sank into her chest. *Great, now I've made her cry.* I couldn't even bring myself to look at Amelia. *I'm such a moron!*

"You ready, sweetie?" Doc spoke up, setting his purchase on the counter.

Without so much as a glance at me, Amelia joined her grandfather, placing her cookies and paperback beside the can of solvent, then twirled and exited. By the time Doc paid for the mineral spirits, the hippie guy stood next in line. I shuffled to the front of the store as Doc exited. *Where's a comic-book character with an 'earth-shattering Kaboom!' when I need one?* I stared at the frayed hem of the hippie's bellbottoms as he stepped forward.

"A packet of Zig-Zags," he said.

Dora wandered from her stool to the stock room as he laid a bill on the counter. I couldn't look at Mrs. Garver when she rung up our groceries and asked, "Some penny candy, Ben?"

"I guess—" I shrugged, still hot, as if I had been caught lying or stealing, except way worse—I had made Dora cry.

CHAPTER 8

A SQUAWKING CROW ACCUSES ME, ROUSING me back to the present. I still feel bad about making Dora cry, although I was just an immature kid and kids do stupid things. Even so, I had always considered myself above downright meanness. Looking back on that incident—on my reaction to Dora—I'm grateful for having become acutely aware of my flawed character and the need to redeem myself. I didn't view that revelation as progressive at the time; all I felt was overwhelming shame. A tinge of it resurfaces even now and triggers my tick.

As if looking for reassurance, I glance up at where Doc's Cessna once moored and then narrow my vision to the cove. A ghost of a rowboat floats by with fourteen-year-old me at the helm and more passengers than a dinghy could ever hold in real life. Each face comes in and out of focus. In a flash, the apparition vanishes. Mustering a half smile, I wiggle my red and white toes.

Time to get on with it and move ahead. I stand, arching the slump from my back. Might that old aluminum rowboat still be lurking somewhere? It seems unlikely, though it's worth a look. Drawing in a deep breath, I peek behind the shack at a heap of pine needles and layers of decomposing foliage. I kick at the dross of leaves and they return a hollow thud. The upside-down boat doesn't budge. It's now as much a part of the landscape as the nearby boulders. The old relic probably houses a happy family of mice, safe from predators, and I'm not about to disturb it.

While I'm here, I can't help checking the shed to see if the previous owners have left anything behind. Rusted hinges moan as I push open the door. Dust filters the light shining on old coffee cans sitting upon rows of shelving. Mom's old recliner, covered in every god-awful insect and web, is as twisted and misshapen as the shelves above it. Two oars lean in the corner, paddle ends up. I force back a snatch of a memory—an impulse; a swing in the dark; a thud—and wade through bits of debris and a curtain of spiderwebs.

As I yank one of the oars and carry it to the light of the doorway, I inspect the repair I once made to the fractured wood. It was a pretty good fix for a kid—a narrow strip of copper flashing wrapped around the split end of the paddle, and a row of small brass nails driven through to the other side and peened, like little rivets. Dad said it was a waste of copper and threw off the balance between the two oars—as if a couple ounces made a difference.

I deposit my handiwork beside Mom's old recliner. A swatch of yellow behind a pickle jar catches my eye. I chuckle, reaching for the wrinkled *MAD* magazine wedged behind an old bucket. As I pull it out, the faded image of a black Alfred E. Neuman, standing in for Linc of the Mod Squad—that is, Odd Squad of *MAD*—stares back. I give it a good shake, relieving it of any vermin. Between some mindless comic reading, the coffee-stained sketchbook, and some other memorabilia I brought along, I should have plenty to distract me after dark.

I give the cover a second glance. I'm pretty sure this is the very same magazine I bought at Garver's that first week of June. As I tuck the folded magazine in my back pocket, I remember tucking it under my shirt as if it were *Playboy* and smuggled it into my room.

WITH MY CONTRABAND READING SECURE under my mattress, I emptied my pockets of coins and candy. Tootsie Rolls, Bazooka bubble gum, and fireballs. That left me with $3.33. Three singles, three dimes, and three pennies. The number seemed lucky somehow, like a good omen. Like this summer was going to be something special.

As I lay in bed that night, I would have fallen asleep to the image of Amelia staring, of her kissable lips, three aisles away at Garver's, but every time I envisioned her, Dora's voice cut in, bringing with it a heat wave of guilt. I would have pulled out my fresh copy of *MAD,* but even that had guilt attached to it—all those 'bursting bosoms'—and the fact that I had snuck it. Rather than continue to wallow in guilt, I retrieved *The Island of Dr. Moreau* and my flashlight from beneath my pillow and read until my eyes and brain could no longer focus.

In spite of fitful sleep, I still woke early the next morning. Amid the first peeps of songbirds, I listened for stirrings in the bedrooms on either side of mine. By the time each chirp and caw had become an incoherent chorus, I slipped out of bed and into shorts. Careful on the tread that creaked, I snuck down the stairs and then out the back basement door.

I sat for a few minutes at the end of the dock. The ruckus of birds receded as the sun lightened the sky. I had never realized how peaceful the lake could be, the way it looked as if it was still sleeping under a thin blanket of mist, how remote everything felt—how alone *I* felt, but in a good way, as if I were the only person on the lake. Having siblings, I was hardly ever all by myself, but I liked being alone. Solitude made me feel stronger, made me wish I were stronger.

I stood, stretched, and then dove. The water was a lot warmer than I expected. I swam until my muscles strained. Before I knew it, I had reached the mouth of the cove and pushed myself beyond Whispering Narrows and the floatplane. I kept swimming through the mist, toward the island. The water didn't turn shallow at the island's edge, it was more like a drop-off. When I reached its root-bound shore, I hoisted myself up and stepped into thick brush and the dense aroma of pine pitch. A branch bobbed as a crow lighted upon it and cawed, as if curious about my arrival. A fallen tree made a convenient bench below a white pine with evenly spaced branches. Perfect for climbing. Within a minute, I had scaled halfway up, my feet feeling every inch.

I perched upon a high bough and peered at the cove, sleepy and dormant, nestled in the shade. I squinted for a glimpse of Amelia's bedroom at eye level. A loon warbled, skimming the lake's surface and came to rest in the cove. I scrambled down and jumped into a bed of pine needles that stuck to the bottoms of my feet. Trying to scrape twigs and leaves from my tenderized soles, I made my way to the water's edge. One last breath of privacy and I dove into the lake.

If I were to draw a line between our camp and me, Doc's plane would intersect that line. Whenever I ventured out of the cove, I always swam wide so it wouldn't look as if I were messing around near his mooring. As I gained on the Narrows and the Cessna, I slowed at the sight of a figure on the landing. Doc. He spotted me at the same time and waved. I veered toward him, hoping he hadn't overheard my snide remark to Dora the day before.

"An early riser?" he called out. "Good man!"

He still seemed to like me. I closed the gap between us, swimming nearer.

He beckoned toward the ladder. "Come on up."

I didn't dare refuse. As I emerged, goose bumps rose in the chill air, but a rush of excitement quickly warmed my torso as I checked our camp for movement. It remained unlit.

"Wow," I said, walking the length of the fuselage.

Doc folded his arms across his barrel chest. "Yeah, she's a beauty. Wanted one like her ever since I was your age. What are you, just about fourteen in September?"

I didn't take my eyes off her. "Yes, sir. Almost fourteen."

He looked me up and down and seemed to study my face for a moment. "And how's your mom feeling these days?"

It seemed an odd question at first, but then, not so much. For whatever reason, I had always sensed that their estrangement was one-sided. In fact, I recalled a time when I had caught them in conversation. But why did his question, and that fleeting trace of a memory, leave me uncomfortable? I shrugged. "She's good, sir."

He nodded as I stepped closer to the plane and caressed the white and red paint job.

"First time I went up was when I was fourteen. One of my best memories."

I craned to see the control panel. "How old were you when you learned to fly, sir?"

"*Doc*," he reminded me. "I was in my twenties. Perhaps you'd like to go up sometime."

"Me?"

He expelled a throaty chuckle. "Who else would I mean?"

Now I didn't have a single goose bump. "I sure would love that."

"Get permission and we'll take her up."

"Okay," I said, aware that if my parents saw me talking to Doc, there would be a whole lot of explaining to do. It triggered pounding in my chest. Then, to get my pulse screaming, Amelia sauntered down the lawn and on to the mooring, like a model on a runway, flaunting shorts and a snug T-shirt. The heat of my body parched my throat. Even if Doc still liked me despite my rude behavior at Garver's, I knew Amelia had heard me and seen Dora cry.

"I should go," I said, torn between my first real-live encounter with Amelia, and wishing I could take a dive without being noticed. Problem was, the water would sizzle, given the heat that emanated from my chest.

"You coming by later this morning to work on the clock?" Doc asked, his back to Amelia.

"Maybe." My eyes darted and my breathing faltered. "Depends on if my dad's taking me fishing."

Doc glanced over his shoulder at Amelia as she approached. "You've met my granddaughter, haven't you?"

It was odd that in all the years we'd been coming to camp, I had never met her, face to face, let alone talked to her. "Not exactly—I mean, I've seen her around." That was it; that was all the air I had. I could barely make eye contact, and when I did, she acknowledged me with a half-hearted smile. She must have thought I was the biggest moron, ever!

"This is our neighbor, Benjamin Hughes," Doc said.

She offered a quiet, "Hi."

I nodded a greeting and again said, "I gotta go," and dove into the water. If Doc hadn't thought I was rude before, he probably did now. *Idiot.* I was a moron.

Swimming all the way back to our camp, I came up with a hundred ways I should have responded—none of them included 'I gotta go' or running out of breath or swimming away like some scared kid. I could have asked how Amelia liked the book she had bought yesterday, or told her that she played piano beautifully, or that I liked Oreos too. I could have told her I felt bad for what I had said to Dora, but it wasn't Amelia I needed to apologize to. And would telling Dora I was sorry just make things worse? Then she would never leave me alone!

Behind me, the Cessna's engine rumbled into and around the cove. I turned, treading water as the plane pulled away from its mooring, picked up momentum, and skimmed the lake. As it lifted off, it disappeared from sight. I emerged onto our pebbled beach and shook off my shame like a dog shakes off water—not quite dry and still foul smelling.

CHAPTER 9

THE HANDS OF MY POCKET WATCH HAVEN'T moved since 9:42 this morning. As I slip it back into my vest, it occurs to me that guilt is a lot like hands on a broken clock, stuck in the random past. That might sound a bit melodramatic—if it weren't painfully true. In fact, as I reflect on that summer, so much of it seems steeped in melodrama. I've downplayed it over the years—except for the guilt—but there is no denying that I've endured too much drama.

Overhead, the sun has slipped past its zenith and begun its descent. It's after noon for sure, but by how much? Not that it matters. In less than twenty-four hours, I hope I will have accomplished what I came for. In the morning, I'll wait for Oscar's truck and move on. Nothing melodramatic about that.

I gather my lunch rubbish and juggle my boots—time to return to the cottage. Pausing at the basement door, the insecurities of a kid creep back in. After my conversation with Doc beside his plane that morning, I wondered how I would ever get permission to fly in the Cessna. It seemed as unlikely as scoring another four bucks from Dad. The most I could have hoped for was part of an hour with him, fishing like he had promised—like he had promised every year. Not that he hadn't followed through in the past, but his idea of fishing involved minimal time and effort, and a lot of checking his watch. Just the same, I had always hoped, although I can't call it optimism.

ANXIOUS TO MAKE PLANS WITH DAD, I BOLTED up the basement stairs, composing myself, ready to play it cool when I stepped into the kitchen.

Mom sauntered out of their bedroom and posed in the hallway.

Ignoring me, Dad peered up over his newspaper at Mom. "Those are new."

"I got the sandals at Garver's."

He fluffed his paper. "I'm talking about the entire outfit."

Mom's gaze landed on me as I grabbed the Corn Flakes box at the table. "And where have *you* been?"

"Just went for a morning swim," I said.

"When did you start taking morning swims?"

I shrugged. "Today, I guess."

As I sat at the table, Dad's focus shifted from Mom's outfit back to his paper.

I shook cereal into my bowl. "We're still going fishing this morning, right Dad?"

"We'll see." He circled something on the newsprint. "Why don't you get the rowboat cleaned up and we'll see what's left of the day." That was as good as 'Don't count on it!', but I still hoped.

After I scarfed down my cereal, I went to my room, crammed candy in my pocket and counted my change. My $3.33 had turned into $2.22. Maybe I had miscalculated how much candy I had bought, but I had been so sure of the threes. I then headed down to the beach where Frankie and the neighbor kid, Skip, squatted at the water's edge.

"Hey, Frankie, you seen my dollar floating around the room?"

Wiping his nose, Frankie looked up from scooping a bucketful of tadpoles. "Where the heck did you get a dollar?"

"None of your business. Have you seen it?"

He shrugged. "No. You should check under the bed."

As if he would have owned up to seeing it.

"Hey, give me a hand, would ya'?" I said, uncovering the rowboat.

"What's in it for me?"

I dug into my pocket and pulled out a couple Tootsie Rolls. In two seconds, both Frankie and Skip splashed out of the water and stood opposite me, lifting the aluminum boat from upside down onto its side. I took it from there, lowering it to a row of round posts that I had laid on the ground as rollers. My grip slipped and the boat landed with a tunk, adding yet another dent to its underside. Skip squealed with a shiver. A nest of wriggling pink bodies had dropped from under the seat onto the floor.

"It's just a bunch of baby mice," I scooped up a couple with a leaf and laid them back in the nest. "They're no grosser than frogs and tadpoles."

I carried the full nest inside the shed and tucked it in the corner nearest where the boat had sat.

"Will their mama find them?" Skip squatted for a better look and then glanced up at me with big brown eyes full of concern. "Or will something come and eat them?"

"Sure, she'll find them—that's what mamas do. They protect their young. No matter what." There was a good chance she would abandon her offspring and that, in fact, something would eat them, but I didn't want to upset little Skippy. And a part of me needed to believe in the strength of maternal instincts.

I left the boys in the shed—making plans for how to protect and feed the babies until mama could take over—and returned to the boat. I spent the next half hour scraping a wasp nest from the transom and removing mice crap and spider sacks and sweeping earwigs with a half-worn whiskbroom. With the oarlocks in place, I retrieved the paddles from the shed. In the corner, Skip and Frankie had built a fortress around the nest. Beside it, I grabbed both of our fishing rods, the tackle box, and a net. I carried them to the boat, admiring my oar repair, making sure it would survive another summer. I bet it would hold up a lot longer than me.

With the rods and oars in place, I was good to go. Now all I needed was a dad. I bounded up the path to the basement door and flew up the staircase into the kitchen.

"The boat's ready!" I said as I burst into the room.

At the table, Mom jumped, disrupting her coffee mug as she raised it to her lips. Coffee sloshed all down the front of her outfit.

"Now look what you've done, Ben! How many times have I told you …?"

Told me what? To not breathe? "Sorry, Mom."

I grabbed a dishtowel from the sink and went to mop up the table. Snatching it and blotting her front, she huffed with impatience. "What do you want?"

I mumbled, "Where's Dad?"

"He had to run a last-minute errand."

"What do you mean?"

"I mean," she opened a random cabinet, "he took off to run an errand, last minute."

"But he said we'd go fishing."

She slammed the cupboard door and faced me, her expression as sharp as her tone. "And what do you expect me to do about it?"

Her eyes gaped and her lips pressed. I didn't dare push it. She gripped the back of the chair and stared at me.

"Fine. I'll go fishing by myself." I knew how to do that. But first, I had to use the bathroom. When I came out, Mom stood at the counter and spun around to face me, pushing something behind her as she sipped her new cup of coffee.

"Have a nice time on the lake," she said with a sweet smile.

"Yeah, right," I muttered under my breath as I headed downstairs and out to the boat.

As I pushed off shore, scraping my way to shallow water, the sound of running feet pounded the dock.

"Wait up Ben! I'll come with!" Penny came up alongside the boat as I neared the dock.

"I already put Dad's rod away. You'll have to go get it from the shed." I steadied the boat.

She stepped inside with her beach bag and plunked down at the transom end. "Who needs a rod?"

"Yeah, right." I had just become her indentured cabby, her ride to the public beach. "Does Mom know where you're going?"

"I told her I took pity on you and that we'd be gone for *hours*, fishing, of course."

It was all the same to me. I could drop her off at the beach and still do some fishing, even if I was all by myself.

With a pivot of my oar, I aimed the boat toward Whispering Narrows, rowing with the bow at my back. As we passed Amelia's beach, I imagined her sprawled on the sand. I used to imagine her sitting at the end of their little beachside dock and maybe having an opportunity to talk, but this morning, that seemed a little too up-close for comfort.

Amelia's vacant dock jutted out about twenty feet into the cove. I could have touched it with my oar as I passed by. Peering across their lawn, I envisioned the grand piano behind the prow-shaped picture windows at the center of the house.

"Keeping an eye out for Amy?" Penny asked as soon as we passed through the Narrows to the privacy of the open lake.

"No. She's not even home."

"Really? How do you know?"

"Saw her taking off with Doc this morning," I said, tossing a glance over my shoulder at the mooring ahead of us. From a set of sliding-glass doors, a slender brunette, wearing a peasant dress and round dark spectacles, stepped out onto the patio and waved. Penny waved back.

I kept rowing. "Who's that?"

"I think it's Amy's cousin from California."

"Oh yeah?"

"Forget it, lover boy. She's like twenty-two years old."

"So?" As if I had any more chance with her than I did Amelia. "What's her name?"

Penny shielded her mouth, "Sunshine."

"Seriously?"

"It's actually Matilda, named after her grandmother, but she changed it. Says Sunshine is what Doc always called her, but she is such a *hippie*—" the word hippie rolled from the curl of Penny's smile. "I think *that's* why she changed it."

"I've heard that hippies don't wash."

"That's not true, any more than it is to say thirteen-year-old boys don't wash."

"I do too." Though I hadn't showered since we arrived, but swimming in the lake was as good as bathing. "So, speaking of hippies, who's at the beach?"

"I don't know what you're talking about."

"Yeah, right." I gave my oar a thrust. "And what's-his-name isn't a lifeguard again this summer?"

"His name is Percy."

"God Penny, what kind of name is Percy? If I had that for a name, I'd change it to Gomer Pile."

She kicked my ankle. "Don't be so intolerant."

"Sheesh. I was just kidding." It wasn't like her to be quite so touchy. "But seriously, isn't he a little old for you? I mean, what is he, about twenty?"

"He's only nineteen. Besides, he barely knows I'm alive."

"He seemed to know you were alive at Garver's the other day."

"Barely. He didn't say two words to me."

"Maybe he's not into sixteen-year-olds."

She folded her arms across her front. "Just shut up and paddle."

I kept rowing for about eight-tenths of a mile—at least that was the distance I had clocked on the station wagon odometer, from the beach to our camp. It was probably less, rowing a straight line across the lake, but with the sun directly overhead, I felt every inch of it. I quit rowing and took off my T-shirt.

"Oh my gosh," Penny gasped.

"What?"

"When did you grow armpit hairs?"

"God, Penny—I don't know." And I really wasn't sure. It was as if one morning I woke up and there they were. And that was the least of it.

She pulled her hair out of her ponytail. "Don't be so defensive."

"I'm not. It's just weird is all, and it doesn't help having my sister point it out."

"Yeah. Sorry." She fluffed her hair. It fell past her shoulders. "I guess we're both growing up, but it's easier thinking of you as a little kid ...."

"Yeah, well ...," and there wasn't anything more either of us wanted to say about that.

I rowed closer to shore, near the public picnic area, peering through the low, overhanging trees at the shelter and porta-potty. No one sat at the scattered tables or cooked at the built-in grills. No wonder. Not a single ray of sunlight warmed the dismal setting.

"That part of the park gives me the creeps," Penny shivered. "That's where the pervs hang out. They say it's haunted, you know—by the Picnic Ghost."

I laughed. "What happens? Do sandwiches mysteriously disappear?"

"Beats me."

"So, have you ever seen any?"

"What—ghosts?"

"No. Pervs."

"No, that's why they're pervs. They sneak up and peek

in through holes in the back of the porta-potty, when you're, you know ...."

"Gross."

"And only pervs use them. Us normal people use the nice restrooms." She pointed to the opposite end of the beach, behind the boat launch. I had used that restroom. It didn't smell bad. And every year, they painted over nasty stuff written in the stalls. I rowed harder to arrive at the public landing quicker. Penny kept her eyes to shore and broke a smile. She had spotted what's-his-name.

She adjusted her button-down shirt, which was no longer buttoned, revealing the top of a two-piece suit. "Were you planning on sticking around?"

That meant she didn't want to hurt my feelings by saying, 'You're not sticking around, are you?' I could take a hint. Since I had already done my own scoping-out of the beach and found no one of interest, I said, "I'm just gonna mess around on the lake. You want me to come back in an hour, or what?"

"How about two?"

She was stretching how long we could be away without Mom panicking. I checked my Timex and glanced at Percy Wade who hadn't taken his eyes off Penny since we beached. Then *our* eyes met. I stared him down, which surprised me. I mean, what was I going to do, go over and tell him he best not mess with my sister? I looked back at Penny. "Where'd you get that swimsuit, anyway?"

"Never mind that. Hour and a half?"

"Sure. But not a minute longer."

Three hours, three fish, and a sunburned-back later, I braced myself as I rowed up to our camp's dock with Penny. Giving my oar a calculated twist, I landed the stern against the dock with a clunk, holding my breath at the sight of Mom on her recliner.

She sat up and waved with a smile. "Did you kids have a nice time?"

Penny and I exchanged wary glances.

I held up a couple yellow perch and a bass. "Yeah."

"That's so sweet. It warms my heart that the two of you play so nice together." She lay back and closed her eyes, smiling all the while, her paper cup in hand.

Later on, when Dad returned from errands, he passed out Nutty-Buddy cones. A pretty pathetic apology for skipping out on me, but that didn't stop me from grabbing two.

That night, I double-checked under the bunk bed for my other dollar. Lo and behold, there it was, way back in the corner.

Chapter 10

WIPING MY SWEATY PALMS, I AGAIN BYPASS the basement door and make my way up to the Saab. A wave of heat engulfs me as I open the front passenger side where a stack of paperwork lies atop an armload-of-a-cardboard box. I glance at the dashboard. 3:10. As I lift the package from the seat, my gaze settles on the ruined artwork. I put down the box, grab the sketchpad, and toss it on top of everything.

Inside the kitchen, I lay the box on the table and set aside the paperwork. With the overlapped flaps of cardboard pried open, I remove a layer of crumpled newspaper and then lift Doc's clock. She still runs as good as the day I finished regulating her in his shop.

At my apartment in Denver, I allowed her main and chime springs to unwind before packing up for the journey. She survived the humidity of Missouri, the chaos of dorm life at MIT, and the Rockies' high altitudes. Her case is a little worse for the wear, but she has been the constant in my life, resting only during those short intervals when I had to pack her up for a move. Something in her continuous tick-tock stabilizes my 'works'—my main spring. Inserting the thumb-worn key, I give it a few turns and then open the back, hook her pendulum to the spring wire I once repaired, and set it in motion. Focusing on the gentle ticking, I close my eyes, imagining myself standing in front of Doc's workbench, listening for the slightest irregularity in each tock, as if it were her heart beating.

Thinking back on my mechanical aptitude, I have to admit it was a clever repair for a thirteen-year-old.

I DIDN'T BOTHER SNEAKING AS I RIFLED through our shed for an old bucket of tools. Dad had taken off again, and Mom dozed on her recliner with her paper cup as usual. All I needed was a strip of fine-gauge steel and some cutters.

Laying out an old piece of cardboard, I glanced over to the corner where Frankie and Skip had built a barricade around the mouse nest. It was empty. Probably ended up as snake lunch. I shuddered at the awful nature of things—the brutality of life and death. Survival of the fittest.

Dumping the coffee can of nuts, bolts, corroded screwdrivers, and rusty nails, I spotted what I was looking for—a spark-plug feeler gauge. Fanning the gradations of thin metal tabs, I compared them to the split pendulum spring and chose the correct thickness. With stiff tin snips, I cut one. Dad would never notice. Ingenious as improvising the repair was, I didn't feel comfortable telling Doc I had rooked my Dad's tool, yet I hoped Doc would still be impressed.

"I'm going to ride my bike," I told Mom.

"Okay, don't be long," she replied, as if she would notice.

I pedaled to Whispering Narrows' garage, parking my bike down near the mooring, out of sight from the road. I gave the plane a long stare, wishing I could get up the nerve to ask my parents for permission to fly with Doc. I then checked the beach for Amelia. She lay front-side up, her head nested in a halo of strawberry curls. *Perfect.* This morning, I could mess around with the clock and watch her from the window over the workbench.

Inside the garage, I passed the black Jaguar—a 1965 XKE coup. I would have walked all the way around it or even dared touch it, but I was afraid Doc might walk into the room and think I was messing with his stuff, so I moved to the workbench. As I bent to open the tool drawer, the door between the house and garage creaked opened.

"Oh. Hi." A smooth female voice stood me straight up. A brunette approached, removing her round sunglasses—the same lady I had seen on Doc's patio a few days ago. Big brown eyes looked me up and down. "Sorry. I didn't mean to spook you."

I tried not to stare at the sway of her hip-huggers as she moved in my direction, yet as soon as she stood beside me in the hazy sunlight of the window, it was her gauzy, see-through midriff that I couldn't quit staring at.

I swallowed hard. There was no way I could control the surge of heat. "Hi. Doc said I could be in here."

"No, you're cool." As she combed fingers through her hair, long straight tresses shimmered bluish-red and covered her front. Whereas her dark coloring did not match Amelia's, her features did. "I'm Sunshine. I think I saw you the other day, out on the water."

"Yeah." I tried to catch my breath. "I'm Ben."

She held her hand out. I offered mine with hesitation and she gripped it—not firm but not limp.

"It's nice to meet you, Ben." She smiled and let go. "I'm just taking the Jag out."

I nodded. "Oh."

"What'cha working on?"

"Doc's clock."

She laid her hand on my shoulder as she stepped closer for a better look at the disassembled clock parts drying on an old newspaper. She stood about my height and smelled like a combination of citrus and burning leaves. Earthy, but not in a bad way. "Far out. You're one smart kid, Ben."

I liked that she used my name, as if it were worth remembering.

She tucked a few strands of hair behind her ear. "Hey, I've got a pair of earrings that busted. You think you could fix them for me?"

"I could look at them."

"What a sweet kid," she patted my flaming cheek and turned away.

A second later, she slunk into the front seat of the Jaguar as the automated garage door opened. Shifting into reverse, she looked behind and backed out.

"Goodbye, Ben." She waved and then peeled out of the driveway as the door lowered.

Wow, my first up-close encounter with a Jaguar coup *and* a hippie, all in one morning.

Once I had the clock put back together, I wound the spring and wrote a note to Doc, telling him it still needed regulation. Not that I couldn't have taken it to our camp and done it there, but I couldn't hide the ticking and didn't want to have to explain where it had come from. Besides, leaving it in Doc's garage gave me an excuse to come back.

I signed my name and glanced out the window. Amelia had been gone from the beach for a while, so I wouldn't get a final look before I left. I wiped my hands and stepped out the side door to retrieve my bike. I pushed it uphill toward the pea stone and rounded the corner of the garage just in time to catch Penny talking to Amelia in the driveway. They waved goodbye with a smile before Penny pedaled off on her Schwinn. Not that my sister striking up a friendship with Amelia would better *my* chances, but maybe Penny would say something nice about me, and maybe Amelia wouldn't think I was a complete jerk. Since I hadn't thought a whole lot more about my last encounter with Dora, maybe Amelia hadn't either.

CHAPTER 11

NOW THAT I HAVE THE CLOCK TICKING, I return the key to my pocket. It clanks against the marble. Rolling its smoothness between my fingers like a worry stone, I inspect the aggie and set it on the table. It rolls across oak and onto the floor, continuing its path to the wall. The house always had a tilt toward the lake. One good shove and the whole place would probably collapse into the basement. That accounts for the clock's uneven ticking.

If I tuck a few pages of that sketch pad under one end of the clock, that should regulate her enough to keep her ticking the night through. With that done, I again pull out my pocket watch. Still no movement. Guessing that it's close to 3:30 by now, I nudge the clock hands into position.

From the cardboard box, I remove a yellowed envelope and scrutinize it the way I did the first time I laid eyes on it. It's addressed to me, care of my aunt, Mrs. Wanda Biggs, RR#2, Kingsville, Missouri. Back when I received it, I would have torn into it, but when I read the return addressee, I kept much of the envelope intact. With the same anticipation, I blow out a slow breath, lift the flap, and slip the card from its sheath like a sacred emblem. Water-colored daisies wrinkle the paper, even after years of having been pressed between pages of an old calculus textbook.

> *My Dearest Ben,*
> *We love you and know you will rise*
> *above it all ... I hope Penny is doing better ....*
> *Love, Sunshine*

I ached when I first read that, and even now it triggers regrets. Yeah, I should have written back—should have kept in touch. Then again, it was all so overwhelming. Who could blame me for withdrawing from everything and nearly everyone I knew before I turned fourteen?

There were a lot of legitimate reasons why I never kept up with Amelia—other than through Doc—but there would have been nothing 'complicated' about staying in touch with Sunshine. I have always felt bad that I didn't respond to her note; granted, I didn't receive it until three years after the fact, when I was deemed "old enough." Ironically, the arrival of her card coincided with Doc contacting me— a phone call I happened to pick up on before it could be intercepted. Finally receiving word from Sunshine and hearing from Doc within the same week dumped me into a bout of depression, not because *they* had disturbed me, but I learned they had made several other attempts and I had been "shielded" from supposed upset. Strange, what people will do—will withhold—in the name of protecting the innocent.

Sunshine would be pleased to know I at least kept her card. In fact, after this weekend, I'll do my best to contact her—she could likely use a little encouragement. Perhaps I'll quote her own words.

Although it's with an ache in my heart, I smile, recalling my second encounter with Sunshine.

MIDWEEK, MIDWAY THROUGH JUNE, I WOKE early again. No one stirred when I snuck out. Dad had returned to Massachusetts over a week ago, which meant no more hopes of fishing with him but a lot more freedom. Just the same, if Mom caught me messing around where I shouldn't, she would keep a tally of my misdeeds and report them to Dad. He might forget or ignore Mom's complaints, or he might choose to address them at the most humiliating moments. I would have preferred a beating in private than the demeaning way he treated me around others.

I jumped on my bike and pedaled away from Safe Haven, down around the curve, looking for any activity at Whispering Narrows. The old patchwork Rambler I had seen the day we arrived was parked in front of the garage. Walking my bike past the car, I read the bumper stickers— *Make Love, Not War*; *Flower Power; Daisy Hill Home*— surrounded by peace signs and sunflowers painted all over the replacement tailgate. That would take a lot of bottles of Testors—at 69¢ each, covering maybe a square foot per bottle, well, that would eat up a year's-worth of hot lunch money. Besides that, Dad would kill me if I ever painted anything on the Galaxie.

I rounded the corner of the garage and parked my bike out of sight. It was 7:07 when I unlocked the door. When I reached the bench, the hands on the old clock corresponded exactly to the numbers on my Timex. My job was complete.

I scratched my head, killing time. How was I going to come up with another excuse to be at Doc's place? Just then, the door to the main house flung open.

"Oh good! I'm glad I caught you, Ben." The smooth voice belonged to Sunshine. This time she wore a smock, speckled and smeared with paint. "Would you mind looking at my earrings?"

"Sure," I said as she glided toward me.

She held out her closed fist, bright blue and yellow under her fingernails. "Sorry about my appearance. I've been up early, painting."

"What are you painting?"

"A landscape on canvas." She dropped several large hoops and beads into my hand. "Can you fix it? You might have to redesign them a little. I think I lost a couple parts."

"Sure."

Through the open door, a blond-bearded, shirtless man

in bellbottoms stepped into view. "Sunshine, how about some bacon and eggs?"

"In a minute," she replied as if singing the words.

The guy raised a brow at me and exited.

"That's Lenny, my boyfriend," she said. "Would you like some bacon and eggs? Have you eaten?"

"No, that's okay. I'm fine."

"Oh, come on," she smiled and grabbed my arm, pulling me toward the door. "I'm making pancakes and everything."

"I couldn't. Really." I pulled back. Just then, Doc appeared in the doorway.

"Ben. Perfect timing. Come on in, son." Now he had a hold of my other arm. I had no option. My heart shot into my throat. I couldn't have uttered no if I had tried. Doc ushered me beyond the garage and in through another door, into the kitchen. I scanned the room for Amelia, but only Lenny sat at the table, peering at me through round spectacles.

"Ben," Sunshine said, "this is Lenny."

"So you're the kid who fixes stuff. *Fixer-man*," he said, lifting a banjo from the seat beside him. "Come on and sit. Be comfortable."

Outside the sliding-glass door overlooking the lake, a girl—that is, someone around Sunshine's age—turned toward the house carrying a camera with a huge lens. Her wild, dark hair hid a lot of her face, although I could still tell she was cute. Her tie-dyed T-shirt stretched across her huge chest.

"Hey," she said, stepping inside and flipping me a peace sign.

Sunshine gestured, "And that is Candace."

I returned a quiet "Hi," and sat beside Lenny, a banjo nestled in his lap. He didn't have a Southern twang, but he could have passed for a hillbilly.

Sunshine shed her painting smock and traded it for an apron that covered little of her bikini top. As she lifted the neck loop overhead, I caught a glimpse of dark wisps at her armpits. *Holy crap!*—girls grew hair there too? I had never seen that on my sister or Mom. If it hadn't been for the view of so much boob, maybe the hair would have seemed gross, but it didn't.

Candace meandered around the kitchen, snapping pictures of household objects as Lenny cradled the banjo and plucked a tune—it sounded nothing like the Beverly Hillbillies. He glanced up at me and responded to my quizzical stare. "Bach, man. Classical. Cello suite in G."

"Oh," I nodded, more impressed with how fast his fingers moved than with the actual song, but the longer he played the more it grew on me. Sunshine hummed along at the stovetop. Candace moved to her side, photographing Sunshine from odd angles as she turned bacon and cracked open eggs. Then Candace turned the camera on me.

"For posterity," she said as I turned away. That was all I needed—evidence. Not only was I completely out of my element, but I was inside Doc's house.

Doc carried on as if this whole scene was nothing out of the ordinary; half-naked, non-family members hanging out, while a Northern hillbilly played classical banjo, and some lady collected evidence, clicking away with her camera. My mom would have freaked out.

Lenny set aside the banjo and tucked a cigarette between his lips. *Oh crap!* Mom would definitely smell that on me if she didn't smell bacon first.

As he lit a match, Sunshine chimed in, "Not inside, Lenny."

"Oh, right. Sorry," he chuckled, his voice as deep as Doc's. He snuffed the flame, scratching his blond beard that matched the hair on his meaty chest. He wasn't super tall like Doc, but he had veins that popped across his biceps and forearms when he rested them on the table.

Doc's hand settled on my shoulder. "Well, son, I'm taking her up today. What do you say? Did you get permission yet?"

"Pretty much. I just gotta double-check," I lied. I didn't mean too—it just came out.

Candace set a full coffee cup in front of me. I had never drunk coffee before. I mean, I had tasted it, but Dad said it would make me hyper and wouldn't let me drink any at home. The idea of defying him made the coffee all the more tantalizing. Besides, there was nothing illegal about a thirteen-year-old drinking coffee. Careful not to spill it, I smiled and sipped. It didn't taste half bad. I sank back into my seat, scanning the room and sipping.

On the opposite wall, an open doorway led to another large room. It had the feel of a den or living room, with a sofa and chairs. I tried to place it, given where we were in relation to the cove. Both the kitchen and den—or great room—were part of the lake-facing wing, whereas the center piano room separated the east from the west wing.

I had gone back to sipping when a spout of strawberry blond hair yanked my attention to the great room doorway. Amelia wandered toward the table, rubbing her eyes and yawning. Her hair stuck out in all directions, and her faded pajamas hung from her shoulders, skimming her chest. Wow, what an incredible sight. When her squint landed on me, she gasped, smoothing her hair and trying to cover her boobs at the same time. "What is *he* doing here?"

"I invited him," Sunshine sang out from the stove.

Amelia rolled her eyes in Doc's direction and huffed, then stomped out of the room.

I withered and slurped another sip of coffee. My appetite left with Amelia.

Doc nudged me. "Oh, don't worry about her, son. Fifteen-year-old girls don't like being seen in their jammies, that's all."

Sunshine set a plate of eggs, bacon, and a pancake in front of me. "She just likes you. If she didn't she wouldn't care. Now eat up!"

Did she say Amelia liked me? At once, my appetite returned. I forked a piece of pancake and bit into unexpected texture, chewing with hesitation.

Squinting at his plate, Lenny spoke my mind. "What the hell kind of pancake is this?"

Sunshine called out, "Whole grain, stone ground wheat. Eat up. It's good for you."

Lenny doused his with more maple syrup and passed the pitcher to me with a grin. "Eat up, man."

Doc gulped down the rest of his coffee. "Well, son, I'm taking off to check out my new radio, so if you want to come along, be here by ten."

"Yes, sir."

Amelia didn't show up by the time I left, which was about ten minutes after I started eating. As I pedaled home, I didn't know if I was more excited at the prospect of flying with Doc, or having seen Amelia in pajamas. I had forgotten about smelling of bacon and maple syrup, until I stepped into our kitchen and caught a whiff of burnt toast.

Mom stood at the counter, opening and slamming cabinet doors above and below the sink, rifling behind boxes of cereal and cans of Spaghetti-Os. She glanced over her shoulder at me.

"Where have you been?"

I kept a safe olfactory distance. "Out riding my bike."

She rubbed the deepening creases across her forehead and then reached for her coffee cup, her hand trembling. Penny stepped out of the bathroom and headed for the table.

Mom dug through the contents of her pocket book. "Penny, I need to go to town. I'm leaving you in charge."

Penny glanced at me with a sly smile. "Sure, Mom."

"Have you seen my wallet?"

"No."

Just then, Frankie burst out of our room. "I wanna go!"

Mom sighed, her eyes shifting all around the kitchen. "Where is that purse?"

"I saw it on the front seat of the car, Mom. Can I go, *please?* I never get to go."

"Fine," she relented with a sigh. "I'm going to put on my face. Go change into something decent and meet me in the car. Don't keep me waiting."

He jumped up and down. "Yippee!"

As soon as Mom and Frankie stepped out the front door, Penny returned to her room and emerged wearing beach attire.

I gave her a once-over. "So, where are you headed?"

"As if you didn't know."

"Not that I would ever tell." I smiled. "Anyway, since you're in charge, would it be okay if I went up in Doc's plane with him this morning?"

"Are you serious?"

"Sure."

"I don't know, Ben. Mom wouldn't like it."

"Yeah, probably not any more than she'd like you hanging out at the beach with Percy."

She glared. "You wouldn't tell."

"Of course I wouldn't. No more than you'd tell if I went flying with Doc."

Ten minutes later—and with permission—we hopped on our bikes and went our separate ways, but not until after she had left a note on the kitchen table.

> *Mom,*
> *In case me and Ben aren't here when*
> *you get back, we went for a bike ride*
> *together. Be home soon.*
> *Penny*

At exactly ten o'clock, I skidded around the hippie car to the side of the garage. Doc ducked to clear the wing as he strode to the end of the mooring. I put on my best casual posture and wiped my sweaty palms.

He bellowed, "Ben! Right on time. Good man."

"Hello, sir." I planted my hand in his and he gave it a firm shake.

"All set then?" he said, opening the cockpit door.

"Yes, sir." He stepped aside and I climbed up and into tight quarters, scooting over the pilot's seat.

"Buckle up, son," he said as he shut the door and sank into his seat.

The instrument panel gleamed before me; gauges, knobs, dials, and needles. A control yoke in front of me and two pedals on the floor. Doc handed me a set of headphones and placed his own over his ears. "Let's see how the radio works, shall we?"

He flipped a switch, pulled a knob, turned a dial, and then the engine revved. "Clear," he called out at nobody on the mooring and pulled the yoke. Working the pedals on the floor, we turned toward the widest part of the lake, passed the island, and gained momentum. In less than a minute, our ride went from bumpy to smooth as we ascended. The engine vibrated through my body, like being one with the machine. My heart rose in my chest.

"Whaddaya think?" His voice came through the headset. "Can you hear me okay?"

"Yes, sir. This is great!"

He turned the yoke right and we banked south. As the wings leveled, we circled up and around, over our camp and Whispering Narrows.

"Wow," I said. "Your place looks even more gigantic from the sky."

"Kind of crazy," Doc chuckled. "Once upon a time, I thought I'd fill it with kids and grandkids. Then the wife up and died—left me with just the two."

As enthralled as I was with the view, I glanced at him.

Without further prompting, he continued, "Sure I could have remarried. Had plenty of opportunity, but threw myself into work instead."

"What kind of work?"

"Medical equipment. Probably should have thrown myself into being a father rather than a manufacturer.

What's the point in having a big house when your own kids won't come to visit?"

"But your grandchildren visit."

"Yeah, just have the two of them, though. Sunshine's father lives in California—hasn't stepped foot in any of my houses in ten years. And Karen, well—I'm afraid she's a bit self-absorbed, especially these days with her wedding coming up. Demanded too much from my son and went the other way with my daughter." He shook his head wistfully. "Don't know what I'd do without my baby girls." He glanced at me and laughed. "I'm just a crazy old man with too many regrets.... Never mind me."

Even though he laughed, his mouth twitched, more like a frown than a smile. I looked away in discomfort. How could someone as rich as him have regrets? How could someone as great as him have a son that didn't want to spend time with him? I would have given anything to have a dad like Doc.

We made another pass around the lake, this time continuing on to the east end, all the way over to the beach and circled it. I peered out the window. We flew low enough that I made out Penny by the lifeguard stand and Lenny's rambler in the parking lot. I couldn't pick him out of the clusters of people on the beach, but it seemed odd that he would hang out there and not on Doc's stretch of white sand.

From there, we gained altitude and banked toward the north, up and over the mountain, following the ridge until it tapered to the west. As the hills sloped into a valley, I leaned into the window, peering at the open fields. I easily picked out Garver's Market and the Galaxie parked out front. Mom must have still been inside. Although Doc maintained altitude, I straightened, moving away from view, in case Mom stepped out onto the porch. As if she could even see me all the way up in an airplane.

We made a loop back toward the south and east.

Overall, the flight lasted less than a half hour, but it was the most exciting thing I had ever done in my nearly fourteen years. Someday, I would have a pilot's license and fly a plane of my own.

Chapter 12

Here I am, still wallowing in this dark and depressing kitchen. It's not just the dinge of disrepair—this cottage has always felt confined and dismal, so different from Whispering Narrows; an open amphitheater compared to this casket of a camp.

I trace the outline of painted daisies and hum a stanza of Bach. I'm not sure what it was about Doc, or if it was Whispering Narrows, but the environment over there fostered freedom of expression. Hippies crashed there. Live music played in the background. People hung out, wearing whatever they wanted. They smoked—albeit outside. I imagined they sat around in the evenings, engrossed in philosophical debates.

For years, I wished I had been part of their family. Even after I found out how screwed up they were, I still would have chosen them over my own family. With the exception of my relationship with Penny, I never felt as if I were part of my family—as if I had been switched at birth.

I read Sunshine's note for the hundredth time. No matter how many years pass, I'm still trying to read between the lines; Sunshine was good at that. Was she born with a sixth sense, with the ability to tune into everything around her? Or did her parents—did Doc—cultivate that in her? I've always wondered about intuition. How does a person develop it? What role does genetics play in the way we turn out, and how much depends upon what we choose? Ah, genetics and exposure—nature versus nurture—the age-old psycho-philosophical debate.

According to the odds, I should be a miserable failure,

struggling with addictions, running from the law, screwing up every life I touch. Not that I'm well adjusted, I mean, if I were, would I be sitting here in the dark, twitching away, raking up my past in hopes of some closure? Just the same, I would like to think I've been a contributive member of society, in spite of my upbringing.

Okay, sure, I've been told my "rescuer" personality is some sort of overcompensation, and yeah, I'll admit Gretchen and Penny are a lot alike—maybe too alike. It's not as if I was looking to fall in love with someone like my sister, but I can't discount my need to "fix." To rescue. And how did I acquire that characteristic? It's not as if either of my parents were rescuers, that's for sure.

I reread the card, *I hope Penny is doing better* …. and prop it against the box, knowing I'll read it again over the course of the next few hours.

I stand and stretch. Penny's room is next.

My sister's door remains closed; 'shut down' comes to mind. With my hand on the knob, I half expect that when I open it, I'll find Penny sprawled out on her mattress—her mouth wide open, arms flung overhead. Her latest Nancy Drew book might lie on the floor beside her bed and her clothing would be strewn across the room. I would have to be careful where I step or I'd trip over her sneakers. A gentle whiff of *Heaven Scent* cologne would greet me.

As I lean into the door, it squeaks open. I step into a room swept clean. Closing my eyes, I pick up the slightest scent of Penny. For the first time since arriving, my eyes and sinuses burn, and my throat constricts. I hold back tears but my vision blurs. So much for repressing emotions. I know I'm supposed to go ahead and let it *all* out and have a good bawl, but it seems counterproductive and anticlimactic. I would rather remember Penny and me laughing. We did a lot of that.

I close my eyes again. Tears subside as the memory of Penny's laughter morphs from imaginary to so real I can hear it—light but crisp, like a shard of color bursting from the center of a blossoming flower and then finishing with a snort. She could get me laughing every time.

EVEN WITH THE NOISE OF FIREWORKS shooting off from Doc's lawn, Penny's laugh cut through and echoed back. It was the Fourth of July and we had taken the rowboat out on the cove after dark. Mom sat on shore with Frankie.

I centered the rowboat in the cove, where blue and red burst into a million sparks overhead and mirrored on the water. A breeze rippled the surface, fracturing colors like a sparkling gem and drifting us away from shore. I flicked the oar, wetting Penny's arm as her hand dragged in the lake.

I asked, "Are you going to say 'Ooooo' to every rocket?"

"No," she laughed as green cut across the sky and exploded overhead. "Ahhhhhh!"

I smirked. "Making noise must be a girl thing."

Penny's foot nudged my leg. "Come on Benjie, it's not that hard! Make a little O with your mouth and breathe out! Oooooo …."

I rolled my eyes. The normal response would have been to express awe at the sights and sounds, but mouthing 'Ooooo' or 'Ahhhh' felt unnatural to me, as if showing excitement would leave me exposed, open to derision. But this was Penny—my safest audience—so I exaggerated the O and made my "Ooooo" sound for her entertainment.

"Okay, that's fine, Benjie, but you're supposed to wait for the fireworks."

For the next few minutes, I did my best to Ooo and Ahh at the right moments, and each time, Penny laughed, which made me vocalize with all the more enthusiasm. I had always wished I were more like my sister, uninhibited, taking risks. Not that I was opposed to risk taking, but I always calculated how much pride I would have to pay. Humiliation cost a lot. I preferred favorable odds. But when I hung out with Penny, she could persuade me to do embarrassing stuff I would never risk on my own.

With my back toward the open lake, I didn't notice that we had drifted close to Whispering Narrows.

"Careful!" Penny pointed behind me. "You're headed right for the dock."

Before I had a chance to correct my course, we floated within oar's reach of Amelia sitting at the very end of the dock. She raised her knees to her chest as though she was afraid I would ram right into her. Along the beach-facing side, Sunshine, Lenny, and Candace dangled their feet off the edge, kicking water.

Penny waved. "Hi, everyone!"

I twisted my oar to face them broadside.

"Hello, Ben," Sunshine smiled as Candace waved.

Lenny added, "Hey, Fixer-man. How's it going?"

"*Fixer-man?*" Penny said under her breath. I ignored her.

"Hi, Sunshine. Hey, Lenny. Hi, Candace." I looked directly at Amelia. Her eyes shifted and returned to mine with a reserved smile. Sunshine had said Amelia liked me, but she didn't seem to be sending out that vibe at the moment. It would have been weird if I didn't say anything, and it didn't seem as if she was going to, so I calculated the risk and put it out there. "Hi, Amelia."

"Hi." She offered a small wave as her gaze dropped to her lap. Loud whirring and a bang broke the awkward silence, as another round of fireworks sprayed overhead.

With a thrust of my oar, I rowed away.

"Hey, Ben," Sunshine called out. "When are you coming back for breakfast?"

"Don't know."

"You know, you don't need an invitation!"

My cheeks flamed as I nodded at the group, still visible

under the quarter-moon. As I kept rowing, Penny breathed the word, "*Breakfast?*"

I cringed at the thought of Mom overhearing but doubted she had made out Sunshine's words over all the commotion in the cove and across the rest of the lake. With another loud boom, multicolored light scattered overhead, reflecting on the upturned faces of all on the dock, except Amelia's. Was she watching our boat float away in the dark?

With one long and continuous explosion of sound and color, the finale lasted for less than a minute, but that was pretty long when it came to fireworks. The breeze had shifted, drifting the odor of sulfur toward us. That meant conversation between Penny and I, even if still amplified, would travel to the uninhabited side of the cove, while we could better hear what was going on over at Whispering Narrows. Sunshine's voice carried best. Unfortunately, there were too many people talking all at once, so I couldn't isolate Amelia's words. But that didn't stop Mom's voice from cutting across the cove.

"Penny and Ben! Don't be out too late!" she called.

"Okay," I replied, because Penny wouldn't.

"So, *Fixer-man*—" Penny spoke up quietly "—how is it they all know you?"

The slam of our backdoor echoed across the cove.

"'Cause I'm the coolest kid on the block, that's how."

"C'mon, Ben. Seriously."

"Okay, but it's just between me and you."

"As always."

"I've been going over to Doc's to fix a clock for him. And a pair of Sunshine's earrings. And some other crap." Okay, I exaggerated the 'other crap,' but I was on a roll.

Her eyes bugged out. "And they invited you for breakfast?"

"Yup."

"Who was there?"

"Just those guys." We neared the shoreline, opposite Whispering Narrows. I quit rowing.

"What about Percy?"

"Why would he be there?"

"He hangs out with them at the beach sometimes. I've seen him with that *other* girl—"

"You mean Candace?"

"Yeah—Candace. She and Lenny take the handicap group from Daisy Hill to the beach sometimes. I think he and Candace are in charge of daytrips, or something." She ducked beneath a low-hanging branch as we came too close to shore. "I think Percy likes Candace."

"Probably because she's more his age and she's old enough to, you know, *do it.*"

"Like you would even know anything about *doing it.*"

I quit rowing again. "And you would?"

She glanced over at Whispering Narrows, where conversations had quit. "Not yet."

"God, Penny, that sounds kind of slutty." I hoped I hadn't said that too loud. Fortunately, Doc's yard had cleared. We were safe.

"I didn't mean it *that* way. I have no intention of *doing it* with anyone until I'm at least eighteen and it's true love. It's gotta be just perfect, and he's gotta be *the* one."

My cheeks flamed again.

Penny cocked her head as if trying to get a better fix on my discomfort. "Dad has talked to you about the birds and the bees, hasn't he?"

"Yeah, right," I said, double-checking Doc's lawn—still vacant under his big yard lights, and pulled my oars out of the water. "As if he could be bothered." And if he could have been bothered, he would have waited until I had a few buddies over, just so he could watch me squirm and turn bright red.

I had heard a few things about the mechanics of sex, mostly from friends at school, but neighborhood dogs had solved the biggest part of the mystery a long time ago. In addition, I had gathered a few tidbits of information. You could tell if a woman had *done it* by the way she walked—just a little bow-legged. My friend Freddy insisted that if you blew softly in a girl's ear, she would do about anything you wanted. And Archie said girls couldn't run fast because they menstruate—that had something to do with a girl's 'time of the month' and mood swings.

"Well, you at least know how not to get a girl pregnant, don't you?"

"*Yes.*" My eyes rolled with utter mortification as I thrust my oars back in motion. Of course I knew about rubbers, but I sure wasn't going to discuss that with my sister, any more than I would ever discuss it with my father. What I really wanted was to get off the subject.

Before we ended up too close to Amelia's beach, I steered toward our float. "So how are you going to manage sneaking down to the beach, once Dad gets here this weekend?"

"Didn't Mom tell you? He won't be coming till Wednesday, or something."

I shrugged it off. "No one tells me anything—except you. Besides, it doesn't matter to me if he comes at all. All Mom and Dad do is fight, anyway. And Mom's in a better mood when he's not around."

"You mean in a better mood after she's had her morning *tonic.*"

"You mean her coffee?"

She exhaled a half-snort-half-chuckle. "Coffee? Yeah, *Irish* coffee—but hold the brown sugar and cream, and easy on the coffee."

"What do you mean?"

"I mean Whiskey—or actually, vodka. It's colorless and doesn't smell as strong. That way no one will notice—so she thinks."

My chin dropped. "Mom puts vodka in her coffee?"

"And her lemonade. And her ginger ale."

"Does not."

"Sorry to burst your bubble, Ben, but Mom drinks like a fish."

I flinched, struck by the notion that Penny might be right. But Mom didn't fit my image of a stumbling, bumbling skid-row drunk. Did drinking every day mean she was an alcoholic? Either way, I had an awful gut feeling that it had something to do with me, that somehow her drinking meant I was deficient in some way—like if I were a better kid, she wouldn't need some special *tonic.*

"How do you know?" I said.

"Top shelf, beside the refrigerator. Full on Monday— most of it gone by Wednesday. That's why she's so frantic to get to the market on Fridays."

"Does Dad know?"

"What do you think they fight about?"

I was going to say 'Me,' but said, "Money," instead. After all, I had heard them fight about Mom's spending just as much as they fought about me. "You know, I saw a huge wad of money in Dad's wallet when we first got up here."

"Probably a bonus from work."

"I don't know. He's acting really weird lately."

"Cut him a little slack, Ben. He works hard so we can come here."

"Now you sound like Mom."

She jabbed her finger at me. "Don't you ever say that again."

"*Sorry.*"

She broke a grin and then burst out laughing. "You need to relax, Benjie. Now, take me home. I'm pooped."

All the way back, I kept thinking about what Penny had said, and trying to sort out if what she thought of Mom had more to do with the two of them not getting along, or if it might, at least in part, be true. I would have to pay better attention to that bottle in the cupboard ... although, now as I thought about it, Mom did always have a cup of something in hand.

I beached the boat and Penny climbed out. She ruffled my hair the way she often did to Frankie. I ducked out of reach, dragging the boat farther ashore.

"You go ahead," I said. "I'm gonna stay out for a little while."

As she made her way to the basement entrance, I walked out to the end of our dock. Humidity and the sulfur haze hid the stars. It had to be near midnight, but it still felt like near eighty degrees. I peeled off my T-shirt and dove into the water. Its surface rippled in front of me as I swam. Only a vague outline of the moon reflected on the cove. A light at the end of the floatplane mooring lit most of the waterfront.

As I made a loop from our dock to the middle of the cove, a giggle cut across the water. A figure emerged from Doc's kitchen and sprinted across the lawn. A few seconds later, another body—maybe two—stepped outside. I recognized Sunshine's hushed laugh. They scrambled their way toward the dock as I swam backward, bumping into the float. I couldn't see much, but I imagined it was Candace and Sunshine—probably skinny-dipping.

I swam around the corner of our float, treading water. As they swam out into the cove, their splashing and giggles rolled across the water. Lenny's laughter joined in. Now I worried they might see me and think I was a peeping Tom. Worse yet, what if they wanted me to join them? Tantalizing as the idea was, it freaked me out.

In the shadows of overhanging trees, I made my way toward shore and snuck in the back door. That night, I had the best dreams.

CHAPTER 13

THAT WAS ONE MIXED UP SUMMER. IN retrospect, I realize what a mess I was, even before the *real* catastrophe. I have blamed a lot of it on awkward hormonal stuff—better to put an innocuous slant on 'difficulties' rather than accentuate the tragic. Nevertheless, I've been told that "if one doesn't face the ugly truth, it all catches up." So, that's why I'm here. That said, I'm not going to wallow in the melodrama any more than necessary, because there was a lot of good during that summer. The *Mad* magazine in my pocket is an apt reminder.

I pull it out and hold it toward the light of Penny's window. The "Odd Squad"—one of the many ironies of that summer. When I return to Denver, I'll bring this with me. I know a couple who will find it as amusing, if not poignant, as I do.

Before I leave Penny's room, I crank the window open. A gust of afternoon breeze washes over my face, and when I step into the hallway, Mom's closed bedroom door rattles against its jamb. The stack of papers on the kitchen table lifts and scatters all over the floor. Displaced atmosphere, no doubt, but it sends a chill up my spine, as if Mom could be right on the other side of that closed door, rummaging around her room for some misplaced thing—important papers, keys, or her wallet.

 MOM RIFLED THROUGH HER BEDROOM ON A mad hunt, grumbling under her breath. Between thumps of tossed shoes and the slamming closet door, she called out, "Your father is coming this afternoon, and I need to get to the market! Where is my wallet?"

I rolled my eyes at Penny. Why did I feel the need to check under the table and inspect each seat, as if it were somehow my fault that Mom couldn't keep track of her stuff? Penny chewed her mouthful of Cheerios, unconcerned as always.

Frankie appeared from the basement stairway, licking his chapped upper lip. "I found it!"

Mom dashed from her room. "Where on earth was it?"

He held it out. "Right here, on the second step."

"Oh my goodness, how could I have overlooked that? You are such a good and clever boy, Frankie." She embraced him and then tousled his shaggy hair. "Just for that, you can come with me."

Penny's raised brow met mine, her cereal-crammed mouth twisting into a deviant grin. We would be unsupervised again—two kids on the loose.

A half hour later, I beached the rowboat at the public landing. Even from a distance, I easily spotted Candace. She stood, hands on her hips, beside the lifeguard stand. Her T-shirt rode just above the sliver of her bathing suit bottoms. A camera hung from a strap around her neck and nestled between her boobs.

"That's Candace," I said to Penny as she stepped out of the boat.

"As if I didn't know."

As we gathered our stuff, Candace sauntered away from Percy, over to a blanket where Lenny had planted himself, closer to the pavement than the water. He sat, reading, between Dora on his far side and some gangly guy with one leg, on his other. Dora lay on her stomach and waved at me, while the other fellow arranged short metal crutches in the sand beside him. I took a deep breath and waved back as Penny veered toward Percy. Candace escorted some hunched, gray-haired man with a limp, down to the shore. She aimed her lens over the lake and scanned the beach as the man waded nearby. So, this was The Group a.k.a. the Odd Squad.

Lenny peered over a hardcover book. "Fixer-man," he called out and waved me over.

I was determined to be my best self and headed his way. I spread my towel near the guy with the missing leg—he seemed a safer option than Dora; I couldn't help it—I still dreaded being singled out by her. I hoped she would stay put.

Lenny spoke up. "You know Dora Garver, right?"

"Yeah—Hi, Dora."

"You can call me Isadora."

"Yeah—*Isadora*." I hoped my brief response would appease her.

The one-legged guy snickered as he poked a twig in the sand.

Lenny smiled and gave him a firm nudge. "And this character is Christopher."

I nodded a reserved greeting. How had I ended up in The Group?

Christopher ducked as Lenny went to smack the back of his head, "Watch out for this guy—he'll kick your butt."

Had Lenny actually made a joke about his handicap?

"Ha!" Christopher threw his head back, his eyelids half drooping, and burst out with a spastic laugh as he tossed the twig at Lenny. "Good one!"

Lenny shoved him in response, nearly toppling Christopher, whose long swim trunks crept up his stubbed thigh. He didn't bother trying to cover it up. I caught myself scrutinizing the nub of flesh, a couple inches above where his knee would have been.

Dora pushed herself up, onto her hands and knees, and then stood. Her bathing suit looked as if it had belonged to her mother about a hundred years ago. She pulled the sagging shoulder and tugged at her wedgie. I froze, staring straight ahead, hoping to ward her off. *No good!* She waddled over to me and spread her blanket at my side.

"Hi, Ben," she said, leaning so close that one misplaced glance would scar me for life.

"Hi, Isadora." Sandwiched between her and the one-legged guy, I forced a smile, still staring ahead. Scrambling for something to relieve my escalating discomfort, I glanced at Lenny. "What'cha reading?"

"Pride and Prejudice, man."

Sounded heavy, like some kind of civil rights, activist stuff. "Is it any good?"

"Oh yeah—Austen is a freaking genius."

Christopher's head wagged rhythmically. I wasn't sure if it was a tick, or if he was disagreeing, until he said, "She's no Mary Shelley." At least that was an author I recognized, right up there with H. G. Wells.

Dora swatted away any insect that flew near me, and when she smacked a mosquito that landed on my thigh, I shifted closer to Christopher. Pushing sand into neat piles, I made symmetric designs, wishing I were out in my rowboat. As much as I liked the idea of hanging around the beach, when it came right down to it, it was boring as all get out. And present company made it about as uncomfortable as I could imagine. I was just about to excuse myself and go swimming when Christopher spoke up. "I gotta use the john."

Lenny blew out a long sigh and looked at Dora, then out at Candace with her charge down at the water's edge, and then at Christopher and back at me. The next words out of his mouth were probably going to be 'Would you mind staying with Dora?'. I preempted that disaster with "I could take him."

Both Lenny's and Christopher's brows rose in unison. Were my motives as transparent as my grimacing smile? I came to my feet as Christopher gathered a crutch. Lenny pulled him up and nodded at the other crutch. I handed it to Christopher.

"You sure?" Lenny asked. I wasn't certain if he doubted my ability, or Christopher's willingness.

"Yeah, I got it," Christopher replied, inserting one forearm and then the other into metal brackets on each crutch. The posts dug into the sand at uncooperative angles. I thought for sure he would topple. I would have asked why he didn't just use a wheelchair, but it didn't take much imagination to see the impracticality of narrow wheels sinking into sand. Christopher hobbled along on his own, his upper body wrenching and twisting with each labored movement. Lenny stayed at his side until the sand firmed, meeting pavement.

"You good from here?" Lenny asked.

"Yup." Christopher steadied himself. "Got it."

Lenny returned to Dora, whose admiring glances reminded me of what a jerk I had been to her at the store. But a jerk wouldn't be helping some handicapped kid to the bathroom, would he? Oh, who was I kidding? Even a genuinely nice jerk would apologize to Dora instead of trying to overcompensate and getting stuck wiping some kid's butt. *Oh God!* I hadn't thought of that. What had I just gotten myself into? My face burned with embarrassment.

As Christopher positioned each contraption and hopped forward, I readied myself for a rescue, glancing back at Lenny, whose eyes widened with skepticism—or was that my own insecurity? I had better not screw up. For a few steps, I walked alongside Christopher, keeping a little distance between us, as we made our way to the restroom door with relative ease. I let out a sigh.

Christopher's words came out abruptly—"I'm not retarded, you know."

I stiffened, unsure how to respond. I guessed he could tell that I assumed he was somehow like Dora. I shrugged for lack of a polite, if not patronizing reply. He quit walking and I paused with him.

"I have Muscular Dystrophy—it affects my body, not my brain," he said, slurring just a little.

For the first time, I looked him in the face. Sweat spiked

the straight, sandy-colored hair across his forehead. Blue, hooded eyes studied me and sparked, turning the corners of his lips to a smile that revealed straight white teeth. I still wasn't sure what to say.

He leaned on one crutch and nudged my leg with the other. "I used to be like you."

"Sorry," was the only word that came out.

"What for? *I'm* having a *good* time! Obviously, two legs don't guarantee that. It wouldn't kill you to crack a smile, you know."

I let out a nervous chuckle and moved forward, toward the restroom door, hoping he would follow.

He laughed. "You need to lighten up, Fixer-man."

"*I'm* having a good time," I said, pushing through the door and holding it for him.

"Yeah, taking Frankenstein to the bathroom is loads of fun."

"I don't mind. I had to go anyway."

He shuffled toward the closest stall, nudged it with his elbow, and backed in.

I moved to the urinal. "You need any help?"

"Nope."

There was a lot of shuffling and bumping in the stall, and then one of his crutches skidded beneath the divider. He cussed and then laughed in one breath.

"Seems like someone ought to put crutch hooks in public johns," I said as I finished peeing and picked up the contraption. "Either that, or they need to design better crutches."

"Yeah, maybe around the time they design something better than a peg leg. Mary Shelley had it right. Used parts!" He laughed. "Maybe we could steal some bodies at the local morgue."

Now that was funny. "Ha! We'd need a wheelchair to cart them away. Maybe you could come up with one of those."

"Yeah. One of those powered jobs—with turbo-boosters. They'd never catch us—we'd be the ever-elusive Odd Squad, wanted in fifty states!"

Did he know that's what folks around town called The Group from Daisy Hill? It didn't matter. I was part of the joke and the odd one of The Group. Funny how standing on the other side of a bathroom stall—without the visual reminder that he had an impairment—made Christopher seem no different from me. I liked him.

Back out on the beach, Dora still sat beside my towel. I scoped out Penny. Somewhere between the boat and the lifeguard perch, she had removed her shirt and shorts and her ponytail. I still wasn't sure how she had managed to nab a two-piece swimsuit without Mom knowing. Percy leaned forward from his post as she swayed, chatting and giggling, tossing her hair over her shoulder. Penny would have been annoyed if I interrupted, so I followed Christopher to our spot. I walked along, prepared to steady him if he needed it, while glancing back at my sister. I understood that girls got crushes on older guys, but when Penny pawed Percy's leg, I squirmed. Good grief, did I come across as that desperate when I was around Amelia?

I again sat between Christopher and Dora but remained preoccupied with Penny. Even after Percy leaned back in his seat, clasping his hands behind his head and closing his eyes, she didn't come and sit near my towel—no, she camped out on the sand right beside him. How obvious was that?

"Is that your sister?" Christopher nudged me back from my staring.

"Yeah."

"What's her name?"

I looked at him askance. "Penny."

"Is she nice?"

"Yeah," I said, though my tone questioned what he was getting at.

"She's pretty."

"She's my sister, man. I don't think of her like that."

"Is that her boyfriend?"

"Percy? No way."

"Then I've got a chance."

My brow flicked incredulously. "Yeah, um … well," I tried to come up with a way to let him down easy. "I think she likes older guys."

"How old is she?"

"Sixteen."

"Perfect! I'm eighteen."

I shrugged. Did he really think he had a shot at Penny? *Wow*. I had never met someone so optimistic or just plain cocky. Regardless, any guy talking that way about my sister made me cringe. I needed a subject change.

I asked, "So, you like to read?"

"Yeah."

"Let me guess—"

Before I could say Mary Wollstonecraft Shelley's *Frankenstein*, he pumped his outstretched arms and grunted like the multi-membered monster himself and thumped Lenny's book. "None of that girly Regency Romance for me!"

Lenny nudged Christopher's arm with his volume. "Yeah, well, at least Jane Austen was prolific—what did Shelley publish? Just Frankenstein."

"Shows how much you know. She published plenty, and she was a political radical, besides that."

Lenny shrugged and chuckled. "Smart-ass."

Christopher and Lenny's banter devolved into a dispute over which writer's prose was better. That evolved into a discussion between Christopher and me about the feasibility of animating a Frankenstein from spare parts, versus H. G. Wells constructing a time machine, which escalated into a debate over whether or not Verne had depicted a hot air balloon to travel around the world in eighty days, or some other flying machine. Before I knew it, an hour had passed.

I glanced at my watch. "Wow, I gotta get going."

Christopher jutted his chin toward the public landing. "Is that your rowboat?"

"Yeah, you want a ride?" I asked without thinking about the impracticality of it.

"Hell, yeah—"

Lenny cut in, "Not today, buddy."

"Maybe we could work it out sometime," I replied.

"We'll see."

With that, I gathered my towel, said my goodbyes, and went over to where Penny was still sprawled out next to Percy's station. My shadow loomed over her. She squinted up at me.

"Hey, Pen, time to go."

"We just got here, Ben."

"Did not. You're getting burnt."

"This is not a burn. I'm working on my tan."

I looked up at Percy as he stroked his goatee.

He smiled. "How's it going?"

"It's going fine," I said, without the least bit of friendliness.

I crossed my arms and returned my attention to Penny. "Well, I'm going. You can walk home if you want."

"Fine." She sat up. "I'll be right there."

I glanced at Percy who was now grinning, and then I nudged Penny's thigh with my toe. "Hurry up. Don't forget Dad's coming this afternoon."

"I said I'd be right there."

I never used to embarrass Penny, and it wasn't as if I were some whiny, snot-nosed little kid like Frankie. Just the same, I figured I would give her some space. I gave Percy another stare-down before I returned to the boat. Sitting on the transom seat, facing the water, I heard Penny coming up behind me and didn't move. Her beach bag dropped beside my feet as she gave me a gentle shove.

"You're not going to make *me* row us home, are you Benjie?" The tone of her voice conveyed a smile.

She nudged me again. I didn't respond to her lighthearted change of attitude. I just climbed out, pushed the boat into the water, and held it steady as she took her usual seat. With one more shove, I splashed in the water and boarded. Manning the oars, I avoided eye contact.

I rowed a few feet and set my sights on the beach, on Christopher. Lenny came to his feet beside him and then walked over to Percy on the stand. They talked for a few seconds. Then Lenny passed something to Percy, and Percy passed something back. They shook hands, palm to palm, not the way I shook hands with Doc, but grabbing each other's thumbs. Lenny spotted me, flipping a peace sign before returning to Christopher and the others. I just waved, I mean, how lame would it be for me to make a peace sign? I wasn't a hippie and had no interest in becoming one. That was more than I could say for Penny. Besides, why did they feel the need to come up with all kinds of new gestures and symbols, anyway? What was wrong with a plain old handshake or a wave, and leave it at that?

"Why are you in such a grumpy mood?" Penny said.

"I'm not in a *grumpy* mood."

"You are too."

"Am not."

"Okay, listen, I'm sorry I wouldn't sit with you. Sometimes I just feel like hanging out by myself."

"By yourself?" I rolled my eyes. "Hanging all over what's-his-name is hardly hanging out by yourself."

"I was *not* hanging all over him. And his name is *Percy*, for the last time."

"Yeah? Well, I can't believe that you can't tell he's not into you, but you still throw yourself at him."

"Shut up! I do not."

"God, Penny, it's embarrassing."

"Yeah? Well, I'll tell you what's embarrassing, is watching you making pathetic attempts at getting Amy's attention. I mean, hanging around at Doc's, waiting for a glimpse of her boobs, when she scarcely knows you exist? How embarrassing is that?"

I'm sure my face must have turned every shade from red to purple. She made me want to come back at her with cuss words, the kind I had heard at school—the kind that would earn me three douses of hot sauce. "And what makes you such an expert on Amelia?"

"She and I talk."

"Yeah, right. You just want to be friends with her so you can hang out with the hippies."

"You know what! Sometimes you really are such a— such a *moron*." I had been called a moron plenty of times by Dad and bullies at school, but never by Penny.

"Yeah? Well—*drop dead!*" It felt good saying it, though I immediately wanted to take it back. But I didn't.

Penny folded her arms and pursed her lips as I rowed harder, trying to land us at camp faster. Laughter from Whispering Narrows greeted us as we entered the cove. Doc, Amelia, and Sunshine hovered around the fieldstone grill. All but Amelia waved—well, she might have, but she had stepped behind Doc, so I couldn't tell.

It was a hot and sticky, breezeless afternoon. Sound carried faster than words that just slipped out in anger. Odors hung in the air, lingering like regrets and second-guessing. It wasn't until we passed Amelia's little dock that the aroma of grilling steaks caught up with us. I glanced over my shoulder to check the bow's bearing.

Over at our beach, Dad had arrived and stood at the water's edge. A puff of smoke rose above him as he flicked something to the sand and ground it underfoot. Cigarettes? Mom must have been right about him sneaking smokes. Penny waved as I slowed the pull of my oars. I should have been looking forward to seeing Dad, but I wasn't.

"Hi, Daddy!" Penny called out.

"Hey, Sweet Pea! Where is everyone?" Dad said as I neared shore. I caught a whiff of cigarettes. "I get here and the place is deserted."

I had barely beached the boat before Penny jumped out and flung her arms around Dad. "We just went for a boat ride. Mom and Frankie went to the market."

"Spending all my money, no doubt."

"Hi, Dad," I said.

He looked at me. "I wish you wouldn't beach the boat, Ben. That's how it gets all scratched and dinged. How many times do I have to tell you to tie it at the dock?"

"Yes, sir." I shoved off. The sound of gravel scraping the boat's bottom amplified and echoed across the cove. As I drifted toward the end of our dock, I wished I could keep rowing straight over to Whispering Narrows or back to the beach to pick up Christopher. The boat rocked as I tied off the bow and stern. Dad and Penny walked arm in arm up to the basement door. I couldn't think of a good reason to follow, so I hoisted myself onto the dock and sat at the end for a few minutes, trying to figure out what was so wrong with me that my own father couldn't spare a decent greeting for his elder son, after not seeing him for five weeks. Frankie would receive far better than a hello. I didn't see any point in being around to witness that.

I kicked at the water with both legs. I should have felt grateful to have two legs. What if I had to hobble around like Christopher? Did he have parents who loved him, or did they just drop him off at Daisy Hill, wishing they'd had a 'normal' son? What if people looked at me and assumed I were retarded? Why couldn't I just be glad for having two parents and two legs? I stood, a lump forming in my throat.

Light chatter tripped its way toward me from Doc's yard. Three deep breaths—an attempt at holding back my emotions—and I dove deep. Cutting through the murky light, deeper and deeper into the dark, I pushed harder and harder until the pressure in my ears matched the pounding of my heart. My eyes no longer burned from restraining tears. I hit bottom, skimming through muddy debris. All at once, I ran out of air. Time suspended as I forced my way up, each stroke pulling at my compressed chest. In those few excruciatingly long seconds, I imagined my lifeless, two-legged body floating to the surface. How long would it take anyone to notice? If I were waiting on my family, it might take hours. Doc would be the first one on the scene. He would be sad. So would Sunshine. Amelia probably wouldn't care. Mom and Dad and Frankie—well, that would screw up their summer. But Penny, she would be devastated. I imagined the horror in her eyes, and panicked at the thought of taking a breath of lake water. I wasn't sure which way was up. Propelling myself with decreasing strength, I finally breached the surface.

Gasping for air, flinging water from my hair and face, I wiped my eyes, looking for anyone who might have seen how close I had come. If not for the turtle that ducked under at the sight of me, no one noticed. Now a flood of tears mingled with the water that I had nearly accidentally drowned myself in. What a stupid—selfish—thing to do. I skimmed the calm surface, letting it wash away the traces of my humiliation.

"Benjie—" my sister's voice cut across the cove. "Come help with supper."

All that meant was no one else wanted to carry paper plates and crap downstairs and out the back door to the picnic table. When I swam ashore, I picked up the scent of charcoal briquettes and lighter fluid. As I emerged from the water, smoke from the grill curled from the edges of the cover. That meant Dad had been out getting things started while I was practically drowning. As if he would care.

CHAPTER 14

I'VE THOUGHT A LOT ABOUT SUICIDE OVER THE past eighteen years—not about killing *myself*, of course, but about what it takes. What makes a person like Christopher rise above his circumstances and embrace life, while another becomes so overwhelmed that she wants to end it all? I've been on suicide watch with Penny a couple of times since that summer. Gretchen also had her issues prior to our relationship, but she found a medication that keeps her on an even keel—that, and some short-term therapy. If those remedies work—great! Go for it. That's way better than the alternative. And I suppose if this venture I've undertaken doesn't do the trick, I might have to resort to a bolder tactic, like a shrink and a prescription. But for now, as I collect these papers from the floor, I'm hoping these documents—what they give me permission to do—will provide the perspective and closure I need. Maybe my twitch will even disappear.

These written legalities declare me the owner of this piece of real estate. I wish owning—or disowning—a past could be as simple as papers changing hands. Symbolic gestures, like signing a document in front of a witness, can officially change a person's status. A Marriage License: single to married. Power of Attorney: change in guardianship. A Death Certificate: legally living to certifiably dead.

In fact, that's what this deed is all about. Owning what rightfully belongs to me, and giving myself permission to disown what was never mine in the first place. What makes a thirteen-year-old kid feel like he has signed on to responsibility for everything bad that happens? I took the weight of that summer upon myself, as if somehow I should have seen all the events as they were adding up. As if a kid has the context of adult experience.

A transaction at the beach? How was I to know it was a drug deal? A smoldering 'cigarette' butt—a joint. Hell, I had only recently heard of LSD, or even marijuana or weed. I didn't know what drugs were and hadn't known anyone who used them. Dope was what you called your kid brother when he did something stupid. A buzz was what your mother did to your head at the beginning of summer. And a bookie? Well, what a strange name for someone that takes bets on horses. Those fragments of that summer are my mental memorabilia.

I reach into the cardboard box and pull out another bit of memorabilia. I have mixed feelings about this item, but I've kept it all these years. I remember seeing it for the first time—that afternoon, when Dad came back to camp for his mid-summer visit.

AS SOON AS I STEPPED INTO THE BASEMENT, after my near-death experience and subsequent summons to help with supper, I met Mom's shrill voice from upstairs.

"They were on sale, Frank. I thought you'd be happy with steaks."

"You think money grows on trees?"

"Well, what would you have me do with them? Drive all the way back to Garver's and return them?"

"Just give them to me, Beverly," Dad grumbled and trotted down the stairs. When his sights landed on me, he scowled. "Just like you to disappear when there's work to be done. Go help your mother."

I pushed back the burning behind my eyes and slogged upstairs.

Penny glanced at me from the table where she snapped

green beans. She looked on the verge of tears as her shoulders slacked.

Mom sipped her lemonade and said, "Help your sister."

I pulled out the chair beside Penny. Her chin quivered as she offered a half smile. When I sat, she nudged me and whispered, "Sorry Ben."

We could never stay mad at each other for the simple fact that we needed each other, especially in moments like this.

I grabbed a green bean. "Me too."

"How many times do I have to remind you to wash your hands, Ben?" Mom said, slamming her empty cup on the counter.

As I stood at the sink, Frankie skipped out of the bathroom. "I'll take the plates and stuff down, Mom."

That just meant he would carry down paper plates and napkins on his way to the frog pond, and score a few brownie points while he was at it.

"You are such a good boy, Frankie." Mom grabbed him by the shoulders and kissed his head. "What would I do without you?"

Penny rolled her eyes.

As soon as Frankie left the room, Mom began pacing, then opened and closed the cabinet beside the refrigerator. "I'll finish up the beans. You two take this sack of corn out back and shuck the husks."

"Sure thing, Mom," Penny said, then mumbled, "so you can pour yourself another drink."

"What's that, Penny?"

We both stood. Penny pushed the bag at me. "Nothing, Mom."

I followed Penny down the stairs. We couldn't get out of there fast enough.

"You missed a doozy," she said before we stepped out the back door.

"Another fight?"

"Yeah. Mom's been overspending—"

"Says Dad. Told you it was money they fight about."

"What do you think she's been overspending *on*? I mean, we've had hot dogs or Spam and Spaghetti-Os practically every day since we got here."

"I don't know, we had hamburgers a few times, and she's got a couple new outfits."

"Get real, Ben. Liquor is expensive."

"Maybe Frankie's been dipping into her purse."

She held the door for me. "Maybe."

Dad stood over the grill with a long fork in one hand and the other pressing against his ear. A long, white wire connected his head to a new handheld transistor radio. How much had that cost?

Penny came up beside him. "Oh cool, Dad, when did you get that?"

Preoccupied, he pushed her aside and turned his back on her. Now pressing his finger to his ear, he licked his lips like a kid anticipating a snow cone.

"Come on, *come on*," he said under his breath, ignoring Penny as she backed off. Her whole countenance took a nosedive, like I had earlier. I was used to Dad's rebuff, but the way he had just treated Penny made me want to follow through on his advice to "give it right back to bullies." And what was the deal with the radio? How could he accuse Mom of overspending? I had seen radios like that go for $25 and $30 at Philbrick's Electronics, back home in Massachusetts.

I sat at the end of the picnic table bench. Penny joined me. I would have said something about the radio and how much he had spent on that, but her eyes welled up.

"Here—" I passed her a corn cob and returned to shucking.

Penny kept her eyes on Dad.

I tossed a husk to the ground. "Hey, you wanna sneak out later?"

"What do you mean?"

"You know, like after everyone goes to bed—get in the boat and row out on the lake and look at the stars."

A gradual smile came over her face. "Yeah. After everyone's gone to bed. We can have a secret signal or something."

"That's so lame. No. I'll just come to your room when everything's quiet."

Dad burst out, "Yes! Son of a gun. I *knew* it. Ha ha!" His voice rang out, eyes lit with a broad smile that turned into a laugh as he yanked the plug from his ear.

Penny and I exchanged glances as Dad approached and tossed the radio at me. "Here ya' go, kid. Consider it an early birthday present."

I fumbled with it, trying to gather up the wire as he practically skipped to the back door.

"What the crap!" Penny grabbed it from me as my mouth stayed agape. "Are you going to share?"

"Heck, no."

"Bring it tonight, okay?"

I still wasn't sure what had just happened, but it appeared as if I was the owner of a new radio.

When Dad returned with Mom, they were arm in arm, all lovey and smoochy. It was the weirdest thing. When we sat down to eat, the steaks were a little overdone but Mom didn't gripe, she just sipped her lemonade and smiled at Dad. He was in such a good mood that I almost asked if he and I could go fishing tomorrow, but a lot could change between dinner and tomorrow morning. I would take my new radio and call it better-than-even compensation.

Penny and I cleaned up after we finished eating, while Mom and Dad sat down at the water together, talking and laughing. After that, we took my radio out to the end of the dock, messing with the AM stations, trying to find a few that came in good. At around nine o'clock, Frankie came down in his pajamas and kissed Mom goodnight.

She announced, "Time for you two to get ready for bed."

"Are you kidding me?" Penny huffed.

"Don't sass your mom, Sweet Pea. Go on now. You too, Ben."

"I can't *believe* this," Penny said under her breath as we both stood.

"Never mind that." I reclaimed my radio. "As soon as they hit the hay, we're outta here."

Within a half hour, we were in our rooms, Frankie was snoring, and Mom and Dad made their way down the hall. Their door clicked shut to the sound of Mom's muffled giggling.

A few thumps bumped the wall and Dad whispered, "Quiet Beverly," and then Mom 'shushed' loudly. That's when other noises started. It took a second to realize what was going on and two seconds longer to escape into the hall. I shuddered at the thought.

Poking my head into Penny's room, I gestured for her to follow.

"They're asleep already?" she whispered.

I shook my head and responded in kind, "No, but they won't hear a thing over all the noise they're making."

"Oh, gross!" She rolled her eyes and climbed out of bed, still clothed.

We made our way to the stairs, then down and out the back door. I was glad Dad had made me dock the boat. All we had to do was keep it from bumping and we would be home free.

I rowed so as not to splash, nodding toward Whispering Narrows as we passed, and kept my voice low. "Guess what I saw the other night."

Penny leaned forward, her eyes wide. "What?"

"Skinny-dipping."

She covered her mouth. "No way."

"Well, I mean, they were probably skinny-dipping. That's what hippies do."

"Who was there?"

"All of them."

"Percy, too?"

I rolled my eyes. "I don't think so, but it was dark."

"They were all naked?"

"That's what skinny-dipping is, you doofus."

She sat back, her eyes wandering toward the little dock as we passed by, as if she was imagining them. "Wow. I wish I'd been there."

"Why? So you could join them?"

She grinned and shrugged, then nodded.

I quit rowing for a second. "No way."

"C'mon—you would have loved to, if you weren't so chicken."

Not that I hadn't thought a lot about skinny-dipping ever since, but yeah, I was chicken alright. "Not a chance. What's the point to it anyway?"

"It's just the idea of it—no clothes ...."

Now that we were out of the cove, I asked, "Have you ever gone skinny-dipping?"

"Not yet." Her brows waggled. "You wanna?"

Skinny-dipping with my *sister*? I huffed, "Yeah, right."

"Oh, you're such a stick-in-the-mud."

"I just don't see the point in it." Well, I did but not unless I was with someone other than my sister. Besides, what if a fish mistook my dangling parts for bait.

"Hey," she pointed over my shoulder. "You wanna go to the island?"

"Sure." With a glance, I set my bearing and rowed hard. I liked working my muscles as if that might help my physique. It seemed as though I had improved some since we arrived at camp, but it was probably just our cheap bathroom mirror, like one of those warped ones in the funhouse.

I slowed as we neared the island. Within a couple feet of shore, I twisted my oar, bringing us alongside the exposed roots. Penny looped the line at the transom. I grabbed another root and steadied us while she climbed out.

Standing in the little clearing a couple yards in, she said, "Looks like someone's been here before us."

"Yeah. Me and probably half the lake." I pointed up the pine tree. "I climb this all the time. It's a great lookout."

"You are such a boy." She shoved me and grinned. "Bet you can't do it in the dark."

"Oh yeah? Watch this." I knew the branches by heart. One limb after the other, I scaled my way to the top in no time.

"Can you see anyone coming this way?"

"No. Just a couple people on the end of Amelia's dock, but no one on the water."

"Good."

I glanced down at her as she stripped off her top. I had seen her in a two-piece, but that was way different from seeing her bra. "What are you doing?"

She wiggled out of her shorts. "I'm gonna go skinny-dipping. Don't look!"

"What?" I nearly shouted, averting my eyes.

"Skinny—"

"I got that the first time! What are you, nuts?" She splashed and I glanced down at her pile of clothes.

She let out a giggle that turned into a laugh, which rolled across the lake and returned. She now hushed her voice, "C'mon Ben! It's fun!"

"No way. You're sick."

She laughed and swam out a few yards. I thought she might keep swimming right over to Whispering Narrows, but she then doubled back, giggling the whole time. When she neared the island again, she treaded water. "You're missing out, Ben."

"And you're out of your mind." If I were going to risk a bass nibbling my bare butt, it sure wasn't going to be with my sister. Just the same, I was wishing I were that brave. If it hadn't been for the naked part, she could have talked me into it, but a kid has got to draw the line somewhere—I mean, for crissake, she was my *sister*. What kind of perv skinny-dips with his sister?

She swam a bit more and then announced, "I'm getting out—don't look."

Yeah, right. Like I was going to look. A minute after some splashing and then pine needles crunching, she said, "Done. Come on—let's go rowing some more."

That just meant she hoped someone might still be sitting on the end of the dock, probably one of the hippies, her newfound preoccupation.

"Well?" I said, once we had boarded the boat. "Was it as great as all that?"

She shivered. "If I could skinny-dip every day for the rest of my life, I would."

"*Girls.*"

"You don't know what you're missing."

"Don't care."

As I rowed, Penny kept her gaze fixed over my shoulder—I assumed at the dock. Sure enough, she whispered, "Keep heading the way you are. We'll come just close enough."

"Close enough for what?"

"Oh my gosh. It's Percy and Lenny."

I was only interested if there was a girl, but I glanced over my shoulder anyway, right as Lenny said, "Hey, Fixer-man. How you doin' Penny?"

Percy passed a tiny glowing cigarette butt to Lenny and exhaled, "Hi, Penny," in a puff of smoke. It didn't smell like any cigarette I knew of.

"Hi, guys," she replied, cool as could be, arching her back a little. That's when I noticed her bra on the seat beside her. How embarrassing.

"Nice night for a boat ride," Percy said. "Too bad there isn't room for four."

"Yeah, too bad," I said, glaring at my sister. As we drifted away, I interjected, "Hey, Lenny, when are you going to bring Christopher around so we can go fishing?"

"You serious about that?"

"Heck yeah."

"Okay, I'll work it out."

"Great," I said, steering the boat past them.

Penny waved. "Goodnight."

"See you 'round, Penny," Percy's deep voice carried over the water. I guessed if he hadn't noticed her before, he sure did now.

Penny whispered when out of earshot. "If Lenny wasn't Sunshine's—what a hunk."

"I thought you liked Percy."

"I do—it's just, well, did you see the muscles on Lenny?"

"I don't notice that kind of stuff on guys."

"Of course you do. Guys are always comparing."

"Yeah, to guys our own age. Not to full-grown men. Duh."

She shivered. "Full-grown men … hmmm …."

"You know Penny, you better be careful. Those guys are a lot older than you."

She smiled wishfully. "Yeah … I know."

"I'm serious."

"Oh, Benjie, you worry too much." She dragged her hand in the water. "I'm not a child, you know."

"Yeah, I know. But you're still too young."

She kicked my foot. "So, who is Christopher?"

"Some *older* guy who hangs out with Lenny."

Her brow flicked. "Oh yeah?"

"Yeah. And he's really smart and funny."

"What's he look like?"

"Blond hair, blue eyes."

"Mmmm … I don't remember seeing him."

"You saw him. You just didn't pay any attention to him because he's missing a leg."

She grimaced. "*Him?*"

"Yeah, *him*. And you are not going to hang out with us if we go fishing together."

"Yeah, well, you know I hate fishing—"

"You mean you'd be embarrassed to be seen with us."

"Would not."

"Would too."

"Just shut up and row."

"That's what you always say when you know I'm right."

She growled and kicked my ankle, though it was more of a nudge. I was right, and we both knew it. Just the same, I couldn't accuse her when I felt just as awkward around Dora. The opposite sex always complicated things. Sometimes even having a sibling that qualified as the opposite sex made things a little uncomfortable. To be honest, I liked it better before Penny grew up and got interested in boys—before I ever noticed girls' chests. It seemed as if boobs messed things up, even between the two of us. We used to take baths together in broad daylight, back when I was really little. Now, the idea of swimming naked with my sister—in far more water—in the dark, was too weird even to think about. Weirder yet, she might actually consider swimming naked with guys like Percy and Lenny.

Chapter 15

I'VE NEVER CONSIDERED MYSELF SENTIMENTAL. Yet here I am, standing in a kitchen so full of my past, pulling yet another fragment from a cardboard box. A symbol of something I've lost—an opportunity. A hope. A transistor radio.

Over the years, I've thought a lot about why Dad didn't like me, and I've drawn my own conclusions. It doesn't take much imagination to put it all together. Yeah, there's a chance I could be wrong, but I'll never know for sure. I'm certain Mom knew the reason why, but that's not the sort of thing a mother shares with a kid or even an adult child. That's the kind of secret a mother takes to her grave.

Sentimentality aside, I can't help marveling at what this little transistor radio signifies, technology-wise, and how far we've come. As a kid, I imagined inventions like compact discs but in some Jetson-like future. I had no idea that as an adult I would end up on the cutting edge of technology.

I run my thumb over the raised letters where the white paint of General Electric has worn off the wood-grain face. I click it on and roll the AM tuner. Static and that faraway sound of popular hit music plays …

PENNY'S HEAD BOBBED AND HER FOOT wiggled to the music's beat as she sang the chorus to Creedence Clearwater Revival's "Bad Moon Rising."

She glanced over at me on the float, under the late morning sun. "Hey, Ben—"

I was sulking and didn't answer.

She sang my name, "*Ben*-jie ...."

"What?"

"C'mon, don't be grumpy just because Daddy didn't take you fishing again."

"It's easy for you to say. He actually *likes* you."

"Don't be silly. Who just got a brand new pocket transistor radio?"

"Yeah, I know. But it sort of feels like—I don't know...."
I did know it had been a generous gift, but why did it feel so secondhand, like an afterthought?

"What? Just because he didn't wrap it up in pretty birthday paper with a card?"

"If it had been a birthday present for you or Frankie, it would have been."

"Listen Ben, if you don't like it, I'll gladly take it off your hands." She picked it up from between us, stroking the case. "Don't be so ungrateful. Besides, Dad loves us all the same."

"Yeah, right." I came to my feet, curled my toes over the edge of the float, and dove in. In all honesty, I was grateful. Dad could have just as easily tossed the radio to Penny and entirely forgotten my birthday—but he didn't. And aside from not taking me fishing, he had treated me better, right up until he left on Sunday morning. He hadn't called me moron or idiot more than a couple of times—if he did, I was so accustomed to it that I didn't notice.

When I surfaced, Penny dove in after me as I treaded water. She emerged a few feet away, and we swam to the middle of the cove.

"Did you hear about the wedding?" she said, casting a glance toward Whispering Narrows.

"Yeah, I think Doc said something about it."

"It's a week from Saturday."

"So what."

"So what? It means there's going to be a big party."

"As if we were invited."

"We could sneak over."

I swam backward, away from her, saying, "That's crazy," and then turned, swimming my way toward the mouth of the cove. Penny took that as a challenge and came up behind me. The race was on. I stroked with everything I had, gaining on the imaginary line where the floatplane mooring jutted into the lake. I let out a reserved *whoop* as I passed it ahead of her.

"Nothing quite like the thrill of victory!"

My head whipped around at the sound of Doc's booming voice.

Penny's and my gazes rose to his face, our arms and legs flailing below the water's surface.

"Good morning, sir—I mean Doc," I said breathlessly.

He pushed his hands deep into his chino pockets, facing us at the edge of the planking. "Good morning to both of you! I was actually just thinking about you—" he glanced at Penny "—and your sister."

"Hello, sir," she finally offered.

"Good morning, Penny." His attention vacillated between the two of us. "I don't suppose you have television here on the lake, do you?"

"No, sir, but we have one at home."

"Well, how would you like to see the Apollo lunar landing on Sunday night—in color?" He let out a laugh. "Well, the actual landing will be in black and white, but the broadcast will be color."

Penny and I exchanged wide-eyed looks.

He continued, "Of course, it will be a late night, so you'll have to get permission."

"Yes, sir, we'd love to. Thanks."

"Okay then." He began to walk away and then turned, gripping the floatplane wing. "Oh, and I'm going up again, day after tomorrow. What do you say, Ben? You game?"

"Yes, sir!"

"Ten sharp."

Penny stared at me, her mouth wide as a bass when I replied, without hesitation. "Ten sharp."

As Doc walked away, she shoved me, mouthing the words, "I can't *believe* you!"

"What can I say?" I grinned. "It's your bad influence on me."

We continued to swim in circles, exchanging ideas on how we might finagle permission for a history-making television broadcast at Whispering Narrows. Doc made it halfway up the landing before turning. "By the way, Ben—Lenny mentioned something about bringing his friend by this afternoon. You still interested in taking them fishing?"

"Yes, sir."

"Good man," he said and continued toward the garage.

As far as going up for another flight with Doc, well, permission granted once—albeit roundabout—was as good as a season pass. I would worry about the details later, though ever since Penny had pointed out how Mom consistently went to the market on Friday mornings, I felt optimistic that Mom would follow through. I had also checked the top shelf of the cabinet beside the refrigerator. The bottle's level did drop, day-to-day, the way Penny had said. If I needed to, I could empty some into the sink—that way, Mom would have to go.

As soon as Penny and I returned to camp, I gathered up my tackle and readied the boat for Christopher and me. Mom had already gone inside for lunch with Frankie and Penny. I chomped down the last of my peanut butter and Fluff while paddling around the cove. A couple times, Amelia stepped out of the sliding-glass door, but then went back inside, probably because she spotted me and figured I was just waiting to gawk at her. If she liked me the way Sunshine had said she did, she sure had a weird way of showing it.

The next time the kitchen door opened, Lenny stepped

out, pushing Christopher in a wheelchair. Our cottage remained quiet so I rowed over to Amelia's beach.

Sporting a life jacket and a flesh-colored, plastic-looking leg, Christopher hoisted himself out of the chair. Lenny tossed a lifejacket at me as he assisted Christopher aboard. I never wore a lifejacket. Those were for sissies.

"You coming with us, Lenny?" I asked.

"Nah. You two will be fine. Just stay in sight of the dock so I can keep an eye on you. I'll be in some deep doo-doo if the two of you go overboard, so take it easy."

I gave the lifejacket a second thought. If Christopher did go over, would I be able to rescue him? I strapped the vest around my chest.

Christopher clutched one side of his lifejacket and laughed. "My boobs're bigger than yours."

"You wish," I said, puffing my vested chest as I rowed. "So do you even know how to swim?"

"Sure I do, I'm just not as fast as I used to be," he said, bending his good leg and positioning the fake to balance his weight. No matter which way he shifted, his plastic leg wouldn't cooperate, but that didn't stop him from juggling his fishing rod and a shiner.

I rowed to halfway between the floatplane and the island, wishing we could head out to the middle of the lake where the water was deep and cold.

"Nothing ever bites this close to shore," I said.

Christopher's fake leg buckled at an awkward angle as he cast his line. "We'll see about that. You just gotta know how to wiggle your bait."

"Whatever you say."

I let my line out a few unenthusiastic yards and nudged his prosthesis. "What's that thing made of, anyway?"

"Resin or something."

"Can I touch it?"

He laughed. "Sure."

I thumped it a couple times. It didn't sound quite

hollow, but not real solid either. "It looks kind of like one of my sister's doll legs."

"Your sister's got a GI Joe?"

I rolled my eyes. "No, but GI Joe is what I meant."

"Right," he chuckled. "Well, regardless of how it looks, it's better than no leg at all."

"Seems like someone ought to invent one that doesn't buckle at the knee and with a foot that moves better."

"Yeah, well, this isn't the top of the line. The really nice ones cost a fortune and insurance companies don't like to pay for frills. Besides, I spend more and more of my time in the chair anyway. The leg is mostly for looks these days—my parents want me to feel more *whole*."

I stared at it long enough to be rude, but I was as much distracted with the idea of feeling 'whole' as I was with the prosthesis. "Does it help? I mean, do you sometimes forget that you don't have both legs?"

He was quiet for a long moment before he looked me straight in the eye and answered, "Every morning when I wake up."

Although he said it with a deadpan expression, his words hit like a reprimand for asking such an invasive question. My discomfort didn't keep me from saying, "That must make it hard to get out of bed—" I didn't catch my unintended irony until he laughed.

"Good one," he said.

Now my face heated. "I meant, you know, 'hard to face the day'."

He shrugged, "I'm just glad I have this one." He slapped his good leg.

"So, are you going to lose that one, too, on account of the muscular—you know—the disease you have?"

"Not unless they botch another biopsy, so I get another infection and gangrene and have to have it lopped off."

I wasn't sure if he was kidding, but I chuckled, "Really? That's what happened?"

His eyes darted. The corner of his mouth flinched. "Yeah. Really."

My mouth hung open. "Sorry. I didn't mean to laugh."

"No sweat." He shrugged. "Besides, look at me, I'm out on a lake, fishing!"

"How can you be so positive?"

His brow cocked. "It's like if the boat flips over—what are you going to do? Sink or swim? Me—I'm a swimmer.

"I see what you mean," I said, although I still had a hard time understanding how a person could maintain such optimism and determination.

We reeled our lines in and cast again.

Studying his now-smiling face, I asked, "So, how long have you been living at Daisy Hill?"

"I don't live at Daisy Hill. I live with my parents in Connecticut. I just come up here for a few weeks in the summer so I can have a little privacy and fun on my own."

"When are you going home?"

"They're coming to get me in a few weeks, at the carnival— you know, that way they can have fun with me, too."

"Do you like hanging out with them?"

He shrugged with a grimace. "Yeah, I guess. Don't get me wrong, my parents are great, but they can be a real pain in the butt."

"So, this is like a summer camp for you?"

"Yeah. With a whole different pool of girls to choose from."

I chuckled. "What do you think of Amelia?"

"Amy? She's okay—not my type."

"What's your type?"

"Tall. Blond. Blue-eyes. I want blond, blue-eyed kids. A dozen of them."

I laughed. "I bet you end up with them, too."

"Hell yeah, I will."

His bobber dropped below the surface and popped up. With a yank, he let out a "Whoop" and reeled in a big fat perch. "I'm eating fish tonight!"

CHAPTER 16

THE TRANSISTOR RADIO JOINS THE FOLDER of papers and Sunshine's note beside the box. I wish I had some memento from that afternoon with Christopher. Maybe a big fat, plastic perch mounted on a plaque. My red-and-white-striped socks will have to suffice. Whimsical yet practical. That's Christopher. I learned a lot from him in a short time. I still struggle with implementing that kind of buoyancy, but his example helped me see that optimism exists in real circumstances, with real people, not just in Pollyanna characters.

I may not have a souvenir from that afternoon, but here's a fitting bit of memorabilia that Christopher—my guinea pig and prototype tester—had a lot to do with. My first patent. This piece of paper, with the B-T insignia, is one of my foremost professional accomplishments. Doc was behind the purchase of my patent, but that didn't rob any of its luster; it only supports my speculations about him. Doc ended up being a strong tailwind, giving my life direction—in addition to providing some great aviation metaphors. I'll never forget the first time he put me in control.

RIGHT AFTER MOM LEFT FOR HER FRIDAY morning errands, I met Doc at the mooring. Upon his direction, I climbed into the cockpit, buckled my seatbelt, and put on my headphone. His voice came through loud and clear as he rattled off the instrument checklist: "Flaps, carburetor, throttle, backpressure, and ready for take off."

123

He increased the throttle to 2600 RPMs. We bounced around until the plane gained enough momentum and the nose lifted. The lake shrank in the distance as we gained altitude. My attention refocused on Doc, his maneuvers and how each affected the plane. This time, after we were airborne for several minutes, at about 110 knots, Doc held altitude and said, "You wanna take the controls?"

"Seriously?"

"Sure. I've seen you studying everything I do." He patted the yoke. "What's this for?"

"Pulling makes the nose go up, pushing goes down. Left or right makes the ailerons go up or down for banking left or right."

"Ailerons," he said with astonishment. "You know what they're called."

"I read."

"Good man!" He smiled and leaned back so I could see his feet. "And these?"

"Rudder pedals control the yawing motion, left or right."

"Good. Take over."

Hesitating until he gave me a nod and a nudge, I then gripped the yoke.

"Bank left. Easy does it."

I turned left, my heart pounding right out of my chest.

"Give the left rudder pedal a little pressure," he said. "It will even out the banking."

As I followed through, the plane responded to my command.

"Good ... now hold your course."

My insides leapt as if I had grown wings and burst out of this metal shell around me, soaring under my own power. I had never felt more in control than I did in those moments when I was flying at 7000 feet. I didn't dare take my eyes off the horizon to enjoy the view—who needed a view, with all this power?

"You've got quite a knack," Doc said. "Reminds me of myself when I was your age."

"Did your dad teach you?"

"Hell no—pardon my French! The only thing my dad ever taught me was how to duck."

I didn't know how to respond.

"That's okay, son. A man should know how to duck— comes in handy. No point in getting a black eye if you don't need to. Besides, I wasn't a kid who shriveled up just because my daddy didn't love me. Made me tough. Taught me how to fight for what I want, to stand on my own two feet."

If this was a lecture on standing up for myself, it sure felt a lot different from Dad's 'bully' spiel. I glanced at Doc for but a second as his eyes met mine. There was no sadness or pain in his expression—just a satisfied smile.

"That's right," he said, "the only thing I got handed to me was these—" he held up his big mitts and then tapped his head "—and this. Just like you son. You may not know it, but you're blessed."

My gaze shot to him and back to the horizon. I sure didn't feel blessed, but ever since I started hanging out with Christopher, I thought more about some of the things I took for granted—like legs and hands.

"You think every kid has a brain like yours?"

"I don't know, sir." Mom said we were fortunate not to have mental handicaps, like Dora, but I hadn't ever thought of my brain as anything exceptional.

"You may not think so, but you're special, Ben. You're a smart kid."

I didn't respond.

He continued, "Your potential is limited only by what you believe about yourself, son. Do you know what that means?"

After talking with Christopher, I had an inkling, yet I shrugged.

"If you think you're at a disadvantage because your father doesn't treat you the way you'd like, or your mom has mood swings, you're only right if you believe it. Look at me! I could have believed my father when he said I was no good, but I never believed it. Not for one minute. Everything I have, I've earned it myself—nothing was ever handed to me. That takes mettle, son. And you've got that mettle. I can see it in you."

It didn't matter that I wasn't sure why he was telling me all that. It only mattered that he liked me and saw something in me, something I had never seen. Maybe Christopher was rubbing off on me. Maybe he had planted a seed—and now Doc was watering it. It was a lot to think about.

I tried to picture Doc as a kid and as a young man. How had he put his brain to good use and made a success of his life? I stayed the course we were on and kept mulling over everything he had said. After we had been flying for a while and hit some turbulence, Doc took the controls. I was glad to give them up.

"Don't worry, son—just a little pocket of mixed-up air."

"I'm not worried, Doc."

"Then what's that look on your face?"

"I was just wondering something."

"Well, out with it!"

I sorted through which question to ask. "So, how exactly did you earn all your money?"

He chuckled.

"I'm sorry." *Idiot!* "That was a rude question."

"You should never be sorry about curiosity. I'll tell you how I made my money. I worked for it—that and a little luck and good timing. Treating people the way I want to be treated."

"So, there's money in medical equipment?"

He winked. "Booming business. Ever hear of Burns-Tech?"

"No, sir."

"Well, you're in good health, why would you?"

I shrugged again.

"Quit shrugging, son. It makes you appear indecisive."

"Yes, sir. So, is that why your name is Doc? Are you a doctor or something?"

He laughed. "Just a nickname. I earned it though. Back in the day, I could cut up a machine and sew it back together like nobody's business. Now, I manage all the people who do that for me." He exhaled and continued, "Cutting-edge technology. Makes X-ray machines look like a Brownie camera. You wanna get into a field that's up-and-coming? Medical technology. Computers. By the time you're my age, every household will have one. Focus on your math skills, son, and physics."

"Yes, sir." I didn't understand half of what he was talking about, but I liked the ring of the word technology. It sounded so modern, like science fiction. And I liked math and science. I was good at those. My eighth-grade teacher had said I had aptitude.

"Now, you listen to me, young Benjamin—" he seemed to wait until he had my full attention before he continued, "—when it comes time for you to start applying for universities, you let me know. If you keep those grades up, I'll write you a letter of recommendation that'll get you into any school you want. Understand?"

"Yes, sir."

His eyes penetrated mine until I started to squirm, but I didn't dare look away.

"I'm serious," he said, sternly, squinting at me. "Sometimes, it's not *what* you know, it's *who* you know. And I know people. Don't ever be too proud to ask for a leg up." He paused again. "You understand?"

"Yes, sir."

After a few seconds, he chuckled, "I bet if I were to ask you to repeat everything I just said, you could—word for word."

I grinned, "Yes, sir." And I could. I would never forget—not one bit of it. After a few seconds, a thought occurred to me. He must have read it in my pause, because he looked at me with his raised brow.

He said, "Speak your mind, son."

"You could have fixed that clock easy."

"Sure I could." He winked.

"Why didn't you?"

He let out a long sigh. "I saw potential."

"In me?"

He nodded and gave me a sideways look. "Not just in you, son."

I wondered what he meant, but didn't have the courage to ask.

CHAPTER 17

YEARS OF DEBRIS SPECKLE THE SCREEN OVER the kitchen sink. I look beyond the dreck, beyond this dismal and depressing shell of a house. The poor old place, with its history—who would want to make a home of it? It would have to be someone who doesn't believe in ghosts. Someone with vision. Not that I couldn't see potential in this property if I were inclined to look—which I'm not. Although, it is tempting.

That concept—potential—fascinates me. Years ago, I memorized the definition of the word: *Existing in possibility*—from the Latin word for power.

Potential is a powerful word. Unfortunately, it offers no closure. That's the open-ended nature of it. Always striving; never fully accomplished.

My ability to see things that 'exist in possibility' is an asset in engineering and design, but I'm also inclined to look for potential in other places. The artist woman, for example. It's ridiculous how quickly I could build a scenario—a fantasy—out of ringless fingers on a pretty hand. I didn't even get a real look at her, but I had already provided her with rosebud lips and a face I could fall in love with.

Romantic fantasizing aside, even as a kid, I saw potential in something simple, like the radio on this table. I scroll across staticky stations. This little device represented the possibility that my father might have liked me, that perhaps we could have cultivated a relationship. In some cases, the door closes on potential; it's contrary to the nature of the word, but it happens.

I roll the radio's volume dial until the static dissipates and it clicks off, leaving only the sound of the ticking clock. A half hour has passed since I last checked the time. It seems like a lot longer, maybe because the walls of this cottage are closing in on me. I need some air—a walk down the road.

As I step into the dooryard, I still can't get over how dwarfed everything appears. My calves burn with the strain of walking downhill, even though the distance between camp and Whispering Narrows seems shorter. I come upon the first set of stone pillars quicker than I expect. My heart beats faster, as if I might see Amelia in the yard—or Doc. I hesitate, like a kid afraid of getting caught on the neighbor's property. Passing the cement lions, I make my way toward the front door, walking alongside the recently mowed lawn and trimmed shrubbery.

A chuckle escapes my tight chest. Oh, what the hell! What's the worst that could happen? A spark ignites at the thought of Amelia. Last I heard, she married some guy she had dated for only a few months—at least that's what Doc told me the last time we spoke. But what if she lives here now? What if Sunshine, or someone who knows of their whereabouts, answers the door? I have nothing to lose, so why not knock?

I stand in front of the massive door for a few seconds longer, my heart shooting adrenaline to my tingling hands. Grabbing the lion-head knocker, I give it three loud raps. And wait. And wait. The house and grounds could not be more still. Well, at least I had the courage to try. Then, for the heck of it, I give it one more knock, a timid one, like on the night Penny and I snuck down to watch the lunar landing on color television.

 WITH PENNY BESIDE ME, I RAPPED ON DOC'S front door, afraid that if I knocked too loud the sound would carry up to our cottage and wake

Mom. I didn't have to knock a second time before Doc answered. Amelia stood behind him.

"Well, come on in!" Doc took my hand.

As I returned his grip, my eyes briefly met Amelia's.

"Hello, Benjamin," she said, with her usual half smile.

My heart jumped. "Hi, Amelia."

She quickly turned her attention to Penny. "Let's go up to my room."

"Okay." Penny followed her to the stairs as my gaze followed them up around to the balcony and into one of the front-facing doors. Doc turned, leading me toward an exit beside the piano room, when headlights from the driveway shone through the windows.

"Well, that's curious." He released my shoulder and made his way to the front door. I stood off to the side. At the moment he reached out for the latch, the knocker sounded, and the door flung wide open.

"Hello, hello!" the female voice sang out.

"Karen, sweetheart! You've arrived early!" Doc grinned widely, grabbing hold of the woman. She could have been Sunshine's double but about ten years older and hair about ten inches shorter, pulled back in a brightly colored headband like Mom wore.

"Surprise, surprise, Daddy!"

"Well, this is just wonderful." He seemed genuinely pleased. "What a perfect surprise!"

Behind her, she held a man's hand. As he stepped forward, his blond, Brylcreemed hair glistened under the overhead light.

Doc's smile stretched with tension as he greeted him, "Good to see you, Dick."

"Always a pleasure to see you, sir."

In the wide-open doorway, a tall kid, in a forest green polo shirt, scuffed his loafers on the doormat. It took me only a second to recognize him as the Elmore kid, whose coffee I had spilled—the one who had flicked his cigarette at me. He raked his fingers through a blond tuft of hair, oblivious to my presence. As he stepped in, he looked up and all around the spacious foyer.

Dick spoke up, "Sir, this is my son, Ricky."

Ricky extended his hand, greeting Doc with rows of perfect and gleaming teeth. "Sir. It's a real pleasure to meet you."

Doc maintained his grip for a second longer. "I hear you just graduated Elmore Academy."

"That's right, sir."

Dick chimed in, "With high honors. He'll be attending Yale this fall."

"Impressive," Doc said, but I had heard enough of Doc's motivational discourses to detect a lack of 'impressed' in his tone.

"Where's my baby?" Doc's daughter said as Ricky's eyes fell on me without recognition.

Amelia appeared on the balcony and offered a neutral, "Hello, Mother."

"Come on down here and give me a proper greeting," her mother chided.

Even as Amelia trotted downstairs, her stride lacked enthusiasm. When her mother embraced her, Amelia hugged back, but her grip appeared limp.

Amelia's mother turned her to face the groom-to-be. "Say hello to Dick."

Amelia gave a less-than-half wave—way less than she normally offered me. "Hello, sir."

"Nonsense," he said. "There's no need for formality. Why I'm practically your dad. Call me—"

"Dick," she said. For the first time, I wondered about Amelia's real dad.

"And this is your stepbrother, Ricky—that is, he will be after next weekend."

Amelia's brow rose as Ricky stepped toward her.

"Well, hello," he said, extending his hand.

She accepted it and smiled politely—a bigger smile than I usually received. His eyes were all over her—way worse than I ever gawked.

Amelia said nothing. Her mom's voice cut through the awkward silence as she gestured toward me on the sidelines. "And who is this young man?"

Doc grabbed my shoulder, bringing me into the group. "This is Ben Hughes, the cleverest boy on the lake—come to watch the lunar landing with us."

"Well, Ben Hughes, it's a pleasure to make your acquaintance." She followed through with the same pseudo formality this family seemed so fond of. I accepted her limp handshake.

"Nice to meet you Miss, I mean Mrs.—I mean—"

She tossed her head back. "Nonsense! There'll be none of that! You call me Karen."

"Okay—"

Her plucked brow spiked, prompting my follow-through.

"—Karen."

She smiled with satisfaction. "That's better."

"I'm going back to my room," Amelia announced. "Call me down when they're actually going to step on the moon."

Without waiting for a response, she ran upstairs. This time, Ricky's gaze followed her all the way up and around until she shut the door behind her. Penny was the smart one, staying out of sight in Amelia's room and avoiding all the introductions.

Dick said, "Let's go get those bags, shall we, Ricky?"

"Sure thing, Dad," he responded as his sights landed on me. He squinted, as if it finally dawned on him that we had already 'met.'

Karen slipped her arm around Doc's waist. Arm in arm, he ushered her through a doorway and motioned for me to follow. "Come along, Ben."

I stepped into the large room—the great room I had seen from the kitchen when eating pancakes with Lenny. Only the television and a floor lamp lit the area. Both Lenny and Christopher hunched over a chess table, deep in thought. Sunshine bent behind Lenny, leaning over his shoulder as he studied his next move. At the sight of us, she sprung up.

"Karen," she squealed. "You're here early!"

Christopher's hand hovered over the queen. "Hi, Ben," he said without breaking his focus.

Lenny, fingering his beard, glanced up and flipped me a peace sign. "Fixer-man."

I returned their greetings as Sunshine and Karen embraced.

"Have a seat, Ben." Doc directed me to the overstuffed sofa and chairs forming a semicircle in front of the television, where Percy and Candace sat side by side. Candace, with a large bowl of popcorn in her lap, patted the cushion beside her.

Percy looked up and smiled. "Peace, man. Sit."

I obeyed.

"Popcorn?" she said.

I dug into the bowl as Walter Cronkite's mouth moved; the volume had been muted. Nobody seemed to be paying much attention to the television. At the moment, I wasn't as interested in a history-making broadcast as I was in history-making interactions going on around me. Sunshine and Karen stepped into my peripheral vision. They stood face to face, their profiles like a mirror image.

"Have you talked to your dad—is he coming?" Karen said in a hushed tone.

Sunshine shook her head and shrugged. "Yeah, he said maybe, but that's as good as no." I sure knew what that was like.

"Well, never mind—his loss," Karen sighed, and then added, "I'm going with your suggestion—bird seed instead of rice."

"Cool."

"And you're going to love your maid-of-honor dress—it's so *you*."

Sunshine drew her hair behind her ear. She wore the earrings I had fixed. "I can't wait to see your gown."

"Can you believe? It's a minidress with yards and yards of white chiffon."

I had never heard of a bride wearing a minidress, and I was no fashion expert, but I liked the sound of it. Maybe Amelia would also be in the wedding party—in a mini minidress.

"White?" Sunshine smirked, "Didn't you kind of miss the virgin boat?"

"Hey, this is my *first* wedding. That's practically virginal these days."

Candace broke into my eavesdropping with a nudge, "Whaddaya say, Fixer-man?"

"Huh?"

"You wanna come with?"

I grabbed another handful of popcorn. "Where to?"

Now slumped into Percy, Candace winked. "To a Love-In, over in New York, like we had in Cisco a couple summers ago."

Percy rolled his eyes. "He's too young, Candace. Leave him be."

She jiggled his knee. "You're making the scene, aren't you, Perce?"

His closed eyes fluttered. "If Lenny's got room in the Rambler."

"What's a Love-In?" I asked with my mouth full.

Ricky's voice came from behind, "It's where a bunch of smelly, un-bathed, longhaired, half-naked hippies gather for free love and subversive music."

"Whoa! Whoa man!" Percy craned his neck to look behind. "If I weren't so laid back and opposed to violence, I'd clean your freakin' clock."

Candace giggled, "You mean if you weren't so buzzed that you can't get your butt off the sofa."

Across the room, Lenny came to his feet. "Yeah? Well, I ain't opposed to violence as a means to an end, punk!" He drew in a quick breath. "But I won't disrespect Doc's house."

"Who's the downer?" Candace whispered to me.

"That's Ricky—Amelia's new stepbrother."

She rolled her eyes as Doc spoke up behind us. "Come on now, kids. I'm sure Ricky didn't mean anything by it, did you?" I imagined Doc's heavy hand on Ricky's shoulder, giving him the squeeze.

"Nah, man, I was just kidding around. It was a stupid joke."

"Stupid, alright," Candace snickered between the two of us. "What kind of lame-o-reject is he?"

I shrugged, although I had a pretty good idea of what kind of lame-o he was. I refocused on the television. "So, when do they land on the moon?"

"Oh, that happened hours ago. It was nothing to see, just some tape loop of flames shooting out of a module— then pictures of a staged setup. Pretty boring. The walk is supposed to start sometime soon, though."

I checked my watch. It was 10:30. Across the bottom of the screen, I read, *CBS News Simulation*, as an astronaut messed around with some stuff.

Doc's voice came from behind again, but this time back over where we had come in. I crooked my neck forward as he opened the door. "Amelia! Five minutes! C'mon down!"

"Let's finish the game later," Christopher said. I flipped my attention to the other side of the room as he wheeled away from the game table.

"What!" Lenny remained sitting. "You'd rather watch some government conspiracy on the tube, rather than finish the game?"

"It's history in the making."

"Just another ploy so the *man* can keep his eye on you."

"He's so radical," Candace said to me. "What a turn-on."

Christopher wheeled up beside my end of the sofa. Sunshine sat in the adjacent armchair. Lenny came to his feet and stood behind her, his arms folded like Mr. Clean, giving Ricky—who stood at Percy's end of the sofa—the evil eye. Watching them was way better than color TV.

Light from the opening door caught my eye as Amelia and Penny entered the room. Penny's gaze immediately fell on Percy. Ricky gave Amelia another good long look but she ignored him, moving with Doc to the sofa behind me. I would have given anything for eyes on top of my head.

"Hi, Percy," Penny said, scooting between Christopher's chair and me. Two thin braids framed her face—soon she would probably be wearing gauze and a headband.

Percy leaned forward and winked. "Hey, kiddo."

Penny's wilted expression changed to a smile, as if Candace were no longer snuggling up to him. Penny gave me a shove over to make room. I inched closer to Candace. Christopher cleared his throat.

"Hey, Penny," I said, "this is my friend, Christopher."

She politely offered her hand. "Hi."

His face lit up as he took her hand and shook it. Even though she proceeded to ignore him as she wedged herself between the arm of the sofa and me, I knew he was ecstatic.

Doc raised the TV volume with a handheld device. An astronaut climbed out of the module and started down the ladder, but the bottom of the screen still said it was a simulation. Then all at once, it changed to splotches of black, white, and gray. The words, *LIVE FROM THE SURFACE OF THE MOON,* showed up on the bottom of the screen. It gave me a shiver.

There were some beeps and commentary. Not too impressive. Then they said, "We can see you coming down the ladder now," and I finally figured out what I was looking at. I had a hard time making out any more of what they said. *Armstrong on the moon* appeared on the screen. A few seconds later, Armstrong's garbled voice said something.

Candace asked, "What did he say?"

I shrugged.

Live voice of astronaut Armstrong from the surface of the moon popped up, but the spoken words were just as unintelligible. A few minutes later, the live part ended.

"Well, I'll be …," Doc said.

I wished the broadcast had been more like I had imagined—like from the movies. Just the same, I had witnessed something profound. I wondered about the people behind the scenes, the ones who had figured out how to send a man to the moon. What were those people like when they were thirteen? I didn't stay in my musing for long. I figured that if I was going to have any interaction with Amelia, now was my chance.

I stood and stretched. When I turned to face Amelia, her eyes were already on me. She didn't look away until everyone started milling around and her attention shifted. Christopher backed up his chair. I pulled Penny up out of the cushions as she glanced at Percy, passed out on the sofa, and then directed her attention to Christopher.

"It was nice to meet you," she said. "Thanks for taking Ben out fishing—he needs a friend besides his big sister."

"Sheesh, Penny." I cuffed her shoulder.

Christopher laughed. "At your service. I'm also a great chauffeur."

Penny giggled, "They should call you Hot Wheels."

Christopher's face beamed. He was about to come back with something clever—I knew that much—but Penny cut him off.

"I mean, like those toy cars." Bright red, she turned away, nudging me. "We should probably get going."

"Yeah, I guess, but first I want to find Doc," I said.

Amelia chimed in, "I'll walk you out, Penny."

I was going to miss my chance with Amelia, but I needed to thank Doc. I scanned the room and spotted him stepping into the kitchen. When I pushed the door open, I walked in on him and Karen. Neither looked happy, but both their expressions changed the instant they saw me.

"Sorry," I blurted. "I just wanted to say thanks for inviting us."

"Well, son, I'm glad you came. You know you are always welcome here."

"Thank you, sir." I glanced at Karen whose smile was strained but polite. "And it was nice to meet you. So, anyway, I gotta go."

As I made my way through the great room, Christopher poked me with a grin. "Hot Wheels!"

I laughed, bolstered by his optimism. He knew why I was in a hurry, so I didn't say more than, "Catch you later."

In the foyer, Ricky stood at the stairway landing with Dick. I slipped out the front door without either of them acknowledging me. When I stepped out, Amelia was sitting on the stoop.

As she rose from the middle step, I said, "Did Penny leave without me?"

"Yeah." Her gaze locked on mine.

"Oh." I stepped down to her level—nose to nose. She sighed. I tried to catch my breath. It appeared as though she had waited for me. Was I actually standing outside, alone with Amelia Burns, staring into her eyes?

Her gaze shifted. "Benjamin …."

I liked how she called me Benjamin, instead of Ben— maybe because I called her Amelia instead of Amy.

When her eyes came back to me, I looked away.

"You know ..." she sighed again, "I'm a lot older than you."

"I know you're fifteen." I made myself meet her stare.

"I'm just saying, is all." She bit her lower lip. I didn't know what a girl was supposed to look like if she wanted a guy to kiss her—for real, not just some girl in third grade who said she would give me a fat lip if I didn't. When I caught a glimpse of her tongue moistening her lip, it made me dizzy. I could have sworn she moved a fraction of an inch closer.

I was scraping together the courage to ask, 'So, *what* exactly are you saying?' when the front door opened.

Ricky stepped outside, this time looking me up and down. "Sorry, didn't mean to interrupt anything."

Amelia backed off. "You're not interrupting anything." Quick as that, she rushed back into the house.

Ricky hovered over me. "So. You're the cleverest boy on the lake, are you?"

"Yeah, that's me." The courage that had shrunk with Amelia, now came up from my core. I stared him down, waiting for some other smart-aleck remark.

"We'll see about that." He winked, breaking eye contact first and turning toward the house.

That was it? That was all he had? And why did an eighteen-year-old feel the need to grandstand in front of an almost fourteen-year-old? I didn't move until he stepped inside. I wasn't sure what I was feeling, but it was powerful and strange. The same feeling that made me want to kiss Amelia—that made me think I might have gotten away with it—also made me want to knock his teeth out. That feeling—my own potential—overwhelmed me.

CHAPTER 18

NOTHING IN THIS MANSION-OF-A-HOUSE STIRS. Even if I stand on Whispering Narrows' doorstep until the sun goes down, no one is going to answer my knock. As I pass the sidelight, I half expect to see the reflection of my thirteen-year-old self. My facial hair brings adulthood rushing back. I started growing the beard during my first semester at college. I loved that it changed my entire look—like a disguise. It's been years since I've seen my naked face. I wonder if I'll recognize myself when I shave it tonight.

As I step off the granite, I recall the look on Amelia's face. All those years ago, I wasn't sure if she hoped I would kiss her, but in retrospect, I know that's exactly what she wanted. Even at fifteen, she was such a complex—no, *complicated* person. It was no wonder I never quite figured her out, and no wonder she made such a lasting impression. After that summer, I compared every girl I dated to Amelia. Until she married and there was no chance of 'us', *ever*, I couldn't seem to commit to anyone else. And that was in spite of my suspicion that there was another reason why a relationship with Amelia was out of the question—or at least taboo.

Even now, as I close my eyes and envision her face, the strength and depth of my yearning stirs physical discomfort. The idea of Amelia—the idea of loving that intensely—has never let go of me. As much as I loved Gretchen, I could never quite get *there*. Gretchen sensed it and that was part of why it didn't work out between us.

That familiar ache continues as I walk away from

Whispering Narrows. I've grown weary of suppressing and ignoring what I felt for Amelia, but indulging it is pointless.

A breeze lifts a curl from my forehead, cooling my overheating body. Off in the distance, cumulonimbus clouds gather. Big mushrooms, building and billowing. If I'm going to swim, I had better do it sooner than later.

Before heading to my room, where I've laid my overnight bag, I stop at the kitchen table. The box still holds another item tucked against the inside. I pull out an old Polaroid photo, its colors faded, unlike my memory of that Friday morning before the wedding.

WITH THE UPCOMING BIG EVENT OF THE summer, Whispering Narrows had been abuzz all week. Doc even had a special trellis built for the ceremony. The wedding would take place on Saturday. By Friday morning, a crew of workers had delivered chairs and tables, all waiting to be set up under the tent, which they had not yet erected.

Mom had already left with Frankie for her Friday morning errand run. I was out riding my bike, pedaling about a half mile beyond Whispering Narrows. I met up with Doc's Land Rover, and he stopped as I pulled up beside the driver window. Karen sat in the passenger seat, her eyes and nose red.

"Some mix-up with the party tent," Doc said. "Gotta fly downstate and pick up the missing lines and straps. You game for a quick flight?"

With that, I followed him to his place and parked my bike. Less than a half hour later, Doc and I were at 7500 feet.

Doc was more quiet than usual, and although he did let me take the controls for a little while, he didn't seem to be paying close attention. After ten minutes solo, every vibration or rattle amplified and set my nerves on edge. Was I still on course? Oh God, what if I crashed us?

"Hey, Doc?"

His gaze seemed focused on the horizon. It took a moment for him to respond. "Yes, son?"

"Just wanted to make sure I was doing okay. You're being really quiet."

He scanned all the gauges and dials. "Nope, you're fine."

Not that I minded bearing responsibility for our lives or spiraling 7000 feet to a fiery death, but I had to question the wisdom of a kid flying an airplane for that long, without a license or anything. I held my breath.

"You want me to take over?" he asked.

"Yeah, maybe until on the way back."

"Sure." He grabbed his control yoke, making no adjustment to our bearing or altitude.

Again, silence. I didn't mind being the one who wasn't talking, and I didn't mind periods of quiet, but this was unlike Doc. He sighed a couple times, and then the lack of conversation started gnawing at me. All I could think to say was, "Are you looking forward to the wedding?"

"Oh, sure." He nodded and sighed.

I didn't know why—maybe it was my own nerves, or maybe I had been curious about it for a while—but I blurted, "So, is your son coming?"

As soon as it slipped out, I regretted asking, especially when he stared ahead for a few seconds, blinked, and then looked at me for another long second before answering, "I don't know."

My next, even more stupid question was, "Do you want him to?"

Doc chuckled, though not like usual, and glanced at me again. "It's understandable that you'd be curious about my son, Ben ...." He gave the inside of his cheek a good chew and then continued, "It's complicated. It's not that I don't think you're smart enough to understand, it's just that sometimes trying to explain is ... it's pointless and doesn't change anything. People make choices for their own reasons and they grow apart, that's all."

I nodded, trying to grasp what he meant.

He let go of a deep breath. "It's not that Brad doesn't have legitimate gripes—God knows we all have them—but I can't change the past, and the choices he's making now don't fix any of that."

I had no idea what he was talking about and wished I hadn't asked.

He peered over at me again, his lips pursed. "Sorry. Crazy old man talking again."

"That's okay—not that I think you're crazy."

"Sometimes I am a little crazy, but I do know one thing and the sooner you learn it, the better. Don't get stuck in the past. For your own sake and for the sake of others, learn to let go. Do you understand?"

"You mean, don't stay mad at people forever?"

"Yes. Even if they stay mad at you."

"Is your son mad at you?"

"I guess we're both a little mad at each other. Sometimes I have trouble practicing what I preach." After a moment of quiet, he looked over at me again. "So, let's do our best to live in the present, okay?"

"Okay."

Shortly after that, we landed on a big lake, where someone met us with a large canvas bag full of the rope lines and ratchet straps for the tent. Doc tossed them back into the third passenger seat. He said it was fortunate that the wind was on our side, helping us along on the return flight. Now, the extended silences felt easy and natural.

When we landed on Rockette Lake and moored the Cessna, and after I unhooked my seatbelt, Doc said, "Your whole family is welcome to come over for the wedding reception. Be sure to invite your mom."

My gaze wandered. "Yeah, sure."

I must have sounded a little hesitant, because he added,

"Do you think it would help if I came over and invited her myself?"

Then I responded a little too fast, "Oh, no, sir. No."

He looked at me askance. "Your mother doesn't know you've been flying with me, does she? Or that you've been over fixing things, or that you came to watch TV."

Oh crap. Which was worse—getting caught in an almost-lie right now, or possibly getting caught in a full-out multiple-lie, later on? I bit my lip. "Not exactly sir. I got permission when Penny was in charge, and I kind of used that for everything."

"I see."

"It's just that Mom ... well, she's ... she's kind of ...."

The fragment of a memory, which always seemed to dissipate before it solidified, flashed again. This time it lingered just long enough for me to see them—Mom and Doc, face to face, his hands holding hers ... that is, Mom yanking her hands from his. Or maybe it was Mom and Dad....

"Never mind, Ben. I understand your mom better than you think."

I shook off the memory. "I'm sorry, Doc. I didn't mean to lie. It's just that ... I don't know ... I *need* to be here." I was choking up. Oh God, I couldn't well up in front of Doc. I stared ahead and breathed deep.

"I know that, son." He gripped my shoulder. "Whaddaya say this little part of our conversation—right after I invited you to the reception—never took place."

"Really?"

"One condition." He faced me and waited until my focus landed on him. My eyes must have been watery, but I couldn't look away. His grip tightened. "Don't lie to me again, son."

I didn't answer right away. I wanted him to know I had thought about his words before I replied, "Yes, sir."

As soon as Doc climbed out, I checked our beach for Mom—all was clear—and then followed Doc.

Sunshine met us at the end of the mooring. "I'm so glad you're back. Karen is wigging out."

He ducked under the wing. "Oh no. What now?"

She swung a newfangled camera from a wrist lanyard. "Most of the tent crew had to leave."

Doc rolled his eyes and ran fingers through his silver hair. "Great."

I stood beside Doc. Sunshine gestured for us to pause. "Wait. Let me get your picture."

I shrank back, stepping out of the way.

"No, Ben, you too." She pulled me back over, planting me beside Doc.

Doc put his arm around me and winked. "Get the plane in there, too."

I couldn't help smiling. She clicked and then pulled the tab on a snapshot and handed it to me. "Wait a hundred and twenty seconds, and then peel this back."

I started counting as Doc grabbed the tent lines from the plane and then nudged me forward. "Come along, Ben. Looks as if we'll need some extra hands."

I checked our beach for Mom. Still safe. The three of us walked up the lawn together. They had already rolled the tent out in front of the east wing. The poles lay on the ground. It was going to be huge. Dick and Ricky stood off to the side as Lenny, Sunshine, Percy, and Candace bent at each corner, while some other guy with a long pole pointed and explained what they needed to do. Doc went over to talk with him. Ricky already had his sights glued on me. Amelia was nowhere around.

One hundred eighteen ... one nineteen ... a hundred and twenty ... I peeled the tab slowly. A picture of Doc and me stared back. That was about the coolest thing I had ever seen. Who had figured out how to develop a photograph that fast and without a darkroom? I wished I had a camera like that, so I could take it apart and put it back together.

Doc snagged my attention with a quick whistle and

beckoned me over to between Lenny and Candace at the west end—the end that faced our camp. I tucked the photo in my back pocket.

"Fixer-man. How's it hanging?" Lenny's thumb looped the front pocket of his low-slung jeans. Shirtless, the guy was all muscle. Penny was right—I did notice that stuff. I wished that when I grew up I could look like him. Nobody would mess with me.

"Good," I replied. "How are you?"

He exhaled a puff of smoke with the words, "Good, man," and flicked a cigarette butt into the grass a few feet away and snuffed it with his boot.

On my other side, Candace winked. "Hey, Ben." She wore her standard tie-dye, stretched to the limit, and a long denim skirt.

There were enough of us around the tent that I hoped to blend in, given my proximity to our camp. I glanced up at the second story of Doc's mansion. Amelia appeared in the open floor-to-ceiling window overlooking the yard. When I nodded, she gave me a shy smile and a half wave. I wasn't the only one who noticed her, because when Doc called out, "Ricky—a little help—at the other end," Ricky stared up at Amelia, peeled off his polo shirt, and strutted below her window, over to the pole opposite mine. I couldn't help catching how Amelia's eyes rolled but kept watching him. Not that my gaze followed him for the same reason, but I did notice his build—like he must have been on the football team or something.

Lenny let out a snort under his breath. "Oh, give me a break. Who's he trying to impress?"

I smirked.

It must have finally dawned on Dick that he was the only one not doing anything, because he put down his beer can and filled in a gap on the south, lakeside of the tent.

Once all the lines were in place, we each pulled on the rope, hoisting the pole we had fed through a loop.

"Take my rope, man," Lenny pushed his line at me, "I'm going under."

"No way!"

"Go ahead, you're fine. Just grab it and lean all your weight back."

I centered myself between the two poles, leaning more toward the corner as he disappeared under the red-and-white-striped canvas. My back and arms strained.

On the other corner, Candace grinned at me. "You've got quite the muscles, Ben. You kind of look like Lenny when he was your age."

My confidence skyrocketed like the heat that burned my cheeks. I checked on Amelia—she was still standing at her window. Had she heard Candace's remark? As the tent lifted, Ricky glared at me from the opposite end. I guessed he hadn't forgotten about the spilled coffee.

Now that the center poles were in place, Lenny reclaimed his rope. The tent man walked the perimeter, double-checking the placement of each pole, and ratcheted straps. Lenny pounded stakes. As I backed away, Sunshine brought a tray of lemonade and passed me a glass.

"How did that picture turn out, Ben?"

I pulled it from my pocket and showed her. "Can I keep it?"

"Of course you can, but promise that even though I'm not in it, you'll think of Doc *and* me every time you see it."

"I promise."

She looked into my eyes and stroked my cheek. "You are a beautiful boy."

Moving along with her tray of refreshments, she left me in a full blush. *Beautiful boy?* I wasn't sure what that meant. Even though *beautiful* or *boy* were the last things I wanted anyone to call me, coming from her, they sounded better than great.

Then, Karen came from behind and grabbed my arm.

"Oh, Ben, thank you so much for helping." She gave me

148

a quick hug. Over her shoulder, Amelia came into sight, stepping out of the French doors. At the moment Karen released me, I was going to go over to say hello to Amelia, but Mom's shrill voice echoed across the cove. "Ben Hughes! You come home right this minute!"

The heat of a few minutes ago felt like a cool breeze compared to the furnace that now exploded from my chest.

Doc approached me and fished out his wallet. He passed me a ten. "Here, this might smooth things over with your mom if she knows I hired you to help out."

"I can't take your money, Doc."

"Of course you can!" He grabbed my hand and pressed it in my palm.

I couldn't muster the dignity or words to thank him, let alone look at Amelia. I saw only Ricky's smirk as my mother's voice shrieked again. "Benjamin Hughes! Right now!"

CHAPTER 19

M Y CALVES BURN AS I WALK UPHILL, BACK toward camp. I'm out of shape—that's the problem with spending too much time sitting at a drafting table. Before I know it, I'll need one of the prostheses I designed. *Ha!* Christopher would get a kick out of that—and then he would chuckle at my pathetic pun.

I have never been as fit as when I was a kid, always on that bike. Pedaling up this hill that afternoon—after Mom's screeching voice ordered me home—required so little effort. Maybe it was the adrenaline, turbo-boosting me uphill. As it turned out, aside from the humiliation of it, Mom catching me at Doc's didn't turn out to be the disaster I had imagined. Maybe it was because Mom had downed a stiff drink before I came home, or because I told her I was just trying to be neighborly, or that Doc had paid me for my time, but she didn't have the conniption I thought she would.

Mom could be surprising. We called it moody. Day-to-day life revolved around gauging her vicissitudes and trying to catch her on the upswing when we wanted something. That could be difficult because sometimes her moods lasted for days. Penny tried to convince me that it was as simple as Mom drinking too much, or that it was "her time of the month."

The afternoon when Mom ordered me home, providence handed me one of her good moods. The only reprimand I received was a warning—I was "not to pester *that man* or go over to their house uninvited." That provided me with all the license I needed for the rest of the summer—after all, Doc had given me an open invitation. And now that I was on his payroll, it would be a whole lot easier to explain the clock when I brought it home. Even the Polaroid snapshot could be explained away should my mother come across it. As I hold it up for inspection, I think of Doc and the plane, and of course, I think of Sunshine—her cool hand on my burning cheek.

I kind of fell in love with both Amelia and Sunshine that summer. The cousins were so different in some ways, and yet so similar. I couldn't help looking at Sunshine and imagine Amelia at twenty-two. Sunshine, the unattainable ideal, and Amelia ... well, I suppose in the end, she turned out to be just as unattainable.

Perhaps it's the heat of late afternoon, or the memory of them, but I'm now warm—too warm, like I need to get rid of layers.

In the bathroom, I stand in front of the mirror staring at a face I've grown tired of. The beard always made me look older, and maybe I'm hoping that shaving it off will also shave off a few years, now that I'm on the verge of my thirty-second birthday. That's not old, I know, but I feel old. Or perhaps I just feel jaded. Either way, the beard is coming off.

I remove three straight razors from my kit and lather up. Two razors down, and moving on to my neck, I already feel lighter. I rinse my face and can't help smiling at a glimpse of someone I used to know. Aside from a few fine lines, I look like a kid—like a beautiful boy. I blink and blink again. The face returning my gaze is no longer mine. The harder I look, the more it pleads for answers. As my own eyes water over, the image staring at me blurs. I look away. Time to change into my swim trunks and move on.

Down at the cove, I step out of my Birkenstocks and make my way to the group of boulders, counting off each one until I stand at the launch pad. A light breeze reminds me of the storm rolling in, and that I no longer have facial hair. I stroke my smooth cheeks. As long as I don't look at my hairy chest, it's as if I'm thirteen again. I breathe deep and dive. When I emerge, my sights settle on Amelia's dock beside her sandy beach. In a way, that's where all the trouble started, though the buildup had been in the works since the day Amelia and I began our staring game at the beginning of that summer. Up until her mother's wedding, everything was largely fantasy, fed by my big imagination. Fantasies tend to embolden a person. If the mind dwells on it, the idea is more likely acted upon, and that doesn't go for just kissing a girl, because boys don't fantasize about girls alone, but about being strong and brave and clever, too.

PENNY AND I WATCHED THE WEDDING FROM our float. I wasn't sure why, but I didn't mention to her that Doc had invited us to the reception. Maybe I was afraid she would make good on crashing the party. That would have been fine, except I didn't like the idea of her being around a bunch of older guys, especially Percy. I had the feeling he would be there.

When the procession music began, Penny grabbed me as if I were her best girlfriend. I reclaimed my arm with a yank.

"What's the big deal?" I said, when in fact, ever since I had heard the word "mini," I couldn't quit envisioning Amelia's thighs in something super short.

Penny sighed. My own jaw dropped when Amelia stepped out the French doors. Then Ricky swaggered out beside her. She looped her arm in his and began the stiff, measured walk toward the floral trellis.

"Hot pink," Penny whispered, as if I didn't know my colors. Actually, only the part across Amelia's chest was hot pink; the fluffy-looking fabric over the loose-fitting skirt looked like a cloud passing over a sunset. It wasn't as short as I had hoped for. Just the same, it did show her knees and a couple inches of thigh. Her strawberry tendrils cascaded from a pile of curls atop her head and brushed her shoulders.

Penny giggled, "And spaghetti straps."

"What?"

"That's what they're called."

Amelia wasn't smiling, although Ricky was all teeth, posing for the photographer.

Another lady stepped out in a dress similar to Amelia's, and then Sunshine joined them in bright and cloudy blue. After a longer pause, Doc stepped out, looking like Sean Connery as James Bond—except for the silver hair. He held out his hand. Karen grasped it as she emerged, her veil covering as little of her face as her dress did the rest of her. Penny gasped again.

"Can you believe that!" Penny said with a streak of awe. "There's practically nothing too it! Oh my gosh! It looks like a négligée."

What it lacked in length, it made up for in plenty of billowy fabric, and the breeze sure had a way of playing with the hem. If Karen had been built more like Candace than Sunshine, the low V neckline would have been what Mom called obscene.

Doc strolled Karen down a red carpet as guests threw white petals in front of them. When they arrived at the preacher, Doc bent and kissed Karen's cheek, placing her hand on Dick's. It was just a dumb wedding, but all at once, the impact of it hit me. Doc was giving away his little girl—turning her over to the care of another man. And if any of my gut instincts were accurate, Dick was not the man Doc would have chosen. And how did Doc feel about Amelia's father?

Penny sighed. "I can hardly wait to get married."

"I thought you wanted to go to college and be a nurse."

"Women these days can do both, you know."

"I know. It just seems like after you're married you would want to be a wife and not a student."

"That's about the stupidest thing I've ever heard come out of your mouth."

I shrugged. Maybe a wife could do a whole lot more than

just cook and clean and watch soap operas. Now that I thought about it, I liked the idea of a wife who had lots of other interests. Then we might not get bored with each other.

Penny sighed, "What a perfect day for a wedding. I hope when I get married, it's just like this—clear blue, sunny skies—then everything will turn out perfect."

Penny was thinking about the weather she hoped for on her wedding day, but if I were ever going to get married, that would be the least of my concerns. How about worrying if I had picked the right girl, or how I was going to pay for a house and a car and my wife's college education.

Once the wedding procession ended and the ceremony began, I swam around the cove until Dick kissed his bride. Even from a distance, it seemed a little too long and passionate for a public kiss. Made me wonder all the more about Karen.

I swam back to shore as Penny continued watching. Mom didn't rouse when I walked past her recliner on my way to the cottage. Now my main concern switched to whether there would be any Marshmallow Fluff left—and the reception, of course. I didn't plan to sneak over until Mom went to bed, which was around 9:00 most nights. That night, I turned in near 8:45. About a half hour earlier, shortly after sunset, the chamber music switched to a heavy bass beat. Would Mom fall asleep with all the music and noise from across the cove? At 9:30, I snuck out into the dark, wearing my decent shorts, a button-down shirt, and sneakers—not wedding attire, but it was the best I had at camp.

I thought about walking to Whispering Narrows, but rowing over gave me more opportunity to scope out the party before showing up. Once I boarded the boat, I sat in the shadows beyond our float for a long time, staying close to shore. I swatted mosquitoes and watched the crowd, half of them under the big lit-up tent, dressed in formal-looking outfits. Another bunch—mostly younger people—talked and danced barefooted out on the lawn. It was easy to pick out Sunshine. Lenny hovered nearby, wearing only jeans and a black vest but no shirt. I also spotted Percy. I scanned the group for Doc but couldn't make out his figure or the sound of his laugh. And of course, I looked for Amelia.

As much as I wanted to see what it was like at a big fancy wedding, with an open bar and white-gloved waiters serving hors d'oeuvres, I sat there feeling very awkward at the thought of beaching the boat and walking up to the party alone. Then Amelia emerged from the crowd, in that cute little dress, padding barefoot down the lawn and out to the end of the dock. She stood for a few seconds and then sat, shoulders slumped and swinging her legs. I was about to start rowing over when Ricky came down the lawn. Sometime between the ceremony and now, he had lost his tuxedo jacket and tie. His shirt was unbuttoned halfway down, and his sleeves rolled halfway up. Carrying two party cups, he swaggered out to where Amelia sat.

With the oars in my lap, I watched under the nearly full moon and crisp black sky. How would she react to him showing up? When he offered her a cup, she drank it down fast, passed it back to him, grabbed his other cup, swallowed it down, and then held it away. She looked at it and then up at him. If there hadn't been so many other noises echoing around the cove, I could have heard what she said when he sat beside her. There wasn't a whole lot of room for her to move over, even if she had wanted to. She leaned away from him.

They chatted back and forth for a couple minutes, but he did most of the talking. Somehow, he managed to make her giggle, which cut through the other echoes. Whatever he had said made her relax enough that he closed the gap between them. When he pointed at the curls on top of her head, she patted them down. He made like he was going to fix something in her hair. That's when he moved in closer.

It wasn't as if he had done anything more than touch her

hair, but the way he looked over his shoulder, as if to check for onlookers, made me start rowing just enough to set my boat moving in that direction. By the time he stroked her cheek to lean in and kiss her, I had cut my distance to the dock by half. She didn't react for a second. I slowed—if she liked him, she would think I was a jerk for interrupting—but when she started pushing him away, and he grabbed her shoulders and kept kissing her, I was a few boat-lengths away. I heard her words, "Get *off* me!" clear as could be.

That overwhelming feeling I'd had the other night—my unrestrained potential—again possessed me. I called out, "Hey, Amelia!"

I startled then both, allowing her opportunity to give him a big shove. He backed off. Now that I had her attention, I called out again, "Amelia, you wanna go for a boat ride?"

Shadows hid much of their expressions, and I wasn't sure if hers showed anger or fear until I came nearer. At the sight of me, her grimace changed to something like a smile of relief. Ricky squinted. His face registered recognition and then disdain.

"Benjamin—" She swung her legs to the beachside of the dock where I approached, giving my oar a twist and maneuvering the transom end so she could board if she wanted.

Ricky came to his feet, smirking as usual. "Hey, kid, you showed up just in time. We'd love to have you paddle us around the lake, wouldn't we Amy?"

I did my best to steady the boat as Amelia—all legs—hopped in, mouthing the words, "Go. *Go!*"

At the very moment Ricky made to board, I pulled both oars with all my strength. By the time he realized I hadn't stuck around for him, he lost his balance, arms flailing and one leg straight out. He landed in the lake with a splash. Wide-eyed, Amelia's head whipped around to look. She covered her mouth. I steered us into the shadows of the cove, away from where he continued to thrash in the chest-high water, cursing. He traipsed toward shore, sopping wet. I let out a nervous laugh—what the heck had I just done?

"Serves him right," I said as Amelia panted, staring at me with alarm. I didn't think she was mad, but I wasn't sure. I swallowed hard. "Don't worry. I'll stay right in the cove so if Doc looks for you, he'll be able to see you're with me."

Her eyes squeezed shut, sending a tear down each cheek. "He won't even notice."

"What do you mean?"

"My stupid Uncle Brad showed up ... and him and Sunshine had a fight and Grandpa kicked him out, because Brad had too much to drink ... and my stupid mother thinks my screwed-up family is all normal ... and she thinks stupid Dick is wonderful and Ricky—" she took a deep quivering breath, "he's such a conceited creep and now he's my stepbrother ...." That's when she really started crying.

I wished I had a handkerchief or something, but she didn't need it; she just lifted a layer of fabric from her dress and wiped her eyes and nose. It should have grossed me out but it didn't. I was more concerned about coming up with something to say. All I could muster was, "Gosh, Amelia...."

She rubbed both cheeks. "I feel dizzy. I think there was something in Ricky's drink or something .... Am I drunk?"

"I don't think so."

"Then why didn't *I* just push him in the water?"

"I don't know." I tried to keep from smirking, but one corner of my mouth curled. "Maybe you *are* drunk."

"It was *gross*." She grimaced through her tears, wiping her mouth. "He slobbered all over me."

"Maybe he knows he's a lousy kisser and that's why he has to get a girl drunk first."

She let out a small huff that was almost a chuckle and then closed her eyes, sending tears from their corners. Drawing her knees together, she wrapped her arms snug around her waist and continued leaking tears. Even with a red nose and puffy eyes, she still made my insides crazy. I didn't say anything more; I simply kept rowing around the cove as the bass beat of "Light My Fire" rolled across the water.

Her strawberry brows scrunched as she opened her eyes and yanked pins from her hair. "And I hate this *hairdo* and this *dress* and my *mother* and this whole *stupid* wedding." One by one, she threw pin after pin at the water. "She just wants me to look like a Barbie doll. She even wanted me to wear fake eyelashes. Can you believe it? I mean, I'm only fifteen years old!" She threw another with even more force. "If it hadn't been for Sunshine, she'd have made me wear gobs of blue eye shadow and mascara." She plucked another pin, wrenched it wide open, and hurled it. "I'm just so mad!" Half of her hair had come down. She tried to comb her fingers through it as her eyes slowly met mine. "I must look horrible. You must think *I'm* horrible."

"No I don't."

"Well, I *am* horrible."

"No you're not."

She stared at me as tears streamed down her cheeks, but her face wasn't all twisted as if she was crying. She said, "Why are you being so nice to me?"

"I don't know. I guess I'm just a nice guy."

She kept staring, maybe holding out for a better answer.

I continued, "And because you're Doc's granddaughter and I think Ricky's a creep, and I hate to think of you being sad. I mean you have everything—you should be happy."

Her brow narrowed. "How would you know what I have and how I should feel?"

"I guess I don't, really, seeing as I've only talked to you once. And I don't know your mom, but, well, how would you like to have mine?"

She went from frowning to a half giggle, "No way," and then turned serious again, "but I don't want mine either. I wish it were just me and Doc and Sunshine, all the time."

"I wish Doc was *my* grandfather."

She cocked her head. "How come I hardly ever see your dad around?"

"He's got a job."

"What does he do?"

"He's a salesman. What about your dad?"

Her gaze dropped to her lap. "I don't want to talk about that."

"Okay. What *do* you want to talk about?"

She shook her head as she looked over every inch of me, blinked a couple times, and then swallowed with a grimace. "Sometimes ... Benjamin ...," her voice trailed off with her gaze.

"Sometimes, what?"

She bit her lip as if trying to keep it from trembling as she shrugged. "Sometimes ... I'm afraid of turning out like my mother."

I tried every which way to figure out what she meant, because as far as I could tell, she was nothing like her mother. "What do you mean?"

She shook her head and wiped another tear as it slipped down her cheek. Her eyes pleaded for something I couldn't grasp; it made my heart feel as if it were being grabbed and pulled out of my chest, right through my ribcage. For a second, I didn't think I would be able to keep my own eyes from welling.

All she said was, "I want to go swimming."

I nodded, still trying to understand. "Okay."

CHAPTER 20

EIGHTEEN YEARS AFTER THE FACT, AMELIA—
that is, the fantasy of Amelia—still mystifies me.

As I glide across the cove, my beardless chin
cuts through velvety water—like skinny-dipping, naked
and free. I've only skinny-dipped once in my life, in a
chlorine-bleached pool, with no snapping turtles or
nibbling fish. And it wasn't the way I had imagined it
would be—not like the hippies, all uninhibited and out
there. Swimming naked was nothing short of awkward. I
couldn't wait to get it over with. The whole time, I was
wishing I could have re-enacted swimming with Amelia—
both of us comfortably clothed—that night of the wedding.
Perhaps it was the combination of her vulnerability and my
restraint, but reminiscing on it, I realize just how sensual—
not sexual, but truly sensual—it was, and how moments as
raw as that became my touchstone for future intimacy.

I've never been certain of how sex and intimacy are
supposed to come together for the adult male—for the
well-adjusted adult male. At almost fourteen, I was on the
brink of maturing sexually and emotionally. I assume
that's the way it works; both elements come together
within a few years of each other—the emotional half,
lagging. But what if something interrupts one element? I
continued to mature sexually, with all the normal desires
and functions, but I've always wondered if I got stuck in
my pubescent mindset when it comes to emotions and
expectations. Most guys grow beyond those early, intense
desires associated with their first feelings of arousal. It's
more physical than anything, but pin that to a real-live

girl and it feels like it must be love. Then, we grow up, move out of adolescence, and realize there's a whole lot more to love than hormonal surges. But what if a guy never progresses beyond that? What if he gets stuck in emotional limbo and is always looking to match that intensity? Every sexual experience—every relationship—comes up lacking.

Diving deep, and then emerging at the spot where our float once moored, I brace myself for the swirl of emotion and sensation I'm about to evoke. I've replayed that evening so many times over the years, in spite of how raw it leaves me. But today, I'm right here, right where it happened. And it's not that a whole lot did happen, but it was the first time Amelia and I connected. The moment I fell in love.

I swim in a circle, estimating where I rowed my boat so as to put Amelia's end against the ladder. I remember that keeping her safe was my primary concern.

SHE HADN'T BEEN SLURRING OR ANYTHING, but I didn't know how drunk Amelia might be. I prepared myself for a rescue as she climbed out, her footing unsteady. I secured the line and scuttled from the boat. Amelia swayed at the edge of the float and dove into the water, disappearing for a few long seconds, the way I had on that afternoon when I almost drowned myself. My heart sped until she breached the water's surface with a splash.

She laughed, motioning for me to join her. "Come on!"

Without hesitation, I kicked off my sneakers, slipped out of my shirt, and dove in beside her. When she swam out farther, I followed. She paused and I caught up. As we treaded water, she was so close that the fabric of her dress brushed my hand as it floated upward, like a beautiful swishing jellyfish. The water between us swirled and pushed against me. Moonbeams reflected off her face. She looked at me the way she had the other night and moved closer, so close I felt her breath.

Beneath the water, her fingers grazed my waist up to my chest, then my neck, and then my cheek. The temperature of the water must have risen about a hundred degrees. I came close enough to kiss her—close enough that her breath warmed my lips without them touching—and then I hesitated. I pulled back. Under the circumstances, kissing Amelia seemed wrong. It would have been different if she hadn't been sort of drunk and she wasn't in such an emotional twist. I didn't want her to be embarrassed about any of it later. Just the same, I hated for her to get the wrong impression, like I wasn't interested.

I came out with it, in an exhalation, "I really like you, Amelia."

She backed off. "But you don't know me well enough to like me."

"Maybe. But I wish I did."

She stared at me, as if she was studying my face, trying to figure out if I meant it, and then said, "But if you did, you might find out you don't like me at all. I'm not just boobs, you know."

I choked. "I—I …." I calculated my options and the risks. She was smart enough to know that boys my age noticed boobs first, and that was enough to make us like a girl, so there was no use denying it. But I couldn't think fast enough to be anything more or less than honest. "I mean, sure I noticed, but right now I kind of wish you were flat-chested so you would know that I would have beat the crap out of Ricky and taken you in my boat, even if you had no boobs."

She threw her head back and laughed, treading water. "You actually think *you* could beat the crap out of Ricky?"

Still treading water, I grabbed my bicep, made a fist, and grinned. "Well, maybe not. But if I had to, I would have tried."

She smiled—a shy but real smile. "Thanks for rescuing me."

I shrugged and swam a loop around her. "No problem."

She spun with me. "I really like you, too."

"Even though I'm a lot younger?"

She glanced away and then back as I continued my circle. "That was a stupid thing for me to say the other night."

"Sometimes we all say stupid things, right?"

"Yeah."

"And you know, I'm not really that much younger."

"I guess a couple years just seems like a lot."

"It wouldn't seem like that much if *I* was older than *you*. Why is it that girls can like older guys, but not the other way around?"

"Don't you know that girls mature sooner than boys?"

"That's not always true. It's just something they say in health class."

"Well, I guess there are exceptions. Penny says you're mature for your age. She says that sometimes you're more grown-up than she is."

"Really?"

She nodded, following my eyes as I completed another ring, sending a wake around us like a halo. "You should bring me back."

"Okay."

We swam close to each other, over to the float. As she climbed up, her dress clung to her thighs and her hair hung down her back in coiled tendrils. She reeled and I thought I might have to catch her, but she rebounded. I grabbed my shirt, leaving my sneakers on the float, and held the boat for her as she climbed in. I then climbed in after her. Sitting on my bench, I slipped my arms into my sleeves. She stared at my chest.

I grinned, buttoning up my shirt. "I'm not just boobs, you know."

"Yeah, I know—boobs *and* brains," she snickered.

Now I understood a little of how she felt. What if she liked my chest better than what was in it? Hoping she would focus more on my brain, I said, "I just like mechanics and reading, is all."

"Me, too—I mean reading, that is."

"I know. You've always got your nose in a book when you're on the beach."

She giggled. "Are you always watching me?"

I nudged her foot. "Not *always*."

As I took my time rowing back to Whispering Narrows, we traded off staring at each other. What would happen after tonight? Would we spend any time together, talking about all the things we liked, and what we wanted to do when we grew up, and where we wanted to live, and what places we wanted to visit? I really did want to know her.

With a glance over my shoulder, I steered toward shore and beached.

She stepped over the transom, her skirt creeping up her thigh. A light breeze caught her dress. She looked mostly dry, if not a bit limp. "You're coming up, aren't you?"

"If you want me to."

She nodded and I dragged the boat farther ashore. Instead of heading up to the big tent, we veered toward the hippies, out in the open and under an overhead haze. Halfway up the lawn, Sunshine rushed down to meet us, her curled hair bouncing above her shoulders. She took Amelia's face in her hand, as if examining her young cousin's state of mind, and then hugged her and grabbed my arm. In one swoop, she wedged herself between the two of us, escorting us to the tiki lights staking the area surrounding guests on the lawn. Another set of torches lit the perimeter of the tent.

Percy and Candace danced together. At the edge of the group, Lenny waited for us, swaying to the beat of "Crystal Blue Persuasion*." His snug vest, buttoned up to his collarbone, made his biceps look even huger. And it wasn't like any vest I had seen in Sears and Roebuck's—more like something a swashbuckler would have worn with a flouncy shirt in a sword fight. The vest might have looked frilly on some other guy, but not Lenny.

"Hey, Fixer-man," he said. "Smooth maneuver down there at the dock."

At least Lenny, if not the rest of the guests, had seen or heard about Ricky's 'swim.' I blushed. "It was an accident."

He winked. "That's right, man. Take the fifth."

I was unsure of what "the fifth" was, but if saying "it was an accident" was *the fifth*, I was sticking to it. I scanned the other faces for Ricky but didn't see him. I didn't know what the repercussions of his 'swim' would be, but I expected something, though not while I was anywhere near Lenny.

Amelia plunked down onto the grass, her dress tucked between her widespread-crisscrossed legs. Sunshine watched with concern. The filmy sheath of Sunshine's dress covered her knees like an umbrella as she squatted beside her cousin. "Amy, did you have something to drink from the bar?"

"I don't know—I mean, Ricky gave me some lemonade. It tasted funny, but I was so thirsty."

"When's the last time you ate?" She sounded motherly, but in a good way.

Amelia shrugged. "Last night? Wait, I had toast this morning."

Sunshine rolled her eyes and sighed as she stood. "Ben, you hungry?"

"Sure."

"Okay, you stay here with Amy, and don't you dare let her wander off." She squinted, but not as if she were mad. "Do you understand?"

"Sure."

"Okay, I'll get you guys a plate. I'll be right back."

As I sat beside Amelia, Sunshine strode across the lawn toward the tent. I glanced at my watch. *Ah crap!* I had forgotten to take it off before I went swimming. Oh well. It was worth it. When I glanced up, I saw Ricky's back at the edge of the tent. He wore Bermuda shorts and a polo shirt. Sunshine headed straight for him. Her pointed finger jabbed his shoulder, snagging his attention. I couldn't hear what she was saying over the loud music, but her finger shook in his face, and her squint could have shot poison darts. He flipped both palms up and backed off. After one last jab, she spun around and made her way toward the kitchen door.

Ricky glanced around. A few faces showed curiosity but then returned to their partying. That's when Ricky's eyes met mine. He smirked, then turned and disappeared deeper into the tent crowd. My heart thumped.

Amelia leaned into me. "I feel dizzy."

"Are you going to barf?"

"My stomach feels okay—just hungry." All at once, a giggle exploded from her chest. "Did you see the look on Ricky's face?"

I wasn't sure if she meant just now, when Sunshine was reaming him out, or when he had come out of the water, realizing a thirteen-year-old had made a fool of him. I tried to laugh along with her, but my bravery had peaked and since subsided. I mean, it *was* an accident. It wasn't my fault he had tried to climb in the boat uninvited.

Amelia flung herself back, flat into the grass, holding her chest and laughing. Yeah, Ricky's 'swim' was funny, but now Amelia was rolling and laughing as if she couldn't stop. Then her laughter turned into crying, and quick as that, she was laughing again. I glanced around to see if anyone noticed. No one's eyes met mine or gazed at Amelia. Were outbursts a normal part of rich peoples' wedding receptions? I wasn't sure what to do. She wasn't hurting anything, but her skirt began hiking up her thighs. How would it look if someone caught me trying to fix that? She needed to settle down and quit thrashing.

I lay on my side next to Amelia and stroked her face. Her cheek warmed my palm as I brushed hair from her forehead and wiped tears. She took a deep breath and opened her eyes, though they were merely glazed-over slits.

She reached over and her finger hooked my lower lip. "Did you know you have the most kissable lips? All curvy and full." Her finger dragged down to my chin, and her hand dropped to her side as if it weighed ten pounds.

Her lips looked like two little, red rose petals. I pulled a few strands of hair from the corner of her mouth. Since I had decided not to kiss her out on the water, I sure wasn't going to kiss her right now, though she probably would have let me.

Sunshine arrived and knelt beside Amelia. As I sat up, she passed me the plate, heaped full, and then helped Amelia to sit. Sunshine shook her head, adjusting her cousin's dress and looked at me. "It's just a good thing you came along when you did, Ben."

Amelia grabbed a chicken wing.

"Slow down, kiddo." Sunshine tucked a napkin in Amelia's hand. "Chew it good or it will all come back up."

I poked a shrimp in my mouth. "I saw you with Ricky," I said, trying not to talk with my mouth full. "What did he say?"

"He said it was just a misunderstanding—that he brought her lemonade, she downed it, and then grabbed his screwdriver and drank it before he could stop her." She turned Amelia's chin to face her. "Did your lemonade taste funny?"

Amelia shrugged. "Sort of. I don't know …."

Sunshine shook her head. I didn't know if I should say something about how Ricky was all over her. I didn't want to embarrass Amelia. That was girl talk, and if Amelia wanted to tell Sunshine, that was her place, not mine. Besides, probably everyone saw it anyway.

I stuffed a wedge of something in my mouth. Whatever it was, it tasted good. I helped myself to another. For every one bite I ate, Amelia scarfed down two.

I nudged her. "Slow down—quit hogging it."

Now that Amelia had simmered down, Sunshine asked, "You two okay over here?"

I nodded.

"Okay, well, before you leave, bring her to me. Got it?"

"Got it."

She patted my cheek and, in the most ladylike way, came to her feet. Her hips swayed all the way over to Lenny, who passed her one of those funny-smelling, odd-shaped cigarettes. She took a long drag off it and then passed it to Candace. What was it with hippies and sharing their cigarettes?

Between the two of us, Amelia and I cleaned the plate. As I licked my fingers, she lay down and sighed, "I'm tired. I could sleep forever."

I scooted a little closer to her head but remained sitting. Bringing my knees to my chest, I faced the tent. The crowd had thinned a lot in the last hour. Men had removed their suit jackets, and their ties hung like nooses. A few women padded around without high heels. Most of them looked as if they weren't in much better condition than Amelia. The band still played, and a few people hung off each other on the dance floor. Some swayed by themselves. If it weren't for the frequent sound of laughter, from both the lawn and tent, I wouldn't have guessed that people were having a good time. It didn't look like *fun* to me.

At the far end, way under the tent, I spotted Doc. I couldn't make out if he was having a good time or not, but if he'd had to kick his son out earlier, after not seeing him for so long, I imagined that even if Doc was putting on a happy face, he was not enjoying himself. Then again, maybe Amelia misunderstood and Doc hadn't kicked Brad out at all. Maybe they just had words. What had Sunshine and her dad fought about? She seemed tense, but maybe it was just the 'misunderstanding' between Amelia and Ricky.

I continued scanning the crowd—both under the tent and the fringes of people on the lawn—looking for Ricky. I found him on the dance floor with some middle-aged lady. I was safe for the time being and slacked my posture, allowing my gaze to wander. I happened to glance over my shoulder and did a double take as Penny came around the corner of the house, in rolled-up shorts and a tank top— without a bra.

What the crap! She had snuck out, too. That was bad enough, but then she walked right over to Percy Wade. I kept my sights glued to them as they made their way to some fold-up chairs and sat. Penny played with one of her thin braids—the way she had fixed her hair the other night—with a bead attached to the end. She hadn't seen me yet. I didn't know if I should call out—which would have mortified her—or if I should just watch.

While I considered what I ought to do, Candace joined them. She sat beside Penny and passed Percy the cigarette. He inhaled and then passed it to Penny. She looked at it for a second, took a small puff, and then let it out. Candace giggled and shook her head, then took the cigarette and demonstrated how to suck it in and hold it. Penny tried again. This time, she did just as Candace showed her. Penny coughed a little, sending two small puffs out her nose but held her breath and then let it out with a laugh.

Great. Now my sister was smoking. Oh well, just more ammunition for blackmail—not that I needed it. When Percy again passed what was now a skinny little butt, Penny took another drag and didn't cough, until her eyes landed on mine.

Chapter 21

FOR PENNY AND ME, THE WEDDING AT Whispering Narrows was where all the trouble started—that is, it marked the point of no return. We were both so naive. If I had to serve a day sentence for every time I beat myself over not knowing what was really going on, I would be locked up for life. Over the years, I've come up with a hundred different ways I could have—should have—handled that night. I have replayed a thousand scenarios. I should have told Sunshine that Ricky kissed Amelia—I should have told Doc. I should have pulled Penny out of the pot-smoking group of older kids. I should have beat Ricky senseless or taken a beating or anything that would have called attention to the fact that he was a scum predator.

Even now as I swim the cove, I want to pummel something, but my blows strike only water. And what does venting accomplish? Nothing. Besides, it's too late for anger. I can't change any of what happened. I was only a kid. How was I supposed to know? Just the same, I have to acknowledge the role I played even if it wasn't my fault—directly. Penny had to learn to take responsibility for her own actions, which I'm sure was far more difficult than me trying to reconcile my own culpability. And she has also had to learn how to let go.

So, where did it all really begin? That's as difficult to determine as defining 'it'. Probably *it* began years before that summer, right in our own family dysfunction. So, if it didn't start at the wedding, it certainly gained momentum there. My involvement might have gone back to weeks before I 'helped' Ricky into the lake, back to when I spilled coffee all over him at Garver's. For Penny, it might have launched at the moment she took the drag from that "funny little cigarette." A manifestation of *it* was that look on her face, the way her gaze shifted—the way her whole person shifted—as she turned her back on me.

I STARED AT THE BACK OF PENNY'S HEAD AS she again faced Candace and Percy. My chest dropped into my stomach as I slouched over my knees. It was ridiculous to let my feelings get hurt over it. Maybe I just needed to grow up and accept the fact that Penny had older friends who were more interesting than I was.

Beside me, Amelia snored quietly. She looked like Penny when she slept, with her wide-open mouth. That was definitely not how I had pictured this night turning out. My visions of slow dancing with Amelia, and stealing a kiss of my own out at the end of her dock, evaporated like the wisps of smoke rising above Penny and her new friends.

On the bright side, I was sitting beside Amelia, even if she was passed out. She still looked beautiful as her head lay in a nest of strawberry curls. Her lips were closed but relaxed and her cheeks, flushed. I could have been in a hundred different places, but I wouldn't have traded sitting beside her, watching her sleep and guarding her, for anything.

One dainty hand lay atop her tummy and the other tossed overhead. Her fingernails matched the hot pink of her dress. They weren't long and fake looking—just trim. Her skirt draped over her slender thighs. She had pretty feet, with pink toenails. Had her mother made her paint them, or did Amelia like them that way? I hoped it was a special-occasion thing. The more I hung around with hippies, the more I liked the natural look of a girl without all the make-up and stiff hair. Amelia sure didn't need the extras—she was perfect the way she was. If there hadn't been people around, I would have lain close beside her and listened to her breathe—maybe I would have dared to lay my hand on hers.

After a few minutes, she roused, rubbing her eyes. She looked up at me. Propping herself upon her elbows, she asked, "Was I snoring?"

"A little."

She grimaced. "How embarrassing."

"It was cute. At least you weren't drooling."

She shifted to sit, tugging at her skirt. "I don't drool."

"Of course you don't." I chuckled.

"I gotta use the bathroom."

"Are you going to barf?"

She squinted with annoyance. "No. I gotta pee."

"Okay, well, let me help you up." I stood. She took the hand I offered, and I pulled her to her feet. She didn't hesitate or stare into my eyes or anything; she just started toward the house. I looked for Sunshine. She spotted us at the same time and came over to me as Amelia kept walking.

"I'm going to put her to bed." Sunshine kissed my cheek. "Thanks for taking care of my little cousin."

"Sure."

"Why don't you get yourself some cake? There's plenty left."

"Okay."

I actually had a mind to leave, but I didn't like the idea of taking off while Penny was still there. So, I scanned the dwindling crowd for Ricky, and since he was nowhere around, I shoved my hands in my pockets and strode over to the tent. I ducked under a bracing line and stepped beneath the big top, when Doc called, "Ben!"

He stood in front of the bar with half a glass of something golden in one hand and a cigar in his other. He stepped toward me as I approached, poked the cigar between his teeth, and grabbed my hand.

"Hello, Doc."

"I'm glad you could make it." He swept a wide gesture. "Whaddaya think?"

"It's pretty big."

"Yep. The best of everything for my little girl." He didn't smile when he said it, and his breath smelled like liquor. "How about a drink, Ben?"

I shook my head, "Oh, no sir. I don't drink."

He burst out with a guffaw. "I mean ginger ale or Coke or something, not the hard stuff."

Idiot! "Yes, sir, that sounds good."

He escorted me to the bar and landed me in front of the bartender.

"A Coke," I said.

"On the rocks," Doc added, grinding the cigar butt underfoot.

As soon as I had my drink in hand, Doc led me to a table at the far end of the tent. Crickets chirped and a refreshing breeze cooled my neck. Doc let go of a long sigh as he pulled out a chair and sat.

"Oh, I'm getting too old for this." He nudged the chair beside him. As I took my place, he stretched his legs and leaned back, taking another sip. Setting his unfinished drink on the linen tablecloth, he arched a brow at me. "Have you had a good time tonight, Ben?"

The whole night flashed in front of me. "Yeah." I didn't consider it an untruth. There was a lot about tonight that had been great.

Between the house and the tent, the happily married couple stepped outside in travel clothes. Karen hugged guest after guest as Dick followed suit.

Doc folded his hands above his belt. "My girls sure looked beautiful today, didn't they?"

I nodded and sipped my Coke.

Doc took another gulp and sighed again. He rubbed his chin.

"Fathers and daughters ...." His eyes watered as he stared off in Karen's direction. I looked away but glanced back as he continued. "So much easier than fathers and sons."

"I know what you mean."

His questioning gaze flashed at me.

I elaborated, "I mean, my sister gets along fine with my dad. But not me."

"I hope the two of you can mend things while you're still young. It can make or break your adult relationship."

I just listened.

"It's a shame to have regrets ... when things could have been different."

I wanted to ask about Brad, about what had happened tonight, but it wasn't any of my business, and I didn't want to stoke a sore subject.

As if Doc sensed my curiosity, he looked at me askance and said, "My son came today."

"Is he still here?"

He shook his head. "Guess he didn't have the nerve to show up without a few drinks under his belt, like I'm some kind of horrible monster." He continued staring off in Karen and Dick's direction as they hugged their way through the few remaining guests. "Don't know where I went wrong with my boy, what made him go the way he did ...." His eyes shot back to mine, as if catching himself rambling. "It's a long complicated story, and I've had more to drink than a man should when trying to explain family history, especially when there's no explaining it. Besides, you don't need to hear all the sordid details."

I wanted to say something helpful or reassuring, but mostly I didn't want to talk about his son anymore—or about my father. I squirmed in the chair and downed the last of my Coke.

As Doc sat forward in his seat, he patted my back. "You're a good boy, son."

I swallowed hard. I wished I were Doc's son. I would be the best son in the world, and I wouldn't disappoint him, ever.

Just then, Karen called out, "Daddy! We're ready to leave!"

With a grunt and his hands on his knees, he pushed himself up and out of his chair.

I rose with him. "Thanks for inviting me, Doc."

"You're welcome." He arched his back, gave mine another pat, and headed toward Mr. and Mrs. Dick— whatever-his-last-name-was.

Doc gave his daughter a bear hug and wiped his eyes. I hoped they were happy tears, but I sensed they weren't. Seeing him all emotional tugged at my own composure. As I drew in a deep breath, Ricky joined them, which added to my discomfort.

I had seen enough of Doc's weird new family members for one night and took a roundabout route over to Penny. At that point, I was tired and didn't care if I embarrassed my sister. I came up behind her as she hung on Percy, giggling and making an all-out idiot of herself.

"Penny—" I firmly nudged her shoulder. "We should go home now."

She turned. I expected her to be mad, but she burst out laughing. "Benjie!"

"Come on Penny, it's late."

She swayed and giggled, "Late? What time is it?"

Percy and Candace drifted toward a bunch of other guests.

"I don't know." I tapped my crystal. "My watch is busted."

She grabbed my arm and grinned. "Oh, no…that's too bad…."

I squinted and tried to make her look at me. "Are you drunk?"

"Me? No, I haven't had anything at all to drink."

"Then what's the matter with you?"

"Nothing. I'm just happy." She stood up straighter and yawned. "Yeah, I guess it's beddy-bye time."

She walked over to Percy and the others, said a few words, waved goodbye and came back to me. "You coming?"

"I've got the boat. You wanna ride?"

"Nah. I'll walk," she said as she turned and waved at me over her shoulder. She sauntered back to the corner of the house and disappeared into the shrubbery and shadows. I scratched my head, befuddled at her mood. Maybe it was infatuation. *Girls.*

I wasn't in the mood for saying goodbye to everyone, but I looked for Sunshine. When I caught her eye, I waved. She blew me a kiss and smiled. That was about as close to a goodnight kiss as I could hope for.

I scanned the group one last time to make sure Ricky wasn't lurking somewhere. My path to the beach was clear, so I headed down the lawn to my boat. When my feet sank into the sand, I let out a sigh. *What a night!* I couldn't wait to climb in bed and replay all the best parts of the evening, the way Amelia looked and smelled, and how close I had come to her rosebud lips.

As I stepped toward my boat, a voice came from behind. "Hurrying off without saying goodnight?"

Ricky. *Crap!*

I turned, stared into his face, and squared my posture.

He stepped closer. "I guess you think you *are* pretty clever."

I said nothing and glanced over his shoulder.

"Looking for your buddies? They're all too wasted to notice you down here. But you could squeal and I bet they'd come running."

I still said nothing. I wasn't sure what to do, but screaming like a girl was out of the question. Bad enough that my heart was freaking right out of my chest.

Now Ricky loomed over me. I stepped back. He wouldn't fight a kid, would he? I mean, I would fight him for all I was worth, but I didn't think he would throw a punch, unprovoked. He didn't. Instead, his big mitt came at my head as he shoved my face, pushing me back.

"Twerp," he laughed.

I fell backward onto my haunches at the water's edge as he shoved my boat out into the cove. My whole body ignited like a torch. As he turned to strut away, he walked smack into Lenny's vested chest.

"What the hell is this? You pickin' a fight with a kid half your size?" Lenny's voice rumbled. He didn't touch Ricky, but he could've walloped him for the way Ricky reeled back.

Ricky rebounded, getting in Lenny's face, "You wanna fight me?"

"Actually, I really do. I ain't a peace-lovin' brand of hippie."

"Come on then." Ricky raised his fist like a boxer, ready to deflect a punch and plant one of his own.

Lenny chuckled as he took a step closer. Face to face, Lenny looked like he had the size advantage, but his movements were sluggish, whereas Ricky was all hyped up, even if he also appeared unsteady. I came to my feet and stood off to the side, unsure of what my role was in all this. Somehow, it was no longer about me.

As Lenny stepped closer, he swayed and Ricky laughed but didn't let down his guard. "You're so stoned you couldn't hit me if your life depended on it."

Lenny smiled. "Yeah, I'm pretty wasted, but I still know two things—" his voice was low and lazy. "Even if you whoop me, I can still rearrange your pretty teeth. So you gotta ask yourself how much you like your dental work. And second—Percy is up there just waiting for my signal. So, do you feel like having both our unwashed, free-lovin' hippie bodies pummeling your pretty face?"

Sure enough, Percy stood halfway down the lawn. Ricky wavered and backed off.

Lenny closed the distance between them. "Now, apologize to Ben."

It struck me that Lenny had called me by my name, and not Fixer-man, as if this was far from lighthearted banter.

Ricky snorted, letting out an incredulous huff, his fist still up. His footing faltered. For the first time, intense anger flared Lenny's nostrils and came up into his eyes as he removed his glasses.

"*Apologize*," Lenny said through gritted teeth.

Ricky shot a glance at Percy and then at me. His jaw shifted and tensed. "Sorry kid." His words came out stiff and angry. "It was a misunderstanding."

Lenny stepped aside. "Now, get the hell out of here."

Ricky backed away, staying well out of fist-throwing distance and took off for the big tent, cutting a wide girth around Percy who paused and watched him.

"You okay, Fixer-man?"

I brushed sand from my hands. "Yeah."

I couldn't bring myself to say thanks, because I wasn't sure if I was grateful or not. If Lenny hadn't shown up, Ricky would have walked off, feeling the victor, leaving me humiliated, yeah, but it would have settled the score. Now—well, I wasn't sure how Ricky would try to even things up.

"Okay, then," Lenny said and walked off, up toward Percy who had started back to the group.

I waded into the water to retrieve my boat, cooling my overheated body. With the bowline in hand, I tied it to my waist and swam as hard as I could, hitting the water with all the force I wished I could have unleashed on Ricky. I might not have been any match for him, but I could have rearranged his nose for sure. Contrary to Dad's impression of me, I was capable of standing up to bullies; it just made more sense to walk away—unless they were picking on some defenseless weakling. Then I knew how to land a punch. Problem was, every bully bigger than me took that as a challenge, and I didn't like fighting. I would never forget the feel—the sound—of my fist smashing into flesh and bone. It made me sick to my stomach.

When I snuck up into our cottage, I stumbled into an overturned chair beside the table. I righted it and then cracked open Penny's door. She lay on her bed, still in her clothes, snoring. At least she was safe.

Chapter 22

O N THE LAUNCH-PAD BOULDER, LYING ON my back with my eyes closed, I still see the party lights twinkling on the cove. When I open my eyes, that twinkling is flickering sunlight, creeping into treetops and dancing on my eyelids. I sit and breathe the scent of an incoming storm. The barometric change pushes a breeze from the east, through the Narrows, and ruffles the water. It cools my chin. That's right—I shaved. My sights return to Whispering Narrows. I envision the big tent and the music. I could indulge another fantasy about Amelia, given the freshness of the memory, but I'm no longer in the mood.

Ever since that night, I have always had a hard time at weddings—funerals too, but not as much as weddings. Funerals are the consequence of bad things that happen; weddings are the incubators of trouble.

Looking back on it, planning my own wedding was where my relationship with Gretchen unraveled. She wanted a big wedding with all the accouterments. Her parents are loaded and wanted to dote on her, which was fine. I had heard enough of Penny's talk about a woman's dream wedding to know how important a day it is. It seems a girl's entire childhood revolves around the fantasy of her wedding, from the gown, to the cake, to the bridal party, right down to the lacey blue garter. I, on the other hand, would have been happy to elope. Or at least to have restricted the ceremony to immediate family, but that posed a whole other dilemma.

Gretchen knew most of the milestones of my life. She

also knew about Dad, but I never filled her in on all the finer details of what had happened. And Mom—she was old, so residing in a nursing facility didn't spark questions; I lapsed into silence there, too. As for my sister, Gretchen knew only sketchy details regarding Penny's past. It didn't seem like my place to talk about my sister's history. And Frankie. Well, lots of siblings don't keep in touch— nothing unusual about that. Consequently, all the subtleties of my past didn't start to surface until it came to picking out a reception hall and caterer—and narrowing down the guest list. I wish I could say that what drove Gretchen and me apart was her shock and horror over what I had told her about my past, but no, it was my inability to open up and share any of it. She walked away because I couldn't bring myself to tell her the truth. That's when my tick started. Go figure.

Gretchen and I had spent so much of our relationship sorting through her past dysfunction and need for validation, that we conveniently overlooked mine. I am pretty good at seeing to the needs of others; it makes me feel as if I have something worth contributing in a relationship. I'm a great support and I know it. I'm not saying that isn't a fine quality, but it might be subterfuge. My safety mechanism. A sly way of sidestepping and overlooking—a way of not dealing with my own dirty secrets. Maybe subterfuge and hiding secrets is in my blood. Or maybe it's a learned behavior. Like denial. Mom had honed those traits to perfection.

THE MORNING AFTER THE BIG WEDDING AT Whispering Narrows, Mom said she had heard Penny stumbling around in the middle of the night—heard her right through the ear plugs she had worn to snuff the party noise. I could imagine the huge crash and clamor of the toppling chair, which would have sent most parents rushing from their room to investigate.

"Did you get confused and lose your way to the bathroom?" Mom asked.

Penny glanced at me, the front strands of her hair crimped from the braids she had worn the night before. "Yeah, um, I must have been sleepwalking. I stubbed my toe on the kitchen chairs. Sorry I woke you, Mom."

"Oh, I dropped right back off, thanks to the little sleepy pill I took."

Sleepy pill? Since when had Mom been taking sleeping pills?

"Really Mom?" Penny scrunched her nose with an air of condescension. "Barbiturates?"

Mom cocked her head and squinted.

"What!" Penny shrugged, "I learned about downers in health class."

Mom placed the milk bottle in the refrigerator. "Oh Penny, it's just a little over-the-counter pill. No harm in that."

That accounted for how easy it had been to sneak out at night. I filed that bit of information for future reference.

"Sure, Mom." Penny rolled her eyes and brought her cereal bowl to the sink.

As Penny sidled past, Mom touched the fringes of her kinky hair. "This is new."

"Yeah …." Penny glanced at me. "I was thinking of getting a perm and thought this would be a good way to see how it looks."

"Nonsense. You'd have to use rollers. I brought mine. Maybe we could have some fun with them, later."

"Yeah, sure," Penny's voice trailed as she made her way to the bathroom.

Frankie came out of our room, rubbing sleep from his eyes.

Mom tousled his hair. "Did all that party racket keep you awake last night, Frankie?"

"Huh? I don't know. I don't remember."

Nothing ever kept that kid awake at night—not even a bad conscience.

After Mom went down to the water with her *Ladies Home Journal* and her lemonade, Penny invited me to ride bikes, which meant providing her with an alibi for the beach, as if she needed one these days. Mom seemed not to care where we were as long as one of us kids—usually me—could round up the others for supper.

Since I didn't want to miss an opportunity to see Amelia, I declined Penny's invitation and hung around camp, swimming and messing around with Frankie and Skippy. I had forgotten how much fun it was doing kid stuff, like catching frogs and skipping stones. Promising we would stay within arm's distance of shore, I convinced Frankie to let me take him in the boat, along the edge of the cove, to find more spawning pools.

He and Skip piled into the rowboat with their buckets and nets. I grabbed a fishing pole and beached the boat to make it easier for Frankie to climb in. The poor kid was white with anxiety. He clutched the sides of the boat as I stepped in. We sat there for a minute so he could get used to it.

"See, it's just like being in the bathtub," I said as I dug the oar into the sand and pushed off with care.

"It's rocking—It's *rocking*!" he squealed.

"You're fine," I said in my most soothing voice. "We can turn back anytime you want."

Mom glanced up from her reading. "Oh, Frankie, I'm so proud of you! What a brave boy."

Now bolstered, Frankie shook his head, "No. No, I don't want to go back."

"Okay." I continued rowing, keeping us close to shore, making my way toward Whispering Narrows. Anytime I came close to a branch or boulder, he grabbed it, but when we found a colony of frogs or a turtle, he seemed to forget all about sitting in a tippy boat.

My mind drifted as the cleanup crew disassembled the party tent, tables, and chairs, until all that remained was trampled grass. During the time that I rowed around the perimeter of the cove, Amelia didn't come out of the house once. Did she have a hangover? Did she remember the things we had talked about and that she had said I had kissable lips? Just thinking about the way she had touched me under the water ... I shivered, quickly remembering where I was and making myself fake interest in Skippy's turtle. I sighed. Maybe Amelia remembered all of last night. Maybe she was too mortified to leave her room.

Reeling me back in, Skip asked, "Did you bring any bread crumbs, Frankie?"

"Oh, yeah." My little brother excitedly shoved his hand in his pocket. "I almost forgot."

As he yanked out a baggie full of torn-up bread heels, a pocketknife clunked onto the bottom of the boat. A tightly folded greenback stuck out from one of the knife's crevices. I snatched the bill as Skip grabbed the knife.

Fondling it, he frowned, "Hey, this is *my* knife."

"Oh, yeah," Frankie cut in, "I found it for you—I had it in my pocket to give to you."

"Boss. I thought I'd lost it for good."

Frankie looked at me as I held up a crisp ten-dollar bill and raised my brow.

"What!" He stared me straight in the eye without flinching. "I found it floating to shore this morning. Someone from the party must have lost it."

Did he think I was that stupid? I would have to check my new hiding place on top of the rafters in the unfinished room to make sure he hadn't rooked the ten bucks Doc had given me.

"Yeah, well, we should return it." I stuck the bill in my pocket. "Ten bucks is a lot of money, and if someone lost it at the party, Doc will know. I'll give it to Mom, so she can hold on to it."

"Yeah, sure. I was going to do that anyway."

Just then, Mom called the boys for lunch. It was just as well. I had lost interest in rowing my klepto brother around the cove. Besides, I was hungry.

I made a Spam sandwich in the kitchen, and when Mom started to stress about Penny being gone so long, I scarfed down my lunch about as fast as she gulped her lemonade. After lunch, I hung around the cove, keeping an eye out for Amelia.

A couple hours later, Mom's lilting voice carried to the float. "Ben, would you please go find your sister. I'd like some help getting supper started."

"Sure, Mom." That would at least give me an excuse to ride my bike past Whispering Narrows.

Five minutes later, I coasted down the hill. The old Rambler wasn't parked in Doc's driveway and neither was Karen and Dick's Mercedes. Just the Jaguar. If only Sunshine had been outside. A chance to talk to her would have been almost as good as seeing Amelia.

Each push of my pedal weighed more than the last as I passed on by. Just beyond Whispering Narrows, I veered to the side of the road and slowed at the sound of a car behind me. A dusty black Cadillac Eldorado rode alongside my bike. Its window rolled down.

The driver smoothed his greased hair. "Hey, kid, nice bike you got there."

I eyed him with suspicion. What was he going to do next—offer me candy or something?

He cocked his head. "Hey, you must be the Hughes boy. Frank Hughes' kid, right?"

"Yeah?"

"Well, that's one slick paintjob you've got on your ride."

"Thanks."

"Did you do that yourself?"

"Yeah." If he knew my dad, I guessed it was okay to

talk to him even if he was technically a stranger. "I really like your car."

He stroked his steering wheel. "Oh, yeah—she's a cherry."

"Automatic transmission?"

"You bet." He gave me a two-finger salute. "Well kid, you have a nice afternoon."

"Okay."

His car inched forward, and then the brake lights flashed as he called out, "Oh hey, you be sure to tell your dad, Irving said 'Hi.'"

"Okay."

"Bye-bye, now." He stuck his hand out the window, his big, gold ring sparkling in the sun.

As he drove away, I took note of the Massachusetts plates. Lots of people from Massachusetts had camps on Rockette Lake, including us. Was Irving someone Dad knew from work? I didn't give it a second thought except to attach a rhyme that would help me remember his name. Swerving Irving.

When I pedaled into the public lot, I spotted Penny not too far from Percy's lifeguard stand. I skidded my bike up to the rack in front of the split-rail fence that separated the beach from the lot. The shooting gravel drew Penny's attention. I stayed put as she scrambled to her feet and met me at the bike rack. Catching a whiff of that same cigarette smoke I had smelled at the wedding, I glanced around, looking for the Rambler.

"Have Lenny and Christopher been around?" I asked.

"Yeah. They just left. They said to tell you 'hello'."

"Oh yeah?"

"Yeah, and Christopher asked when the three of us are going for a boat ride. I hope you haven't been giving him any ideas about me."

"You're the one who called him Hot Wheels."

"Yeah, well, I didn't mean it the way it sounded. Besides, you know I like Percy."

186

I huffed. "Percy isn't into you. He likes Candace. Besides, Christopher is more your type."

"You don't know the first thing about who's my type," her eyes rolled, "and I'd appreciate it if you wouldn't talk to him about me behind my back."

"And you don't know the first thing about what I say behind your back," I retorted with the same snotty tone.

She pursed her lips. "So why'd you come down here, anyway?"

"Mom wants you home to help with supper."

She gave me the same annoyed look as she always gave Mom. "Fine."

I sneered, more frustrated at having missed Christopher than at my sister's surprisingly witchy attitude.

"Well, go on Ben. I can find my own way back."

Without a word, I spun out on the road. Somewhere between passing Whispering Narrows' first stone pillar and approaching number two, I made a split-second decision to pull into the driveway. In less time than it took to decide that, I stood on the front stoop and grabbed the lion-head knocker. Two raps later, Sunshine opened the door wide.

"C'mon in, Ben."

"I can't stay," I said as I stepped inside. "I just wanted to check on Amelia."

"That's so sweet of you." She closed the door and glanced up at the balcony. "She's not feeling so good today."

"That's too bad." I scanned the foyer and peered into the open great room doorway. "Is Ricky still around?"

"No. He took their car back down to New York. He won't be here for a few weeks, not until Karen and Dick come back from Rio." She cocked her head sympathetically. "Lenny told me you had a run-in with Ricky down at the water."

My gaze shifted. "Kind of."

"You know, Ben," she stroked my arm, "violence isn't the way."

187

"I know. But sometimes I wish I were bigger. Like Lenny. Then everyone would leave me alone."

She shook her head. "Lenny would never hurt anyone. He just talks like he's tough. You know, love is more than just words on a bumper sticker."

"I know," I said, but I had seen the anger in Lenny's eyes—even if he wasn't inclined to beat the snot out of Ricky, he could have. That was the confidence I wanted.

"Of course you know that, Ben. You're a gentle soul, too."

I wasn't so sure about that. "Yeah, well, I gotta go."

"I'll tell Amy you stopped by."

"Okay."

As I stepped outside, a green Chevy Malibu pulled into the driveway and came to a stop in front of the stoop. A man, with eyes like Sunshine's, opened the car door and climbed out as I mounted my bike. He looked at me and smiled with reservation.

I said, "Hi."

He nodded politely and then glanced at Sunshine, still standing on the steps. Half of his mouth fell with an awkward twitch.

"Daddy," Sunshine said.

As I pedaled out to the road, I looked back. The man stood on the step for a moment, saying something, and then Sunshine embraced him.

CHAPTER 23

BACK WHEN I WAS A KID, I CONSIDERED myself a gentle soul, even if at times I felt compelled to use my fists. I hated violence and I still do, but ever since that summer, I've had reason to second-guess the person deep within me—my core self. Do all of us have some primal monster just waiting for the right—or wrong— circumstance to propel us into an out-of-control madman?

Sunshine was the gentlest soul I have ever met. She meant well with her admonitions against violence, but she didn't understand what it was like to be a guy, to have one's courage and sense of right and wrong challenged— what it's like to *have* to fight, to so completely lose control that it goes beyond violence and becomes a sublime vindication of righteousness.

Maybe she sensed something in me—not only the good, but also something seething and waiting for that combination of circumstance and motivation. Maybe she hoped to alert me to my own weakness, to nurture my better self before it was too late.

I like to think Sunshine saw the goodness in me—my gentler side. Yet it was Amelia who drew out the tenderness from my deepest insides, from a place I didn't then know existed in the male psyche. She stirred that tenderness out on the water as we swam the night of the wedding and as she lay in the grass beside me on the lawn, but that was only the first tug. Those feelings surged through me the following day and night. Fed by my imagination and uncertainty, I ached—literally ached—not knowing what she was thinking and feeling.

Over the years, I have felt a twinge of that every time Amelia came to mind. Even as I sit on the launch pad, I think of her and wonder where she is, at this very moment. I ache not knowing. It's just as well we never connected after that summer, though Doc said she did ask about me. Not that I hadn't asked about her too, but I figured it would never work out. In spite of the potential complications, I finally did scrounge enough courage to ask Doc for her phone number. I was also testing whether he would allow me to pursue his granddaughter—his blood relation. Would he discourage it and offer a confession, answering my suspicions?

It was around three years ago when I decided to ask Doc how I might contact Amelia. I wasn't sure if I should write first or show up on her doorstep unannounced. Either way, it was a huge leap. Even as I dialed Doc's number, my heart sped as fast as if I had been calling Amelia. After an uncomfortable silence, Doc told me she had just eloped; I still don't know if the pause on the telephone was Doc's relief or regret. To twist the knife, she had run off with someone he scarcely knew. The news left me chilled, like the evening air rolling in through the Narrows. It raises goose bumps, like so many unresolved questions.

Is Amelia happy? Has she come to terms with her history? Did she think about me after that summer? I'm sure she must have, but I'm probably the only one still stuck in the past, still thinking about us and wishing things had been different.

THE DAY AFTER I STOPPED IN AT WHISPERING Narrows to see how Amelia was feeling, she finally came out of the house. I had been hanging around our float all morning on the chance she might make a showing. As soon as I spotted her walking across the lawn toward her dock, I got a fix on Mom snoozing, and I dove into the water.

I swam around the end of Amelia's dock to where she sat on the side hidden from camp. Lifting my torso, I rested my elbows on the planks, inches away from her thighs. She offered a weak smile when I said, "Hi."

She hugged her knees.

"You must be feeling better," I said, eyes traveling from her oversized T-shirt to the loose ponytail atop her head.

"Sort of." She shrugged. "Mostly embarrassed."

"I was hoping you wouldn't feel that way, though I can see why you might."

She rolled her eyes.

"No, I don't mean it in a bad way, I just meant, well, it was kind of a crummy night all the way around," I said, "except for hanging out with you."

"Yeah, I bet I was a real hoot."

I cocked my head. "C'mon, you have to admit swimming was fun."

"I guess." She blushed and her cheek dimpled. That was the first time I noticed she had a dimple on her left cheek.

"And the night could have turned out a whole lot worse. You could've barfed."

Her dimple deepened as she sighed. "Listen, I'm going to be away for ten days. My grandpa's got some business out west, and Sunshine's taking me with her to an artists' colony on Monhegan Island."

"Where's that?"

"Off the coast of Maine."

"Are you looking forward to it?"

She shrugged. "Yeah. I like hanging out with Sunshine."

"Are the other hippies going?"

She chuckled. "Hippies?"

I guessed that wasn't what she called them. I hoped she didn't think I meant it in a negative way. "Yeah, you know, Lenny and Candace and Percy."

"No. Just me and Sunshine."

"Oh. So, um, what's up with their cigarettes, anyway?"

Both her eyebrows rose. "You mean joints? Weed?"

I shrugged and swiped at a mosquito in midair. "I guess."

"It's pot—you know, marijuana. Kind of like alcohol, only you inhale it instead."

"Have you smoked it?"

She shook her head. "Sunshine says I'm too young— like too young to drink. And after the drink I had the other night, I have no interest in alcohol *or* weed. I didn't like how it felt, not one bit."

"I've never had alcohol, and if it tastes like it smells, I don't care if I ever have it."

"Grandpa says some people just don't know how to handle their liquor, like Uncle Brad."

"So, the guy that came yesterday—was that Brad, Sunshine's father?"

"Yeah. He came to apologize."

"So, are things between him and Doc better? I mean, I know it's none of my business. You don't have to say."

She shrugged. "I don't know. They talked privately for a long time. I think it had something to do with the reason for Uncle Brad's divorce. He left right afterward, looking like he had been crying. Grandpa's been really quiet ever since."

"Why don't they get along?"

"They're just really different. Sunshine says Uncle Brad's artistic—too much like his mother—and Grandpa is more practical. But that's not really it. That's just what they tell me."

I didn't mean to question it, but when I said, "Oh," it might have sounded like I was fishing for more.

She continued, whispering, "Uncle Brad has a boyfriend, but they think I don't know it."

Now when I said, "Oh," I'm sure the gravity of my tone conveyed my befuddlement, if not discomfort. I had heard about stuff like that but had a hard time comprehending two men—together.

She half-rolled her eyes. "Told you I had a weird family."

"I guess every family is a little weird," I said, wanting to change the subject. "So when do you leave?"

"Tomorrow morning," she said as she came to her feet. "I've gotta go pack."

"Okay."

Up close and in daylight, Amelia had even prettier legs with the most delicate freckles all the way down to her slender, now-unpainted toes. I looked back up at her face. The sun was mostly behind her, giving her hair a pinkish halo.

She gazed down at me. "I just wanted to say thanks for rescuing me the other night."

"You already thanked me."

"I know. I remember everything I said."

"Everything?"

She blushed. "Yes, *everything*. And everything *you* said, too."

"Good. Because I meant *all* of it."

Her big toe nudged my forearm. "Me too."

As she turned to walk away, a crazy idea came into my head. "Hey, Amelia."

She turned to me. "What?"

"You want to go for a boat ride later? I mean after dark, when everyone's gone to bed."

"You mean sneak out?"

I nodded.

Her gaze wandered and then she grinned. "Okay."

"I'll be right here at ten o'clock."

She walked away and then glanced back with a wave.

I could hardly lift my tingling hand to respond and pushed off the dock, falling backward into the water, kicking my legs and shaking blood into my numb arms.

My whole body rushed with expectation. I had just asked Amelia on some kind of a date—and she said yes.

The image of candlelight and wine on a checkered tablecloth flashed before me. No, that wouldn't work. Maybe I could take her out to the island and spread a blanket over pine needles under a pine-tree canopy. No, that seemed too much like something Ricky would do. I traded that idea for maybe a small campfire in the clearing. Should I gather a little kindling and a split log or two and bring them out beforehand, or bring them along when I picked her up in the rowboat? Even though I was, in fact, calculating everything, I didn't want it to appear that way, like it was all some kind of set up.

Was this how dating was going to be for the rest of my life? Trying to anticipate the outcome? How I should act, what I should talk about? Hoping I wouldn't say something stupid? How clever could I be without embarrassing myself? Just the thought of whether or not I should try and kiss her hiked my anxiety beyond discomfort. It had been easier when it all happened spontaneously, but now there was so much to consider. So much preparation. My excitement turned to angst. My stomach didn't feel right for the rest of the afternoon.

"Are you okay?" Mom had asked when we sat down to eat, and I only picked at my Spaghetti-Os.

"I'm fine." I forced myself to stuff a forkful in my mouth, chewing for a long time as Mom brought her empty plate to the sink.

"I'm going to the market tomorrow morning," Mom said, rummaging through her purse. "If there's anything you're in the mood for, add it to the list." She pulled out a pen and went back in, I assumed for paper. Had she come across that ten I had tucked in her purse yesterday? I didn't wonder for long.

"Oh—for goodness sakes—there it was the whole time," she said, waving a ten-dollar bill. "I thought I'd lost my money or my mind. What a relief."

Frankie kept chewing as if he hadn't heard Mom, which convinced me he had swiped it from her in the first place. It was bad enough that he had been so bold as to lift a whole ten and not just pocket change, but he showed no remorse or embarrassment—his cheeks didn't even turn as red as his chapped upper lip. And Penny was oblivious to it all as she filled her mouth, staring off into space, probably fantasizing about Percy Wade.

By 9:30, Mom was snoring and so was Frankie. The full moon shone through our window like a streetlight. I slipped into the hall where a bead of light came from under Penny's door. I stepped extra careful so she wouldn't hear. Not that she would snitch, but I didn't want to share this with her. Simple as that.

It was weird—in little more than a week, Penny and I had gone from being accomplices to having our own secrets. I didn't worry too much about her smoking weed any more than if it had been regular cigarettes. The idea of filling *my* lungs with smoke didn't appeal to me at all, and after thinking about Mom's drinking, and how bad alcohol had made Amelia feel, I wasn't curious about that, either. Perhaps that was the difference between being almost fourteen and being sixteen-and-a-half. No, it wasn't the smoking that bothered me, but rather, whom she was smoking with, or why she was smoking in the first place. At school, she had always been popular without smoking or dressing trashy, so I didn't understand why she felt the need to do it now. Maybe she wanted to fit in with an older, looser crowd. I didn't know a whole lot about free love, but I had a couple friends with older brothers, and I had heard the way they talked about girls—about the boy-crazy kind that would *do it*. I cringed to think of my sister being that kind of girl. But then again, she was smart, and she had told me she wanted to wait. She wouldn't do anything stupid.

CHAPTER 24

Y BUTT IS NUMB FROM SITTING. AS I STAND and stretch my back, the evening breeze picks up. Stroking my naked cheek, I'm glad I shaved, even if it does leave me exposed. In the dimming light, the island and thickening clouds reflect on the lake. I wish the boat were in better condition—I could row out to the island and look for remnants of our first date there, or the next. I would close my eyes and replay everything that happened.

Although the content of my fantasies about Amelia have changed over the years, many details remain the same—as long as I filter the bitter from the sweet. Of course, none of the bitter was her fault, it was only circumstances as they unfolded, things we had no control over. But prior to our first date, and even the second, there was nothing to taint my imagination. It was pure indulgent fantasy at its best because it was based on something I perceived as reality.

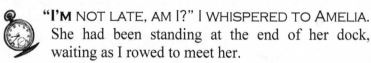 "I'M NOT LATE, AM I?" I WHISPERED TO AMELIA. She had been standing at the end of her dock, waiting as I rowed to meet her.

She shook her head as she tossed a blanket at me and eased into the boat, her bare feet meeting the floorboards without a sound.

I rowed through the Narrows and nodded back toward her house. "Which window is Doc's?"

She pointed to one that overlooked the lake. I weighed stealth against speed. The last thing I wanted was for Doc to catch me sneaking off—speeding off—with his granddaughter. Not that this was a breach of trust, and if he later asked me about it I would fess up, but I didn't want him to think I was the sort who would ever try to corrupt Amelia. I opted for stealth and slowed, doing my best to keep the splashing to a minimum and the oar from creaking against the lock.

"I thought it might get chilly," she whispered, hugging the blanket against her sweatshirt, "—you know, on account of the clear skies."

"Good idea." I was glad I had also brought my jacket.

"It's so still tonight … sounds carry."

I rolled my eyes. "Yeah, I know."

"We could always hang out on the island—I've seen you go out there."

"You have?"

She nodded.

We didn't talk the rest of the way over. We were storing up for the privacy of the island. The moon behind the treetops cast a shadow over where I usually moored. I tied off the boat and kept us steady as Amelia climbed out.

"Too bad we couldn't make a fire," she said, inspecting the charred remains and ashes from my last visit to the island.

"Who says we can't?" I held up matches.

She looked around and began collecting kindling, while I pulled out my mini flashlight and scavenged for a few larger sticks in the wooded brush. When I returned, Amelia crouched over some dried leaves, pine needles, and twigs, arranging them in the small stone-encircled firepit. She then sat on the nearby log, smoothing the still-folded blanket on her lap.

I deposited my scant bundle in front of her and fished the radio out of my jacket pocket. "Do you wanna listen to some music?"

"Sure."

I tossed her the radio and inspected her pile of tinder.

"You did a good job," I said as she scrolled through

stations. She zipped past and then returned to "California Dreaming," lowering the volume. With the strike of a match, the pine needles caught fire and crackled. Perfect.

She set the radio on the ground and looked up at me with anticipation. "Are you going to sit?"

"Sure." I tried to gauge how close was too close, but the short log didn't provide a whole lot of leeway. My bare arm brushed hers as I sat.

We gazed at the fire. Her head bobbed to the music's beat. My toes tapped in my sneaker. I sucked in a long breath and exhaled. "This is kind of weird."

"Actually, I was thinking it's kind of nice."

"Yeah, I mean, it's really nice, but kind of weird too. I've never actually hung out with a girl—I mean except for Penny."

"It must be nice to have someone to hang out with."

"It's nice most of the time."

"I always wished I had a brother or sister. But that was pretty much impossible, because I don't have a—you know, 'cause my mom wasn't married, and now it's kind of late for her to give me a brother or sister. Besides, I don't feel like being a babysitter—and now that I *have* a brother, I'm stuck with Ricky."

"So, do you ever get to hang out with your dad?"

She hesitated, shaking her head, and then looked at me. "I've never met him."

"Is he dead or something?"

"I don't know. My mom won't tell me anything about him. I don't think she knows where he is. Or if he even knows I exist."

"Oh." I then understood why she hadn't wanted to talk about her father the other night. I added another stick to the fire and poked at it with a long twig. Cream's song, "Crossroads" played. "Well, sometimes knowing your father isn't all it's cracked up to be, either."

"Yeah, but if you didn't know him, you'd want to."

"Sure I would." I looked her in the face. "I bet your dad has curly red hair, bright blue eyes, and a dimple on his left cheek."

She smiled. "That's what I think. It's funny, because whenever I'm in a crowd and I see a man with red hair, I always look to see if he has just one dimple. Sunshine says it's my best feature."

"It's pretty cute, but it's not your best feature. It would be pretty hard to pick out *the* best feature on you."

She smirked, making her dimple really stand out. "Stop it."

I grinned. "Am I embarrassing you?"

She blushed and unfolded the blanket, spreading it over our laps, even though I didn't feel the least bit cold. We continued staring at the fire until her leg bumped mine, drawing my eyes to hers. That look came over her. Now I couldn't turn away. I studied her moonlit face as she gazed into my eyes and moved closer. Her lips brushed mine. It wasn't a kiss to begin with, just our lips touching, but my heart beat so fast it became too hot beneath the blanket. It didn't take long for our touching lips to turn into a real kiss. She tasted so sweet, not like sugar, but like cool water when you're really thirsty. As soon as I felt her tongue, she pulled back.

I could hardly catch my breath.

She stared at the fire, smiling. "I never kissed a boy before."

I shot her a glance.

"I know what you're thinking, but Ricky doesn't count." She hugged her knees.

"You should forget it happened, then."

"Okay, but you might have to kiss me again." She straightened up and waited for me to lean in. I kissed her. Again, I tasted her tongue and she backed off, smiling. "You kiss really good. I bet you've kissed a lot of girls."

I shrugged. "I kissed Robynne Flynn in third grade. She

said she'd give me a fat lip if I didn't—I mean, I'd have been stupid not to. She actually kissed pretty good. Then, in fourth grade, I tried to kiss her again and she did give me a fat lip. I figured I probably wasn't any good at it, so I never tried to kiss another girl."

Amelia giggled. "Is she still in your school?"

"Yeah. She kisses lots of guys, though. Not my type."

"I wish we were in the same school."

"You wouldn't be embarrassed to be seen with a ninth-grader?"

"Normally, I guess so, but not with you—I wouldn't be embarrassed at all."

I looked at her askance. "How come all these years that we've been coming up here, you pretty much ignored me?"

"Because you were always *staring*. Do you have any idea what it's like to be stared at—especially after I got these?" She glanced down at her chest.

Now my cheeks heated. "Sorry about that. It's just that—well, in my defense, you did wear those two-piece bathing suits."

"Yeah well, if a girl can't wear what she wants on her own private beach—sheesh."

"Okay, it was rude. I am sorry. But you made it really hard not to stare, even if you didn't have—" I pointed "—those. Don't you realize how pretty you were, even when you were a lot littler? And yes, I know you're more than that, but I never had a chance to find out about the rest of you."

She stared at me and smiled. "Okay, I have a question for you."

"Yeah?"

"Why do you always call me Amelia instead of Amy?"

I studied her whole face. "You look like an Amelia."

"What's that mean?"

"It's kind of like the way 'Amelia' *feels* when I say it, like there's something to it. Amy is just, well, it sounds flat." Her eyes grew wide and I realized I had just said *flat* after talking about her chest. I rebounded. "Not like *that*. I mean, Amy sounds silly compared to Amelia. Amelia has character."

She cocked her brow.

I continued my bailout. "It's like the difference between oyster crackers and an ice cream sundae. Or peanut butter and jelly, and a lobster dinner. Or sardines and …."

"Oyster crackers?" She giggled. "I guess it's just like the difference between Ben and Benjamin. Benjamin has substance. It suits you."

Nothing sounded better than her saying my name. "I really like you, Amelia Burns."

"I really like you, Benjamin Hughes."

With those words lingering in the embers and sparks swirling up into the trees, we stared at the fire for a long time, holding hands under the blanket. We didn't kiss again that night, not even when I dropped her off at her dock, a little past midnight. I didn't want to take a chance on Doc catching us. As hard as it would be, what we shared on the island would have to last ten days while she was away.

Chapter 25

I T'S TIME TO PULL OUT OF FANTASY WORLD AND move on with my evening. Again, I'll take the roundabout route up to the cottage. As I climb the rickety old stairway, I give the handrail a good shake to see just how bad off it is. That was a mistake. With a creak and a groan, the long stretch of railing falls over. It crashes and folds, its spindles splayed like bicycle-wheel spokes. I step more carefully, more reverentially, lest I further anger the god of loose nails.

At the top of the stairway, I veer toward the old lean-to, lured by a memory of wheel spokes. Perhaps my stingray is still where I left it.

I'm surprised this old shed hasn't folded in on itself. It tilts worse than forty-five degrees toward the property line. Parting vines of overgrowth, I peer into a tunnel of greenery, old boards, and broken storm windows leaning against my bike. What a sad old relic, its spokes and rim as mangled as the stair railing. *Oh well.* There's no fixing some things. With a sigh, I turn and head for the cottage. Supper awaits.

Standing at the kitchen sideboard, I set aside the Marshmallow Fluff and assemble the Wonder bread and canned Spam on the counter beside the clock. Its tick has an even tempo and appears to be keeping good time. Only 6:06. This is going to be a long night. If only I had brought a more substantial supper. And Marshmallow Fluff? What was I thinking? *Sentimental sap!* I would have been better off with a fifth of something.

I don't mean that, not really. As tempting as it might have been during several episodes of my life, I have never resorted to alcohol or drugs—except that one time in high school. I'm not sure how much I drank, and maybe it was the combination of cheap beer and blackberry brandy, but I have never been so sick. As for pot, I had no desire to try it. I don't like feeling out of control, of not having all my wits. Situations come up when you least expect, and alcohol puts you in a vulnerable position if you're caught off guard. And I'll never forget that hangover. Just the thought of it makes my stomach queasy—or perhaps it's hunger. Time to fill my belly.

I inspect the can of Spam, wishing it were salad or antipasto. I think I've become a food snob over the years. I liked Spam as a kid—a comfort food—but at this moment, it isn't all that appetizing. I guess it's too late to take my upset stomach into consideration.

I dig around in the bag. No knife, just a spoon. Dora must have been too flustered. I could forgo the Spam, but even if I opt for Marshmallow Fluff, I still need a knife. I pull one under-the-counter drawer and then another. A few utensils clank forward. Butter knives lie among a few bent forks, a rusty spatula, and some stained sugar packets. A piece of faded red paper catches my eye. Carnival tickets. The highlight of our summers. I unfold it, flipping it over. A series of handwritten, repeating numbers fills the back— that, and the words, Finnegan's Favor. So much for that happy little memento. I begin to tear it up, but no, I'll add it to the table and dwell on a happier memory—even if it did end poorly.

THE DISTINCT BUZZ OF SUNSHINE'S JAGUAR carried across the lake sometime around midmorning. I waited a few minutes, so I wouldn't appear too eager for Amelia's return from Monhegan Island, and then hopped on my bike. I arrived in their driveway just in time to catch Amelia yanking a small suitcase from the Jag's trunk.

She smiled over her shoulder as I pulled my bicycle up beside her. "I could help you carry your stuff, if you want."

"Just because I'm a girl doesn't mean I'm not strong enough to carry my own stuff, you know."

I guessed I had said something wrong. "I know. I was just trying to be nice."

"You don't have to try that hard, Benjamin. I already think you're nice."

The sight of her dimple reassured me. "You sure packed light."

"Well, it wasn't some big fancy vacation. It was more like camping." She grabbed the handle of a flat wooden box, tucked it under her arm, and then reached for a small canvas bag.

"You may have muscles, but you don't have three hands." In one quick move, I dismounted, laid my bike on the grass, and snatched the suitcase from her grasp. She gave it up with a smile.

"Shut the trunk for me?" She stood close, a glint in her eye.

"Sure." At that second, I thought I might kiss her, but then she turned.

"Follow me."

As we approached the granite steps, the front door flew open and Sunshine walked out. "Hello, Ben."

"How was your trip?" I said, swatting a mosquito as we continued through the door.

"It was a gas!"

"Far out," I said and Amelia gave me a one-raised-brow look.

I shrugged. "What!"

Amelia shook her head and continued on to the staircase landing. It then dawned on me that I was going to be following her up to her bedroom. I glanced around the foyer as if we were sneaking and should be on the lookout for someone—maybe Doc. And what would I do if Doc was to appear? I didn't have to wonder for long. By the time we climbed halfway up the stairs, he came through the great room doorway and shot us a look.

"Hello, Ben. Helping out are we?"

"Yes, sir."

"That's fine, but Amelia, you keep your door wide open."

She rolled her eyes. "Yes, Grandpa."

He walked out through the service entrance—through the door where he had led me the first time I was there. He didn't appear to have any qualms about me hanging around his granddaughter, which was great, but then the responsibility of it hit me. The last time I had gone flying with him, he and I had entered an honesty pact. If he was ever to ask about stuff between Amelia and me, I couldn't lie.

As Amelia's cute butt wiggled up the stairs, I had a hard time focusing on it—well, for a few seconds, anyway. When she opened her door wide, we entered a room ten times the size of my room at home.

"Where do you want this?" I said, glancing all around.

"On the bed."

I laid the wooden box on her blue and white bedspread—not lacey, but very girlish. The space wasn't as fancy as I had pictured, but she did have a small radio and record player with a large collection of 45s. I had also imagined a lot of pink and a bunch of stuffed animals, but only a worn-out bunny lay on her pillow and not a stitch of pink anywhere. "I like your room."

"Thanks."

"You don't like pink."

"Hate it. It's all my mother used to let me wear." She opened her closet door. "The stupid bride's maid dress was the last pink I'll ever be seen in."

My whole bedroom at Safe Haven could fit inside her closet. Clothes hung evenly spaced, not crammed full the way I would have envisioned a rich girl's wardrobe. She even had her very own bathroom.

I walked over to the big picture window overlooking the lawn and a full view of our float. The sight of it made me queasy. When she stood beside me, her nearness gave me goose bumps.

I exhaled. "Nice view."

"Yeah. I always know when you're out on your float."

My face heated. Had she sometimes stayed inside if she saw I was outside?

She glanced at me. "You're not the only one who knows how to stare."

I didn't want to talk about staring—mine or hers. "So, are you going to the carnival on Saturday?"

"Maybe. Depends."

"On what?"

She grinned. "On who's going to be there."

"Well, maybe if you end up going, we could go on a couple rides together."

"I like the Ferris wheel."

"What about the Turkish Twister?"

"I love that!"

The excitement that beamed from her face turned to *that look* again, but I sure as heck wasn't going to get caught kissing Amelia in her bedroom. And even if I had tried, we would have been interrupted two seconds later, when the front door squeaked open.

"Hello, hello!" Her mother's voice echoed around the foyer and up into Amelia's room.

Oh, great! That meant Ricky had also returned. Amelia closed her eyes with a huff. "They weren't supposed to be here until tomorrow. I *hate* when she does that—just assuming everyone will drop everything for her."

"Aaaammeeee …" Karen's voice echoed again, "Where aaaarrrrre you?"

"Coming Mother." She glanced at me. "Come on."

I wasn't sure if it was a good idea to have Amelia's mother see me coming out of her daughter's room, but I obeyed. I stepped out onto the balcony behind her. Karen and Dick stood below.

Karen gave me a curious look. "Well, hello, Jim."

"His name is Benjamin, Mother."

"Well, I was close," she laughed. "Sorry, *Ben*."

Doc came out through the service doorway. "Well, this is a nice surprise." His voice didn't carry the same enthusiasm it had the last time they arrived early, but he hugged his daughter anyway and then shook Dick's hand. "How was Rio?"

"An absolute blast," Karen said, glancing up at us. "Well, aren't you going to come down and hug your mom?"

"Yes, Mother."

"Where's Ricky?" Doc asked as I lagged behind.

"Oh, he's parking the car and getting our bags. He's such a fine young man, Daddy. I can't wait for you to get to know him."

Amelia exhaled a cough and although I couldn't see her face, I was sure her eyes rolled. At that moment, Ricky stepped through the front door. His gaze landed first on me, then Amelia, and then on Doc as Ricky approached him with an outstretched hand. "It's nice to see you again, sir."

Doc offered a tight-lipped smile. How much did Doc know about the wedding night fiasco?

With her arms limp at her side, Amelia surrendered to her mother's embrace.

"That's no way to greet your mom," Karen chided.

"Sorry. I just finished lugging my bags upstairs."

"Oh, never mind. Let's go have some lunch." Karen looped her arm through Amelia's and ushered her toward the great room door.

Amelia offered a weak smile as she looked back at me. "See ya', Benjamin. Thanks for helping."

Dick and Doc followed the girls. Ricky stalled as I made my way to the exit.

"Hey, Fixer-man," Ricky said as I passed by. "Listen, I'm really sorry, guy—I accidently ran over your bike. But you're so clever, I'm sure you can fix it."

I spun to face him. "You what?"

His smirk turned to a chuckle. "You really shouldn't leave your junk lying around in the middle of the driveway."

I'm sure he enjoyed every shade of red coloring my face. As he walked out of the room, I said nothing, only because I was so mad I couldn't spit out a word even if I had been able to think of something.

I let myself out. My bike lay on the lawn beside the driveway, right where I had left it. A tire print flattened the grass leading up to my crushed front rim and spokes. Ricky had bent the whole wheel so bad that I had to carry my bike up the hill. How was I going to explain that to Mom? I dragged the crumpled mess to the overgrown side of the lean-to and tucked it out of sight. I could fix it, but it would never be right. If there were any consolation, I hoped that would be the extent of Ricky's payback.

CHAPTER 26

T HE KITCHEN WATER FAUCET GASPS AND sputters, spewing rusty liquid. I don't wait long enough for hot water to travel from the basement. With my hands rinsed, I grab for a yellowed paper towel hanging under the cabinet and think twice. *Gross.* Instead, I blot my hands on my shorts and reach for the Spam. I pop the key off the bottom and insert the tab. As a kid, such a simple mechanism fascinated me—a machine in its most basic form. I loved twisting the metal band as it coiled around until it returned to where it started. *Voila*, the can opens.

As I go through the motions, the metaphor, Can of Worms, comes to mind. Best not to think about worms, since I'm about to consume this can's contents. Here's a better platitude: What goes around, comes around. On second thought, I'm not sure I like that any better. It's a little misleading in its simplicity. Over the years, I have learned that resolution, or Karma as Sunshine would say, is never simple and it does not take collateral damage into account.

It's true that innocent people end up in the wrong place at the wrong time, but who can claim complete innocence? I have had difficulty sifting through what I was—*am*— responsible for, and what I'm not. I can claim only my own stupidities and deceits, not anyone else's—Penny's, to be specific. Perhaps 'innocence' is better defined by lesser degrees of guiltiness. Of course, in some cases, guilt can be unequivocally assigned.

My stomach still doesn't feel quite right. Perhaps I'll change out of my swim trunks before I eat.

Mom, Penny, Frankie, Skip, and I crossed the field beside Garver's Market where we had parked the Galaxie. We passed Lenny's Rambler a few rows over. I hoped that meant Christopher would also be at the carnival. As we walked through the archway entrance on our way to the short line at the ticket booth, Mom doled out three singles to each of us. I pocketed mine and scanned the crowd for Christopher and then surveyed the parking lot again, hoping for Amelia. I didn't find either of them. Instead, my sights landed on Ricky standing by the Turkish Twister. Our eyes met. His usual smirk morphed with curiosity as his gaze settled on Penny and then back to me.

Had it just occurred to Ricky that Penny was my sister and more of a hippie groupie, rather than a full-fledged member of their crew? Penny had always shown up and left before or after me—at the lunar landing broadcast and the wedding—and she appeared enough like one of the hippies to be overlooked; clearly hands-off.

From the shift of Ricky's eyes, I read his thoughts: She's your *sister*? She's *your* sister!

At that moment, I wished I had told Penny about what a lecher Ricky was and how he had molested Amelia, but Penny and I hadn't been talking as much lately. I glanced at my sister as she tucked stray hairs behind her ear and scanned the grounds. To my relief, she seemed to overlook Ricky in her search for Percy.

Just then, I heard the Jag. It rolled into the field and parked. Sunshine climbed out first, and then a familiar pair of plaid pedal pushers poked out from the passenger seat. Next came sleeveless shoulders and strawberry curls. Amelia.

Mom grabbed my arm and then Penny's. "I'm going to stay with Frankie and Skippy, but I want the two of you to stick together, do you understand? And meet us back here at nine o'clock."

Penny gasped, "Nine o'clock?"

"All the lowlife come out after nine," Mom said, clutching Frankie. "I want my babies back here at nine sharp."

"Nine-thirty—*please* Mom?"

"Nine. And that's that."

Three hours was better than nothing. I yanked my sister's arm. "C'mon Penny, let's not waste time."

I wanted to lag behind and wait for Amelia to catch up, but Penny had spotted Percy and was on the move. She ambled right past Ricky. I ignored him, though in my peripheral vision I caught him watching.

Christopher called out from his wheelchair, drawing my attention to him. He sat beside Lenny who wore his unbuttoned vest, jeans, and army boots. They both watched Percy at the high striker. Penny and I wove through the crowd toward them as Percy hurled the sledgehammer onto the pad. The red weight climbed to the line between Good Girl and 1000. That seemed pretty decent to me. I would have been thrilled with 900.

"Hi, Penny," Christopher said with a smile. "Hey, Ben."

Penny offered a barely audible, "Hello."

As I greeted everyone, Lenny took his place, lifted the hammer with ease, and let it drop. The bell rung instantly. Both Lenny and Percy grinned, slapping each other on the back, as if neither cared who was stronger. It was all in good fun.

Christopher nudged me. "Are you going for it?"

I was curious to see how close I could come to grown men. As I thought about it, Penny came up behind Percy, but Candace, who suddenly showed up, beat her to it and grabbed Percy's arm, planting a huge kiss right on his mouth. Her chest flattened against his—well, nothing could entirely flatten her chest. Penny stopped in her tracks. When Percy spotted her, his expression wilted. Penny turned away and began to wander off. Percy said something to Candace and then caught up with Penny. As Percy led her away, Christopher's gaze remained upon them.

"I'll be right back," I said to Christopher.

I followed them to where they slipped in between two nearby game booths, and I stood between them and the moving crowd. Percy stroked her arm, exuding sincerity as he said a few quiet words, trying to catch her gaze. I turned away to give them more privacy. Stuffing my hands in my pockets, I studied my feet and the trampled grass and cigarette butts. I glanced over at Christopher. He still had his eye on Penny.

To my side, T-shirts and gauze skirts hung from a rack beside baubles and cigarette lighters. I poked at a troll hanging from a key chain, trying to look as if I wasn't straining to listen in. Even if I couldn't make out every word or see gestures, I picked up on the tone of the conversation. Since Percy was doing most of the talking, I speculated on what he might be saying, though Penny gave it away with her high-pitched voice. "I'm *not* too young!"

"I'm sorry, Penny—" he said as she rushed past, tears streaming down her face. Percy looked at me and shrugged, wagging his head contritely. I turned to catch up with my sister and strode beside her as she disappeared between another couple of booths, out of the way of foot traffic. I followed.

She muttered, "Jailbait—what is *jailbait* anyway?"

"I don't know."

"He just thinks I'm some little kid."

"I think he does like you, Penny, it's just you're not as old as Candace. He probably likes older women, is all."

"Don't tell me 'I told you so.'"

"I wasn't going to." Even though I wanted to.

She wiped her eyes. "I'm *not* too young."

"Penny—"

"Shut up Ben—you don't know how it feels."

I folded my arms across my chest, angry and sympathetic at the same time.

She fanned her face. "Do my eyes look puffy?"

"A little. But not bad. Let's go on a ride and then you'll be all better. Well, you'll *look* better anyway. Pale and green will camouflage your red nose."

As we stepped out from between the booths, Christopher wheeled up on his own. I looked for Lenny; he offered a nod.

Christopher grinned. "Let's go on some rides."

Just then, Amelia approached the three of us.

"Hi guys." She looked my sister in the eye. "You okay, Penny?"

Penny snarled, "*Yes!*"

Amelia backed off, directing her attention to Christopher and me. "You guys wanna go on the roller coaster?"

As I said, "Yeah," Penny said, "My stomach doesn't feel like the roller coaster right now."

It didn't occur to me that Christopher might not be able to get on—or even handle the roller coaster.

"How about the Ferris wheel?" Amelia stepped closer to me.

Penny shrugged. "Okay."

Christopher nodded.

I started off with Amelia on one side, Christopher on the other, and Penny trailing close behind, but it wasn't long before the wheelchair lagged and ended up beside my sister. *Smooth.*

The four of us made our way through the wafting aroma of hot dogs, cigarettes, and buttery popcorn.

"You want some cotton candy or anything?" Christopher asked, directing his question to all of us.

"No," Penny said. I didn't want any either. We continued onward, bumping people, weaving our way through the crowd. By the time we arrived at the Ferris wheel, three buckets remained empty. When it came our turn to board, the scrawny carnie cut in front of Christopher's chair, a cigarette drooping from his mouth.

"Sorry, man—no cripples allowed."

"I'm not a cripple. I just want a ride."

"Sorry, buddy." He took a long drag off his cigarette and slowly blew it down at Christopher. "No can do."

Before the smoke had a chance to dissipate, Lenny stepped out of the crowd and landed his big mitt on the carnie's pointy shoulder. Lenny's chest expanded and his biceps strained. "He's going on the ride."

The carnie coughed out a puff as Lenny lifted the bar. Without thinking, I reacted, helping Christopher out of his chair and into the bucket. Lenny climbed in beside him and winked at me. "It's the boots, man. No one messes with the boots!"

I need to get me some boots like that!

Penny hung back. "You guys go ahead—I don't mind sitting by myself."

"You sure?" I asked, still stunned at what had just taken place with Christopher.

She nudged me forward. "Yeah, you two go ahead."

I tore off a couple tickets. The carnie avoided eye contact as I handed them over. As Amelia and I took our seat, the attendant pulled the bar down in front of us. He hit the lever. Our bucket rocked and rose forward, then paused for Penny to board in the seat after us. At the last second, Ricky showed up.

Without a word, he slipped into the seat beside Penny, and then asked, "Do you mind if I share the ride?"

Penny smiled bashfully. "I guess not."

I couldn't believe how brazen he was, especially with Lenny so close by. Amelia and I glanced down behind us at Ricky's wide grin.

Amelia's fingertips dug into my bare knee as we exchanged concerned looks.

"Did you tell her?" Amelia said under her breath.

"You mean about Ricky?"

She nodded.

"No. I haven't told anyone."

She leaned into me. "You have to talk to her."

I let out a long sigh. "Yeah."

Her hand, still on my knee, relaxed. I let go of the bar and took her palm, lacing her fingers through mine. She squeezed back.

As our bucket elevated, with Penny and Ricky down behind us, I sensed his staring eyes. The gradual ascent put them below, and when they came into view beneath and in front of us, the two of them faced each other. A serious expression fixed Penny's brow as Ricky spoke. She shook her head and rolled her eyes, but not with annoyance. Instead of focusing on each other, both Amelia and I leaned forward as if we might catch the drift of their conversation, but as the ride peaked, we lost sight of them. I shrugged. Amelia snuggled closer to me, looking all around the fair grounds as the cycle repeated itself.

I glanced up behind at Christopher, whose smile tensed. Every time Ricky and Penny came into view, my insides withered with disappointment for Christopher. My sister's smile curled with increasing ease, although Ricky hadn't inched any closer.

On our last ascent, as we overlooked the park, I would have sprung a kiss on Amelia, but I didn't want to make Christopher feel any worse. Besides that, I caught sight of Dora below, waiting her turn in line with Mrs. Garver. As Dora stared up at Amelia and me, her usual smile twisted to a frown. I hoped she wasn't going to start bawling.

Lenny and Christopher came off the ride first. It took a minute to wrangle Christopher into his chair and move aside so others could take their bucket seat. Amelia and I were next. As I waited for Penny—hoping to pull her aside—Dora came up to me.

"Hi, Isadora," I said, hoping that might bring back her smile.

"Do you want to go on the ride with me?"

I just couldn't make her cry again and chose my words carefully. "I wish I could, I mean, I'd really like to, but—"

With a sympathetic glance, Mrs. Garver intervened, "Dora, it would be rude for Ben to leave his date," and moved her ahead, into the seat vacated by Penny and Ricky.

As soon as the Garver's rail lowered, I grabbed my sister's arm. "Penny—"

"I'm fine, Ben. Ricky and I are just going to hang out together."

Amelia cut in. "Then we'll come with."

Penny rolled her eyes. "It's a free country."

As soon as Lenny had Christopher repositioned in his chair, Lenny put it in motion. Christopher waved. "Catch you guys later."

It seemed as if everyone I wanted to keep track of was scattering.

"Hold on," I said, catching up. "Can't you stick around for a while?"

"I know when I'm a fifth wheel." He laughed, but it had to hurt—not just the thing with the carnie, but with Penny.

"You're not a fifth wheel."

"And you can't count," he smiled. "Besides, I gotta meet up with my folks. They'll be disappointed if they can't wheel my butt around."

"Well ...," I folded my arms, "okay."

"Don't worry, I'll catch up with you later so you can meet them."

I nodded, hesitant to let him go.

He flung his arm forward, as if leading the cavalry. "Onward, men!"

"I'll catch you later," I said as Lenny wheeled him away.

I returned to Amelia and my sister—and Ricky.

His brow rose as he smiled at me with fake sincerity. "It's a real shame they won't let a kid like him on rides."

Penny shook her head. "It's just wrong. Makes me mad."

"Oh well, can't let that spoil our evening," he said. "Come on, it will be fun, just the four of us."

Amelia rolled her eyes and grabbed my hand as we walked behind them. Ricky pocketed both hands, keeping a respectable distance between him and Penny. As we approached the basketball hoop booth, Ricky turned to me.

"Whaddaya say, Ben—think you can show up an old man?" He grinned like we were longtime buddies.

I replied with an unenthusiastic, "Sure." I had no intention of trying to show him up, as if I could.

Ricky slapped down twice the tickets required, tossing a look over his shoulder at me. "For me *and* him." He winked. "No hard feelings, right?"

Amelia let out the quietest huff that sounded like the word 'jerk' and squeezed my hand. I didn't reply. I had all I could do not to laugh at the absurdity of it. The bristly man behind the counter laid three basketballs, slightly larger than softball size, on the counter. Ricky picked up the first, posed like a high school basketball star, took aim, flicked his wrist, and aced it. Repeating his routine two more times, he nailed each one. Penny bounced with glee.

"Beginner's luck," Ricky said as the attendant passed a purple ape to Ricky. He passed it on to Penny and then stepped aside. "Your turn, my man."

If it had been only Amelia and me, it would have been fun trying my best, even if I botched it. Now, I was torn between caring at all and wishing I could hurl each ball at Ricky's perfectly straight teeth. I felt Amelia's hopeful attention at my right and Ricky's smirking gloat to my left. I took the stance, eyed the basket, and tossed. One in. Ball two. Aim, toss, right through the hoop. I took a deep breath. In thirty seconds, I had gone from not caring to wanting this more than knocking Ricky's teeth loose. I flicked my wrist; the ball made a respectable arch, bounced on the rim, rode it for two seconds, and then tumbled outside.

"Too bad. That was *so* close," Ricky said, as if he were my mentor. "I'll tell you what—that was a little unfair. To be honest, I was the basketball captain in school, so why don't you pick the next game, Ben."

I started walking. "I'd rather go on the roller coaster."

"Oh, come on, Benjie," Penny piped up. "You've got a really good pitching arm. Let's find the Ball Toss game."

"I don't feel like it."

Ricky nudged my shoulder and grinned. "Don't let my experience and size intimidate you, Ben."

I held my ground. "You don't intimidate me and the games are boring."

"You don't want Amy to go home without a stuffed animal, do you?"

I didn't realize I had closed the space between him and me, until Amelia slipped her hand in mine and pulled me back, saying, "I don't even like stuffed animals."

"Fine then," Penny yanked Ricky's sleeve. "We'll just let the two of you go off on your own. That's all you really want anyway."

I looked at Penny in disbelief. When had she turned so snotty?

She gave him another tug. "C'mon, Ricky."

"You kids have fun," Ricky said over his shoulder as the two of them walked away.

Amelia stepped forward, as if to follow. "We shouldn't let them out of our sight, you know."

I didn't move. "I'm sick of being my sister's babysitter."

"You don't think she'll wander off to someplace secluded with him, do you?"

"No. Besides, we won't be staying much past dark. My mother says that's when all the lowlife come out."

"Well, then, let's go on some rides."

I bit my lip and let out a sigh. "Okay."

Amelia smiled. All at once, I couldn't believe I was standing in the middle of the carnival with the prettiest girl I knew.

Chapter 27

As I tug my comical socks onto my feet and button up my vest over my bare chest, I can't help thinking of Lenny. I'll never fill out my vest quite like he wore his, at least in the formidable way I remember him. No one messed with Lenny. He could be so intimidating but was always for the underdog. Maybe it was my personal run-ins with bullies that made me want to emulate Lenny—not necessarily his ability to intimidate, but rather his desire to defend and assist.

The happenings of that night at the carnival gave momentum to so many events that had already been set in motion, but the most profound for me as an impressionable adolescent was the way Lenny defended Christopher—even the way I perceived Christopher's disability. Sure, the carnie had let him on the ride after Lenny put the 'heavy hand' on him, but Lenny couldn't always rush to Christopher's side.

I knew Christopher was disabled from the moment I had laid eyes on him, but it didn't take long for me to overlook his limitations and view him as plain old Christopher, especially when it was only the two of us hanging out. Yet, I had no idea what it was like for him in the real world outside of Rockette Lake.

Now, with all the legislation for disabled and handicap access, people tend to take for granted things like restrooms with wide doors and stalls, and handicap parking. Today, a carnie would think twice before denying access to a disabled patron for fear of a lawsuit, but for years, Christopher had been the victim of a lot of ignorance, insensitivity, and downright stupidity. Worse yet, people in general tended to dismiss him. Even Penny—one of the most fair-minded and progressive people I knew back then—didn't view Christopher as a viable romantic interest. Why couldn't people see beyond his broken parts? Maybe that's why I connected with him. Beneath the surface, emotionally I was as much a part of the Odd Squad as he was physically.

That evening, when I said goodbye to him, I promised him—and myself—that I wouldn't lose track of him. In fact, I didn't. During those first few years after that summer, when I tried so hard to disconnect from my past, he was the one person, aside from Penny, who I kept close and confided in—albeit through letter writing at first. We ended up rooming together at MIT and shared an apartment right up until his wedding. Of course, I was his best man. He would have been mine, too, if my engagement hadn't fallen apart.

FOR THE NEXT COUPLE OF HOURS, I SPOTTED Ricky and Penny at some booths and rides. To my relief, neither of them clung to the other or held hands or anything. Even though I had also been keeping an eye out for Mom and the boys, I didn't notice when they came up behind us.

Frankie poked me in the back. "Hey, Ben, look what I won!"

I inspected the unopened Lunar Launcher package, too big for Frankie to have swiped it. "Pretty nice."

"See," he pointed at the red, blue, and green disks, "these go on the shooter and they fly!"

"You and Skippy will have a lot of fun losing those."

Mom folded her arms and looked Amelia up and down.

Amelia smiled. "Hello, Mrs. Hughes."

"Hello, Amy."

"We just ran into each other," I said, glad that we hadn't been caught holding hands.

Mom looked around. "And where is your sister?"

"She went off with Amelia's stepbrother, Ricky."

"She what?"

Right then, Penny and Ricky came into view over her

shoulder. I pointed. Mom turned, cocked her head and when she looked back at me, a smile had replaced her frown. "Well, he looks like a very nice young man."

I wanted to burst out laughing. "Yeah—well, we're going on the rollercoaster now." I picked that ride so Mom wouldn't pawn Frankie off on me. He hated the rollercoaster worse than riding in a boat.

Mom eyed Amelia once more. "Okay, well, don't lose track of time."

I refrained from rolling my eyes and walked away with Amelia close at my side.

She kicked a paper cup in her path. "Your mother hates my guts."

"She doesn't hate you, she just hates your—you know—that you look older than you are."

"That's not fair."

"Yeah, well, she's really into appearances."

"You mean she's shallow."

"I don't know—I guess."

"Then, how come you're not?"

I shrugged. "Sometimes I am pretty shallow." I thought back to how I had treated Dora a few weeks ago. "But at least I know it and I'm working on it."

"Well, I don't think you're shallow. I think there's lots more to you than people see."

"That's true of everybody, right? I mean, even psycho killers might look perfectly nice on the outside."

Our lighthearted laughter trailed to a nervous chuckle when we both realized what a disturbing notion that was.

Amelia looked around. "Where do you suppose Ricky and Penny are, anyway?"

"I don't know. Let's check out the rollercoaster—maybe they are over that way."

As we arrived at the end of the line, Christopher approached with a parent at each side. His dad's hand rested on his shoulder.

Christopher gestured, "Consider yourself officially introduced to the Cunninghams—my parents."

Christopher had his dad's hair and forehead, and his mom's eyes and smile. I shook hands with both of them and so did Amelia.

"You planning on getting on the roller coaster?" I asked.

"And sit in other people's vomit? No way!"

"Suit yourself." I laughed because he laughed, but I had a hunch he would liked to have gone on the ride, but either his parents didn't want him to, or he had already suffered enough humiliation for one evening.

"We're headed back to Connecticut, but I wanted to make sure you have my address." From beside him, he pulled a hardcover book with a piece of paper tucked between pages.

"What's this?"

"What does it look like?"

I read the cover, "Frankenstein? Is this so I can further my research on replacement parts?"

"Ha!"

"And I didn't get you anything."

"What! No troll doll?"

"Sorry."

"Just make sure you write—I've got some more book recommendations."

"I will," I said, even though I had never been much of a letter writer.

Christopher's parents wheeled him away. He didn't look back, but I couldn't take my eyes off them until they disappeared into the crowd.

Amelia slipped her hand in mine. "You're really going to miss him."

I nodded. It was strange how I had connected with Christopher after having spent only a few hours with him. Maybe it was just a want—a wish that I was more like him, as unaware of my shortcomings and limitations as he was of his own.

Amelia and I didn't talk about much of anything as our car clicked up to the top of the rail. When it let loose, she screamed the whole way down and around, laughing and raising her hands overhead. I wished I could yell out the way she did, without something inside holding me back. It was that same reservation I always felt when watching fireworks. Christopher wouldn't have let anything hold him back—he would have been hollering the entire time.

Amelia and I ended up riding the rollercoaster twice, and the Turkish Twister. I scored her a stuffed kitten at the ball toss. The guy tried to get rid of another ape, but she traded it for a small white kitten made from rabbit fur.

"It will always remind me of you," she said, giving it an affectionate hug.

"But you don't like stuffed animals."

"I can make an exception."

As we shared some popcorn, Candace and Percy walked past with Lenny and Sunshine. They paused.

"Hey, Fixer-man." Lenny winked at me. "You two having a good time?"

"Yeah."

"Is Ricky leaving you alone?"

"More or less."

"Well, don't worry—" he took a drag from a normal cigarette. "We've got our eye on him."

I took consolation in that, for Penny's sake, and nodded as they moved along.

Amelia asked, "What is Lenny, your personal bodyguard or something?"

"I don't know. I think he just really doesn't like Ricky."

"Well, I know that's true. And neither does Sunshine."

I gulped down the rest of my soda. "What about Doc?"

"He hasn't said anything about Ricky." She sipped her drink.

How much had she talked with anyone about that night? "Hey, Amelia?"

"What?"

"Does Sunshine know Ricky tried to kiss you?"

"I don't think she saw, and I didn't say anything ...." Her eyes shifted. "Could we not talk about that?"

"Sure. Sorry."

"It's just that it's *so* embarrassing."

"I promise I won't bring it up again."

I tossed my cup into a trashcan as we walked by, wishing I hadn't drunk anything. In the last five minutes, my bladder had gone from feeling fine to making me want to cross my legs. I surveyed the perimeter of the crowd, looking for the blue towers—I hated porta potties. "Listen, I really gotta use the john. Would you hang on to my book?"

"Okay. I'll wait right here."

I left Amelia at the corner of a tent. Peeing was a natural body function, but it was embarrassing at the same time. I hoped she wasn't watching me walk away. As I grabbed the door handle and held my breath, I looked over my shoulder. Penny and Ricky had joined Amelia. I guessed she would be okay. I stepped inside, unzipped, and peed as fast as I could. Even without breathing, the stench made me want to barf. Still holding my breath, I zipped up, shoved the door open, and finally inhaled to the sight of Ricky standing in front of me.

"Jeeze, Benny, did you leave that stink?"

"Screw you," I said. As I walked past, he laughed. Made me want to use real swear words. I no sooner heard the door shut and lock behind him when Lenny and Percy came out of nowhere. Faster than I could put together what was happening, each stood on one side of the porta john and started rocking it. Ricky hollered, cussing his head off as it tipped back and forth a few inches off the ground. Amelia came to my side, her mouth covered and eyes

225

wide. I could hardly believe it either. As quickly as it had begun, they quit and ran away, holding their stomachs and laughing. When the door flung open, Ricky wasn't completely covered in crap, the way I had imagined, but enough of it has spotted his Bermuda shorts and polo shirt that it had surely spattered his legs and loafers, too. As soon as he stepped out, his eyes landed on me. I grabbed Amelia's hand, backed off, and then ran. Neither of us could hold back our laughter.

Hiding behind one of the booths, I bent, gripping my knees and trying to catch my breath.

"Did you see the look—" Amelia said between gasps as she hugged my book, "—on his face?"

"Oh man! He looked right at me." I panted. "Not good." I sure hoped he realized I wasn't strong enough to tip the john—that it wasn't me. My next thought was my sister. "Where's Penny?"

"She missed it all—said it was nine o'clock and time to go."

"Oh crap!" I looked at my watch. "I'm late. Give me my book—I've gotta go."

I was about to take off when Amelia grabbed my hand, yanked me back and gave me a huge kiss. "Thanks for the kitten, *Benjamin*."

Her fingers trailed from mine as I glanced back and smiled. "Bye, *Amelia* …."

Looking both ways, I trotted over to the entrance where Mom, Penny, and the boys waited. "Sorry Mom. I had to pee really bad."

"Well, alright," she said.

Penny stared off, distant and dreamy, clutching her ape and a paper sack. She seemed oblivious to the porta-potty incident.

"What's in the bag?" I asked, as we walked to the parking field beside Garver's. Penny began to open it when Mom interrupted.

"I'm going into the store to call your father. You kids go get in the car and wait."

Penny rolled her eyes as Mom split off. "Hurry up and wait—that's Mom for ya'."

I nudged my sister as we approached the car. "So, show me."

"Oh, yeah." Penny dug into the bag and pulled out some gauzy fabric that I recognized from one of the racks. "A skirt like Sunshine's."

"Wow, where'd you get the money for that?"

Frankie and Skip piled into the back seat of the Galaxie, leaving the door wide open.

"Ricky bought it for me. And—" she pulled out another wad of fabric, "—a matching top."

"Are you kidding me?"

"What's wrong with that?"

I shut the car door to give us some privacy. "Penny, Ricky's not what he appears to be."

"Oh, Ben, he told me you'd say that. He also told me that he accidentally ran over your bicycle and you'd probably still be mad at him."

"What?"

"I know, it's kind of embarrassing, but you really shouldn't have left it in the middle of the driveway. Sometimes you're so absentminded when you're around Amy."

"I did not leave it in the middle of the driveway! He backed over it on purpose."

"Honestly, Ben. Why on earth would he do that?"

"Because I caught him trying to kiss Amelia."

She sighed. "He told me all about that, too. How Amy got drunk and threw herself at him—I mean, really, Ben. I saw her passed out at the party myself. Remember? You were sitting right there next to her."

My mouth dropped open and before I could do more than let out a huff, she continued, "Seriously, Ben, Ricky has every right to be mad at you for making him fall in the water, but he's not mad at all. He likes you in spite of it. He thinks it's sweet that you're so protective of his baby sister. And I have to tell you, I was a little embarrassed by your behavior tonight. Ricky was no less than a gentleman this evening—and I mean *all* evening—he couldn't have been more respectful and kind to me. And you acted like— well, like a miserable brat. You should be ashamed of yourself. I'm not saying that to be mean, but you embarrassed me tonight."

With that, she climbed into the front passenger seat and shut the door.

Oh my gosh! When had my sister turned into Mom? I was so mad and my heart was beating so fast that I wanted to scream, but the knot in my throat wouldn't let me. How could Penny have been so taken in by Ricky? I paced behind the tailgate, trying to calm down.

In the distance, but not so far that I couldn't see the whites of his eyes, Ricky walked to his car, peeling off his shirt. Bare chested, his muscles flexed as his gaze kept fixed on mine. Standing at the rear bumper of his dad's Mercedes, he stripped to his underwear, wadded his clothes into a ball, and tossed them into the trunk. He slammed it shut, flipped me the bird, and climbed into the front seat.

I glanced at Penny in our wagon. Her head tipped back as if she was dreaming, completely unaware as the Mercedes drove off, right as Mom came around the corner from Garver's. She tucked a small envelope in her purse and blotted her eyes.

"Good news," she said as she approached, carrying a tall paper sack. Her lips trembled as they formed a thin smile. "Your father is coming up early. On Thursday afternoon. Isn't that nice, Ben?"

"Yeah. That's great." *Just great.*

CHAPTER 28

SPAM HAS A VERY DISTINCT AROMA. AS I squeeze yellow mustard from the condiment packet and smear it over a slab, it evokes some memory that catches and then slips away, like a fish that nibbles but doesn't snag—like a gag reflex that subsides. It's something from a long time ago—maybe from the last time I smelled or ate it. I didn't eat any Spam all through college, and my aunt never served it. She had a freezer full of homegrown beef, pork, and chicken—no need for store-bought meat. Likely, I ate my last Spam meal during those few days after the carnival—when it rained nonstop for three days straight.

My upset stomach hasn't improved, yet I go ahead and flop a slice of Wonder bread over the compressed-meat-substance. I sniff it again and then hold my breath before taking a bite. I chew, stretching back in my chair at the kitchen table. It's not bad. But as I swallow, my stomach doesn't agree.

As I massage my belly, a gust blows the door wide open. I rise to shut it and the sky opens up, spraying water sideways onto the front stoop. Off in the distance, thunder rumbles. Heavy drops pelt the screen over the sink as I shut the window and the door, and return to my seat. A vague memory surfaces again; this time it snags.

I bite off, chew, and swallow a second mouthful and wait for the memory to congeal. Nothing. I take another bite, chew a few times, and it reminds me of Monopoly, of all things. Now it's coming back. Spam, Monopoly, and Frankie.

AFTER THE CARNIVAL, NOT ONLY DID IT RAIN for three days, but Mom didn't come out of her room. I didn't see a whole lot of Penny, either. That meant I got stuck minding Frankie during those few days while it poured and poured and poured.

It seemed that every summer there was at least one week when rain kept us stuck inside, listening to it patter, hoping it might let up. It always turned into a two-or-three-day-long Monopoly game, and Spam for lunch and supper. At least this time the rain didn't coincide with one of Dad's weeks at camp. It was bad enough that it sent Mom to her room, but Dad would have turned as foul as the weather, pacing from upstairs to the basement and back up again.

During those days after the carnival, Mom's mood lasted a lot longer than usual. At first, I thought she might be sick, but she didn't cough or sneeze or sound congested as if she had a cold. And she didn't rush to the bathroom to puke or ask for the antacid like she would have if it were a stomach flu. I thought maybe it was a hangover, but as far as I knew, she hadn't been to the kitchen for lemonade or a Coke.

When I hadn't seen her for an entire day, I tapped her door. She didn't respond, so I cracked it open. Mom hollered and told me to get out. I sure didn't need to be told twice. It wasn't as if that had never happened before— the really bad mood and the yelling, that is. It just hadn't occurred yet at camp this summer. Dad had said it was her nerves, and after she had gone to the doctor that one time, she hadn't had a "nerve attack" for a couple of years. I had almost forgotten about them.

After she had shrieked at me, I wasn't going to push it and ask for permission to light a fire in the fireplace. She had appointed me the de facto decision maker and I would start a fire if I wanted. Within a few hours, a warm glow heated the concrete and dried the mustiness to a comfortable level. Outside, a stream of water dripped from the overhang above the back door.

Frankie wiped his nose as we leaned over the Monopoly board. I rolled the dice and moved my boot five squares, landing on his property. Pennsylvania Avenue, with a hotel. $1400. I doled out the rent as he bounced up and down, giggling like a girl. Maybe it was because I had the feeling he had been cheating all along, or I would have rather been out rowing around the lake looking for Amelia, or riding my bike if it wasn't all busted up, or the fact that Penny had been ignoring me, but Frankie's nose picking and giggling grated on my nerves more than usual. And if it wasn't that, it was his whining. Then, when I turned my back on him to add another log to the fire, I returned to a much thinner stack of blue fifties. To make it worse, he had just landed on Chance, right before Park Place, drawing the card *Take a ride on the Reading—If you pass Go collect $200*—though I could have sworn that card had been drawn an hour ago. I'd had enough Monopoly!

"You little cheat!" I said, my frustration rising from a place so deep it came up and overtook me faster than I could get it under control.

"I am not. You're just a sore loser."

"Is that right? I'll show you a sore loser." I flipped the board and all its contents onto Frankie's lap. With that, he broke out in a squeal, rising in pitch as he ran for the stairs, drawing out "Mom" into ten syllables.

Great. Halfway up the stairs, I caught up with him and grabbed his arm, which sent him to his knees and amplified his cry.

"I'm sorry, Frankie, I didn't mean it. Just calm down."

"Stop pinching me!" he squealed louder.

"I wasn't pinching you." I threw my hands up as he tore his way into the kitchen. I blew out a long breath as his footsteps clopped overhead, all the way to Mom's room. Through his sobs, he spewed accusations of cruelty and violence as I waited for the inevitable.

Mom screeched, "Ben!"

I lugged myself upstairs as Frankie emerged from

Mom's room, snuffling loudly. He rubbed his eyes and smirked, a little too much like Ricky.

"Ben!" Mom hollered again. I stood in her dark doorway. The shades in her room were drawn and it smelled like unchanged sheets and BO mixed with hairspray and maybe liquor. I didn't get a real good look, but her hair stuck out in all directions as if it hadn't seen a comb or brush in days. Her eyes sank into dark circles. She looked like a madwoman on *Creature Features*. I wasn't sure how long she ranted, but after the first round of "selfish, inconsiderate, irresponsible, girl-crazy, cruel, unfeeling, no-good, six-years-older-for-god's-sake" and back to "selfish," I tuned her out. "Now, you go apologize to him, right now! And shut the door on your way out!"

I backed away, closing her door as quietly as I could. When I turned, Penny stood in her doorway, her expression blank.

"What on earth?" she said, as bewildered and perplexed as I must have looked.

I choked back the emotion churning, or maybe it was my Spam sandwich threatening to come back up. "She's in one of her moods."

"Oh God, no. Not now."

"She'll snap out of it."

"I wish Dad was here."

For the first time, I did too.

Penny followed me to the sink. As I filled a cup of water and then drank, she peeked in Mom's paper sack from Garver's, still sitting on the counter.

"It's full," she said and moved to the cupboard beside the refrigerator where Mom kept her stash. A nearly empty bottle sat on the top shelf. "She hasn't been drinking—unless she has a bottle in her room. Did she smell like liquor?"

"How should I know? She just smelled bad."

"Okay, well, we need to keep her calm. You need to go back downstairs and make nice with Frankie. Do you think you can keep from getting him wound up?"

"I wouldn't have gotten him *wound up* if I hadn't gotten stuck with him all by myself for the past three days."

She looked away. "Sorry—I guess I've just been in a mood of my own. I got my, you know—my time of the month."

"Maybe that's what Mom's got."

"Maybe."

"Is that why it seems like you hate my guts these days?"

"I don't *hate* your guts. I just ... I don't know. Everything gets so confusing. I can't even explain it."

"You're not going to wig out like Mom, are you?"

"No. You just don't understand what it's like to be a woman."

"Does this have something to do with hormones and—*guys*?"

"Don't start in on Ricky again. He's really nice and you shouldn't be so intolerant of people you don't know."

I didn't want her to turn on me again, but I had to at least say, "Just be careful around him."

"Don't worry about your big sister, Benjie." She patted my shoulder. "Come on, I'll play cards with you and Frankie for a few hours, okay?"

In the basement, Frankie's face showed none of the telltale red or puffiness of someone who had actually been crying. As Penny dealt a round of *Authors* card game, he poked at the fire with a long stick and then blew on its glowing tip. I grabbed it from him, pushing him away. "What are you trying to do—burn down the house?"

"Why would I want to do that? This place isn't worth anything if it's burnt down."

I wondered if he had ever heard of fire insurance. I didn't know if my parents insured the place, but if they did, Frankie was the last person I would tell. He would probably turn out to be a pyromaniac in addition to a klepto.

Chapter 29

THE FALLING RAIN LULLS ME INTO A STUPOR. I belch up Spam. I knew I would regret eating. And I would have preferred not to remember that episode, either. I glance at the clock—9:59. It feels like 11:00 or later, and I wish it were. My day is catching up with me, and my eyes don't want to stay open. I rise from the table and stretch.

The wind has died and rain patters the roof in a gentle, steady rhythm. I crack the front door, letting in a fresh breeze. Clean air fills my lungs. Thunder rumbles in the distance. In all likelihood, the storm will roll around again.

That's what Mom was like; a storm that always rolled back around. It was only a matter of time. Penny and I had both seen her in bad moods, but we had always assumed she would snap out of them eventually, and she had, as far as we could tell. But who really knew what was going on in her mind? I don't think either of us comprehended the extent of her mental illness. In fact, I don't think we even comprehended the concept of mental illness.

Dora was mentally handicapped—we understood that meant she had mental limitations, something she was born with like a clubfoot, except it was her brain that didn't work quite right. But she was harmless and sweet and predictable. Before that summer, I'm not sure I had ever heard the term 'mentally ill' in a clinical sense. But I had heard of psychos, lunatics and schizos—those were the crazies in the loony bin. I had no idea how people ended up in the psyche ward or institution, but they were scary places with padded cells and straitjackets, hiding behind names like Meadow Brook Acres or Oak Hill Haven.

BY TUESDAY NIGHT, THE WEATHER BROKE. First thing on Wednesday morning, I went for a swim, which meant that if Mom didn't get out of bed again, Penny would get stuck with Frankie for the morning. Or maybe he would go and play at Skip's.

Humidity coated everything. The planks on our dock swelled with rainwater, black and slippery underfoot as I walked to the end. Even as I took in a lungful of air before diving, it felt like nine-parts water to one-part oxygen. I hardly noticed the difference in atmosphere when I hit water. Swimming circles deep into the cove, water washed over every fine hair on my body. Damselflies and pond skaters skimmed the water's surface. All the tension of the past few weeks dissolved into the lake.

Sometimes, it felt so good to be alive—to be a kid on summer vacation with nothing like homework or teachers or school bullies looming over me. Even if my life wasn't perfect, being a kid was great. And even better, I was a kid with a girl who not only liked me, but who liked to kiss.

While thinking of Amelia, I made another pass near Whispering Narrows and spotted her coming out onto the lawn, still in pajamas—the same ones she had been embarrassed for me to see her in a few weeks ago. She waved and I swam to meet her at the end of the dock. She sat, arms folded across her chest. I propelled my way over to the hidden side of the dock and braced my arms on the planks, like last time.

She hugged her knees. "How's it going?"

I rolled my eyes. Part of me wanted to tell her all about what a crummy few days I'd had, but I didn't want to dive into a conversation about how weird my mother was, or that I still couldn't make Penny believe me about Ricky. I wanted to hear about Amelia.

"I guess it's going pretty good," I said, "now that it's not raining. How's it going with you?"

She shrugged. "I'm okay, now that Ricky is gone. He left on Sunday morning. Unfortunately, he's coming back this afternoon." Maybe that explained why Penny didn't bother leaving the house this morning. Amelia continued, "And Sunshine and Lenny are making plans to go to that Woodstock Love-In this weekend. Sunshine's got her, you know—period, so she doesn't want to be there the whole time, so Grandpa's flying her over on Sunday. Lenny's driving the rest of them over tomorrow morning, at the crack of dawn, to get good seats or something."

"So much for my bodyguard," I chuckled.

"So, did you talk to Penny?"

"Yeah. Ricky's pretty sly—he's making like everything was all our fault, and Penny believed it. She thinks I'm being overprotective."

Just then, Doc's voice rumbled down the lawn, reverberated across the water, and rolled back. "Amelia! Breakfast!"

Amelia stood. "I gotta go."

"Hey, do you want to go for another boat ride tonight? Ten?"

She smiled. "Yeah."

I pushed away from the dock as Amelia wiggled her way up the lawn.

I swam a little longer, putting off my hunger, but if I wanted any of the remaining Frosted Flakes, I had to beat Penny to the table, which I did.

When I was halfway through my bowl of cereal, down to the sweet milk and a few soggy flakes, Penny came out of her room and joined me at the table. She shook the box and frowned at me. "Hog."

"There's Rice Krispies."

She rolled her eyes, disappeared behind me, and returned with the new cereal box, prying the top open.

"Mom still asleep?" I asked.

"I think so, I mean, I haven't seen her yet."

"What about Frankie?"

At that moment, he came out of our room, yawning. "Hey, Ben, Mom says you have to help me strap my sleeping bag on my bike and ride with me down to Skippy's today. "

I muttered, "I can't. My bike's busted."

"Mom *said*," he whined.

"Fine. I'll walk you down." I glanced at my sister stuffing spoonful after spoonful in her mouth. "What are you doing today?"

"I might ride my bike later. Too bad you can't come with—you know on account of it being all busted."

I didn't want to get into the reason *why* it was all busted; that would just bring up the subject we couldn't talk about without me seeming like an overprotective, jerky little brother. I continued eating in silence, thinking about what a great evening I had planned with Amelia. Nobody's bad mood was going to interfere with that.

By midmorning, Penny had already left on her bike, and I escaped to the end of the dock for some alone time with my *MAD* magazine. Even though I had to fend off a new hatch of pterodactyl-size mosquitoes, I didn't mind. Any encounter with the lake's 'wildlife' was a welcome change after three days of Frankie duty. Besides, from where I sat, I could also keep an eye out for Amelia between the stimulating and mind-broadening encounters of *Spy vs. Spy*.

In the middle of black powder and kabooms, Frankie called out, "Ben, I'm ready."

I stood and stuffed the magazine in my pocket. Frankie struggled with his sleeping bag and a paper sack full of clothes. He was such a pathetic, wheezing little spaz. How could I have wanted to choke the life out of him only twenty-four hours ago? Poor kid. As brazen as he could be about thieving, he was a bundle of fears—that and boogers.

I grabbed the bag so he wouldn't drop it. "Looks like you packed for a week."

"Only two nights."

I looked at him behind me as we walked up the outside stairway to the dooryard. "You gonna be okay, away for two whole nights?"

"Yeah. I'm not a baby, you know. I haven't peed the bed in a long time."

"Yeah, I know." At least not since we had been at camp as far as I knew, but our room was beginning to smell a little funky. I flopped his bedroll onto the rack. "Just make sure you use tissue and not your finger, okay? Or else Skippy's mom won't invite you back."

He tugged a wad of toilet paper from his pocket.

"Good." I fastened the strap. "You know Dad's coming up to camp tomorrow?"

He shrugged. "Yeah?"

"Just thought you might miss him."

He shrugged again. "So?"

"I'm just saying, is all." I tucked his overnight bag into the front basket. "C'mon. Let's get going."

He mounted his bike, wobbled over to the road and took a left turn. A few feet down the road at the bend, he waited until I caught up.

"Keep riding," I said. "You have a quarter-mile stretch ahead. Skippy's house is before the next turn. You know their car, right?"

"Yeah."

"I'll keep walking till you get there."

As soon as Frankie skid to a halt at Skip's driveway, he waved. One less complication to my day, and for the next two days.

The rest of the afternoon would have gone pretty well if at 3:30 I hadn't gone into the house for a snack. Avoiding the last can of Spam, I smeared some Marshmallow Fluff on a slice of bread and was about to take it outside, when

Mom came out of her room. I cringed as I looked up, expecting the worst.

She smiled. Now her hair, even though greasy looking, lay flat and smooth under her headband. She hummed her way over to the sink as if she had been behaving as normal as ever for the last three days.

She poured a glass of plain lemonade and asked, "Where's your sister?"

"She went for a bike ride."

"Well, would you please go find her and tell her it's time to come and help with supper?"

Supper? Now we were going to eat supper together? "What are we having?"

"Oh, never you mind," she said, chipper as could be. "Just go get your sister."

I stared at her for a moment as she continued smiling, her bright pink lipstick a little off its mark. She smoothed her hair.

"Okay, Mom. But it might take a little while to catch up with her."

"That's fine, Benjie. Now run along."

I stepped outside, taking a bite of my sandwich and scratching my head. Maybe Mom wanted me out of the house so she could spike her lemonade. Without my bike, the three-quarter-mile walk to the beach would take forever, but at least I might see Amelia or Sunshine at Whispering Narrows.

On my way downhill, I thought about tonight, about me and Amelia on the island. About what a great time it was going to be. The closer I came to Doc's place, the more my imaginings turned into cautious glances and hoping the Mercedes—Ricky—had not yet arrived. To my relief, only the Jag and Lenny's ride sat in the driveway. Candace came from a door beside the garage, carrying a couple sleeping bags. When she saw me, she waved. I guessed she was packing up for the big love-fest.

Now that I was in the clear, I started a slow run for the beach. I barely had a chance to work up a sweat before a car came up from behind. I recognized the sound of the black Eldorado I had met up with a few weeks ago. Its grill and hood came into view, and then the whitewalls. It slowed as the automatic window rolled down.

Swerving Irving leaned over the passenger seat. "Hey! How ya' doin', kid?"

I paused and bent to look in. Candy-red interior. "Good, Mr. Irving."

"Just plain Irving," he corrected as his cigarette smoldered. "Hey, where's your bike today?"

"It had an accident."

"Oh, that's a real shame—she was a cherry." He took a drag off his cigarette.

"Yeah. I can probably fix it when I get home."

"Where ya' headed?"

"Down to the beach."

"Well, I'm going right past there," he said in a puff of smoke. "Why don't you hop in and I'll give you a lift."

The door swung open.

"Sure. Thanks, Irving." I climbed in, scooting onto the seat. "Wow." The dashboard looked like the Cessna control panel. "This is really boss."

"You like Caddies, do ya'?"

"Yes, sir." I chuckled. "Right now, I like pretty much anything mechanical, but this is sweet." I stroked the red leather.

He smiled, a gold tooth glinting. "A clever boy like you will have cars like this and better when you grow up, I bet."

"I wish."

"What'cha gotta do is stay away from fast women and vices—" he nodded at the cigarette butt he held up, and then flicked it out his window. "They'll squander your money faster than anything."

"Yes, sir."

In a few seconds, he pulled up and stopped beside the beach parking lot. "Well, here we are."

"Thanks." I let myself out, shut the door, and leaned back in. "I appreciate the ride."

"No problem." He put the car in gear and then paused. "Oh, hey, when's your dad coming up again?"

"Actually, he's coming tomorrow afternoon. You should stop by."

"I just might do that!" He smiled and then drove away.

If I hadn't been so taken with the Cadillac emblem centered on the broad rear trunk between two slender vertical taillights, I would have noticed the Mercedes, sooner.

Chapter 30

BESIDE MY HALF-EATEN SANDWICH, THE small jar of Marshmallow Fluff remains unopened. On an impulse, I unscrew the red top and give it a quick whiff. After the visceral reaction I had to Spam, I would have thought the sweetness of Fluff might smell good, at least benign. Instead, the mingling aromas turn my stomach. Now the mere sight of the blue and white label makes me queasy. I tighten the lid back on and set the container in the sink.

I turn to my memorabilia sprawled across the table. An unused carnival ticket, a heap of papers, a radio, a faded old Polaroid—and a card. While I'm tempted to spread out my bedding here on the floor and rest my eyes and maybe doze, I reach for Sunshine's note, instead.

… I hope Penny is doing better ….

I stroke the painted daisy. How had I, in the course of a few weeks, lost my sister? Not only had I lost track of her, but I think *she* lost track of her, too. I got my first real sense of that on the night of the carnival and over the course of the next few days, but it really struck me that afternoon when I went to look for her at the beach, after my ride in the Eldorado.

A LOT OF THINGS SEEMED OFF THAT DAY; Mom's mood, and even Frankie's—the fact that he was staying over at Skip's when he knew Dad was coming up. Then there was my ride in the Eldorado—I mean, it wasn't as if Irving had tried anything weird, but now that I thought about having climbed in a car with a virtual stranger—it creeped me out. What if he had been a molester? And to top it off, some other guy sat in Percy's lifeguard stand. Maybe Percy had quit and planned to go off to Woodstock with Candace and Lenny.

Worse still, when I looked for Penny's bike on the rack in front of the split-rail fence, it wasn't there. The only other bike rack sat far across the lot, over in front of the spooky picnic area. Sure enough, her blue Schwinn stood alone—but for a silver Mercedes.

Penny had always said that creeps hung out over there—pervs. I guess she was right; not that my sister was a perv, but sitting right next to her was Ricky. As far as I could tell, neither of them had noticed me yet. Ricky lit a cigarette, took a long drag, and then passed it to Penny. I had seen enough of those cigarettes—joints—to recognize how they differed from Pall Malls or Marlboros. People who smoked joints didn't wedge it between their fingers, waving it around nonchalantly as they talked, but they always pinched it with its glowing end hidden in their palm. Until that day, I had assumed only hippies smoked weed.

I walked closer to the picnic-area bike rack, hoping Penny would spot me sooner than later, but she had her back to me as she faced Ricky. It was he who spotted me first. I forced myself to keep moving ahead, though I didn't know what I would do if I ended up standing right in front of them. Ricky stared at me, took another long suck, passed the joint to Penny and exhaled as she looked over her shoulder at me. I stopped walking and waited. She took another puff and said a few words to Ricky before she stood. She smiled as she made her way past the divider fence toward me as I neared the bike stand.

She folded her arms, standing in front of me with a condescending tilt to her head. "What, Ben?"

"Mom wants you home to help with supper."

"You can't be serious."

"I am serious."

She glanced over her shoulder and back to me. "Just tell her I'm not hungry."

"*You* tell her you're not hungry."

She waited a few seconds as if hoping I would reconsider. When I didn't, her tone changed from flippant to concerned. "Is she out of her room?"

"Yes. And she's acting weirder than usual."

She clicked her tongue and rolled her eyes. "Hitting the bottle again."

"I don't know, Penny. She hasn't even put away the last bottle she bought. I think you should come home. She's going to be really upset if you don't."

"Fine," she sighed, more sympathetic than irritated. "Wait here a sec."

I had a good mind to start walking but I wanted to make sure she would follow through. Ricky remained sitting on the tabletop as she walked over and stood before him, swaying as she talked. He said a few words. She giggled. He said something else and then she leaned forward and kissed him. I wanted to barf. How could my sister like him, let alone kiss him?

As she strode over to the bike rack, he smirked at me, licking his lips. Now I really wanted to puke.

Penny yanked her bike from the slot and mounted it. "Do you want a ride on my handle bars?"

"Yeah, right," I said with disgust.

"Suit yourself." She flung her hair back and took off. I followed, glancing behind at Ricky who hadn't taken his eyes off me. I picked up my pace; the last thing I needed to top off my afternoon was another run-in with the Mercedes.

I lost track of Penny as she cycled her way around a bend where the road forked at the gigantic boulder. I needed to do something about Penny and Ricky. I had to convince her of how evil he was. My anxiety drove me forward. I picked up my pace and started to jog, but by the time I reached the sign, Swaying Pines—Private Drive, I was winded. Up the road, Whispering Narrows' roof poked above distant treetops, but Penny had disappeared. Perhaps she had already made it to camp. As I reached the first stone pillar marking Doc's driveway, I heard girls' voices, but not until I approached the second pillar did I see Penny behind it. She straddled her bike, gripping the handlebar as she talked with Candace.

"Okay, bye," Penny smiled and waved as she pulled away, "Have fun!"

I caught up to her and asked, "What was that about?"

Penny came off her bike to walk it up the hill.

"Oh, Candace just wanted to apologize about the thing with Percy. She really feels bad that I might have gotten my feelings hurt." She sighed, short of breath as the incline steepened. "I told her I was over it."

Should I try to say something about Ricky? About how she needed to get over him, too? I was just about to open my mouth when she cut in. "Candace really is pretty nice."

"Yeah," I said. Although I didn't consider Candace a good influence, I was more concerned about Ricky.

"She even invited me to go along with them tomorrow morning, if I wanted."

"To the music thing?"

"Yeah." She let out another sigh, dreamily rolling her eyes, clear to the back of her head. "Oh, how I wish I could."

"Yeah, well, you can't."

"As if I didn't know."

I kicked a stone in our path. "So do you still want to be a hippie or do you want to be with Ricky?"

"What are you even talking about?"

"Ricky hates hippies."

She huffed. "He does not. He has never said an unkind word about anyone. And he's never been anything less than a gentleman with me."

245

"You've gotta be kidding me."

She quit walking and stared me down. "Ben. You are obviously too young to understand these things, and I know it's hard to see your sister spending time with someone besides you ... but that's part of growing up. You'll get over it."

"I'm *already* over it," I said as we walked the rest of the way in silence. How did she always manage to turn everything around and make me seem like the immature jerk who didn't understand the grown-up world?

When we reached the dooryard, she leaned her bike against a tree near the cottage and asked, "What's for supper, anyway?"

"Beats me," I said with attitude. "The cabinets are getting pretty bare. I think there's only a can of Spam and some other crap."

She stepped onto the front stoop. "*Great.* Hopefully Dad will pick up some groceries on his way up tomorrow afternoon."

She pushed through the front door and I followed.

"Hello, children," Mom sang out, swooping around the table, laying down plate after plate—four in all. She looked like some TV commercial set to music, except for her smeared lipstick. Penny glanced at me. I shrugged.

"What do you want help with, Mom?" Penny stood over the sink, washing her hands as I went to the bathroom.

"Nothing dear. It's all ready."

I listened for conversation as I took care of business and then washed my hands. I heard only the sound of chairs dragging the floor as they took their seats. When I stepped out, Mom sat in her usual place with her back to me. Penny's shoulders stiffened, her eyes wide and mouth agape as she looked at me. I glanced at Mom as I sat, and then noticed what lay on my plate.

"Oh, dear—we forgot to call Frankie in for supper. Would you mind, Benjie?"

246

My stomach tightened. "Mom, Frankie's at Skippy's. Remember?"

Mom twitched. "Of course I remember. He's staying for two nights. Just slipped my mind."

Penny stared at her plate, and then both of us warily set our sights on Mom. She picked up two slabs of Spam, sliced like bread and stacked, with Marshmallow Fluff oozing from between them. Holding it like a sandwich, she took a big bite and chewed.

With her mouth full, she said, "Mmmm. Eat up, children," dipping the Spamwich into her glass of lemonade—like a cookie into milk. Her cheeks bulged as she crammed another bite. Marshmallow syrup seeped from the corner of her mouth. She wiped her chin with the back of her hand.

Penny pushed away from the table, wide eyes filled with horror. "I'm not hungry, Mom."

A wave of nausea turned my stomach. "Me neither." I barely made it to the bathroom in time.

Chapter 31

ALL AT ONCE, MY STOMACH CONTRACTS. I toss the card aside and fling the front door open, pushing through the screen just in time to grab the stoop railing and throw up into the bushes. Rain dripping from the overhang wets the back of my neck. The sight of my mother returns in flashes. With each image, I puke again. Oh God, how did I bury that memory for so long? Combining the sweet, salty, and sour, of Fluff, Spam, and lemonade was revolting enough, but the notion that its abnormality did not register with Mom—that she had checked-out—horrified me. At that moment, I knew my mother had lost it.

Now that I understand the term Borderline Personality Disorder, I can, in hindsight, see the signs, but for the most part, I didn't pick up on her textbook behaviors as they were occurring; they were simply part of our life. Just the same, I had always suspected our home life wasn't normal. I gathered that much from hanging out with my friends. Their mothers weren't moody and didn't have hairy fits. Then again, Mom usually managed to behave normally in front of my friends, and so I assumed that behind the scenes, their mothers probably behaved badly, also. Normal became a relative concept.

The clinical descriptions of Borderline Personality Disorder also cite binge spending and abandonment issues. Sure, there were money disputes that often flared when Mom came home with new shoes and purses ... and there was that fur coat that Dad made her return, the cruise she booked on a whim and had to cancel, not to mention the constant redecorating, including new furniture. But there was always food on the table and a roof overhead, so why would I question the family finances? Besides, I think both Mom and Dad competed for the Poor Money Management Award.

As for abandonment issues—who wouldn't feel abandoned if they had been left up in the boonies with three kids for the entire summer? That aside, Mom never talked much about her childhood. Most of what I know—about her growing up in the Dust Bowl during the depression and being passed around to abusive relatives—I learned from Mom's sister. But even Aunt Wanda didn't like to talk about their miserable childhood.

And then there's a more prominent manifestation of a borderline personality: Promiscuity. I hate to say it about my own mother, but I do believe she slept around. From the parental arguments I had overheard, and my own speculations, I think there were reasons why Dad wanted her up in the sticks, away from her social element. Dad had quit paying for the tennis lessons, and he never liked the milkman or the mailman or the grocer or any other young and good-looking fellow around town. I guess Dad figured that the hick locals like old Earl Garver or even Doc were not her type.

I had always found Mom's flirting embarrassing and hypocritical, especially given the fuss she made about Penny's decorum. I suppose Mom was also the queen of subterfuge. What's the saying—"The lady doth protest too much, methinks."?

Looking back on it, there were a lot of symptoms that fit Mom, but none of that matters at this point. The proof of Mom's illness sat in the dayroom at Pleasant Meadows up until last year. Now she's out of her misery, resting in an urn, buried at Birch Acres cemetery.

If I understand Mom's diagnosis correctly, the actual psychotic break didn't occur until after the Spam episode.

And given the final events of that pivotal week, it's no wonder I recall the milestones and blocked out some of the 'minor' events.

I step inside, my stomach empty. How many more of those small details will come to mind as the night progresses? Do I dare venture into my parents' room? I give it a long stare and blink. As a kid, I rarely went into their room, so I don't know that there's any point to visiting it tonight. Yet the closed door draws me. Perhaps later—right now, I have a more profound, if not bittersweet memory awaiting me.

I glance at the clock, hoping for past-midnight, but it reads only 10:15. By that hour, I had already snuck out of my room that night to pick up Amelia. I recall that both Penny and I turned in early that evening.

PENNY HAD ALREADY EXCUSED HERSELF from the table when I came out of the bathroom, still queasy. Mom had cleared the table, piling the plates—unfinished Spam and all—in the sink, and then returned to her room as if everything were normal. Penny rushed straight to the 'liquor cabinet' and flung it open. The bottle remained undisturbed since we last checked. She looked at me and I shook my head. She said nothing. She simply went to her room and closed the door behind her.

I proceeded to scrape plates into the trash as if they contained something as ordinary as chicken bones and unfinished mashed potatoes or Spaghetti-Os. I then washed and dried the dishes. That would please Mom. When she came out in the morning, she would see how I had cleaned and she would be happy and back to normal. Everything was fine. I was going to see Amelia, build a small fire, maybe steal another kiss, and talk about all kinds of stuff. It was going to be the best night of my almost-fourteen-year-old life. And Mom was going to snap out of it.

After I finished destroying all evidence that anything out of the ordinary had happened at dinner, I roamed our yard, munching down a full packet of Saltines and collected kindling.

Just before ten, I passed Penny's closed door. Her light was out. As I pushed away from the dock, I glanced at her window; her curtain shifted, as if she had been waiting and watching. Did she have sneaking-out plans of her own? I dismissed the thought—and its implication. Nothing was going to interfere with my perfect night.

Fireflies speckled the cove, reflecting on the still water. The heat felt like midday. Humidity diffused Whispering Narrows' yard light and created a halo around each glowing firefly. It was surreal, as if I were entering a fantasy realm. It looked like, well, like fairy dust. I rolled my eyes—what kind of guy thinks about *fairy* dust?

Squinting, I detected movement over at the end of Amelia's dock. When I rowed close enough, she came into full view, hugging the blanket. Tonight, she wore a sleeveless T-shirt and shorts.

"Hi," she whispered as she boarded and then gestured toward the cove. "Look at that ... like fairy dust."

There was no getting around the description. Fireflies surrounded us, continuing to hover—yes, like fairy dust; or diamonds on black satin, or twinkling stars, or any other less-than-manly description.

I smiled, letting the boat drift for a minute, and snatched a fly from the air. It glowed through my closed palm as I held out my fist. She pried my fingers open and blew on the little creature, sending it on its way—yeah, like fairy dust. And then she kissed my palm, and I thought my heart had stopped.

After that, I had a hard time remembering how to row. As soon as we left the cove, the fireflies thinned to an occasional flicker. Now, only the few lights from the perimeter of the lake reflected on the water.

Propelling us away from Whispering Narrows, I headed straight for the island. Neither of us spoke, not even when we had cleared the Narrows, not until I tied off the boat. I climbed out first. "Hand me that bundle of kindling, okay?"

I helped her up and out. Standing in front of me, and without hesitation, she kissed me—but nothing big.

"It's kind of hot for a fire right now," she said, stepping back.

"Yeah, but it's dark. We should at least get it going."

"Okay, but then let's go swimming. I wore my swimsuit under my clothes."

Hoping it was her two-piece, I moved quickly. Within a minute, the twigs ignited and I laid a couple split logs over them. As I crouched by the flickering light, I heard her shorts unzip. I turned as she wiggled out of them, revealing bottoms. With her back to me, she raised her shirt overhead, exposing the swimsuit top. Her hair tumbled down her back. I swallowed hard as she slowly turned. My eyes traveled up her body and I forced them to land on her face as I stood.

"Your turn," she said.

I had difficulty catching my breath. By the time I pulled my T-shirt up and over, she had already moved past me to the water's edge.

She turned halfway around. "Is it okay to dive here?"

"Yeah, it's pretty deep, but dive shallow, just in case."

With that, she sprung into the water, cutting through the dark. This time, I had the good sense to take my watch off before diving in, and stuck it in my shoe. Quick as I could, I followed as Amelia swam a wide loop.

"The water is so warm," she said. "I love it like this."

I caught up. "Yeah, me too—until I hit a pocket of cold."

She swam on her back. I was enjoying that view when she pointed to the sky. "Look! It's cleared off."

I treaded water and took in the view. The humidity had dissolved into a smear of stars overhead. With no moon to outshine them, each star came into focus and sparkled. All sounds of the lake ceased in that moment. We glanced at each other. Her eyes twinkled. "Wow."

The water around us mirrored the black sky. She sighed. "Doesn't it make you feel really small … and insignificant?"

I chuckled—at both the notion and at the 'older' words she used—*insignificant*. "It doesn't take a million stars to make me feel that way."

"You shouldn't feel like that, Benjamin. You are one of the best people I know."

I couldn't think of a response. I wanted to thank her but that seemed too *insignificant*. She swam closer, near enough to study my face. Was she memorizing mine the way I was hers?

She asked, "Do you think it's possible for kids to fall in love?"

"I don't know."

"Romeo and Juliet did, and they were practically kids— he was sixteen and she was only thirteen."

"Yeah, but they were made-up people."

"But don't you ever wonder about falling in love?"

"You mean falling in love? Or—you know—" I was going to say *doing it*, but that sounded so immature.

"You mean sex?"

My face heated as I nodded. "Sure I think about all that. A lot."

"I think I'm going to wait until I get married—like Sunshine."

"You mean she and Lenny don't—you know—"

"No. She's kind of old fashioned, but I think I might be, too."

I hadn't ever thought about if I was old fashioned or not. I just figured that when the right girl and the right time came along, we would just *do it*. As much as I fantasized about sex, I guess Amelia had given it a whole lot more consideration than I had. As we treaded water, she kept staring. I wondered if she had ever thought about me and her—together.

"So, what do you want to be when you grow up?" she asked, squashing my fantasy.

I nodded. "I used to think I wanted to be an astronaut."

"What about now?"

"I'm not sure, but I think I want to design stuff."

"Like an architect?"

"No. More like an inventor."

"You'd be good at that." She swam a circle around me.

I rotated with her. "What about you?"

"I don't know. Sometimes I want to write books, or be an artist, or travel all over the world—like a stewardess. Maybe even learn to fly or … I don't know …."

"How about playing the piano in an orchestra?"

She shrugged, beginning a second loop. "I don't like it enough."

"Are you going to college?"

"Oh, sure. Doc will see to that. Not that I don't want to, it's just that it seems kind of crazy to me."

"What—going to college?"

"No—that grown-ups expect us to figure out what we want to do with the rest of our life when we're only seventeen or eighteen, but they think we're crazy if we fall in love. It seems that if you're old enough for one, you should be old enough for the other."

"Yeah, but you can't change who you're married to— that's for life. People change their jobs all the time."

"Maybe. But lots of people get divorced these days."

"Not me. I won't marry someone unless it's forever."

"How will you know when you've met the right person?"

I shrugged. "I'll just know."

Right then, she let out a little yelp and it echoed across the water as she lunged toward me.

"I think something bit my toe." Now, she was clinging to me.

"Well, there are snappers in this lake."

"What!"

"You know, those biting turtles."

She pushed away from me and left a wake as she made for the island. That gave me the heebie-jeebies and I swam quick as I could, back to safety.

She kicked water at me. "Why didn't you tell me there's snapping turtles?"

"I don't know." I laughed as I hoisted myself out. "I've been swimming in the lake for years, and they've never bothered me."

She shivered. The glow of the fire drew us closer to the heat. As we stood, side by side, she turned to face me, her hands flat against my chest. Could there be a more intense feeling than what surged through me at that moment before I kissed her? This time, her tongue found mine; neither of us pulled away. I'm not sure how long we kissed, but my knees weakened. I led her over to the log bench. We sat and kissed some more. It was hard to control myself, to keep my hands from wandering. She had made such a big deal about liking her for more than just her boobs that I didn't dare touch them, but she didn't seem to have any qualms about feeling every inch of my body above my shorts—not that I minded, but it was making me crazy. I could hardly breathe. This time, I pulled back.

We stared at each other while I caught my breath. I held her hand. "I wish this summer wouldn't end."

"Me too. But we could write to each other. And there will be next summer."

I nodded. I hated to think about how many months away that was. But we could write. Even though I hated writing letters, now I would be writing to Christopher and Amelia. It made me sad to think of this summer ending.

255

The fire had died down and a breeze picked up. I shivered.

Amelia grabbed her shirt and slipped into it. "Wow, it really cooled off fast, didn't it?"

I grabbed my shirt, too. "No kidding. I wonder if there's a storm coming in. That usually happens when there's a big change in temperature."

"I don't hear any thunder."

"Yet—"

Sure enough, a few seconds later the sky flashed. We both counted off together, "One-1000, two-1000, three-1000, four-1000 ...." We didn't hear any thunder, which meant it was still miles and miles away.

"Maybe we should head back," she said, pulling her shorts up.

I held my watch toward the few glowing embers. "Well, it is almost midnight. Let's get in the boat and just row around for a little while, until the thunder gets closer."

I covered the fire pit with sand and then helped Amelia into the boat. I passed her the blanket and boarded.

She spread the blanket over our legs and nudged my foot with hers. "So, when's your birthday, anyway?"

"September first." I rowed around the island.

"Will you still be here?"

"As far as I know. We usually stay until Labor Day weekend."

"I'll have to give you something special."

"More special than tonight?"

"Maybe."

I wasn't sure what kind of special she had in mind, but there was a whole lot of special between making out and the ultimate special.

Peepers sang to us from across the lake and I headed toward the east end, out by the beach. All around us, fireflies danced. Again, lightning flashed, but more than ten seconds passed before the next round of thunder. Even still, it rolled across the lake, mingling with the chorus as bullfrogs joined in.

"I love that sound," Amelia whispered.

"What—the frogs?"

She nodded.

"Me too." The boat drifted closer to where the beach came into view. "If you listen real close, you can hear the sound of the Picnic Ghost. Wooohooooooo ...."

She giggled. "Stop it! You're not scaring me."

"WoooHooooooo ...."

"Stop!"

"Okay," I chuckled.

She turned serious. "No, listen ... did you hear that?"

"What?"

She gripped my knee. "Listen ...."

I rowed closer to shore. "Yeah ... I hear it ...." It sounded like a cry, but muffled. Then it stopped. "What is that?"

"It sounds like ...."

At that moment, I looked over toward the beach where one light on a tall pole lit the parking lot. Beside the picnic area, I spotted a lone car. The Mercedes.

Chapter 32

MIDNIGHT. The clock on the counter gongs twelve ominous times, like in Saturday night *Creature Features*. Irony does not disappoint—on the twelfth strike, a flash of lightning punctuates the hour with a near-simultaneous crack of thunder. I'm too tired to be startled. I wish the previous owner had left a recliner or comfortable chair I can collapse into. I'm not ready to unroll my sleeping bag, but my body aches, threatening to give out.

Instead of sitting, I pace, shoving my fists into my pockets. Time to check the time. I pull the watch from my vest, but rather than flip the front cover, I pry open the back and rub the inscription.

I've been in possession of this watch for a few weeks and haven't learned all of its quirks yet, but already it feels as if I've owned it for years. Time is such a relative thing, moving fast or slow, contingent on so many factors. In one second, it's moving as if in slow motion—a sleight of time that exaggerates every detail; you need to move fast but your body mass can't catch up with what's speeding around you. And in the next second, you're the blur, whirring past everything like a screaming rocket.

That mid-August night—those pivotal moments probably lasting all of eighteen minutes—protracted through eighteen years, suspended in time, waiting for me finally to catch up. I can't stop the memory of it any more than I could have stayed the events of those final thirty-six hours. Adrenaline courses through me, even as it did when I spotted the Mercedes in the parking lot.

IN LESS TIME THAN IT TOOK TO SHIFT THE boat's direction with a flip of my oar, the worst-case scenario flashed through my mind. Ricky. Penny.

The only sounds I heard were my oars thrashing the water and my own pounding chest. Amelia said something indistinguishable, which pushed me harder, closing the short distance between the shore and us—between me and unleashing my rage on Ricky.

Amelia leaned forward in her seat, squinting. "I see them." She scrambled to the edge of the boat, still seconds away from land. "He's *on top* of her."

I twisted in my seat, straining to see through the thick of dark under the approaching trees that twisted with a sudden gust. Not until I detected movement below the boughs did I pinpoint the bodies on the ground, a few feet from the water.

I ran aground on a patch of gravel. I didn't have time to think. Bare legs flailed beneath Ricky. I yanked an oar from the oarlock, and in those few seconds as I lunged forward, raising it overhead, I saw Penny's arms restrained at her shoulders as she struggled against his mouth on hers. In the moment that I shouted, she cried out as he turned his face and my oar met the back of his head simultaneously with a flash of lightning.

He rolled off her in one direction and she rolled in the other, her skirt up to her waist. Ricky moaned, sitting up as I tossed the oar aside. My fist landed on his face as I climbed on him, straddling his body. I planted another punch—coinciding with a boom of thunder—before he grabbed hold of my arm and twisted me to the ground with a thud. His knuckle hit my cheek as I struggled under his full weight, half-shielding myself, and half-swinging back. Before he could land his fist again, I heard a crack and he tumbled off me. Amelia stood over us with the oar, ready to strike again.

I leapt to my feet, dizzy and disoriented, looking for Penny through a sudden downpour, a blanket of dark. Amelia yanked me toward the lake, where my sister was already climbing in the boat. I flew to Penny's side. Behind me, Ricky cussed just once before I heard another crack and a thump. Amelia joined us, and then the two girls clamored into the boat together as I shoved us into deeper water. I then jumped inside, dropping to my seat. Amelia passed me the oar. It settled in the lock, seemingly of its own volition and I pulled with all my remaining strength.

By the time Ricky stumbled into view beneath the overhanging trees, I had rowed several boat-lengths away as he fell to his knees. His vague outline dissolved into the murk of shadows.

With each thrust of my oar, water sloshed inside and outside the boat. Penny buried her face in her gauzy skirt, the torn fabric of her blouse leaving her shoulder bare. She shivered and sobbed. Behind me at the bow, Amelia panted and passed the blanket forward.

I quit rowing and spread the blanket over my sister's half-bare back, pressing my forehead against her tangles of wet hair. "You're safe. It's okay. I'm here."

As I settled in my seat, her eyes rose to meet mine as her sobbing slowed to a whimper.

"Did he—did he hurt you?" It was the stupidest question I had ever asked.

She lifted her face. Even in the dark, her cheeks and mouth and chin were bright red, and her lip was split.

Behind me, Amelia let out a gasp, breathing the words, "Oh my God."

My heart came up out of my chest as fury in my nostrils. "I'm gonna kill him. I swear to God, I'll kill him."

Penny's mouth trembled, "No Ben, you can't tell anyone. Swear to God you won't tell!"

"Penny—"

Her sobbing started again, "Ben, please—*please* don't tell."

"Penny—did he—did he—?"

She sobbed harder. *"Don't tell."*

I threw my head back, tears seeping from the corners of my eyes, searing a path through the cool rain pelting my face. I could hardly breathe.

Amelia came close, her arms wrapping around my waist, her chin resting on my shoulder. She sniffled and sighed. Her breath warmed my ear. "Just get her home for now."

I continued rowing, letting my anger fuel the boat, propelling it forward. Lighting split the sky, refracting into shards of light bouncing off the lake, like some bizarre fireworks display. A second later, thunder crashed like a million tons of sand falling on a metal roof. If lightning struck the three of us, we would all be out of our misery, taking the secret to our grave. When a jagged bolt tore through the dark, illuminating the island as it touched down on the tallest tree, the static prickled my skin. As much as the idea of perishing sounded like relief a moment ago, the thought of Ricky getting off the hook powered me forward as we passed the floatplane mooring and cut through the Narrows. Amelia's landing was only yards away.

I put the bow against the ladder. She climbed up and onto the dock. As I pulled away, she ran toward the lawn and didn't look back. I continued to row hard, making for our beach. Gravel scraped the bottom of the boat, its sound muffled by bilge water and pouring rain. I didn't worry about the noise. If the storm hadn't already woken Mom, nothing would. Even if it did, there was no turning back. My main concern was helping Penny to bed.

I hopped out and pulled us further ashore. Penny quit crying but trembled, breathing heavily. She didn't move.

"C'mon. We're home."

She didn't budge.

"Don't worry, it's dark inside. No one is up. No one knows."

She roused slowly, still trembling. I helped her up and out of the boat, snugging the blanket around her. We made it into the house and up the stairs without Mom hearing. I brought Penny to her room and whispered, "Do you need any help? Can I get you anything?"

She shook her head. I backed out as she dropped to her bed, wrapped in Amelia's blanket.

I stepped into my dark room, shed my clothes and climbed in bed, my body buzzing with a trace of adrenaline. Now that I lay still, I became aware of pain in my hands, my shoulders, my legs—my chest. My cheek throbbed. A few minutes later, Penny crept from her room to the bathroom. The toilet flushed. Turning my watch crystal to catch the beam from my flashlight, I read, 1:01.

I shut my eyes. A tape loop replayed the events of the last hour. The image of my knuckles smashing into Ricky's face played over and over, in slow motion at first, and then speeding so fast the images blurred, protracting the moment of impact, suspending it in time. Images of him on top of my sister—me on top of him—him on top of me. His fist coming at me. His crazed eyes. It was as if I were watching a movie—as if it weren't me out of control yet completely in control. Every action premeditated yet exploding spontaneously from within. Where did that person come from? How could *I* be capable of such violence? My stomach roiled. I wished I had just thrown up and got it over with, but my body wouldn't let me off that easy.

I stared at my ceiling for a long time.

CHAPTER 33

THE TENSION IN MY BACK PINCHES THE NERVES from my neck to my skull. My head is throbbing. Have I been standing here for a full hour, staring at my watch? I stretch my muscles and set the pocket watch—the back and front open—on the table, but first, I read the top line of the inscription.

Douglas "Doc" Burns

The first time I read Doc's given name, it wasn't a complete surprise. I had heard one other person call him that. Doug—just a small word but words can be funny that way; one tiny word in a certain context can carry more import than an entire novel. Words have meanings, if not implications. That's what swearwords are all about. As a general rule, my family never used profanity. "That's how lowlife talk," Mom would say. "Makes a person sound uneducated." Consequently, I didn't grow up hearing much cussing, and only when I started school did I learn some doozers. Even simply asking Mom about a 'new' word was enough to earn a douse of hot sauce. From the context of a term, I quickly figured out if it was dirty, and I made my personal list of words never to use around Mom.

From the time I started school, I had heard the word "perv" but didn't even know it was an abbreviation of pervert until I was eleven, and I had only the vague understanding that it had to do with men who behaved inappropriately with children—Mom called them molesters—and it somehow involved private parts. I knew what sex was, more or less. I had also heard the word "slut" from friends at school; those were the girls who would *do it* with anyone. But we didn't use those words or discuss those topics around adults. We snickered about them in private while gaping at second-hand girly magazines. Or when we chose to walk around the block, rather than take that shortcut through the overgrown lot where pervs hung out, waiting to lure children with candy.

The day after Amelia and I rescued Penny, it seems I heard those words more times in a twenty-four-hour period than I had heard them in my entire fourteen years combined. In reality, those words came up only a few times, but the circumstances seemed to amplify their frequency.

In the weeks that followed, I learned a new word. I was one week short of my fourteenth birthday, but I had never heard the term rape. That's how naive I was. And how does a kid explain what he saw when he didn't know what he was seeing—when his own sister wouldn't admit what happened; not until after years of drug abuse, rehab, and therapy, that is. Even then, she never confessed it to me. I never knew—still don't know—just how far Ricky went. Not that it matters anymore. The damage was done and she has moved on. I'm proud of how far she's come and couldn't be happier about her progress. In fact, it was she who encouraged me to return here—both she and Christopher—so that I can figure things out and move on with my own life.

WHEN MOM SHOOK ME OUT OF A SOUND sleep the following morning, I knew it was bad. I hadn't slept most of the night. I remembered only the first chirping birds at twilight and then exhaustion must have caught up with me. I woke to Mom's screeching voice, her hands gripping my aching shoulder.

"Ben! Ben, wake up!"

I rolled toward her, rubbing my eye. It burned. "What?"

"What happened to your face?"

"Huh?"

"Your sister is gone!" She gripped a sheet of loose-leaf paper, shoving it at me. "Get up! We're going down to those people's house this instant! Get your clothes on, young man! You have a lot of explaining to do."

Insane as she sounded, she seemed less nuts than last night at supper. "Where did she go?"

"As if you didn't know! I'm sure you were in on this, all along. Now, get yourself dressed."

I had no idea what she was talking about, but I obeyed, hopping off my bunk and pulling on shorts as she stood guard at my door.

I grabbed my shirt off the floor and pulled it overhead. "What's the letter say?"

She gasped. "Is that blood on your shirt?"

I glanced down at the dark reddish-brown smear and spatter and then peeled it back off.

She leaned against the doorjamb. "Oh dear God! What has become of my children?"

Without a word, I yanked a button-down shirt from a nail on the wall, slipped my arms in and grabbed my sneakers. My mother shut her eyes, one arm falling limp at her side. Her other hand met her forehead with all the drama of a silent-movie leading lady. I snatched Penny's note and read quickly:

> I've gone with Candace and the others to
> Woodstock. I'll be back Sunday. Don't worry.

I sent the paper to my bed as I scuttled to tie my laces and zip my shorts. I needed to get down to Doc's place. Maybe they hadn't left yet. I set my mind to that, although I had no idea how I would explain any of it once I arrived there. Instead of leading the way, Mom trailed behind. I broke into a jog as I flung open the screen door and took off.

"You come back here and wait for your mother!" she called out after me between gasps.

I picked up my pace, trying to steady my eyes on my watch—7:something. Doc would surely be up and around. I sped down the hill, the sheer momentum nearly taking my feet out from under me. I slowed enough to maneuver between the first set of stone pillars. Out of breath, I leapt up the granite steps and gave the doorknocker four consecutive thwacks. I glanced behind, at the road. My mother had not yet caught up, but her hysteria mounted as she neared.

She yowled, " ... My *daughter* ... *Those* people ... *Rebellious* children ...."

I leaned against the doorjamb. "C'mon Doc—c'mon."

With that, the front door flung open. Just as quick, Doc stood in front of me. Across the foyer, Sunshine and barefooted Amelia appeared in the great room doorway, both in pajamas. I didn't have time to read more than alarm in their wide eyes.

Doc held the door wide open as he glanced at my face and then over my shoulder. "Ben?"

"Is Penny here?"

"Penny?" His gaze vacillated between Amelia and my approaching mother. He shook his head, matching his granddaughters' alarm.

My mother stumbled up the steps, gripping the note and thrusting it out in front of her. "Where is my daughter? She's run off with those hippies of yours!"

Doc patted Mom's arm and gently pried the note from her fist. "Let's just simmer down, Mrs. Hughes."

Mom panted, now crying, "Oh, my baby ...."

I rubbed Mom's back, trying to calm her as Doc read quickly and then flashed a look at Sunshine who had approached. She took the note. Amelia stayed where she was, her eyes full of angst.

"Now, now, Beverly, don't you worry." Doc took Mom by the arm and directed her to a chair inside the front door. "We'll get this all straightened out. I promise."

Mom sat, clutching her chest as Doc crouched beside her. "Amy, go get Mrs. Hughes a glass of cold water."

Doc looked me up and down, his gaze landing on my face. "That's quite a shiner you have there, Ben."

"Is it, sir?" I touched below my eye, flinching at the rough scab and its tenderness.

Amelia padded over to his side. Mom accepted the glass with a sigh.

"Would you like to explain where you got that?" he said, coming to his feet.

I glanced at Amelia, hoping to figure out whether she had told him anything. She took a deep breath as her eyes shifted with dread. Shrugging, she shook her head. She had told him little, if anything. I opened my mouth. Nothing came out.

At that very moment, the service door opened and Ricky backed through the doorway, as if he had hoped to sneak into the house undetected. The door clicked after him. He turned and flinched at the sight of an audience, all staring at him. His eye, swollen shut and his fat lip, split.

Mom gasped, "Oh dear God!"

I had all I could do not to leap across the room and pound his other eye shut. I stepped forward, jaw clenched.

Doc raised his bushy brow and placed his big hand on my chest. "Ben?"

I swallowed hard, emotion welling up. "He was on my sister, Doc. He was all over Penny—he was all over her, pinning her down—"

My mother let out a cry as glass shattered on the slate floor.

Ricky backed up. "He's a lying son of a—"

"Ricky!" Karen's voice ricocheted off every wall as she appeared on the balcony in a négligée wrap, mascara circles under her eyes.

Dick stepped out behind her in a short satin robe. "What's going on out here?"

Doc's hand had not moved from my chest as I leaned into it. "Hold on now. Let's get to the bottom of this." He glanced at the shards of glass on the floor. "Amelia, don't you move."

Mom sobbed as Sunshine, in slippers, rushed to her side and ushered Mom through the great room door.

"Ben," Doc continued, "I want you to tell me exactly what happened."

"We were out rowing around on the lake last night and we heard crying over by the beach—"

"Who was out rowing?"

I shot a look at Amelia. Her eyes filled with tears as her gaze cut overhead and then returned to me, pleading. She shook her head. Did she expect me to keep quiet about it? To somehow leave her out of it? She might never talk to me again, but I had to tell the whole truth, didn't I?

I looked Doc in the eye and swallowed. "Me and Amelia."

"Last night?" His brow arched higher. "Just the two of you?"

I let out a sigh. "Yes, sir. That's when we heard sounds. And when I got near the shore, I saw the Mercedes, and then I saw Ricky attacking Penny."

"He didn't see anything," Ricky interrupted. "He's lying—he doesn't know what the hell—"

Doc flung his arm at Ricky "*You*! Shut up!" and looked back at me.

I continued, "When we got closer to shore, I saw him on top of Penny—she was struggling—I jumped out of the boat and hit him with the oar."

Ricky burst out laughing. "His slutty sister and I were just having a little fun and all of a sudden this maniac was all over me!"

Doc took one step toward Ricky and bellowed. "I told you to *shut up!*"

"*Daddy!*" Karen shouted.

"And *you*!" he pointed up at the couple on the balcony. "Not a word!"

I took a deep breath. "Her skirt was…," I couldn't bring myself to say it "…and her blouse was ripped and she had a bloody lip."

"Oh my God," Ricky muttered, rolling his eyes. "What a freaking bunch of lies. If all that's true, where is your slut sister?"

Doc turned to Ricky. "If I hear that word come out of your mouth one more time—" he then looked at Amelia with all sternness. "Did you see all this?"

She hesitated, glanced at me, and then nodded, tears streaming down her face. Her chin quivered. "He even tried to kiss me at the wedding. Benjamin saw it all."

Doc's eyes flew open. "What?" Now his voice echoed around the room, the chandelier above almost shook as he shot a look at Ricky and back at me. "Is this true, Benjamin?"

Even as I nodded, Doc moved across the foyer, glass crunching beneath his feet. In a matter of seconds, he had Ricky against the wall. Karen cried out as Dick swung around the balcony and made his way down the stairs. The painting beside Ricky shifted as Doc grabbed him by the shirt collar, raising him inches off the floor. His other hand squeezed Ricky's red cheeks, as Dick landed on the floor, swearing at the glass.

"Get your hands off my boy." In two steps, Dick yelped, his foot bloody. He fell to the stairs as Karen rushed down.

Doc still had Ricky by the jaw, lifted him away from the wall and let him drop. Ricky slid down, past the chair rail into a crumpled mass on the floor, shaking, his knees bent and palms pressing his eyes. Now Doc moved across the room toward Amelia and me, his face still ablaze with fury.

As soon as he stood before his granddaughter, he swept

her trembling body from the glass shards and carried her across the foyer to safety. Planting her in front of the great room door, he jabbed his finger in Ricky's direction. "*You*—don't move a muscle, or I'll come over there and finish you off." Doc then turned his finger on me. "Ben—in here. Now."

Was the anger in his tone now directed at me? He had every right to be mad. I was screwed. He waited in the doorway, breathing heavily as I stepped through. Amelia moved to the picture windows. On the sofa, Mom buried her face in Sunshine's shoulder as she stroked Mom's hair. As soon as Doc sat beside them, Mom turned to him, tears streaming from her eyes.

"Oh, Doug—my poor baby ...," she whimpered and pressed her face to his chest as he pulled her close.

Did Mom just call him Doug?

His demeanor and voice turned from angry to tender. "Don't you worry, Bev. I will get your baby back and that boy will pay."

Did Doc just call Mom, Bev?

He turned his attention to Sunshine and pointed at a roadmap sprawled across the chess table as Mom covered her face.

"You and I are going to New York this morning," he said to Sunshine as he rose, and then pointed at me. "You and I are not done. We'll talk about *this*—" he glanced at Amelia and back at me "—when I return."

"Yes, sir." I couldn't catch Amelia's eye before she turned, facing the cove.

In three steps, he landed in front of the map and turned to me. "When is your father coming up?"

"This afternoon."

"Alright, you need to take your mother home now. You stay with her every second until he gets here, do you understand?"

"Yes, sir." I moved to Mom's side as she came to her

feet. Taking her by the arm, I led her toward the door. Doc followed. As we stepped into the doorway, I glanced back at Amelia who had not turned. She probably hated me for telling—not for telling on Ricky, but for telling that she and I had been sneaking behind Doc's back. Maybe she was afraid Doc would think she was like her mother.

In the foyer, Ricky still sat, crumpled on the floor. Karen wiped tears as she sat with Dick at the stairway landing, picking glass out of his foot.

She looked up at me. "This is all *your* fault."

I tried to form the word *What?* but when I opened my mouth, nothing but a breath came out.

Doc spoke for me. "Don't you dare try and put this on Ben."

"I can't believe you would take their side. I'll never forgive you for this, Daddy."

Doc shot a gesture toward Ricky. "That boy over there is a pervert, and he preyed on your daughter, too. What kind of *mother*—what is the matter with you?"

Doc rushed us across the foyer to the front door. As he opened it and stepped through, he touched Mom's shoulder. "I'll have Penny back by the end of the day. Don't you worry."

Chapter 34

A FLASH OF LIGHTING SNAPS ME OUT OF MY trance, and if it thunders in response, I don't hear it. I've been procrastinating, pacing around the table for too long. Of course, I could wait until daylight, until a few minutes before ten when Oscar's truck is due to arrive. As much as I want it over with, I'm not ready to venture downstairs. I reach for Sunshine's card, flicking the edge before reading it again.

...We love you and know you will rise above it all....

Sunshine, the person who epitomized all that was good and pure in the hippie movement—a true flower child. It's ironic that she never even experienced Woodstock, the icon of a generation.

I SAT IN OUR KITCHEN, FINISHING OFF THE box of Saltines. Mom had sequestered herself in her bedroom as usual. I was so exhausted, I had forgotten to check what time we left Doc's, but I figured it was around 7:30 or 8:00.

At 9:00, Karen's hysterical voice echoed across the cove, and then the floatplane started and took off. I went into the bathroom and looked at my face in the mirror. This wasn't my first black eye, but it hurt far worse than the others. I leaned closer and examined my cheek as water ran in the sink until it turned hot. As I wet a washcloth, I noticed my bruised and scraped knuckle. Loosening the dried blood on my cheek, I winced. The eyes of someone I didn't recognize stared back. Someone older. Someone angry. Someone very tired.

I returned to the kitchen and sat, laying my head on the table. With my eyes still open, I stared sideways at the Saltine box. Every sound amplified through the tabletop—

like a soundboard, even the tick of my Timex. Crumbs and salt crystals magnified into boulders, shifting each time I breathed. If my body had ached last night and when I woke this morning, it now felt as if I were being torn, limb from limb, as if every muscle had gone through a meat grinder. In addition to the pain, I didn't have the strength to keep my eyes open. I fell asleep.

When I woke with a stiff neck, and crumbs and salt pressed into my cheek, my Timex read 3:33—three consecutive threes. I hated the numbers, the way they jumped out at me as if they meant something. Right then, everything that was supposed to mean something had twisted and warped until I was no longer sure what I could rely on. For the first time in a long time, I looked forward to Dad's arrival. Even if he ignored me or called me moron or idiot and blamed everything on me, at least that would be 'normal' and there would be a responsible adult in the house.

Every movement outside, or car that drove by, sent me to the kitchen window, but it was never the Falcon pulling into the dooryard. I would have liked to go for a swim just to pass the time, but I took Doc's words not to leave Mom for one second, very seriously. I had already disappointed him. I knew that much. Somehow, I had to redeem myself. Just the thought of Doc talking to me about Amelia was enough to make the cracker mush in my stomach feel as if it would come back up.

All that aside, since when had Mom and Doc been on first-name terms? Now, those vague memories began to solidify—an image of an occasion when Mom had pulled off the road because she'd had something in her eye. Doc had stopped—drove up beside us in his truck—to see if there was a problem.

And Doc at our camp. In the kitchen—no, standing in the hall, outside of Mom's bedroom, as I came up the basement steps carrying the truck I had received as an early fourth-birthday present. An embrace. Mom crying. Doc stroking her back. Mom's eyes landing on me, yanking her hands from his. Or was that Dad? It must have been Dad, because what would Doc be doing in our cottage?

But as another memory surfaced, it was again Doc's face, now on our beach, farther away this time, as if I was looking down from my bedroom window. Mom, so close to him that it looked like a hug. She clung to him until Doc pushed her off him, wagging his head. Mom shoved him and then covered her face as he walked away.

Was that the falling-out? The reason why Mom had held an inexplicable grudge against Doc? As the memory congealed and gained clarity, I recalled Doc's face with increasing certainty. I made the connection between my parents' arguing—the way *my* name always seemed to surface when they fought—and those intimate moments between Doc and my mother. That would have explained why I was never good enough. For chrissake, I was Dad's firstborn son—why wasn't I named Frankie? It was Doc who called me son when my own father wouldn't.

... No, no ... I couldn't have been remembering it correctly. I rubbed my good eye. My head was just playing tricks on me. That had been ten years ago—I was just a little kid and didn't know what I had seen. I forced myself not to think about what it all meant.

Three o'clock passed and my anxiety grew, but not until four did my head begin to pound. I was hungry. Going from one cabinet to the next, I found only Rice Krispies. I looked inside at the handful in the bottom of the box, and then opened the refrigerator. About a swallow of orange juice remained. I grabbed that and swished it down, right from the bottle. Again sitting at the table, I popped one Rice Krispie kernel at a time into my mouth, chewed and swallowed. At around four, I dozed off to images of Ricky—and Penny—and Doc in my kitchen holding Mom.

I didn't check the time when I woke to the sound of Doc's plane coming in for a landing. I flew to my feet and rushed to Penny's window. I had difficulty seeing and headed downstairs and out the back door in time to catch sight of three figures stepping onto the mooring—Doc, Sunshine, and then Penny.

I ran into the house and upstairs. "Mom—Mom! Doc's back—with Penny!"

She came out of her bedroom, puffy-eyed and clutching her heart. "Oh, my baby! Where is she?"

"They just landed. They'll be here in a minute."

Mom didn't wait. She ran out the front door and met them in the road as I watched from the stoop. Penny stood limp as Mom sobbed, hugging her. Doc continued to make his way toward me, leaving Sunshine at the road.

"Let's step inside," he said, his voice grave. I supposed it was time for our talk. He followed me in, making sure the door closed behind us before he turned to me. He continued, "I want you to know that I called the police. Ricky is in custody and they're holding him at least overnight until his lawyer arrives."

"What?"

He took a breath. "Your sister does not want to testify against him, but yours and Amelia's testimony are enough for the DA to press charges. You need to come down to the police station, but your father should be there for that. As soon as he gets home, we'll all go down together. Do you understand?"

"Ricky's going to jail for hurting my sister?"

"It's hard to say what sort of bargain they'll plea, but if I have anything to say about it, it's going on his record."

"Do you think he—you know—my sister?" there was one word I could think of to describe it, but it was the most vulgar word I had ever heard and I had never used it in my entire life. "Did he—"

"The word is rape, son—and I don't know. What we do

know is it's at least assault and battery and that's enough to get him locked up overnight. Maybe even longer than that, if we can get Penny to talk."

I nodded, although I still wasn't clear on what all that meant.

Mom and Penny and Sunshine came onto the porch. Doc opened the door. Penny stepped through first, her eyes glazed over. She wouldn't look at me; she simply headed for the bathroom. Mom stepped in next, as dazed as Penny. Doc touched her arm. She looked up into his face and stepped into his embrace, whispering, "I don't know how to thank you, Doug."

The image of him holding my mother outside my parents' bedroom flashed from memory.

She pulled away and moved over to the table and dropped like a ragdoll into her chair. Doc stepped outside, his hand on my shoulder, leading me out with him.

"Ben, I think it's best if you don't say anything to your mom about our little conversation, just yet. Let's wait till your dad gets here."

"Yes, sir."

He stepped down and turned, his brow raised. "And you and I still need to have that *talk.*"

I swallowed. "Yes, sir."

Sunshine next came out of the cottage, gave me a hug, and then held me at arm's-length. She brushed the hair from my sweaty forehead and smiled sympathetically. "I love you, Ben. You are a good person. Don't you *ever* forget that."

My eyes burned and misted over as she walked away. When I went back inside, Penny came out of the bathroom. Without a word—and without looking at me—she shut herself in her bedroom. Mom walked to her own room, closing the door behind. It was almost 6:30. Where the hell was Dad?

Now I headed for my room—though I could have just

as easily ended up in the bathroom, but I had nothing to throw up. I collapsed onto Frankie's bed. When I finally woke in the dark, it was to the sound of stumbling in the kitchen, or was it thunder? I sat up so fast my head spun. Then Mom came out of her room and screamed. I had heard so many of her emotional outbursts that it scarcely registered. I opened my bedroom door.

Dad hunched over the kitchen table. He glanced up at me, his face a bloody mess—way worse than what I had done to Ricky. His shirt was torn and bloodstained. His hoarse voice ordered, "Get out of the house, Ben."

"What?"

"Oh my God!" Mom cried out, "First Penny and now this!"

Dad let go of his arm he had been holding and pointed at the stairwell. "Get the hell out, Ben. Go down to the beach or something." He didn't shout. It was as if he hadn't the strength.

I shuffled past him as Mom wept at the table. I made it to the bottom step, proceeded to the door, opened and slammed it without stepping through, and then returned to the bottom step. It was hard to make out what Dad was muttering, but Mom seemed to hit all the high points, repeating them shrilly.

The horses. The house. The car. The bookie. The mortgage. The camp. Then the single word punctuations: Everything? Nothing? Bankruptcy? And the final question—Irving who?

It was as if someone had turned up the volume in my head and switched the station to static. Louder and louder, until the pressure in my head felt like it would pop my eardrums. I sat for a long time, until I couldn't stand it any more. I crept upstairs, met by the scent of cigarettes, and peered around the corner at my father slumped over the table. A butt smoldered on its surface—no ashtray. The liquor bottle sat in front of him as he turned a paper cup, bottom side up, into his mouth and then refilled it. I didn't move or make a sound. I just watched. He began to sob. Mom rushed down the hall, slamming their bedroom door behind her.

CHAPTER 35

YES, I'VE BEEN AVOIDING MY PARENTS' bedroom. I'm still not certain why I need to go in there, except it's where Mom spent so much time. It's the one remaining place where she guarded her secrets—secrets from Dad, secrets from her family—from me. Perhaps even secrets from herself.

I massage my neck and stand, arching my back. One more time, I look at my pocket watch but not to check the time. In a way, this overnight journey is as much about Doc as it is about Dad.

Maybe I'm deluded, but I believe—that is, I've convinced myself—that Doc might be my biological father. Maybe it's just wishful thinking, but if he were, that would answer so many questions. Why had Doc taken such an interest in me? Why did he bother to keep track of me through those years of silence after we had moved in with Aunt Wanda? Although my suspicions festered over the years, the notion of him being my father truly sunk in at my graduation. He hugged me for the first time.

"I'm always here for you, son," he said. He had tears in his eyes. "I'm so proud of you."

He also followed through with that letter of recommendation. I think he even pulled a few strings so I could secure that scholarship at MIT. Not to mention, paying a hefty dollar for the patent on my robotic prosthesis.

Now that I'll never have the chance, I wish I had come right out and asked about him and Mom. I never had the courage—the audacity—to confront him. Confessing an indiscretion would have been an affront to Doc's character. In fact, it would be out of character—that's why it could have been only a one-time thing. A moment of weakness.

My last chance to ask Doc evaporated about four months ago. I attempted to contact him when Gretchen was still my fiancée, and the wedding was still on. In fact, I didn't actually talk to him. I talked to his answering machine. I don't recall exactly what I said, but something to the effect that I had met someone, that we were engaged and had set a date—May 30th—and I hoped he could attend.

I didn't hear back for a week but smiled at his number on my caller ID. When I picked up, a female voice replied, "Hello, Benjamin—This is Amelia."

Stunned, my breath caught in my chest. Before I responded, she continued with a sigh. "I'm so sorry to have to tell you. Doc died of a heart attack a week ago." Her voice broke. "His funeral was today. I was just listening to his unanswered messages and—and there you were."

"Oh God ...." It took me the longest time to catch my breath. A pang of sadness gripped my insides, but it was Amelia's loss that choked me; I could not begin to process my own. "I'm so sorry. How are you doing?"

Her voice trembled. "Horrible .... Listen, I simply can't talk right now, except to say there is something he wanted you to have, if you'd tell me where to send it."

Stunned, I rattled off my Denver address.

She repeated it after me and then added, "Oh, and congratulations on your engagement."

"Thanks ...," I said. I thought of a hundred things I wanted to say—to ask—but before I could, she cut in.

"Listen, I've got to go. It was nice talking to you. Some day, perhaps we'll catch up."

"Yeah, I'd like that."

"Goodbye, Benjamin," she said softly and hung up.

Over the years, I've wondered if Amelia ever came to

terms with that summer. Likely, her life also blew apart, setting off a sequence of events she had no more control of than I did. Doc had told me that Karen and Dick divorced a year after they married. Karen remarried twice since. I could imagine what that did to Amelia. It was no wonder she never stayed in one place for long. At least she had Doc and Sunshine—and Lenny; he and Sunshine ended up marrying and moving to California. The last time I saw Sunshine, she was waving at me as I looked out of a car window, driving away. And Amelia, I didn't see her again. My final memory of her was in the great room at Whispering Narrows, her back to me, probably dreading her own 'talk' with Doc.

I didn't—don't—blame her for not saying goodbye. Everything happened so fast those last few hours at camp that I didn't say goodbye to her either. If she and I had ended up having to testify—to corroborate our testimonies against Ricky—we likely would have had occasion to see each other, perhaps even talk. But as it turned out, Ricky copped a plea. He didn't serve time, but his father paid a heavy fine and it went on Ricky's record and ruined his admittance to Yale. None of that brought any satisfaction, and it still doesn't. There wasn't, and will never be, any satisfying justice for that summer.

A month after I talked to Amelia on the phone, a small package arrived in the mail. I opened the box as carefully as Amelia had wrapped it, and found a small velvet pouch. I slipped its contents into my hand—an antique, gold pocket watch with an inscription on the back's inside:

Douglas "Doc" Burns
April 4, 1904 ~ January 20, 1987

He was just short of his eighty-third birthday.

CHAPTER 36

BEFORE I VENTURE INTO MOM'S BEDROOM, I need one last reminder that in spite of everything, good things can come out of tragedy. It's my final memento—a framed photograph. I lift it from the box and stare at it for a long moment before setting it on the table, facing my parents' room so both Christopher and Penny can watch my bravery. As I walk away from their wedding portrait, I glance down at my red and white socks and back at Christopher's single, striped sock and brand new prosthetic limb.

Now fortified, I push open the door at the end of the hall. It's just as dark as I expected. I feel around inside for a light switch, but it's just like the other bedrooms—no overhead light. Opposite the bed, over on Mom's old oak dresser, just one step away, I make out the silhouette of a lamp. With the room now illuminated, I turn slowly. It's as musty as all the other rooms—perhaps more so, or maybe it's some lingering scent of hair spray and claustrophobia. The closet door is open and I peer inside at the floor and up on the shelf. Nothing. The room is unadorned but for the bed, dresser, and lamp.

I sit on the bare mattress. Well, this is a bit anti-climactic. I guess my trip to the unfinished room remains the primary attraction of my overnight.

A couple of feet away, my reflection stares back—already I have a five o'clock shadow, but I hardly recognize my own face. It's going to take a while to get used to my chin as opposed to the whiskers. I rise and peer into the mirror. I want a better look at the man I've become.

The silver oxide coating behind glass is splotchy with age and disintegrated in places. As I adjust the lamp, moving it aside a bit, the lighting changes and one of the splotches at the corner appears more rectangular than irregularly shaped, as if something behind the mirror has pulled the silver away from the glass. I've heard of crazy people hiding money in old picture frames and mattresses. Maybe I'm about to strike it rich! Shifting the dresser away from the wall, I peer behind it at the thin veneer of wood that backs the mirror. Brads are missing at the corner, and it's easy to pull the thin layer of wood away enough to insert my finger. There's definitely something shoved behind the glass. With a little encouragement, it falls into my hand.

Illumination from the lamp confirms that it's an envelope. Closer inspection reveals one charred corner, as if someone put a match to it and changed their mind. Although I'm pretty certain neither of my parents would burn money, I pry the flap open as if a million dollars awaits me. Nope! Just a tri-folded and singed piece of paper. I open it carefully, hoping whatever it contains will remain intact. I hold it to the light. The body of the note is unmarred but for some mildew and burn marks that have encroached upon the date.

I squint, reading aloud:

> *August 23—*
> *Dearest Beverly,*
> *I'm writing this letter—rather than speaking face to face—because I don't know of a discrete time and place to say all I need to say. In fact, I think it would be best if you read this letter and then destroy it so it will never fall into the wrong hands and cause anyone hurt.*
> *You know that I care for you—this has been true for many years. You also know I love my family and I know you love yours—*

this is why our secret flirtations must end—the notes, the stolen kisses, the secret meetings. My conscience can no longer bear it, when so much already weighs it down. I will always care deeply for you and I will always remember the love we shared—how could I ever forget? Ben is a constant reminder. I don't regret that he came out of our weakness—that one glorious and terrible moment of weakness. I always wanted a son—a son I could be proud of—and you gave me one, even if I could not claim him in front of the entire world as I would have liked. He is a good boy and I am proud to call him MY son.

I knew it! This confirms all my suspicions. This is the last missing detail I've been waiting for, and to think I nearly missed it!

I continue reading, but not aloud—I don't have enough breath to spare:

Please, Beverly, don't beat yourself up over the past and what can't be changed. And please don't respond to this letter. Please—let me be at peace with myself.

Love always,
Earl

Wait! *What?*

Earl? Earl *Garver?*

I can't catch a breath—can only exhale, Earl. *Earl?*

The letter slips from my grip as I step back and drop to the mattress.

Earl?

After my lungs finally expand and I draw in a breath, I reach forward and snatch the letter from the floor. I must not have read it correctly. It's the bad lighting.

I skim the first half and reread the end and then reread the entire letter, slowly, analyzing each word as a single entity—as if misreading just one word might have altered the entire letter's meaning. I trail off after the word "Earl." *Oh God.* Earl Garver was my father.

The muscles between my shoulder blades constrict. The lamplight fades until it extinguishes as I fall back on the mattress and close my eyes. I don't see or smell or hear anything. I'm just the memory of a boy running down the stairs, wishing Dad were not my father. Wishing I could disown him and all the implications of being his son.

I spring to my feet and run out of my mother's room, heading for the stairs, for the basement, just like I did those eighteen years ago. I yank the door open, rushing headlong through years of dead and hanging filth, wiping rain and debris from my face and arms as I run toward the rickety old dock. Tripping across its loose boards, I slip, twisting my ankle. Coming to rest at the dock's end, I sit, staring out over the cove, my breathing rapid but even. Measured. Controlled, until it slows, like the drizzling rain. Water droplets fall from the trees, their sound amplifying and then blending with peepers and bullfrogs. I lie back, gazing at the black sky. I resist closing my eyes, but I no longer have control and drift off into darkness.

Chapter 37

THROUGH MY EYELIDS, I SENSE THE SKY beginning to lighten. A few birds are already peeping. It takes a moment to remember why I spent the night on the dock. I have awakened to this heaviness of dread too many times in my life. I don't want to open my eyes. If I lie here long enough, maybe the truth will all go away. But I know better—the truth never goes away. Truth ruins wishes—twists and distorts them into undeniable reality, and the reality is, Earl Garver is—was my father, not Doc Burns.

What does that truth change? I open my eyes. It didn't change the sunrise. It didn't transport me anywhere. It doesn't change that I'm cold and wet and that even if I don't want to go in the house, I have to if I want to get warm and dry. And it doesn't change the fact that I have not completed what I came here to accomplish, or that Oscar will be here by 10:00.

My aching body doesn't want to cooperate. I force myself to sit—it's time to get this over with. Inhaling courage, I stand and face the cottage at the end of the twisted dock. It's amazing I didn't break my neck last night. Now that would be ironic, though I'm not laughing. Balancing with each precarious step, I make my way back to shore, just like I did that early morning, eighteen years ago.

 I HAD TO PEE, BAD. I WOULD HAVE GONE right off the end of the dock, but I waited until I landed on shore and found the cover of nearby bushes. I took my time. I dreaded going into the house, of having everything I had surmised, confirmed.

Had Mom told Dad about Penny? *Oh crap!* We hadn't gone with Doc to the police station. And Dad wouldn't be in any shape to go this morning. Doc must have thought I came from such a loser family. I was sure Amelia knew it too. No wonder she was mortified that Doc found out she had been sneaking around with me. All my fantasies were pissing away. I zipped my fly and turned toward the house. My heart raced as I trudged to the back door, the slight incline feeling like Mount Everest.

I swiped at a dew-speckled spiderweb across the doorway and grabbed the knob. Condensation made it slick. It slipped in my hand. I gripped it tighter as I peered inside. A thin bead of light ran across the floor beneath the unfinished room's door and up its side. Morning ambiance crept in behind me as I stepped in. Strange that the light was on—that I hadn't noticed it the night before. I walked toward it, staring at the floor. The stillness of the house above made me hold my breath. I reached out and merely touched the door, pushing it open a fraction of an inch more—just enough to see the muddy toe of Dad's wingtip shoe, hovering, perpendicular, a couple inches above the concrete floor. It seemed so odd. What was my father's shoe doing in the unfinished room? I did not react until my sight traveled to his unfolded trouser cuff and up the side seam to his limp, gray hand.

I cried out, calling Mom, but I heard no noise, not even my own voice—nothing until the upstairs floorboards thundered overhead. Then Mom was behind me, shoving me out of the way. I backed up, turning away as she pushed the door open. I rushed through the back door and ran outside ahead of her, covering my ears, trying to block out the shrieking, the continuous screams of a madwoman.

She dashed past me down toward the water, her nightgown billowing as she ran into the lake. Wet cloth clung to her body as she splashed, flailing her arms and cackling, her voice echoing round and round the cove. Every bird, peeper and bullfrog ceased—froze like me, standing outside the basement door, watching my mother go berserk. It was the strangest sensation. I was sort of out of my body, watching myself watching my mother. Why was she screaming her head off—what was wrong with her? What had I done now?

Next thing I knew, Doc was behind me, gripping my shoulders, planting me between the house and the shore.

"Do not move," he said.

He then rushed to my insane mother, grabbing her and holding her tight as he called out into the cove, "Call the police."

That was it. Mom had gone insane and calling the police was the right thing to do. I nodded. Yes. That was best. Mom had finally lost it, and the men in white suits would take her away to someplace safe.

I turned around and looked up at Penny's window. She stared out between the parted curtains and I nodded, as if to tell her it was okay. Everything was going to be okay now.

CHAPTER 38

SHIVERING, I STAND OUTSIDE THE BASEMENT, all grown up, facing the truth. I don't know how long I've been stalling, but the sun has crested the treetops and warmed the air. I had better get a move on it.

Pushing through the basement entrance, I step inside and move to the unfinished room without hesitation. I open the door and flip on the light switch. Shelves to my left. Washer to my right. Exposed rafters overhead. Back when I discovered Dad, I never opened the door more than a crack, or looked upon my father's face as he hung there. Doc wouldn't allow me back in the house through the basement. As I stand here now, I feel no otherworldly presence, nor the prolonged panic I expected. I suppose my racing heart is leftover from the anticipation of remembering—that and last night's revelation. And now, that's all they are—memories. Yes, my eyes twitch and I feel a pang of nausea. My chest is as tight as my neck and shoulders, and a bead of sweat runs from my hairline, but that's the worst of it. I haven't lost my mind, and I'm not running out of the basement screaming like my lunatic mother.

I inhale the must and mildew and turn the light off. In the utility room, I shut everything down and make my way to the stairs, through the aftermath. The events that followed—after the police arrived—all happened so quickly. There were the ambulances—one that took my father's body away and one that took my mother. Penny and I had about twenty minutes to pack our things. I packed Frankie's too, and then the cruiser drove us to the station. I wondered if we would see Ricky there, but Doc, who followed, must have seen to all that, to spare us. He and I never did have that talk.

After a blur-of-a-week, the three of us kids ended up at Aunt Wanda's farm in Missouri. Dad ended up in a cemetery in New York, buried without pomp by his brother. We did not attend.

A psychiatric evaluation landed Mom in Pleasant Meadows, a peaceful institution near Aunt Wanda's, where Mom could recover. But she didn't recover. We visited every Sunday afternoon—that is, Aunt Wanda and I did. Mom babbled incoherently when she wasn't completely non-responsive. At times, she recognized me, seemed to want to tell me something important but couldn't get the words out. Whenever I visited, I hoped she would have a lucid moment and would confess to me that Doc was my father; but her coherent moments were few and far between. The last intelligible statement she spoke to me was on a spring afternoon just before I graduated from high school.

On my own, I drove to Pleasant Meadows to tell Mom I had been accepted at MIT and would be going away to college. I would be leaving in a couple weeks, moving into an apartment with Christopher—that he and I would be attending MIT together. Whether she could comprehend it or not, I needed to let her know I would no longer be coming to visit every week.

I hoped to make my visit a special occasion and first stopped at the florist. Her face lit with appreciation. Hugging her bouquet with one arm, she looped the other in mine as I led her outside. We sat on a bench under the leafy canopy of an ancient oak. Something in the warmth of the breezy, flower-scented air, in the way Mom's smile disarmed me, sparked my hopes, made me feel as if she might provide some motherly bit of advice or reassurance. I took her hand and returned her smile. She was still beautiful. She was my mother. My Mom.

I opened my mouth to speak, to tell her I loved her, as if I had forgotten all the ugliness—in that moment, I had—but before I could utter a word, she became agitated, rocking back and forth, digging her fingers into my arm. She threw the flowers to the ground. Her tormented eyes begged for something I could not understand.

"What, Mom? What is it?"

Her face contorted and she blurted, "It's your fault—it's all your fault!"

I don't know who was crazier—my mother, or me for believing a crazy woman. For months, her words rung loud in my ears, day after day, night after night, until they faded to a drone of background noise that I took for granted and came to ignore.

From that afternoon on, I visited Mom twice a year, every year—until I moved to Denver. Then, I couldn't make myself go at all. Gretchen never understood how I could abandon my mother in a nursing home, or why I needed to see to Mom's cremation and burial arrangements without her. "Mother was private and we weren't close," I told Gretchen. "This is the way she would have wanted it."

Under the bleak November sky, Aunt Wanda, Penny, and I interred Mom. Our frosted breath formed no words, yet hovered and dispersed over her grave like a prayer. We stood there for all of a minute as Penny shook her head, her nose red from the chill air, not from crying. Only Aunt Wanda dabbed at her eyes with a hanky. I grabbed Penny's hand and led her back to Christopher who waited in his wheelchair at the cemetery drive.

And Frankie? We made an attempt to notify him, without success. Truth was, neither Penny nor I wanted him there. Besides, Frankie was never a person to form attachments or to need closure. When we moved in with Aunt Wanda, he had no trouble adjusting, aside from another bout of bed-wetting. It was as if Mom's being taken away and Dad's suicide were mere inconvenient blips. In fact, he turned them into misfortunes that elicited sympathies he could manipulate to his advantage.

Creeps me right out, how Frankie used people, how he had always been all about the money—even as a little kid. I didn't know he was pilfering my meager savings until years later. Last I saw him, he still owed me $3000. *Owed*, because I've accepted the fact that he'll never pay it back. I've learned to let it go, but I feel so sorry for all the other people he swindled. It's sad when someone that dishonest turns out to be an overachiever in his profession. I suppose it's a badge of honor for him to be wanted in three states. I have no idea where he lives, and I'll be happier if I never see him again. In Frankie's case, it is like father, like son.

Leaving all that behind, I head toward the kitchen. As I step onto the first stair tread, I think of Earl Garver. He was a good and kind man. Aside from the illegitimacy of it all, I feel no shame about having his genes.

I step again, wishing I had known him better.

It takes three steps before it dawns on me that Dora is my half-sister.

On the forth—that means Penny is my *half*-sister, also.

Step five. Does Mrs. Garver know? Has she ever suspected? How could she not?

Six. So, that's why Earl was always so nice to me.

Seven—and why every time Mom showed up, Mrs. Garver always took over the register.

Eight. I'm back to the letdown of Doc not being my father.

But by the ninth step, it occurs to me that Doc took an interest in and supported me because he liked me—because he believed in me, not out of guilt or pride, but because he saw something special in *me*!

I revel in that notion for the next couple of steps and not until I reach the top does it hit me—Amelia and I have no genetic connection whatsoever!

As I round the top stair into the kitchen, I step into the

muted colors of a new day. Exhausted as I am, I can't begin to think of catching a few minutes of shut-eye. I glance at the clock, 8:00. Time is running out, but I'm not going to hurry these last moments.

With Penny and Christopher's wedding portrait in hand, I'm grateful. Yes, I feel a wave of something like optimism. If Penny could pull her life together, even obtain her nursing degree and stay clean, I can deal with my disappointments. And Christopher—he had other opportunities with some stunning blonds, but he held out for Penny. I couldn't be happier for both of them. Of course, I did feel compelled to give them the conversion van—my customized Transformer—as a wedding gift; after all, I did customize it for Christopher and his Hot Wheels.

Time to turn my attention to the clock. 8:35. I open its back, stop the pendulum and lift it off the hooked wire. With a glance at the drawing pad, I carry the clock and pendulum to the table, ready to wrap and carefully lay them in the box, all set for transport. But first, I fish out one last memento—my last connection to Amelia—to Doc.

Sure, it's just the small box in which she sent Doc's watch, but inside, neatly folded, is the brown paper she wrapped it in. I guess I am a sentimental sap after all. I open the box and smooth the paper. It's just a scrap with my name and address sprawled across it—her looped letters, full and feathery. Artistic handwriting. I imagine her penning my name—*Benjamin Hughes*—and what memory it might have conjured. I hope it evoked something pleasant, though likely it was as bittersweet as my own memories.

Over the years, I've thought about and analyzed just why Amelia made such a profound impression upon my tender psyche. Was it simply the newness of all those hormonal feelings? Did we actually share a bond, an understanding? I've heard the term 'soul mate' as if there exists just one person who completes us. My pragmatism argues against the concept, but my inability to let go of the notion of Amelia causes me to wonder. Perhaps she and I were soul mates. Or perhaps our lives converged at a terrible moment in time, leaving a shared scar—a constant reminder of that awful night—of what we each saw, of how we each participated. Is that injury our bond?

I pass my thumb over the ink as if the letters might rise like a scar. Again, I wonder where she is right now. If only she had provided her return address, but she simply wrote Amelia Burns above Doc's post office box.

Wait—Amelia *Burns*?

I can't believe it's only now occurring to me that she kept her maiden name. Or could it mean she's now single? *Huh*. I shake my head. Just like me to jump to conclusions. Of course, lots of women keep their own name. Just the same, that might be something worth looking into.

For now, I need to keep packing. I place the clock, the portrait, the small box, then Sunshine's card, the paperwork, the radio, and then the Polaroid snapshot in the cardboard carton and close it up, leaving the carnival ticket on the table. The $50 drawing pad on the counter—I can't take the time for it right now, that will have to wait until later. I place it atop the box. Next, I need to retrieve my shaving kit.

As I stand in front of the bathroom mirror, I scrutinize my facial features and stance, looking for traces of Earl Garver. I always thought I had my mother's nose, but it could just as easily be his. My loosely curling hair now make sense, and so does my jawline—funny, but I never paid attention to my dimpled chin, even before I grew the beard. Even my hands appear different, not as meaty as Doc's, but more elongated like those I had watched at the cash register, making change so many times.

I rub the scruff on my jaw. It feels good. I'm looking forward to shaving—to the ritual of it—but not this morning. That's enough mirror time for now. I need to keep moving or Oscar will bulldoze this place with me in it.

It takes a few minutes to pack all my belongings in my car. I shut the passenger door and glance down the road, more at the sound than the sight of Oscar's Demolition and Excavation truck and trailer rounding the corner and coming into view. It downshifts to climb the hill. I pull Doc's pocket watch and flip it open. Eighteen minutes before ten—the same as I read the last time I looked—the moment it stopped twenty-four hours ago. I glance at it again—of all things, the second hand lunges forward. Tick after ironic tock.

The truck comes into view. I step out of the way as he pulls up to the dooryard, trailing a large piece of yellow equipment.

Oscar pokes his head out the window. "You sure you want to bulldoze the place?"

I laugh. "I'd have set it on fire if it weren't illegal."

"Okay, well, it'll take a few minutes to unload," he said and ducked into the cab momentarily, emerging with a covered Styrofoam cup. "Here, I thought you might like some coffee."

"Thanks." I reach for it. After the night I've had, I need it. "I think I'll take it down to the water."

He gives me a two-finger wave and puts the truck in gear. I may as well look over my $50 investment while I'm down there. I snatch the drawing pad on my way.

As I walk down the path to the stairway, my memory of yesterday comes back to me. It has been less than twenty-four hours, but it feels like a whole summer—no, a lifetime—ago. I can't help smiling. Not only did I survive, but I've accomplished what I came for—short of caving the cabin in on itself.

Even as I gingerly make my way down the rickety old steps, my exhaustion is transforming into euphoria. A second wind. Doc would be proud of me. In fact, I now know that Doc was never anything less than proud of me. And I'm proud of myself.

I clutch the coffee cup in one hand and the sketchpad in the other as I arch my back, breathing in full lungs of brisk morning air. I take my time, walking through dew-laden weeds that haven't yet seen sunlight. I can't stop smiling as I step from one boulder to the next, until I reach the launch pad.

The kink has left my neck, and I'm all at once aware that I'm not blinking or twitching. When I breathe, I'm conscious of how full and unconstricted my lungs feel. I exhale—long and slow—waiting for a twitch. Nothing.

Balancing myself, I sit, my legs outstretched, wiggling my toes like a kid. The cove looks fresh and new. All the frightening echoes, the screams and shrieks, fade to a distant memory, like a whisper traveling out through the Narrows, leaving me at peace—finally.

With the pad in my lap, a mist of gratitude and resolution blurs my vision. I pop the cover from the coffee cup and sip. It's still warm enough to be drinkable.

Now, for the pad in my lap. I sip again and flip to the first drawing. Perfect—a waterscape. Sunlight beaming through pine trees and a nice reflection. A pretty good rendition. Lots of attention to detail. The spilled coffee has discolored the edges, but not enough to spoil the image. Same with the next, only this one is of a small rowboat on the water. Funny. It looks so much like mine—the one buried under a ton of pine needles. It tugs at my heart. Already, this pad is beginning to feel like a bargain. I flip the page. A little more discoloration around the edges, but now the image—that is, the view—evokes an even stronger reaction. Setting the coffee aside, I hold it up, trying to catch better light to examine it.

In quick succession, I fold back page after page, each one stealing more of my breath, until I can only gasp. I hold up the last page, turn to my right, and compare the view. The cove. *This* cove. Nearly a dozen sketches, all from a familiar vantage point—from Whispering Narrows.

My heart is racing so fast I can't make out a singular beat. Surely, the artist has signed her name somewhere in here. I leaf past page after page, pausing at the coffee cup drawing—*Spilled Coffee*—and all the way to the back, and I start at the beginning again, where coffee has stuck a page to the cover. I peel them apart, reading the factory print:

THIS PAD BELONGS TO:
Amelia Burns

As quick as I glance up from the pad, a reflection across the cove catches my eye. The kitchen door at Whispering Narrows flashes with sunlight as it shuts. A slender figure, with bobbed, black hair, stands outside and stretches in a loose-fitting white top over leggings. Carrying a mug, she ambles down the lawn and strolls to the end of the dock. She sits, bringing her knees to her chest. Hugging her legs, she sips. Her gaze travels from the sky, around the cove, and finally lands on me. Her head cocks and her hand covers her mouth. Her whole posture changes as the coffee mug tumbles to the dock. Coffee seeps between the planks, trickling into the water as the faintest whisper travels across the cove.

"Oh my God, *Benjamin?*"

THE END

NOVELS BY J.B. CHICOINE

PORTRAITS TRILOGY
BOOK I
PORTRAIT *of a* GIRL RUNNING

ALL LEILA WANTS IS TO GET through her senior year at her new high school without drawing undue attention. Not that she has any big secret to protect, but her unconventional upbringing has made her very private. At seventeen, she realizes just how odd it was that two men raised her—one black, one white—and no mother. Not to mention they were blues musicians, always on the move. When her father died, he left her with a fear of foster care and a plan that would help her fall between the cracks of the system. Three teachers make that impossible— the handsome track coach, her math teacher from hell, and a jealous gym instructor. Compromising situations, accusations of misconduct, and judicial hearings put Leila's autonomy and even her dignity at risk, unless she learns to trust an unlikely ally.

Straw Hill Publishing

Available as a trade paperback and e-book from your favorite online bookstore

PORTRAITS TRILOGY
BOOK II
PORTRAIT *of a* PROTÉGÉ

FOUR YEARS AFTER THE CLOSE of *Portrait of a Girl Running*, Leila is twenty-two and living on a pretty, little lake in New Hampshire. A new set of circumstances throws her into a repeating cycle of grief that twists and morphs into unexpected and powerful emotions. Leila must finally confront her fears and learn to let go while navigating the field of cutting-edge psychology, protecting herself from the capricious winds of Southern hospitality, playing in the backyard of big-money art, and taming her unruly heart. Even her 'guardian' has a thing or two he must learn about love and letting go.

Available as a trade paperback and e-book from your favorite online bookstore

PORTRAITS TRILOGY
BOOK III
PORTRAIT *of a* GIRL ADRIFT

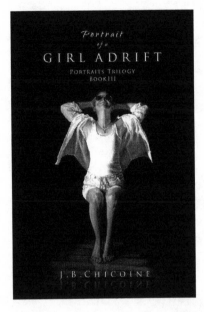

JUST WHEN LEILA THINKS she has everything under control, her deepest insecurities resurface when she must confront her unresolved issues surrounding the mother who abandoned her as a baby, and the men who raised her. Not even Clarence Myles can show her the way, and so Leila embarks on a journey of self-discovery that sends her drifting from place to place in search of answers.

In the process of zigzagging her way between North and South, Leila encounters a series of intense psychological twists and turns that send her reeling, grappling with more questions about her identity. Embarking on a final quest for what it means to be 'whole,' Leila risks everything she knows about maintaining control; on a calculated whim, she boards a boat with a young woman who is everything Leila is not. While navigating her own heart, nothing could prepare Leila for the biggest truth she's about to learn.

Straw Hill Publishing

Available as a trade paperback and e-book from your favorite online bookstore

SPILLED COFFEE

BENJAMIN HUGHES IS ON A mission. He has just bought back the New Hampshire lake cottage his family lost eighteen summers ago, in 1969, just before he turned fourteen— just before his life blew apart.

Still reeling from a broken engagement, Ben has committed himself to relive that momentous summer for the next twenty-four hours.

Every summer as a boy, Ben has gawked at the pretty redhead Amelia, granddaughter to the richest man on the lake, Doc Burns—owner of a Cessna floatplane and the Whispering Narrows estate. During the summer of '69, Ben not only sneaks around with Amelia, but he learns how to fly with Doc, and meets an eclectic cast of characters that will change him forever. The best summer of Ben's life turns out to be the worst as the Burns' family dysfunction collides with his own family's skeletons.

Straw
Hill
Publishing

Available as a trade paperback and e-book from your favorite online bookstore

BLIND STITCHES

NIKOLAI SOLVAY HAS BEEN dreading his sister's wedding, but when his father dies unexpectedly two weeks beforehand, his return to New Hampshire promises to rake up his worst nightmares.

Meanwhile, talented young seamstress Juliet Glitch has been putting the finishing touches on the wedding dress. Mother of the bride—former prima ballerina and Russian expatriate—asks Juliet if she 'would hem her blind son Nikolai's trousers for the funeral' … and the wedding.

When Juliet meets Nikolai, he draws her into the whirlwind of his unraveling family that makes her own quirky domestic situation seem normal. Confronted with the Solvay's delusions and narcissism, Juliet must decide if her developing relationship with Nikolai is worth the turmoil as she deals with her own unreconciled past.

Either way, Nikolai cannot stave off the repressed memories surrounding his mother's defection from the Soviet Union twenty years earlier. Against the backdrop of autumn 1989, during the Glasnost era, Nikolai's family secrets crash alongside the crumbling Berlin Wall.

Straw Hill Publishing

Available as a trade paperback and e-book from your favorite online bookstore

UNCHARTED:

STORY FOR A SHIPWRIGHT

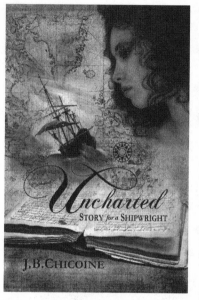

WHEN A PECULIAR YOUNG woman shows up at the Wesley House Bed and Breakfast with a battered suitcase and stories to tell, shipwright Sam Wesley isn't sure if she's incredibly imaginative or just plain delusional. He soon realizes that Marlena is like no other woman he has ever met. Her strange behavior and far-fetched tales of shipwrecks and survival are a fresh breeze in Sam's stagnant life.

Sam isn't the only one enchanted by Marlena. With his best friend putting the moves on her and a man from her past coming back into her life, the competition for Marlena's heart is fierce. In the midst of it all, a misunderstanding sends Marlena running, and by the time Sam learns what his heart really wants, it may be too late to win her back.

Straw Hill Publishing

Available as a trade paperback and e-book from your favorite online bookstore

About the Author

J. B. CHICOINE WAS BORN ON LONG ISLAND, NEW YORK, and grew up in Amityville during the 1960s and '70s. Since then, she has lived in New Hampshire, Kansas City and Michigan. New England is her favorite setting for her stories, though she does love to explore new places.

When she's not writing or painting, she enjoys volunteer work, traveling and working on various projects with her husband.

She blogs about her writing and can be contacted via her website, www.JBChicoine.com and her J.B. Chicoine author page on Facebook.